Beautiful to the Bone

A NOVEL

PG Lengsfelder

Woodsmoke Publishing

Bigfork, Montana

Woodsmoke Publishing
Montana, United States
www.woodsmokepublishing.com

Cover design by BookDesigners.com
Internal book layout © 2015 BookDesignTemplates.com

Beautiful to the Bone/ PG Lengsfelder. -- 1st ed.
ISBN 978-0-9972513-0-2 (Paperback edition)
ISBN 978-0-9972513-1-9 (eBook edition)

For Brooke and Linda,
and people of compassion everywhere.

CONTENTS

PROLOGUE   1

CHAPTER ONE   2

CHAPTER TWO   15

CHAPTER THREE   22

CHAPTER FOUR   30

CHAPTER FIVE   43

CHAPTER SIX   51

CHAPTER SEVEN   61

CHAPTER EIGHT   67

CHAPTER NINE   74

CHAPTER TEN   83

CHAPTER ELEVEN   89

CHAPTER TWELVE   95

CHAPTER THIRTEEN   102

CHAPTER FOURTEEN   107

CHAPTER FIFTEEN   113

CHAPTER SIXTEEN   120

CHAPTER SEVENTEEN   128

CHAPTER EIGHTEEN   138

CHAPTER NINETEEN 144

CHAPTER TWENTY 151

CHAPTER TWENTY-ONE 160

CHAPTER TWENTY-TWO 164

CHAPTER TWENTY-THREE 169

CHAPTER TWENTY-FOUR 175

CHAPTER TWENTY-FIVE 183

CHAPTER TWENTY-SIX 188

CHAPTER TWENTY-SEVEN 197

CHAPTER TWENTY-EIGHT 203

CHAPTER TWENTY-NINE 210

CHAPTER THIRTY 218

CHAPTER THIRTY-ONE 230

CHAPTER THIRTY-TWO 236

CHAPTER THIRTY-THREE 244

CHAPTER THIRTY-FOUR 248

CHAPTER THIRTY-FIVE 256

CHAPTER THIRTY-SIX 265

CHAPTER THIRTY-SEVEN 269

CHAPTER THIRTY-EIGHT 275

CHAPTER THIRTY-NINE 281

CHAPTER FORTY 289

CHAPTER FORTY-ONE 295

CHAPTER FORTY-TWO 299

CHAPTER FORTY-THREE 304

CHAPTER FORTY-FOUR 309

CHAPTER FORTY-FIVE 313

CHAPTER FORTY-SIX 317

CHAPTER FORTY-SEVEN 328

CHAPTER FORTY-EIGHT 331

CHAPTER FORTY-NINE 338

CHAPTER FIFTY 344

CHAPTER FIFTY-ONE 352

CHAPTER FIFTY-TWO 364

CHAPTER FIFTY-THREE 373

CHAPTER FIFTY-FOUR 385

CHAPTER FIFTY-FIVE 392

CHAPTER FIFTY-SIX 400

CHAPTER FIFTY-SEVEN 408

ABOUT THE AUTHOR 416

ACKNOWLEDGEMENTS 417

"It's not
what you look at that matters,
it's what you see."

Henry David Thoreau

If I had been a real mermaid, all the other darkness might have been beside the point. Dark water would have sufficed. But I was caught between —neither land nor water— unable to know my natural origin. Which was Momma's point from the very beginning. And what the encyclopedia could not tell me was what it was like out *there*, beyond the wetlands and mazy waterways, where I was dangerous to others.

But I couldn't help myself. I had what every mermaid has had since the beginning of time. Look it up. We appear of good intention *and* we're ravenous. Many would say we're predatory. But, as I said, I wasn't a real mermaid. I wasn't sure what I was.

CHAPTER ONE

"Come with me." Momma cracked open the door to our '67 Dodge.

I jumped, I giggled. "Really?"

"Get in the truck," Momma said. As if a gun was at her head. "You smile, you got craters in your cheeks."

I sat back, the coil of the bench seat poking through, stinging me where Momma's cigarette had charcoaled and blistered open the seat. Layers of dust settled behind us as we drove past our rusted caboose and bounced out of the clearing, the rutted road rattling and shaking me till we hit the Route 15 asphalt. Momma was taking me away from the farmhouse. For the very first time: an adventure. "Where, Momma, where?"

"Keep your head down, look at the pretty people in the magazine." Momma pulled the jacket hood onto my head even though Minnesota's August lay hot and thick on my skin. She shoved a tattered copy of Life & Style Weekly into my lap. Brigitte Bardot looked up at me.

My excitement lasted till the doctor's office when everything changed forever.

"It's genetic. Is there anyone else —in your family? Is the father albino?" Dr. Childress smiled pleasantly at me. His boney face caved in at the cheeks. An angelic face. I sat quietly on the examination table. At four years old what else would I do? I smiled back. Al-bi-no? Even then my snowy eyebrows and hair were striking on a palette without pigment, except where the blotchy brown birthmark divided my face under my left eye all the way to my chin.

"We don't know the father, but no, I would never . . ." Momma's voice was husky and irritable. "She's so . . . white." The room was white. Doctor's uniform was white. Before momma peeked my way, I felt her pain. I remember thinking,

I'm stabbing momma again.

"Any other children?" asked the doctor.

Momma straightened, still seemed unnaturally bowed. "Oh yes, Carly —my younger daughter— and a son. They're normal." She hesitated. "Different father than Eunis. They're great, healthy. Carly's quite beautiful. Some say she reminds them of—"

"Eunis is healthy," said the doctor. "It's only a pigmented birthmark, nothing malignant." I lifted my head and smiled at him again.

"You have lovely dimples," he said. "Like crescent moons."

The October sun streamed into the office. I blinked hard. The doctor stepped to the window and drew the shade. Momma eyeballed me then away, but not at Dr. Childress.

"She's so —you know. Will she be dumb?"

Dr. Childress' cheeks sucked closer to his cheekbones. I imagined he could be sucked inside out. What would a person look like sucked inside out? Would I look better that way? He took a deep breath without turning to me. The room tightened. Astringent was in the air cutting at my nose. I studied the dull gray linoleum, hoping to become invisible.

"Mrs. Kindsvatter, your daughter is fine. You and her father had genes –"

"—This is *my* fault?"

"There's no fault here ..."

"*My* fault." She showed pitted teeth.

"Eunis is healthy and probably very smart." He glanced at me but I twisted left and right, straining against a current that began dragging at me. I counted small black squares in the cloudy gray floor one after another, hoping they'd never run out, hoping they'd keep me afloat.

"I guess you can't help me." Head down, Momma swept me off the table. I peeked up into her panic.

"Please, Mrs. Kindsvatter ..." I heard the doctor in earnest. My chubby left leg whacked the door on the way out. Lightning bolted through me, ankle to shoulder. I knew better than to cry, I knew better than to draw the attention of the waiting room patients.

〉〉〉

I began to create lists. My first one was this:

Beauty is	Ugly is
Grace Kelly	Bats
Olive Newton John	Evil Skekses
Richard Geer	Me

〉〉〉

"Stop fidgeting!" Momma shoved her knuckle into my spine, straightening me up. "Be brave like Freyja, the mermaid, the goddess of beauty. Or Karen Carpenter."

"Freyja is a mermaid?" I asked.

"Yes, she is. Sit still." She finished combing my hair, the same long, white corn colored hair that's always followed me around. Her hand was stiff and jerking. Like she was stabbing me back. She glowered across the mirror at me. I looked away to the clippings taped and framing the mirror, photos torn from Momma's celebrity magazines. And laid out on the mahogany vanity in front of us, a forest of bottles all sizes. Pink, purple, gray, brown. "Better than the beauty shop," Momma told me. "Maybelline and Revlon made a fortune offa me. Max Factor too, thanks to you."

I can do anything, I thought, I'm five years old! I'm smart. The doctor said so. I can be blank if that's what Momma wants. I can be brave; I can be Freyja.

Momma paced behind me like she didn't know what to do with herself, like she could hit me or something. I peeked at my reflection. My eyes, same as now: pale pale yellow, twitching side to side. *Skrämmande*, Momma said, meaning *ghostly*. Then my features: oversized, especially my nose and mouth. She shook her head.

"Let's see what we can do." Momma reached for the first bottle, sniffing it. "Farrah Fawcett has hair kinda like yours. Nicer, fuller, but let's try this, give you a tan. Farrah's a beauty. A Texas gal. You know she was an angel." Momma shook the cream-colored bottle, started dabbing the color onto cotton balls and then onto my face. A burning, synthetic smell. "Don't move a muscle."

I'll be good, Momma. I promise.

I watched the clock. Never took my eyes off it. Within an hour Momma had added long imbalanced eyelashes, ghoulish eye shadow, and a streaked uneven tan. The result was even more terrifying than the original: I was a miniature gargoyle, part Frankenstein monster cobbled to a badly scarred crash victim. Barely human. *Unbelievably ugly.* I didn't want to, but tears cut across my pudgy cheeks adding the appearance of mutilation.

"Damn you, Eunis, you ungrateful little piss. Now look what you've done."

I clutched the seat. I kept my big fat ugly lips tight. I didn't breathe.

"I'm trying to help you and you've ruined everything. You got any fuckin' idea what this shit cost me? Goddamit, get the fuck outta my sight. You'll always be what you are, and lookin' like that what use are you ever gonna be to anyone? I ain't gonna try helpin' you no more."

I hid in the hallway closet under the stairs. Sobbing. Knowing I'd let her down. Feeling smaller and smaller. Drifting. Until I almost disappeared. Until . . . for the first time, completely alone with my body, darkness became a quiet, dissectible space. My breath steadied.

I leaned against the wall's recycled wainscoting, aging cedar came to my nose. My back warmed as if another body was leaning back-to-back into me, supporting me. Perhaps Momma's enchanting mermaid, the goddess of beauty, combing her golden hair. Perhaps combing mine too.

I didn't move a muscle. Imagining, I suppose. It was easy, basking without light for an hour or so, as if underwater, numinous. When finally I heard Momma ascend the stairs above me, I moved to the closet's center and settled easily into that space. A flutter, a ripple? Giggles? Titters of a water nymph? The joy of hiding? It wasn't *my* warmth or *my* laughter. It was leftover from something or someone else.

☽☽☽

Not long after that Momma decided to keep me out of view so as not to ruin *everything*. Momma had friends, after all, and needed a social life too, especially with my half-sister and brother starting to demand this and that, and Momma's husband, my step-dad Papa Karl, off at the rail yard or somewhere down the tracks.

So when people were around I was told to go to Carly's room, the small creaky room on the second floor over the back porch. There, at least, I could plan explorations.

I could be invisible; *invisible people can still* see. *I'll see. Like Freyja: I'll explore. I'll slip into the woods. I'll read books. No one has to see* me. *I'll learn beauty. I'll do it, I'll surprise Momma; I'll make her proud. I can even be useful. She won't hurt anymore.*

All I had to do was lift the window quietly —the screen fell off years earlier and still lay rotting in the yard where it had fallen— shimmy over the roof and carefully hug the drainpipe on the way to the ground.

But she discovered my escape route one afternoon while entertaining in the kitchen.

"I'm a de-tec-tive, Momma. I'm in-ves-ti-ga-ting."

"There's nothin' to investigate. Stay inside. And if I catch you again—"

"Then can I go to school?" I'd heard Sarah Pooley asking if Momma planned on sending me to kindergarten. "I won't be around to bother you. Can I, please?"

For weeks, I explained the benefits of kindergarten to my mother. "Badgerin'," Momma called it, but I saw something in her eyes, like she was investigating too. Then, on a raw afternoon when the clouds closed a fist around the sky and wolves set the wind howling, Momma finally understood the logic in it and gave in. Or maybe, given the way she looked at me, she thought it was *my* wind threatening her. Maybe she just figured it gave her time to enjoy her morning soaps and read her Star and People magazines in peace, as long as most folks didn't fully make the connection between her and me. And how many people did Momma see anyway doing alterations? (Not many, I heard Margaret Wheeler say under her breath, seeing how Mary Louise Kindsvatter wasn't very good at it.) I'd learned how to use Momma's needs to suit mine. And she'd be happy later because of it.

In class, I was asked to sit in the back so I wouldn't distract the other children who mostly kidded me at first and then lost interest. It helped to stare straight ahead. Even so, at recess I was restless to join the other kids.

"But Mrs. Olson, why can't I?"

Olson wouldn't face me; she peered into the sunny schoolyard. "You're sick, child." The school doctor told the teachers and Momma to keep me out of the sunlight.

"I want to play with the other kids. I feel fine."

"But you're not."

"Please, I need to go out now, it will rain soon. Hard. There'll be lightning."

She frowned. "No dear, I don't think so. Anyway, you still can't go out."

Within a half hour the sky went black and it poured. The kids came screaming in; claps of thunder shook the classroom. From a far corner, Mrs. Olson studied me.

☽☽☽

Momma dropped me at the church. "Pastor Thomas is expecting you." She drove off, leaving me dwarfed by the cloudless sky and the towering rock steeple and cross. She was an infrequent parishioner, going only when Papa Karl was home or when it suited her needs which included a host of seemingly unconnected events, until I began to understand her crude marketing for sewing and alterations, her penchant for male attention, and sometimes the convergence of the two. But I was never invited to attend those Sunday congregations even when Papa Karl "strongly encouraged" my participation. He didn't win those battles. Or many others with her.

When I asked Momma why I was visiting the Pastor, she was vague, saying he wanted to get to know me. But even at that age I had the sense that I was being evaluated. Again. And that Momma was hoping for some sort of holy absolution, something she and Papa Karl argued about frequently.

I had difficulty opening the great dark wine-colored doors and when I stepped in, the temperature dropped and darkness pooled around me. My legs seemed to weaken. The door swung shut behind me sending echoes bouncing off the stone walls and stopping me in place. I expected a musty odor, but instead it was the hint of melted wax. Past the twenty or so pews to the large cross, backlit against the arched window, there was a simple Martin Luther rose of stained blue, white and red glass.

"And you must be Eunis," came a voice, not from the altar but from my right. A bald man, young now that I think of it, although at the time I thought he was old, perhaps forty. He wore a chasuble of vermillion and white crosses, and I thought he looked grand. "Please sit." He shuttled me into the nearest pew. "You're a little early," he said. Then patting his garment, "Do you like it?"

I'd never seen anything so beautiful. I nodded.

"I was just fitted." He lifted his head; a car skittled across the gravel parking lot out back and drove off. Then he fell silent and watched me with soft eyes and an almost smile. He sighed. "I hear you're in school now. Do you like it?"

Again I nodded.

"Have you made friends?"

My eyes dropped to my lap.

He reached for my shoulder. "It's hard when you're new to a school."

"What's beauty?" I asked.

His mouth opened, he sat back, startled. "Beauty?" He shook his head, he chuckled. "Tough to say."

"What does God say it is?"

"God sees beauty in many things, in all people." He put his hand on my knee and began rubbing it.

"But what is it? What does it look like?"

"That's a great question, Eunis. Everyone sees it differently."

"But people like it when they see it."

"Some. Some people are afraid of it." He studied my face. "Saint Augustine thought it got in the way of seeing God's beauty. Sometimes it does." He pulled his hand away.

I scrunched my face in disappointment.

"I guess I'm not giving you a very good answer."

"No, you're not. I thought you would know a lot."

He smacked his lower lip. "Well, I know some things." He

moved closer to me. "You have lovely hair." He reached for it. His breath was sour like Momma's. I pulled back.

"Why am I here?"

He straightened up, his eyes widened as if he was being inflated. He took a deep breath. "Your Mom thought we should get to know each other."

I shook my head. "No," I said. "You can't help her. I want to know and you don't know very much."

His mouth tightened, his eyes suddenly withdrawn. "Now really, Eunis, that's no way to talk to me. I'm trying to be your friend." He put his hand back on my knee.

I pushed his hand away. "Then tell me."

"Tell you what, Eunis?" He was breathing harder. He rubbed his hands.

"What is beauty?"

"It's not that important."

"It is to me." I slipped out of the pew.

He stood up. "Where're you going?"

"Home."

"Don't be rude. Sit down. I'm talking to you."

"I don't want to talk to you, I want to talk to someone who knows beauty."

"Well then, sit down." He patted the back of the pew. "You can't go alone and we can talk about it." His face moved in different directions all at once.

"You don't know, I can tell."

"Sit down!" He slapped the pew hard. Echoes rang all the way to the cross.

"I'll wait on the steps. Momma'll be back. She doesn't want me showing myself off."

"That's not true."

"Now you're not even telling the truth."

"Why you devil—!"

I turned my back on him and walked out.

"How'd it go?" Momma asked when she picked me up.

"Fine," I said and watched the wetlands dissolve into thickets of forgotten places.

꠲꠲꠲

At home, my sister Carly wasn't interested in playing with me or hearing about my investigations. I overheard her telling her friends, "She's not my real sister."

"Half," Momma would say. "She's your half-sister."

My half-brother, Lyle, was too young.

Full of each day with no one to listen, I held on to the day's discoveries until they evaporated, although no one spoke of beauty. After a while, however, the information piled up, became too much to hold. I think of it now as physics but back then it felt like a balloon that would explode. Filled with matter, I *had* to let it out.

I began to speak it, just to myself. Whispers at first, but since I was alone most of the time sometimes I forgot, and soon I talked to myself in a slightly louder voice, to an audience eager to hear what I learned that day: "The new word: 'Or-der-ly.' Means well behaved. Also means neat. Then mistakes don't happen."

)))

But mistakes did happen. There was an incident. I was seven, maybe eight. Lyle four, Carly five. Except for school, Momma never took me away from the house. You'd think I'd be excited. Yet I was mysteriously resistant. The man with Momma had a face like brick, pockmarked and baked dark red. Not Papa Karl.

Momma said, "Take the kids for a walk." She pointed: the path into the tall summer grass was fragrant, honeyed and toasted. It disappeared quickly from the shore. "And don't come back for at least an hour." She rested her small hand on Brick's broad thigh and stroked the stitching of his jeans. His head dipped almost imperceptibly in ascent, eyes torpid, like Momma had drugged him.

"How will I know?" I asked.

"Look at the sun. When it goes over there behind that tree. Now go on."

I secured the broad-brimmed hat the doctor told me to wear and reached out my hands. The kids backed away. I wasn't thrilled to babysit them and I was already worn thin by people's revulsion, but once out there I *was* thankful to be in new territory. Back along the shore, where Moose River met Thief Lake, Momma's laughter drifted above the crickets. Brick's little boy —*Hully*, I think— gripped Carly, terrified of me, his pale, squashed face marbled in yellow mustard and dried snot. She pushed him away.

I herded the kids forward, Brick's boy the most resistant, challenging me every thirty yards as the sun shot lasers through my dark glasses, blinding me as I struggled with him. Carly pulled Lyle to the side. In the distance Brick called out and Momma moaned, and Brick's boy started back toward them. I grabbed him.

"You're ugly," he said. "I don't have to listen to you." And when he kicked me, I spun him around. He kicked me again and I shoved him down the small slope. I don't remember anyone warning me there was quicksand in the bog.

At first it was quite funny watching him struggle, mud caking around his hands and in his hair. Even Lyle and Carly laughed. The lime muck climbed to his waist. He bawled.

"Now will you stick with me?" I said.

He shrieked. Out of nowhere a turkey vulture took flight, his outline rippling across us, the beat of his wings heavy, settling like a cloak.

"Shall I leave you here?"

"Good idea," said Carly. "Let's go." She started up the grade with Lyle.

But with another turn the sludge was to his chest. He reached his arms to me. Now the terror was pulling him down and I wasn't looking so bad. I remembered from the encyclopedia. "Stop moving." And to my surprise, he did. I surveyed the area. "Give me that limb," I motioned Carly to a fallen branch. She complained. "Give it," I hissed. And she brought it to me. Finally, I ruled!

I began to extend the limb to him. But before he was able to grab hold, Momma and Brick came storming down the incline. Brick grabbed the limb, pushed me aside, and sucked his son out of the liquefied earth.

☽☽☽

By age ten, when Momma and Sarah Pooley and the old witch

Solveig Trollkjerringa huddled in the kitchen sharing stories of *vardøgers*, spirit premonitions, I wanted to join them. I wanted to tell Momma what Miss Drakker, the science teacher, said about crickets; how their chirp rate could predict temperature. And if that was true, and if Momma's back and shoulder pain really did forecast wet weather, and if birds flying low meant a storm was coming and giant oarfish could predict earthquakes, why couldn't I feel special things and predict things too?

Momma couldn't have cared less, but I knew what I wanted and how to get it.

"You little pest, I see you there," Momma said, spying me peeping behind the grease-stained door. "Get your long-sleeved jacket, your Hollywood dark glasses . . ." She smirked at her friends. "And your hat and go play in the damn yard. Just get outta here."

Thirty yards from the back door, fortified by the odor of decomposing wood, I approached the old water trough. Momma and the women in the kitchen had pulled out a bottle of something. They cackled and snorted, their backs to the yard.

Beyond the yard was mystery. I felt wicked and I liked it. Taking a final peek at the women, I went forward. *I'm a de-tec-tive!*

I reached the buckling tool shed, surrounded by cockleburs and tall weeds, its single window boarded from the inside with weathered plywood. A remaining glass shard reflected my blotchy ugliness. I looked away.

The shed wasn't pretty; it wasn't 'orderly.' Poorly built and deserted because of its flaws, Momma said to stay away from it; there were *tussers* in it, goblins —a mixture of bones, moss and twigs. They'll promise to marry you, Momma said, and bring us all misery. But reject them and you'll die an ugly maiden and your family will die in poverty, she said, so stay away. I didn't want Momma and Carly and Lyle to die in poverty. But what did the shed look like *inside*?

Stepping through the burrs that pricked and stuck to my legs, I entered the shed, full of errant nails, dust vapors, and abandoned darkness. I stood motionless just beyond the threshold.

"Go on, you scaredy-cat. Detectives can't be afraid." But I was, a little.

I moved farther in and found a patch of open dirt, just enough to scrunch myself on. As I lay in the cool blackness picking off the husks my senses expanded again. Currents moved in my chest.

"Someone's coming to be my friend," I told Carly when she got off the school bus. "I'm just like a cricket or a low-flying bird." But Carly had many friends and didn't care about such things. No one wanted to be around me.

The next day Nemo limped into the yard into the shed and into its shadows, and plunked himself down next to me as if he had always done so. A wiry mutt with only three legs —"nasty looking," said Momma when she finally saw him— he had a high comic yawn that others called maniacal but that made me laugh, every time. I found it lovely.

For the first few months, even when it turned cold, we met secretly in the shed. I'd discovered the remains of a small pine dinghy in the corner and this gave us minor elevation from the damp floor. We settled next to each other for hours in the decaying boat and the broken darkness, Nemo forcing his icy wet nose to my ears, extracting muffled explosions of delight with his tongue, me pulling cockleburs off him and stroking his withered body till he sighed in great relief.

I'd sing a song I'd learned in kindergarten, quietly, so Momma wouldn't hear:

> *"Row, row, row your boat*
> *gently down the stream;*
> *merrily, merrily, merrily;*
> *life is but a dream."*

Then I'd tell him about all the things I'd learned that day, all the mysteries solved. "And you know what's a great mystery?" I said. "Beauty. No one gives me an answer, so *I'm* going to figure it out."

He grinned up at me. His three-quarter grin. The right ear flopped over. His coarse spikey hair, brown and charcoal, white down the center between those eyes, those expectant eyes.

"And someday, when I do, I'll be useful, won't I? I'll be a doctor or something and make everybody beautiful. Maybe even you." I couldn't have known back then that I was stepping into my own quicksand.

He tilted his head.

"Otherwise, why am I here?"

Nemo stood, shook himself out, and with his wet mattress breath, licked my face. He was my first and only friend.

CHAPTER TWO

Momma spluttered and coughed over the sound of the TV. "Where's my tea?" she called.

"Here, Momma." I set the cup next to the Kleenex on the scarred cabin trunk, our coffee table.

"Bout time." She grabbed a tissue and blustered into it. "You missed the last part of 'Guiding Light'."

I didn't recognize momma's soaps one from the other but I knew "Guiding Light" and "General Hospital" were important to her.

"Phillip really loves Beth, always has," Momma said, sipping her tea. "Shit, this is goddamn hot."

"Sorry, Momma." I couldn't seem to get things right.

"Should be, I'm the only momma you got. They look *so* good together. They'd have beautiful children."

"Who?"

"Phillip and Beth. All of them on this show, they *all* look pretty good. But Alan . . . he's a nasty sonuvabitch." She blew on her tea. "You don't mind missin' school to take care a me, do you?"

"Of course not, Momma." I *was* disappointed. Miss Drakker had promised to bring in frogs. How did frogs breathe in and out of water? "What makes them beautiful?"

"Who?" Momma picked up her pack of Luckies and put them down. The walls were already oily with her tobacco.

"Them, on Guiding Light."

"Just look at them."

"They all look different."

"They just are, okay. Now be quiet."

"Momma, can I ask you something?"

"What?" Her eyes still on the screen.

"Who was my real father?"

Momma turned to me, her face pinched, then quickly returned to the screen. "Not sure."

"What do you mean?"

"I don't know who it was," she said, her face cool and hard as stone, a map of wrong turns. "Don't matter." She pressed stiffly on the remote. "He ain't comin' back."

"Was he like me?"

"No. Heavens, no." She turned to me, disappointment in her eye. "I'm sorry."

I'd never seen that before, or maybe I'd never noticed it. I reached for her arm and patted it. "It's okay."

Momma quickly regrouped. "You'd never let me be sick by my lonesome. You'd always come take care of your momma, wouldn't you?"

"Yes, of course, Momma."

"Promise?"

"I promise, Momma."

"Good. Now sit down and no fussin'. 'General Hospital's' comin' up."

☽☽☽

After Momma fell asleep, with Carly and Lyle soon due home from school, I dragged a volume of Papa Karl's incomplete set of encyclopedias from under the stairwell and met Nemo in the shed. Even in the rising spring temperatures he nuzzled into me as I read:

> *"Freyja is the goddess of beauty and the patroness of women who attain wisdom, status and power. She protects the human race."*

He seemed to enjoy that.

"Not sure what a patroness is. Another mystery. We'll look it up later."

He also enjoyed the smell of my pocket, sniffing and nudging me until I pulled out the small piece of exotic cheese I'd found abandoned on the kitchen table, next to the bottles of schnapps and rum. I unwrapped it and took a bite. He stared at me, hopeful.

"Yes, you're an explorer too." I gave him the rest, his small tail a fast-moving metronome thumping against the sides of the marooned dinghy. The rough odors persisted on my fingertips and within a short time Nemo created unbearable clouds for which he showed no effect or ownership.

I held my breath. "Maybe we should adventure today." I could be diplomatic. With the sweetest tilt of his muzzle, he grinned up at me.

We ventured out of the shed and into the fresh May afternoon. We cut through the tangle of dappled woods behind Nemo's owner's house. On his three spindly legs, Nemo kept up with me as tenaciously as any four-legged dog. Farther and farther away from the farmhouse we bush-wacked, two other homes and the Johansson's peeking through the forest knot, stepping on wintergreen releasing its clean smell, over the poison baneberry and through wild sarsaparilla vines until we reached a creek and the small lake pooling from it, winter's ice a memory.

In full sunlight as we explored the creek, I saw sores festering on his legs. "Sit with me." I tapped the ground. He trusted me and that made me love him more. I washed his legs and patted them dry with large aster leaves.

"I'll bring mercurochrome the next time." I tousled his head, a cute head, really. "You're the bestus dog." I kissed him between his ears and smelled his raw, earthy odor. Somehow connecting with his scent made our friendship special, and I think he felt the same.

We wandered down to the lake. "Come on, let's go in." I checked the shoreline, then quickly folded my clothes in a pile and waded in. "Come on." I waved to him.

But Nemo refused to swim, watching me and whining from the shore as I first struggled against the chilled water, then against my own intuition, stopped resisting and stayed miraculously afloat, not exactly swimming, but paddling. "Look! You can do it too!"

He was there as my witness when, on my back, ears in the water, I first heard myself really breathe. He barked his comic approval and after fifteen or so minutes I finally coasted to shore as if I'd been swimming all my life. As if I'd always been free and magical, like Freyja. It came so naturally. I'm still unsure how I did it.

And then, even out of the water, I enjoyed my nakedness and the sun on my skin. It was bad of me, I know, but I didn't want to dress. So we climbed the stubby hill above the lake and I lay there drying.

We lolled quiet and flat on the hillside, thin webs of cloud drifting lazily above us with the occasional buzzing of the first bumblebees —until I heard rocks skitter. I quickly dressed and returned low to the ground in the sweet smelling grass. Nemo remained still beneath my outstretched arm.

From the opposite direction along the lake, an Indian from the reservation wandered slowly out of the woods and found a spot below us. He sat motionless. Staying silent, I noticed my own breath and a tide gliding through my heart. Like the time under the stairwell and the time I forecast rain, and the time I anticipated Nemo. Reciprocal. Natural. Peaceful.

Then the Indian pulled a small bottle from his back pocket. He drank and smoked and talked in rhythmic bursts to the sky. *I can talk to the sky!*

He went on this way for maybe an hour or so in some sort of celebration. It *felt* good to me, so I just lay there with Nemo until the Indian left as quietly as he'd come, my head bigger yet lighter, my body tingling. The crickets chirped. I was lucky to be in such a beautiful place.

"We'd better get going," I whispered to Nemo. I stood and stretched. He stood and stretched. We trekked homeward, the sound of rushing water filling my ears.

On the lip of the forest the hair on Nemo's neck stood up. He stopped and growled. I heard voices.

"She's here, I'm tellin' you." It was the younger Johansson boy, a year older than me.

And then the voice of his older brother. "I gotta see this."

"She's a *hek*, you'll see."

They appeared in the clearing, their cropped blond hair reflecting the fading sunlight. Their large Rottweiler saw me and showed teeth. "Oh, god," said the older Johansson when he saw me.

"Told you," said the younger.

The Rottweiler took an aggressive step toward me and snarled. Nemo stepped between me and the Rottweiler and growled protectively. An obvious mismatch, the first sour tang gnawing my belly.

Before I could call Nemo the Rottweiler was on him, tearing at him. Horrific yelps. "Stop him!" I shrieked.

"He's our right hand," yelled the older boy. "He protects us from evil."

Nemo squealed in agony below the larger dog. Blood surged from his neck and shoulders, and his right eye torn from its socket. The Rottweiler's teeth deeply embedded in his stomach, Nemo flopped from side to side, wounds tearing wider with each swing, the Rottweiler's eyes in a hellish world. I grabbed a rock and hurled it at the Rottweiler, striking its head with a surprised squeak and stunning it.

"What'dya doin' to our dog!" screamed the older boy. "Erobreren, come!"

The Rottweiler pulled away from Nemo and wandered to the boy's side.

"Oh my god." My legs weak, I rushed to Nemo, who lay barely panting on the ground, blood pooling around him. "Oh my god!" I laid my hands on him and bore into the Johanssons. "Do something!"

The older boy took in the carnage. "It's your own fault, witch. Come on," he said to his brother. He swatted at the Rottweiler and the three of them disappeared quickly into the woods.

"Oh my god." I convulsed, tears dropping freely on Nemo. I could barely see. I scooped his limp body into my arms and threaded my way through the forest, holding him close so the branches wouldn't slap at his wounds. My shame grew with every measured step. It was my fault. All of it.

I reached the rear of his owners' house and called for help. "Nemo's hurt, please come! Hurry!" But no one came, not until I crossed the backyard and pounded my fist against their screen door. "Help!"

He winced at my small thrusts so I kicked the door with all my might, but my legs were feeble. "Get out here!"

An older woman, hair in rollers with bulbous eyes, came to the door. "Oh my," she said. Then "Oh my!" at Nemo's bloody body and dangling eyeball.

"We need to get him to a hospital. Right away." I was encased in cold sweat.

"Lay him there on the grass, I'll get my husband."

And when the husband came, a gnarly old man with his own scraggily hair puffing from his ears and nose and sleeveless white t-shirt, he looked aghast.

"He was attacked; the Johansson's dog. We've got to get him to the vet!" Spasms in my chest and throat were out of control.

"Okay, okay," said the hairy man. "You go home now. We'll take care of him." He knelt by Nemo and shook his head.

"He can make it," I said. "I know he can. He's stronger than he looks."

"Go home," screamed the man. "Now!"

I eyed Nemo. He saw me; I know he did. "You're going to be okay." I held my tears so he wouldn't be afraid and tried not to look at Nemo's crimson splashed across my arms and shirt. I backed into the woods. "You're gonna be fine," I called one last time and began home, crying. Then suddenly I stopped, a force telling me to retrace my steps.

I wiped my ears and nose, smearing blood onto my cheeks and hair. At the edge of Nemo's backyard, hidden behind a large box elder, I watched the hairy man and his wife.

"I'll call the vet," said the woman.

"Wait," the man said.

"Shall I get the truck?" she asked.

"I don't know," he said. "It could be expensive."

"We've gotta do something."

"Yes," he sighed. "Get the truck."

And when she did, he picked Nemo up reverently and, sliding carefully onto the tailgate and into the back of the pickup, he sat with him in his arms. He said something to his wife, but over the truck's engine I couldn't make it out. They pulled slowly away, so slowly that I was able to follow at a distance without much effort.

In a half a mile they turned off rutted Smith Road onto a barely visible, little-traveled spur that led back down to the lake. I scrambled to the spot Nemo and I enjoyed that afternoon, the crickets more present, the chill of evening descending on the hillside.

The truck looped around the small opening and stopped. The man called to his wife. She turned off the engine. He slid out of the truck bed and stood at the edge of the lake. I saw Nemo raise his head for a moment, and then the man hoisted his arms and Nemo above his head, and with a strength that seemed super-human, heaved him —a small wail emitting from my little friend— into the center of the lake. It was if the earth below gave way and I was falling, falling.

Before I could scamper down the hill the man and the wife and the truck were gone, and well before I swam to the spot, Nemo disappeared below the surface.

I have no memory of swimming back to shore or of walking home. There was no real footing anymore.

CHAPTER THREE

I washed away Nemo's blood but not his disbelieving eyes. His death was my fault plain and simple. I *was* bad luck. Demons followed wherever I showed my face. I caused misery, just like momma said. Momma was the expert.

In my dreams I saw bloated bodies bobbing in brown water —Nemo, Hully, the old witch *Solveig Trollkjerringa* and other faceless people— distended bellies, hands, feet and cheeks bursting like ripe fruit, gulls and ravens riding them, pecking as the skin popped, split open and peeled back.

But a promise was a promise. I needed to make good on mine to Nemo, even as it gave me the jitters. And at some point I had to make the Johanssons pay. I was sure of that. I bided my time.

My first Experiment & Observation was with my 7th grade classmates, comparing the classical standards of beauty. Mrs. Petrick, our English teacher, read us Greek myths because she said many Greek and Roman myths were the basis for how we lived our lives and related to each other. Which gave me the idea. And maybe I'd finally make a few friends.

Photocopying images from Papa Karl's encyclopedias, I created posters contrasting the Greek Aphrodite —goddess of beauty, born out of sea foam and worshipped as the goddess of the sea— with Venus, the Roman goddess of beauty, the famous painting with her hair blonde and long as her body, born out of a seashell. For the girls, I pulled images of both the Greek (bronze) and Roman (plaster) statues of Adonis. Both naked. Roman Adonis bigger, in *every* way.

At recess I sat quietly on the school's low stone wall, the poster headline 'Pick the most beautiful, win a prize.' The other 7th graders always avoided me, but with a prize at stake they took their chances. I took mine.

Del Green approached. "Hey look, the beast runs a beauty

contest."

His buddy Smitty jumped in. "Eunis, you mind turning away while I vote, I just ate lunch."

And Angela, the youngest of the Johanssons, added, "With a nose like yours, can't you smell what I'm thinkin'?"

Laughter.

I tightened. *Stay on purpose.* "You want a prize or not?"

In a landslide the boys voted for Venus. Del summed it up. "She ain't that hot."

"Then why Venus?"

He leered. "Can see more skin."

Most of the guys avoided Adonis, but those that observed him claimed *they* had the bigger package.

The girls' vote was closer, bigger beat bronzer, but I had a smaller sample because Irene Kelmer with the wandering eye — the *second* ugliest girl in our class— asked me, real loud, "Did your parents lose a bet with God?"

She got laughs from a couple of girls. That started it.

"Yeah," said Christian Hames, "but God didn't give you the hooters he gave Eunis."

"Shut the fuck up." Mandy G. shoved Christian.

Then Barbie, Christian's girlfriend, shoved Mandy. "Maybe if you had tits you could put hands on your own guy. Or maybe the other way round."

That's when Mary Bakke raised her sweatshirt to flash Mandy, three other girls jumped in slapping, and Irene spit in my face. I'm told I kind of snapped. I can't remember exactly, only that I must have shoved her. Hard. I wasn't sorry; she had it coming.

She fell backward over the stone wall and started screaming at me. Next thing I knew, Mr. Price, the junior high Principal, shut me down. "Eunis! What do you think you're doing?" He grabbed the poster and crushed it closed.

"It's just research."

"Inappropriate! Nudity! Lewd behavior!"

I wore jeans and a blue work shirt, buttoned up.

A few kids got detention, *plus* the drawing for the prize —a couple of Momma's old issues of Star and People magazine—

never happened. The kids hated me even more after that.

Mr. Price called Momma to pull me out of school and Momma saw the four confiscated naked bodies. She went ballistic, tossed the poster and ballots into a small bonfire of accumulated garbage long overdue for burning. She threatened to lock me in my room for a month if I ever humiliated her like that again. Sounded pretty much like the status quo to me. I got a busted lip and a week's suspension from school.

What I learned: Beauty may change with the times, but the trends don't render the previous beauties ugly. Oh, and showing skin helps. Just not *my* skin.

〉〉〉

A warm amber light —the only light of the day in my cellar bedroom— was thrown on the tiny wash basin in the corner, and above it *inserted* into the wall, was a mirror on which the late afternoon sun shined, illuminating dark, silver oxidizing stains — caused by moisture and condensation, research I discovered as I continued my rule of reading one encyclopedia page every day. But I was full of books, what about the real world? What about what I read in Momma's magazines? What about *that* real world? What about people and the strange things they did? Like the "Black Widow," 23-year-old Pamela Ann Wojas in New Hampshire? Momma read everything about her. "Fascinating," said Momma. She killed her husband. With her 15-year-old student lover. Why would she do something like that?

Anyway, whether it was the wet Minnesota weather or steam drifting from the tap to the mirror that caused the mirror's disfiguration, I never found out. But its disfigurement was a *reminder*, it taunted me, and if I could have I would have removed the damn thing. Instead, over it, I taped a scrap of thin muslin tablecloth dotted with yellow marigold I found stashed in the shed.

"I'm up to here with my life." The stone basement chamber absorbed my words. Safe, but useless. Research couldn't be accomplished simply crouched in the corner surveying my bunker. "I gotta get out."

The teenage fantasies I'd sprinkled around the room —the

Michael Landon and Andie MacDowell photos, and The Little Mermaid poster— had lost their charm. Out of time. Only the news clipping with its rare photo of Jane Goodall talking in a circle with African teenagers still seemed relevant. She was saving monkeys, sitting and watching, staying out of the limelight.

At dusk, wind leaked into my bedroom, lesions in the windowpane. The light socket swayed. Upstairs Momma huddled into the mossy couch, wary of the wind, of me, what lived inside both the wind and me. Dread. It was contagious.

The foreboding was barely audible at first, the wind choir quietly humming. Restless, like me. The chorus rose and fell, filling my room, wailing and warning. The gypsy wind, well traveled, where did it come from, where was it going? Did it start in Minnesota and end up in some exotic place like Hawaii? Comforting trade winds? Or come for us, Moroccan and dry? An Indian monsoon, still whetted by tidal waves? A South American williwaw, fresh from sinking ships?

I shivered in the corner. "Give me a clue, I gotta get out of here."

It lasted all night, only the darkness protecting me. And there was my answer: darkness.

☽☽☽

The auditorium speakers blared a rap/R&B song:

> *I sense there's something strange in your head*
> *And you can't get it out*
> *It's heartless, aint it*
> *A poisoned starkness, that's the thread*
>
> *Are you schemin' on me*
> *Are you dreamin' on me*
> *Will I fall for your dark screamin' charms*

The crowd screamed for me to do it again. Swathed in darkness, just the two holes into the light, I raced across the court, rolled, bounced, cartwheeled into a back handspring, and vaulted myself into the air before gliding (like in water) into a split ten feet from the stands. Nuts! They went nuts! Cheered; shrieked; applauded. Coach Westmore smiled and clapped too.

Hands on hips watching me. Did he get my note?

"Go, go Beavers!" The crowd on its feet. The cheerleaders at the far end of the court padded toward me. Would the coach let me use his new gadget? Two in the whole school, the perfect research tool. Was The Beaver enough?

I jumped to my feet. More shouts of encouragement. "Beaver, Beaver, Beaver!" Stands full all around: watching, cheering, the team, *me*. All those people *with* me, almost at my command, but they didn't see me. Ideal. My whole body alive! Free! They loved me. They loved The Beaver, my oversized tail and head, my eight-inch eyes, my giant bucky teeth. *I* raised their energy, controlled their flow with *my* movements. To the right, hands up. Their hands went up. Spread "V" for victory. They mimicked me. Smiles and stomping on the bleachers. They felt great. I felt great. And maybe coach felt great.

It was beautiful what they didn't identify, what they couldn't see. If Dr. Childress had seen me, if he'd been inside The Beaver suit with me, he'd have said what nice dimples like crescent moons, but by then he may have been dead.

The second-half horn blasted, basketballs smacked the floor. The teams filtered onto the court. The crowd still buzzing. A championship so near. My time was up. Or just beginning.

Down the ramp, to the boiler room where I usually changed and secretly slipped out of the building. Only I went left into the boy's locker room, along the aisle of lockers. "Eriksen . . . Perez . . . Johansson!" Friggin' Johansson, so proud of his long blond curls. Ready to celebrate the championship in front of all those cameras and adoring admirers after the game.

I opened the locker and, on the top shelf, just like I'd scouted, was his shampoo/conditioner. One last look around. On the court above, a ref's whistle and the crowd booed. "It's the least I can do," I whispered. I replaced his old tube with the one I brought, the one filled with Nair, the hair remover. Let him shampoo with that. Let him rub it in good.

When the triumphant team came filing out of the auditorium to meet the town, the press and the cameras, cheers went up and flash bulbs illuminated the night, the team surrounding me,

The Beaver. I made the "V" for victory. More flashes. Night became day. There was no Tommy Johansson. His senior glory buried, forever.

Coach Westmore came over to me and gave me a hug. "You're on," he said. "I'll leave you a key tomorrow. The Principal gave thumbs up for all your hard work. But Sunday only. Then we'll expect the key back. These are some of the first computers in the state. It's only good for research, so I hope you know what you're doing."

"Coach, coach," said the reporter from *The Pioneer*, "can we get a shot of you with The Beaver?" He hugged me again; I was on my way.

☽☽☽

Even from outside the farmhouse, my bedroom appeared dreary, having been a root cellar for the original owner back in the early 1920's, then a storm cellar before the one window, single light bulb and small washbasin were added. It sat below ground of the clapboard building, and with such steep steps that Momma rarely came down. When she did it usually meant trouble.

I descended the worn wooden stairs, sweaty. The Beaver's neoprene smell overrode my own odor and clung to my t-shirt.

"She gives me the creeps," I remember Carly saying to Momma. Neither Carly nor Lyle wanted to sleep in the same room with me. "She's bad luck."

"I wanna be with *her*," Lyle said clutching Carly's sleeve. "Carly and me." She pushed him off. She fought it, fought it hard. She wanted to stay in the room at the top, but she didn't want to share it.

She and Momma argued over the territory, pie tins thrown, cabinets slammed, fear palpable. Carly in a frenzy, pointing at me: "Creepy spirits," she said. "Just look at her!" Momma's face contorted. Wraiths worming in *her* head.

In a fit Carly knocked two candlesticks to the floor. Momma was going to give it to Carly, and I'd get Lyle in the cellar.

But Momma looked at Lyle cowering in the corner then at me, all the while Carly screaming about demons. Anyone could see Momma feared for him, being the littlest and the one with the least gumption. How could he wake up or go to sleep seeing my grotesque face, and how would he stand up to my constant, troubling energy?

So by saying nothing, by letting Carly have her fear-mongering spotlight and Momma her spook superstitions, I got the cellar solo. The smallest room, but at least I had it and my doubts to myself.

"You know what's so terrific being The Beaver?" Still flushed by my success, I let down my hair and plopped on my small bed. I waited for the springs to stop squeaking and the wind to finish its incantations.

"I'm fluid, like when I sneak to the lake. I can go anywhere. Well, maybe not the boys locker room when they're changing." Unfortunately. "I wish I could have seen Tommy Johansson's face as his hair fell out in his hands." It wasn't enough but it would have to do. It would have to do.

Music drifted down through the floorboards from the living room, Johnny Cash, and then Lyle lifted the needle off the record, strumming the chords and singing. *"I don't like it, but I guess things happen that way."*

"No, no one knows *still*, not even the Principal. Nobody knows I'm The Beaver." Ingenious really —I liked the word ingenious. The combined junior high and high schools decided that the mascot had to be strong and super-athletic, like me, and was too important to switch every game. Years before I arrived they had constructed a top-secret system: 'The blind candidate,' so no one knew exactly who was in The Beaver. *Me.*

I sat back satisfied, but really still a bit dazzled. I combed my hair, the hair Lyle called *manila* as a child, meaning vanilla. He put on a blues record.

"I hear people talking about each other, gossiping. Like Christina whatchamacallit always trashing somebody. She shouldn't do that. She doesn't know, nobody knows what goes on at home. Nobody knows the troubles inside." I stopped combing and looked at the covered mirror. All of it together confusing.

Anyway. How casually the boys wrapped their arms around the girls' shoulders; how easily their bodies buried into each other, the girls twining around the boys like fast-growing vines. The comfort. Must be nice. From above, a Lyle blues chord trembled my heart. *Enough! Buck up!*

"I stood next to Victor King today; *the* most handsome hunk of a man . . . a real Adonis. He's a nix, he's *that* beautiful. Everyone wants to get next to him, even the guys. Funny to watch, like everyone's jockeying for position. I just stood there, right next to him. It's like none of them see me as real, like I'm not in the room. But I am! Vic King, what a dream." A front row seat. Better than nothing.

"And it's going to payoff, because you know what I heard the other day?"

Michael Landon and Andie MacDowell were mute.

"Okay. So I'm sitting at the end of the bleachers and I hear that rats have been found in Kentucky Fried Chicken. You know, they fell into the vats. But that isn't why they've changed their name to KFC; it's because their chicken isn't a regular chicken —it's genetically engineered, and I think I understand what that means. Somebody's trying to create the perfect chicken! Using human-engineered genes. Isn't that cool?"

CHAPTER FOUR

My days sheathed in The Beaver lasted only five years. By senior year, when the library and the rest of the school got computers, the Internet became my new encyclopedia. Scientists were manipulating genes, adding and subtracting them to optimize everything from enzymes to animals! That meant *I* could alter genetic make-up if I could understand what nuclease and homologous recombination meant. Which meant I had to get grades and a job to go to college. Momma laughed.

In class I learned to sit up front because my grades suffered when I couldn't see the blackboard: the albinism. I quickly grew uninteresting, which was better than *terrifying*. I was better forgotten.

I barely altered my routine. I swam, I did my homework, I cleaned the farmhouse and I performed in The Beaver for my high school classmates almost every week of every school session and at every sport, even hockey, where Carly was beginning to be a star. Yet not a single person ever asked my name or even spoke to me. Actually, that's not true. Twice, visiting students asked the way to the bathroom. I pointed.

I appreciated that my schoolmates didn't talk to me. I took it as respect for what The Beaver represented, a kind of fairy-tale life force, like one of Mrs. Petrick's fables. And as I say, I could watch, I could listen. It wasn't science, but it was a kind of research. And along with the Internet, I was learning a lot.

Once, I happened on Victor King. Just me and him and a girl I'd never seen before. Under the stands, next to the Zamboni, coming out of the locker room before the game against Moorhead. Victor had his skates and the girl around his neck. I thought he'd welcome me.

"Beave," he said to me, "what're you doin' here? You should be on the ice."

She slipped a small packet into his palm and gave it a squeeze.

"Thanks," he said to her. "My headache feels better already."

She blew him a kiss, opened a side door, and walked away from the rink.

"C'mon, man," he said to me, "this is a big game. We need you to get the crowd psyched."

"There you are." Perfect Teeth Melissa, his girlfriend, trotted up beside him, ran her fingers through his hair. "Coach's already got the guys on the ice taking warm-up drills. Thought maybe you were messin' around with someone down here." She winked.

"No, just me and old Bucky. Some piece of tail, huh?"

"You'd be pretty hard up."

"I'm only hard up for you." He slipped the packet into his skate. "This clown," he said derisively, "is for the crowd." With that he shoved me forward up the ramp into the arena.

Clown!

☽☽☽

In the meantime little was patched or painted or rehabilitated in or around the house, even with all three of us kids taking Momma's sporadic, often chaotic, direction. It seemed to me that she simply didn't want anything to change. Including me.

Momma told us, "We got spirits settled in. We know them; they know us. I don't need no more sufferin'. Long as the wind don't bring in *heks* or *tussers*, we'll be alright. Still, you be watchful, don't bring us no misery." She looked at me and shook her head.

I did my homework. For fun I read more of Momma's magazines. Fascinated by people and why they did what they did. Usually infidelity or money or both played a part. The "milkshake murderer" was one of those. She killed her husband by having her unsuspecting six-year-old daughter serve him strawberry milkshakes laced with sedatives. She drowned him in milkshakes. Then with the children out of the house, she bludgeoned him to death. I went to bed. I slept if the wind left me alone.

Just before I completed high school Momma explained that

she expected me to pay rent for my space underneath the farm-house and that, of course, I would have to get a job. "That don't mean you're gonna stop shoppin' for me or cleanin' this scrap-heap or gettin' my pills neither. You understand that, right? You pay for your food too."

Momma went on to explain that Carly was already making her way just fine and had to keep herself focused on her studies and her sports. Momma had decided the college hockey scholar-ship looked like a sure thing, even if it was a few years away. Lyle was still too young to be useful she said, though he was six-teen, only a year younger than Carly and only three younger than me. He'd started sleeping on the couch.

"You understand, right?" Momma repeated.

I understood. I understood that without a job I'd never go to college and become the next Gregor Mendel or Christiaan Bar-nard. So I devised another of my lists, I put my atoms in order.

<u>Job Search</u>

<u>Best to Have</u>	<u>Possibilities</u>
Beauty related	Not a beautician
Science related	The fish hatchery?
College lab helper	Closed for summer
No contact with public	Internet?
Local	Aide to forensic osteologist?

"That's ghoulish." Lyle sipped a Keystone from Momma's stash.

"Osteologist? It's science."

"Studyin' bits of dead folk's bones?"

"People want to know what killed them."

"They're dead, they don't give a shit."

"I'm talking about their loved ones. In twenty percent of all deaths, no cause is found."

"You tell Momma? I'll bet she'll freak." He cocked his head and saluted with the beer can.

All I could do was close my eyes. Of course he was right, and maybe if I was in St. Paul, but Momma was depending on me. A job like that in Bemidji, doubtful, although . . .

I thought out loud, "How about old man Carver?"

"He gives me the willies. The whole thing does, so it'd be right up your alley." Lyle took another sip, went back to strumming his guitar.

)))

"I don't want anyone seeing you. You stay in the back room," said Mr. Carver after explaining the tools and chemicals I would use to assist him. "Not that you should be ashamed of what you're doing. It's an art. That's why," he sniffed, "you aren't doing any of the skinning."

He adjusted his coke-bottle glasses. Anyone could see Mr. Carver's eyes were going fast. He needed an assistant. He couldn't seem to keep them though, whether it was the chemicals, the dusky physical space, or the gloomy space in Mr. Carver's head. The large dark sign outside said it all, supported by two thick timbers and Mr. Carver's eyes looming over "Carver's Taxidermy." Under that: "Preserve beauty forever."

"You're not squeamish, are you?"

"No." I meant it. Who had the luxury of being squeamish? But I did feel uncomfortable turning beautiful living things into trophies.

"Good." Mr. Carver pushed the coke-bottles back in place. "There's a whole history to this." He stretched a shaking hand over his domain of wings, paws, fins, skins and skulls. He did a brisk business. His tools lay neatly in rows or hung on the pegboard, ready for cutting, pulling and scraping; the same kind the dentist used, though I hadn't seen a dentist in a while. He even had a crochet needle for tugging the skin back or over.

A hanging spotlight illuminated each workbench, making the rest of the sprawling building a series of black holes. My comfort zone.

"The English Victorian Era," he said launching into his homily. "That was the golden age of taxidermy." I was attentive, though he barely laid eyes on me. One-by-one he rested his attention on each body part in the room, all but mine. "The well-educated, or those who wanted to be, placed birds and animals and fish all over their homes. Things of beauty, if the man, the taxidermist, was an artist and not some 'stuffer.'"

Only men were taxidermists? Women could understand beauty too. But back then it probably was a male profession. I didn't ask Mr. Carver. I already felt his agitation.

He sniffed again, as if he had been inside my head, heard my thoughts, and already dismissed them as trivial. "Anyway, I'll not accept rogue taxidermy assignments. You don't need to worry."

I shook my head. "I'm sorry. I don't understand."

"When some jackass creates a Frankenstein, like a jackalope or a *skvader*, that's rogue, not sticking to nature." Momma had talked of the *skvader*, a fictional hybrid, front half and head, hare; the second half —torso, wings and tail— grouse. A flying rabbit.

"I'm no Dr. Frankenstein. I don't care if it's their favorite mystical creature, I won't do it. I won't be part of their sick ideas." This time he filled both nostrils, a hillside of open pores inflating his already sizeable nose.

"Dragons, water fairies, sirens of the deep, chimeras: a bunch of myths and bad luck. I don't like mixing body parts. It brings bad luck." He stared off to a darkened corner of the shop, but still not at me. "If I ever ask you —*assuming* I want to keep you— to help with that superstitious crap —excuse my language— then tell me to 'just remember,' and that'll do the trick."

"I wouldn't tell you no."

"You tell me 'just remember.' Part of your job, assuming you *do* your job."

"Why 'just remember?'"

"End of lesson. Be here six o'clock tomorrow morning." Again he swept his hand over the multitude of half-completed projects. "Plan a long day."

And they were long days. The more Mr. Carver disintegrated and decayed before my eyes, the more taxidermy prep and finishing I took on, though he never asked me to skin, and I was glad of it. I watched him skin a fox, then decided I'd prefer not to see that part of the process again. I turned away from him whenever he started cutting and scraping, and he never mentioned it.

But there was one moment . . . In that second week, arms stretched out in front of him and more willing to glance at me than the pre-historic fish he carried, he said, "Take care of this." He thumped a gargantuan fish on my workbench. Then pulled gloves and a jowl spreader from his back pocket and laid them next to the fish.

"What is it?" I asked, heart rate up.

"Muskellunge." Clear distaste in his tone. "Frozen. Can you handle it?"

It was light-silver, mean looking and the largest fish I'd ever seen, almost 6-foot long, close to 50 pounds with sharp needle-like teeth. "What do I need to do?" I swallowed.

"I thought you weren't squeamish."

"I'm not." I stood straighter.

"Clean it out, don't rupture the skin." He wiped his hands on a rag, threw it on his bench and walked away, then stopped at the office door. "It's a near-record, don't screw it up." Then closed the door behind him.

I starred at the monster. It starred back. Spitefully. But it was a water creature. I needed to make friends with it. Reluctantly I lowered my hands to its skin, then stroked it. "Pals?" It wasn't amused.

I heard Carver already on the phone with a customer.

I slipped on the gloves. They were oversized and too big for me. I inched the jowl spreader into its mouth. A crackling sound. "Oh no, no!" I said pulling my hand back. The crackling stopped. *Breathe.* I removed the left hand glove. I took hold of the center of its body with my gloved right hand, and with my left I slowly and very carefully reached between the teeth into its belly, straining to stay in its center. Deeper. Almost to my elbow. Something furry *and* slimy! My hand flew out, tearing open the skin between my thumb and index finger. I pumped air in and out. "Shoot."

But no damage to the fish. Another deep breath. "I can do this." I steadied my breathing.

This time, past its teeth, my body as frozen as the fish, my arm buried deeper, deeper, until my hand came to rest on the slime. Trembling, I grabbed hold of it, unwilling to even imagine what it was. I pulled at it, and with a sucking sound it detached from the monster's belly and came toward me.

At the monster's mouth I held my breath and dragged it into the dim light.

I screamed. A large brown and yellow snake with a duckling in its mouth fell to the floor, and with them, as the glove slipped away from my hand, the monster fish slid off the workbench and joined them with a thud on the ground.

"Oh shoot, oh no!" I looked to the office door. I dropped to my knees and scooped the huge fish into my arms, quickly laying it on the table as Carver came cursing through the door.

"What the hell is going on?"

"Just startled," I said stroking the monster. I pointed to the floor and the duckling in the snake's jaws.

"As long as the Muskie's okay."

I smiled and kept gently massaging the fish.

"Just get back to work, will you. Just deal with it."

"Yes, sir."

𝔻𝔻𝔻

Before Mr. Carver's complete decline, I found pleasure in keeping his art high quality. I helped make each animal beautiful by salting, pickling, and tanning the skins; transforming the protein skins to non-protein; and preparing them for rehydration. The process was a delight —no spoilage and so purifying, leaving each body germ free.

"Always," he said, "keep them out of the sun and direct heat. Gelatinization and hardening; hair slippage is irreversible. Never stack skins."

I learned to rehydrate the skins in 5% solution, to keep the pH below 2.2. "But not too long," he'd say checking on me. "It loosens the hair."

I handled all the acids, dressing the fur with Formic acid, bleaching with Oxalic, the poisonous powdered one, and Hydrochloric —muriatic is what he called it— which evaporated easily if I wasn't careful. Those fumes were lethal and the drops would eat away the skin.

"Your skin," he said, "if you aren't mindful."

He appreciated my fastidiousness and rarely complained regarding my work or my presence, though he seldom complimented me or looked at me when he spoke, usually keeping an eye on an otter or a black bear as he skinned or sewed or stuffed, as much as he hated that word. "Talk to your subject and it will help guide your hands," he said without looking up.

And it did take me a while, when he broke the silence, to understand that most of the time he wasn't talking to me.

I peeked from the workshop through the space between the hinges and the door, and I saw the delight of his customers as they picked up their trophies, their beautiful things.

As he held on to the skinning, and with diminished coordination he could do less and less of it —he even tore a few skins, ruining them— he began to lose business, and his customers died off.

But I was able to learn a lot about beauty in those nine years, especially in conjunction with Internet research. For instance, in 1883, a guy named Galton, Charles Darwin's cousin, was the first to experiment with categorizing faces. A photographer, he wondered if certain groups of people —vegetarians and criminals— had certain facial characteristics typical to each. A strange choice of categories, but anyway . . . He determined that there was no such match, but he also determined that the composite vegetarian and criminal faces were found more attractive than their component counterparts.

This led to more recent research that I found useful: Exactly 100 years later Grammer, K., & Thornhill, R. ran experiments on "Human facial attractiveness and sexual selection: the role of symmetry and averageness" in the Journal of Comparative Psychology. Their research suggested that a symmetrical face is the most attractive to the most people, and that the features needed to be average, a consensus derived by the greater population, just as Darwin's cousin had suggested with his photographic experiments. In other words, no bloated lips, no mile-wide nose, and certainly no large, brown puddles splitting the face.

)))

Experiment & Observation: Crafting a symmetrically-faced ani-

<u>mal</u>.

A dead skunk came in for taxidermy. "No skunks or mother-in-laws," said Carver, but I convinced him I should give it a try. They're beautiful animals. It took special deodorizer and extra degreasing but I managed. I even did the skinning. I gave it a perfectly symmetrical face. It looked diabolical and mean.

"No, no," said Carver. Despite his failing health I thought he was ready to throw me out physically. "It's *too* static. Beauty is being alive. Make it alive!" He *sounded* like Dr. Frankenstein, but I understood. What I learned: It needed a small touch of fluctuating asymmetry, but not too much.

)))

I put away money those years, working full-time till I was twenty-seven, even paying Momma when she raised the rent and used some of it for Carly, because Carly *did* get the hockey scholarship and she did need nicer clothes for college, especially as she was one of the stars of the team.

"It's part of the mystique," Momma said, something she must have read in one of her magazines.

Lyle still lived at home. Well, in and out without warning, always carrying his prized Martin D-35 guitar and singing for whatever he could get in the Bemidji bars, especially the most notorious —the once grand Markham Hotel— where he scored his drugs until it closed. He started hanging in the Hotel Hell area in Nymore, by the tracks.

Momma couldn't see any of it happening. "His voice will be his savior." But in the latter years she didn't say it with much conviction.

In my little free time I kept swimming and getting stronger. I checked books and the Internet for new research, and I continued my own research scrapbook, a thick three-ring binder of body parts clipped from Momma's magazines, with pages categorized and devoted to celebrity eyes, ears, noses, hair, mouths, facial hair, skins and chins. I'd never thought of chins previously.

But feeling useful to Mr. Carver sustained me as much as the money and the developing research, which was a shift for me. It added the one-on-one human element that I'd never had. And it buoyed my confidence for other encounters.

One Saturday, late in the summer of my fifth year with Carver, I was preparing to leave a bit earlier than usual to see a lecture titled "Endless Forms Most Beautiful" by a PhD named Sean Carroll. I'd been anticipating it for weeks. I'd hoped Mr. Carver would already be gone, but he seemed intent on mounting a moose head.

I waited, time running out. Bent over his workbench he didn't appear to move —at all. I spoke across the room to him. He didn't budge. I came closer and called his name again which jerked him out of his statue-like existence. He was shaky and disoriented.

"Mr. Carver, are you okay?"

"What? Yes." But he wasn't. He eyes scanned his workbench, bewildered.

I thought about Dr. Carroll's lecture: Darwin's dangerous ideas, mutations, hetero vs. homozygotes —fascinating explorations for my research. Carver stumbled off his stool.

"Maybe I should close up today, Mr. Carver. You look tired."

"What?"

"Can you drive?"

He stood taller. His eyes took on some clarity. "Of course, what do I look like?"

I didn't want to say. "You're sure?"

"Of course I'm sure. Okay, you close up today." He grabbed his keys, snorted a lungful of the chemical-infused workshop and left his usual sour mood hanging in the air, along with the hint of choking hydrochloric acid.

There'd be no lecture for me that night. But I felt faithful to myself for taking care of Mr. Carver. I liked the feeling. I know it sounds strange but it gave me a sense of accomplishment, and I proposed to use it as a guide in the future, it felt *that* good.

The August moon rose up almost full. Something moved in my chest and I grabbed it. "What?" I said to the workshop.

It had been years since I'd had one of 'my visits,' and even if there had been others I'd passed them off as stress or the result of Momma's superstitious brainwashing. I had to stay focused.

They usually passed quickly.

"What?" Something might have moved in the shadows, but all I saw were partially dismembered bodies. The smell of the acid burned my throat. The sound of the crickets jumped three-fold. As if guided by their chirping I went out back to breathe before locking up.

A thick, humid night, frequencies radiated around my heart. The crickets grew louder still, calling me to follow the narrow path deeper into the slough where, from time to time, I'd thrown off my clothes after a long day, waded into the water, and glided magically through as if I was the lake's natural inhabitant. Bemidji was a beautiful place.

It was only a quarter mile from the road, which ran along the slough and then forked north as the slough became Kingdom Lake. By the time I passed the fallen jack pines on the left, the crickets had gone silent. The sudden stillness unsettled me as I came to the glade, though the towering flame grass plumes, as always, bade me to join them in romance.

"You want me?" I whispered.

The water lapped against the bank and out beyond the tall grass. The moon rippled over the lake's smooth skin. I pulled off my shoes, folded and stacked my clothes neatly under my favorite white cedar, then waded into the slough, the water gathering around me as it would around any nymph, welcoming my return.

I was in just below the curve of my pubic hair, the moon illumining my naked body, silver in the water's reflection, and my head still in the shadow of the cedar, when I heard the first grunt. Aware of how sound magnifies and travels across water, I covered myself and receded farther into the lake.

Something large and wild waded without grace into the water, then paused. Violent animalistic retching cracked the space, echoing above the lake. I treaded water. The grunting and splashing resumed not more than fifty yards from me, heading toward me as I swam out into the lake. I froze as the silhouette of a man cleaved recklessly into the deeper waters.

"What do you want?"

"You," he grunted. Strong and athletic despite his careless strokes, it shocked me how quickly he gained on me. I continued to retreat. *Across, he'll never catch me across.*

When I stopped and turned back to look, all was still on the water and on the shoreline. Leaves rustled delicately. I allowed myself a breath.

The man shot to the surface next to me, grabbing at my shoulders and breasts, trying to mount me. "Mermaid naiad!" he croaked and tried once more to have me. He slipped over me. He took in water, then spluttered, gurgled, and fought to stay in the moonlight. He went under once, and I frantically swam away toward the shore.

After a few yards I glanced over my shoulder. The water began to settle. His arm pierced the surface. He reappeared, gasped for air, and went under again.

Damn it! The lake was watching me. I had to double back. I swam carefully and soundlessly toward him, fleet as if the crickets still serenaded my gracefulness, only his thrashing to spoil the storybook night. *The Little Mermaid had saved Prince Eric.* Every thought of the millions that swam in my head every moment day and night, emptied away from me as I came closer and grabbed him.

He fought to climb upon me, pulling me under, now without desire but in desperation. I struggled free and resurfaced. I made a fist. I hit him as hard as I could, once and then twice. My own strength surprised me. He went limp. I took him under the crook of my right arm and swam for shore, dragging his mass beside me.

My heart hammering, I took in deep breaths and his, which was rancid with alcohol and vomit. *Blind drunk.*

On the shore I lay his body down in the moonlight, my legs very nearly collapsing. I tore open his shirt and pumped his chest. A mermaid tattooed on his abdomen. I pumped again. Spittle erupted from the corner of his mouth. That once beautiful mouth.

I leaned closer. It had been almost ten years since I had seen him: his face distorted by the years, by the alcohol, puffy but still roughly handsome. It was Victor King.

My hand aching from the blows, I gathered my clothes and walked unsteadily back to Carver's before slipping them on and beginning my long bike ride home.

The feeling of fulfillment I'd felt with Carver, that feeling of helping another, had dissipated, leaving me uncertain again about my own species. And how faithful could I be to myself, really, in the midst of them?

CHAPTER FIVE

The hockey rink at Bemidji State was an unwelcome place for visitors during practice. Cold, the lights kept low and the sharp clatter of bodies hitting the boards, sticks slapping the puck, the puck striking the boards. The jangle. The delicious chill. The controlled anger. A place I could manage, the shelter of The Beaver suit no longer an option, Carver's catacombs now boarded up, Carver in his grave, not preserved.

I'd spent eight years in college studying part-time, cleaning the locker rooms after hours, acquiring research, and tending to Momma; thirty-two seasons coming and going as every leaf unfolded, then fell to the ground to be blown and covered in snow—though to Momma, they were all winters. Secluded years. The quaint magical thinking left in Kingdom Lake that night many years before. Now simply to be around people without being noticed, as long as I stayed in the highest, darkest regions of the bleachers.

"What's 'phlebotomy'?"

I looked up from my book. Players skated in loops, practicing coming off the boards and taking shots at my sister in goal. Carly the coach, Carly the improbable teacher. Carly the Wizard of Fun. Carly the Beautiful. Amidst thuds and grunting, echoing voices and clacking of sticks, I looked over my shoulder, only to find empty bleachers behind me. It took me a moment to understand that someone was talking to me and not looking away.

In that startled instant, his tiny face appeared. "You seem so intent," he said in a whisper. He nodded at my book but didn't take his eyes off me, as if he needed more time to take in my thickness.

His eyes were set so close to each other that at first glance they appeared lopsided. His body pole-thin. His dark suit out of place and ill fitting, and the shirt beneath it a comical candy cotton blue, buttoned at the top but with emptiness surrounding his neck. No tie. His skin had the look of deflated pudding with crevices —like he'd been kneading it. *Not attractive.*

"I've seen you here before, but you don't watch." He moved from one foot to the other like the bathroom was calling him. "Studying?"

Neither pushy nor shy, he looked at me like he was holding a fine cut crystal to the light, a naïve eagerness around his eyes. I liked it, I distrusted it.

His breath caught and he squeaked, reminding me of the screen door at the back of our farmhouse. "Harold Cloonis, you probably know me 'cause my dad is Kiwanis with your aunt." He held out his sausage fingers.

Naturally, I withdrew. *Unclean. In pain. A Tusser, a goblin. Foolishness,* I corrected myself, *but . . .*

Down through the rows of worn gray bleacher planks, I searched for more darkness than the hockey rink already provided. I couldn't breathe, had to get away.

Never as fluid as in the water, I stumbled getting up. I stepped on my own foot and fell backward, my heavy, expensive textbook cascading to the row below and the next, before falling all the way down and meeting the wet rubber floor at an angle, splitting the spine. An excruciating sound, the book damaged and useless. I tumbled toward the next set of planks.

He grabbed my hand. Not my arm, my hand. *How did he do that?*

"You okay?" he asked.

I knew better than to play into Harold's game. *He* was a prank. There had been a few of those: years back, a fake invitation to the high school prom. Momma cautioned me. Taking a chance, I found one of momma's old dresses and Lyle watched me put it on with naked eyes. "You got a nice body," he said. "Big trumpets." I waited. No one picked me up. The boy had a frightful accident sometime later, something about his brakes failing, his car into the slough where he drowned in ten feet of water.

Once on Valentine's Day flowers arrived from a "secret admirer." After a few days the flowers started to smell like shit. The flowers had been planted in human excrement.

"Let go of me," I said.

Harold let go. "Have coffee with me."

He seemed gentle and the way he *looked* at me. But I had considered comfort, if not love before Harold. It was treacherous. I'd seen the practical foolishness of finding someone to hold me. Desperate people found other desperate people for themselves and that was not who I imagined for myself. I had a mission; it came above all else.

"No," I said.

)))

The next time I was at the hockey rink he started again. "You're breathtaking."

Oh please. Not in thirty-six years had anyone equated me with breathlessness. "Please leave me alone. I'm not interested. I have a lot to study."

"They look like research papers." The whisper appeared to be his natural manner.

"They are."

"And?"

"And what?"

"Are they interesting?"

Please stop. "Yes." I bit the inside of my cheek.

"Tell me."

"Really?" He kept ogling me with those googley pea eyes, that pathetic face. "Visual cues of good genes; Scheib, Gangstead and Thornhill." That ought to shut him down.

"For instance?"

I blew a long hot deep breath. I wanted to stop the intrusion. I wanted to push him backward, much harder than I pushed Irene Kelmer. Let him tumble down the damn bleachers. "Do you know what phenotypic plasticity means?"

"No."

"I didn't think so."

"But I'm willing to learn."

I closed my book. I clambered down the bleachers, without tripping this time.

"Hey!" he yelled.

I didn't look back. But deep down, even if it was a prank, I appreciated his resolve.

❯❯❯

He was persistent, so persistent. After five weeks of calling almost every day and tracking me down at the hockey rink, I cautiously accepted an offer for coffee. Why, I have no idea. Curiosity maybe. Always one of my downfalls, I should have known by then.

I insisted on a quiet out-of-the-way place. I got what I deserved. The coffee had been sitting for hours; disagreeable on my tongue, acidic and chewing at my stomach.

"Now where were we?" His eyes were soft and attentive.

"Phenotypic plasticity. It means the ability of an organism to change its observable characteristics in response to environment. In this research, women choose mates based on body and facial features."

He nodded undeterred. The man was a piece of work and seemed to have no shame.

"There's a lid for every pot," he said pouring a mountain of sugar into his cup.

"Listen," I said trying to be efficient with my time, "why did you ask me out?"

My bluntness didn't produce the shock I expected. He looked thoughtful. "You're unique."

"Well," I said chuckling, "I suppose that's true, but still . . .?"

"Maybe I'm looking for a mate."

My mouth dropped open. "A mate?" Mating with him and inheriting his genes was not only impossible but (were it possible) would create something for a sideshow or a large jar of Formaldehyde.

"Why not?" he said.

I placed my hands on the table, just to stabilize.

He continued. "Look at me. What do you see?" He sat back in his chair, folded his arms, then became aware of them and let them drop.

Despite the strain of the albinism I could see him up close:

stubby fingers, dewy, sorrowful eyes, beak nose, undersized mouth, pouty like a child's. He didn't add up. He didn't satisfy any of the *attractive* research I'd been following.

Even putting aside the obvious sexual dimorphism (the difference between male and female of a species), he looked like a goblin. Momma's admonition about the family dying in poverty ghosted by me. I added cream to my coffee. It still tasted like canvass.

Finally, when I didn't answer, he asked, "You *are* interested in why people mate?" He balanced challenge and hope.

Oh god. Be kind. I settled my breathing and observed the frequencies around my heart.

"No," I said, happy he let me duck away from physically defining him. "I'm interested in human beauty. I'm not sure beauty currently has an actual purpose, but I'm going to give it one. I plan to find the coordinates of beauty. And I'm certainly *not* looking for a mate."

"Coordinates? For what purpose?"

At least he showed interest. "It may be possible to create a genetic map. For future generations . . . to be beautiful to the bone."

"Genetically-engineered beauty?" He seemed to understand the concept. "That's quite an undertaking."

That was it, if not a goblin then an undertaker, that's what he reminded me of. Terrible, I know. "It's a long road, but what's the point of all these theories on beauty if, once confirmed, they aren't applied?"

"Hmm."

"What does that mean?" Was he smirking?

"Nothing. Have you found the coordinates?"

"Not yet, but there's more and more research. I'm doing my own as well."

"That's where I come in." He leaned forward, immediately changed course. "I think you will. I think you'll find the coordinates."

A true piece of work. "Well, well, thank you for the coffee." I started to get up.

"Appalling."

"What!"

"This coffee. Next time I'll get you better."

I walked out unsure why I found him interesting.

〗〗〗

I sat in a corner waiting for him. Out the window I watched a flock of low-flying, newly-mated King Cans returning from the south. Perhaps a storm was coming.

Harold entered and I watched people watching him, watching the slow, nervous contractions of his body. They disappeared when, as he sat, he took my hand and rubbed it, apparently confirming something, a satisfied look on his face.

"Can we go someplace?" he asked.

It was almost sixty-one years to the day that James Watson and his colleagues presented the molecular structure of DNA to the world, reaching into the primordial swamp and saying *we are all in there.* The day should've been a commemoration, a celebration. Harold's invitation implied as much.

I said yes.

He drove me south to the forest where we walked surrounded by green new growth. A weekday, hardly anyone else around. I knew it was an exploration.

He tucked his hand around my waist. I didn't shake him off. He turned me around so we faced each other. He cupped his hand behind my neck and pulled me into him, hungry for my lips. I accepted. And his tongue. The hardness between his legs rubbed against my belly. I accepted. *I'll take away his pain.* I grounded him.

〗〗〗

Still, I had doubts. I made lists. I tried to stay rational. But it was such a grand experiment, to have conversation, to dangle ideas, to theorize, to question — and not only about science.

"He's an accountant but not dry, he's not simply about numbers," I said to my bedroom wall and to Michael Landon's replacement: an enlarged newspaper photograph of William Schroeder leaving the hospital with the first artificial heart. "Harold's not dry at all. Maybe not beautiful, but he's clean. It's all research, ay William?"

Soon I was having the fun I'd always imagined. Well, almost.

"Please move your things off the table." He pointed to make way for his satchel and slammed the front door.

"Is it okay that I let myself in?" His edginess entered my body in disagreeable ways, mostly my chest.

"Sure. Of course." With a quick-but-passionate bite of my neck, he went to his stack of accounting ledgers.

"What'd you do today?"

"The usual," he said. "Clients."

Researchers are undecided if smarts impact facial beauty — they doubt it— but they agree that "openness" reflects positively on facial attractiveness. So far he wasn't very open. He rarely left the office except to visit his clients or the house, and then only after much coaxing from me. I got very few details.

He paged through a ledger, his shoulders hunched.

"You look stressed."

"Something's not right."

I wandered over to him and massaged his neck. "Can I help?"

"Not really." His fingers rested on column after column of scribbled figures. "There's just so much of this . . . I'm going to have to go over every one of these damn numbers again, and I'm running out of time."

"I'm pretty good with numbers." I rubbed his shoulders. "At least I can add and subtract. How about I take on some of those columns, cut down your load. Can't hurt, can it?"

"But your studies."

"They can wait for a few hours. Let me be useful."

And after a couple of hours of calculating the two of us found the error. He breathed easier. "You're a life saver." He sat back and let his head dangle.

I ran my fingers down his back. "And I'm taking you out to dinner tonight."

"I don't know . . ."

I'd only seen the inside of a handful of buildings in my thirty-six years: the farmhouse, Carver's workshop, my classrooms, the school library, the locker rooms, the basketball court and the hockey rink. Oh, and that church. But it was time for both of us to explore. I pushed. He gave in. I was terrified.

He took me to *another* dark, out-of-the-way place, Valhalla's or something. It sounded familiar. I'd never seen anything quite like it —candles the color of water marigold, medallions of sage, large goblets of pewter lining the roughhewn shelves, shelves the color of a broad-winged hawk encircling the room.

Throughout dinner he held a shy, little boy demeanor, as shy as I felt with other people sitting around us. We held hands. That helped.

Once back home I found the citation: Valhalla is the mytho-logical 'hall of the slain' for half of those who die in combat and go with the god, Odin. The other half, chosen first by Freyja, goes to her 'meadow of death.' All prepare to be reborn for the next war.

CHAPTER SIX

Harold's introversion didn't discourage me. It challenged me. And I had so much to learn from him. Like any good scientist I explored his patterns.

He lingered as he turned pages, running his fingers back and forth along the paper, sometimes testing the edges. His hands trailed lightly along walls as we walked. He repeatedly smoothed his napkin. Measuring his experience with his fingers, at least that's what I thought. I could understand that, like the prophetic feelings in my chest. 'Psychometry' is what they'd called it in my encyclopedia, the ability to obtain information about a person or an event by touching an object. But it was an old encyclopedia. There might be more recent scientific explanations.

"Do you like to swim?" The research paper slipped off my lap. I'd lost my place. I left it.

"Not really." He was in *Martin Chuzzlewit*, distracted and not looking at me.

I imagined myself sneaking out of the farmhouse at thirteen, stripping off my clothes and slipping naked past the tall reeds into a small pond, the cold April water stoking my flesh to life. For the first- but not the last time. Would he respond to nature like I did, would he open up?

"Do you?" he asked. He closed the book, index finger keeping his spot.

"Hmm, I do. Very much." I couldn't tell him that the waters —swimming completely exposed in those lakes and ponds— were imagined lovers, the only ones safe enough to imagine. Or that once I entered them, I investigated each with abandon; that they never disappointed me with their touch. That I remember the name of every one —Kingdom, Balm, White Fish, Medicine and others— and of most of the birds and animals that watched my nakedness.

"Well, maybe I'll take you swimming someday," he said.

"Yes, that would be nice." I could see he wanted to return to his Dickens. I wanted to know *why*, why that was more important than exploring us and exposing us to new things.

"Where are you now?" I asked.

His lips barely moved. "I'm here. I'm gathering, gathering information." A hint of delight.

He took my hand. In a moment he pulled me fully to him, untucked my blouse and drew his hands along my naked neck and back. I didn't resist.

He's teaching me, in his own way. I breathed heavy, but it was different than in the hockey rink, without fear. It was like gliding through the insatiable water. I couldn't explain it, but the exploration was always new, always exquisite. He unhooked and removed my bra.

〉〉〉

On May 17, a few weeks after the Native People harvested their sugar maple, on an unusually warm, hypnotizing day along the shores of Kabekona Bay in the Paul Bunyan Forest where we courted and first consummated our relationship, Harold Cloonis proposed to me. I wasn't completely surprised. But the greens were greener, the sky bluer than I'd ever seen it, and the sun seemed to catch me and massage me at just the right times as we passed through the variegated light. It was his acceptance of me, of course, and it was my assurance that I'd been right about nature and how it might open us both up, though we still had work to do together.

To the Ojibwe and other Native People it was New Years Day, a new beginning, and it should have been for me too. But I thought about a big city, where I could be involved firsthand in research, and where healthy, attractive people congregated and new ideas germinated daily. Would he fit in? Would he slow me down? How would I be, surrounded by concrete rather than Bemidji's comforting trees and waterways? And realistically, where would I get the money to live in such a place, even if I could find a research job there?

Furthermore, I'd need to tell him that there would be no children. Neither of us had good symmetrical genes, but it was moot anyway. "I need time to think about it." I made steady eye contact with him.

"Really?" As if his world had been swept away, the dark blue rings around his eyes grew darker still.

"I'm not saying no."

"Please don't. I couldn't bear it."

"You want me to be happy?"

"Of course, that's why—"

"Ssh." I placed my fingers to his lips with one hand and placed his hand over my left breast with the other. We were both diverted by the physical. "It will all work out."

☽☽☽

When I could get away from Momma and her prying questions, our evenings were quiet, and always alone, he with his Poe and Dickens and Dickinson, me with my studies in medical technology. A generous time with little said. Lights kept low. Still, he was pressing me for a decision and I was still studying him for answers.

Occasionally he breathed irregularly, with difficulty. I felt it moments before it started. I raised my head, concerned.

"Listen to this," he said and read a passage:

> *"There is nothing . . . no nothing innocent and good, that dies and is forgotten. Let us hold to that faith or none . . . There is not an angel added to the Host of Heaven but does its blessed work in those that loved it here."*

"A bit depressing."

"Really? Well, it is Dickens. Do you think it's true? Aren't we all connected?"

"I suppose."

He flashed a small admiring smile. "I know you do. You care about people. You're one of those who understands instinctively; you feel without being touched. Dickinson would say you're not waiting for Eternity, you're close to it."

I wasn't convinced. "Hmmm."

Despite that his eyes brightened, as if he was releasing a bucket of safe light on me. "And soon we'll formalize *our* connection."

I mustered a half-smile, hoping he was right, but worried how it might end if he wasn't.

"I know, I know," he said. "You think you're systematic, all scientist. Always carrying a measuring stick." He pointed to the book in my lap, *Davis's Comprehensive Handbook of Laboratory and Diagnostic Tests with Nursing Implications*.

"Dickens wrote something in *American Notes*. It's here somewhere." He rose, plucked the book from the shelf and seated himself in one uncharacteristically smooth move. His fingers searched for a certain thickness of pages, then opened the book accordingly. "Here. This is systematic."

Again, he quoted Dickens:

> *"A woman was locked up alone. She was bent, they told me, on committing suicide. If anything could have strengthened her in her resolution, it would certainly have been the insupportable monotony of such an existence."*

He closed the book. A contorted grin seized his face. My pulse quickened; we're biologically evolved to detect deception in facial imbalance. And wasn't Harold 'locked up' in some ways? Wasn't I?

His grimace swiftly vanished. "A report on how Americans deal with the unconventional. Systematic. Not much has changed since Dickens visited in the 1800s and wrote his journal. You don't want to be systematic. It's not for you. It's a kind of confinement. You can't do your good work hidden behind a curtain. You need to be out and about."

"Confinement? Really?" I affected solemnity, surprised at this apparent turnaround in his philosophy but perhaps, like Momma, he'd be okay if I was out and about *without visual connection to him*. I blustered, then quickly swallowed my laughter. But I knew he was right and I appreciated his support. I just didn't know how to get there. Or how I could afford it.

"Just saying," he whispered. "You have a gift."

"You mean," I said, waving my hands above my head and flaring my eyes in mock wonder, "the stuff of myths and legends, like a *vardøger*, some magic spirit?"

Hurt pinned back his eyes and mouth. That was unfair of me. I didn't know where that came from; he was merely trying to be kind and supportive. I changed the subject. "What about you? You're always gathering information."

"I'm not systematic." He said it like a little boy begging to be understood.

"You don't go out. You're happy to read your Dickens." A piece of me was prodding him to change.

"He's taught me all I need to know about out there. Taught me so much."

"About?"

He thought for a moment. "About not looking away, not at the precious things." He bowed to me. I knew then that he would never hurt me. As if again he'd read my mind, he continued. "Forgive me now for all the foolish things I will do in our relationship."

I inhaled his love, completely. "You're forgiven." Could I really be so indulgent?

He bent ever so slightly to me, then glanced at the clock and said no more. He returned to his page. His hands didn't caress the words the way they usually did; they were restless on the page. I went back to my textbook. A cool current passed between us. He wanted my advice, or something more, but didn't ask. Would that come in time? Would it depend on my answer?

☽☽☽

I devised a test for myself and for Harold. Could he live in a city? Could I give up my work for him? And if I did, would he join me in nature?

"I want you to come with me." I rubbed his shoulders. I really wanted this to work.

"Where?"

"The afternoon in Itasca State Park."

"Ah, no." He was anchored to the chair with a book in his

lap.

"It's beautiful down there."

"Yes, I'm sure it is. What's this all about?"

"A geneticist at Stanford replaced myth with science —using fish skin!" Even thinking about it excited me.

"Huh?"

"He and his colleagues proved being blonde was a *controllable genetic variation.*"

"Could be the end of blonde jokes."

"Could be. The same gene in the fish controls pigmentation in humans."

"I guess that gives you hope."

"More than hope. I'm on the right track. Don't you see?" I coaxed him to let go of the book. "If I can isolate the ideal facial traits, controls for those DNA traits will be available within a few years."

"Creating a master race."

I scowled. "No, just a healthy start; a master *face.* Variations will naturally follow. Anyhow, can we talk about it down there?

"No."

"If not Itasca, someplace outside? How about Little Bass Stump? That's closer."

"Why so mysterious? What does this have to do with me?"

"Do you trust me?"

"Of course, but—"

"Then please put that darn book down and come with me."

☽☽☽

In the car I laid my scrapbook of celebrity faces in his lap, and I drove. Might as well be efficient. A captive audience.

"What's this?" His exasperation not well hidden.

"Clippings from Momma's magazines. Remember when I mentioned attraction to healthy genes? The research that posits that people are attractive because they *look healthy* to others, like they'd create healthy offspring?"

"Don't remember, you've got so much of this stuff."

"Look at them." Decades of beauty: Redford, Newman, Cruise, Diggs, Clooney, Deere, Pitt, Bardot, Derek, Locklear,

Lawrence, Berry, and more. "Look closely. Are they all healthy looking and therefore beautiful?"

"I guess so." He closed the scrapbook.

"No, please look. Which ones are and which ones are not? And why? Like if you wanted to have healthy babies with them."

"I want to have a healthy baby with you."

I hadn't told him yet. "Okay, but if you liked men."

"This is absurd. Damn it!" He slammed his hand on the binder, disproportionately irritated. "They're all good looking. Whatever you want."

I pursed my lips. I could wait him out.

He saw I wouldn't be dissuaded. He opened the binder. "Well, I don't think Cruise is so good looking. Or Pitt."

"Why?"

"Don't know. I certainly wouldn't want to have a baby with them."

A joke; he actually made a joke. I laughed. His face loosened. "How about the women?" I tapped the photos.

"Who's that?"

"Jennifer Lawrence."

"She's good looking."

"Why?"

"She's cuddly."

"*Cuddly.* She looks healthy, so she's attractive to you?"

"Yes, sure."

"And the others? Who looks healthy?"

"I'm not crazy about her." He pointed to Kathleen Turner.

"Why?"

"She's kind of hard looking. We'd end up with kids that looked like Mickey Roarke."

"So," I continued, "black, white, blonde, brunette, hair long or short? None of that factors in?"

"Not for me."

I pulled onto the dirt turnoff and parked the car. "Little Bass Stump."

He looked at the surroundings. "It's pretty. Thanks for getting me out."

When he wanted to he could make everything right. I took

his hand. We wandered down a narrow path that appeared to dead-end at a dense orange thicket of wild milkweed. I pulled him through and found a secluded sandbar.

"Take off your clothes. Come swim with me." I dropped my jeans and peeled off my top.

"What do you think you're doing?!"

"Come on." I spread my arms.

He looked around. "Someone will see us. Put your clothes back on."

"There's no one for a half mile or more."

A pained look fixed on his face. "Why'd you bring me here?"

"Swim."

"No." He backed away from the water. "I don't swim." His eyes stuttered with panic.

"Okay, okay," I said reassuring him, still standing completely naked and trying to control my reaction. "Could you live in New York City?"

"Don't be ridiculous. Why would I want to do that?"

Suddenly I felt emotionally naked. "To further my research."

"Look, I've already got a small nest egg. If you get a job in town we'll be fine."

"I don't want to be *fine*. I want to be useful."

"You'll be useful to me. Come here."

"Harold, I'm serious." All the pleasure of my discoveries and my surroundings were ebbing away.

"*I'm* serious. We've got everything we need here."

☽☽☽

On the way home, we said very little. The greenery and the rolling hills had taken on an empty feeling.

Just before I dropped him off at his apartment, he said, "Eunis?"

"Yeah."

"Can I suggest something?"

"Of course."

"I think you should stop talking to yourself in public. When you start quantifying people especially, it's kind of embarrassing."

"Ah, okay." I balled my fist in my lap. This was going to be more difficult than I'd imagined. I guess I'd grown used to my privacy.

"And, I understand."

"What?"

"That you want to stick with your research. I'll help make that happen." He took my hand. I wanted to believe him.

⟫⟫⟫

When I recognized what I was doing —usually because he reminded me— I realized it didn't sound or look reasonable to talk to myself out loud, although his incessant preaching pissed me off. "What do you suggest?"

"Journaling, like Dickens." Apparently unaware of my irritation, he bought me a diary with a burgundy cloth cover and a simple red cedar box to keep it in. He kissed me on the forehead and stroked my hair. Okay, I'd talk to myself on paper.

Eunis Cloonis —it figures, I wrote in my diary less than four months later when he talked me into moving in with him, an experiment. *Even my name will draw unwanted attention if I agree to marry him.*

"As for the living room," he added, rewarding himself with a scan of his library and the small desk, "I'll ask that you not alter this room in any way except by your presence." But then he added, "Your *magnificent* presence." And he wrapped his arms around me and whispered in my ear. "I love you."

The moving-in thing was kind of cool. As I said, an experiment. Like a badge they'd give to exploring Girl Scouts. After putting it off for days I told Momma, "I'm moving out."

"Out where? Don't be ridiculous." She stopped wiping the counter for a moment, shook her head and turned back to stare out the window at the caboose going nowhere on its single length of track.

"It's time. I'll still come see you. I won't be far."

"I knew this college thing was a mistake. You're full of yourself."

"It was okay for Carly and she's gone."

"She's made something for herself. You're mixin' around with stuff that's useless."

I knew I should just shut up and leave. "Because of the way I look."

"You need to take account a that, sure."

"You ever had dreams?"

"I need you here." She muffled a sob, her back still to me. "I would miss you so much. You're my big girl."

"I need to be someplace else." *Anywhere* else. Away from Momma, away from Lyle the reckless man-child. And into Desire, a fantasy I'd only begun to examine.

CHAPTER SEVEN

Smooth with a refined purr, the motor coach to Minneapolis rode like a queen's carriage. I was nervous but glad to be away from Harold, even for a day. I scolded myself for such thoughts. He'd been good to me. I liked soothing him. I liked watching his eyes relax and close. My brain was too busy for its own good.

Over my dark glasses rows of harvested barley fields slipped by, glazed in morning frost, an assurance of harder things to come. Yet I was cozy. Except for tending to my hood and maintaining a divide from the woman seated next to me, I marveled at the ease of escaping Bemidji, the excitement and *luxury* of it. And streaming past at incredible speed was what remained of the immense glacial Lake Agassiz, as chronicled in the encyclopedia. It wasn't the first time I'd imagined it, but there it was. I fantasized again swimming across the legendary lake, it holding more water than is contained now in all the lakes in all the world.

Careful not to draw attention, I stroked the plush-blue, deep-set seat. I nestled into it and considered the questions to ask Matthew Deere. The young actor was bringing his book-signing tour to the large Barnes & Noble in the Twin Cities, and his autobiography *Deere in the Headlights* about his insecurities in public and in front of a camera, compelled me to take the risk that Harold had advocated.

"You need to be out and about," he'd said, and so here I was, surprising Harold with my courage. He'd be thrilled when he returned from visiting a client.

And now I had the chance to ask Matthew Deere, a man sensitive to personality traits, what he'd experienced working with various actors. Did personality reflect attractiveness on a face? Perhaps there would be some actors he'd rather not discuss, but even that would be telling and something I could correlate to my other research, though I was certain I wouldn't be able to stand in line with people milling around, under rows of fluorescent lights, to ask him the questions. I had so many; he'd starred with countless famous faces.

The sight of him surprised me. He was smaller in person than on screen, not only shorter, but also less muscular. I stuck with my plan. At least fifty women —mostly women— had listened along with me to his sweet story of shyness and his ascension to film idol. I pulled his book and my journal closer. Some of the women gathered round him, asking for *additional* signatures, pawing at him, asking questions. And the questions, from what I could hear, were so petty. About clothing, about his alleged affair with Zooey Deschanel, about *nothing*.

My moment was coming. I could see he was bored and tired; this was, after all, the tenth stop on a sixteen-city tour. I'd done the research. I'd spent over an hour scoping out the bookstore's floor plan, like any smart investigator would do. Did he glance out to me, beyond the gaggle of foolish women?

A butch orange-haired woman running interference for him, perhaps his agent, finally interceded into the circle surrounding him and cleared an opening to a side door through which he vanished, inelegantly dropping his pen. The crowd set upon it.

I stepped outside, down the parking lot steps, and back up a smaller set to a doorway. Effortlessly. And then there he was, Matthew Deere, all to myself.

I was speechless, my hands clammy. I tugged at my hood. He gawked at me, aghast, and then tried to regain his calm. "I'm sorry. No more signatures." He waved me off and moved toward the parking lot.

"But wait." I tried to open my journal and run and read the first question. "Wait."

He did not.

"Physical beauty," I called, sprinting after him, "may be a component of personality. I thought . . . you're a beauty. Your insights could provide help to others." I took two steps at a time, fluidly. He was clumsy. I was on him before I even knew it, crashing into him as he stopped and turned, knocking him to the ground where he skinned his hands and face.

"I am so sorry—"

"Merilee!" he yelled. "Merilee!"

"I just need some answers. It's research." I tried to calm him. I read from my journal. "You've worked with Nicole Kidman twice. Is she—?"

"Get away from me." He screamed stumbling to his feet and rubbing his palms.

"But is she agreeable, conscientious—?"

"Get the fuck away."

"I'm a scientist—"

"Get her the fuck away from me!" he yelled again over my shoulder.

What I learned: I still scared people.

☽☽☽

Harold arrived shortly after 10 PM, not making eye contact with me. A bit guilty, it seemed. *I* should talk.

"Shall we watch the news?" he said.

The news? He usually wanted to run his hands over me the minute he walked through the door, or at least talk or read his Dickens. We rarely turned on the TV. "I guess. How was your day?"

"Fine," he said eyes darting away from me. "Fine." He dumped himself unceremoniously on the couch and faced the TV. He picked up the remote. "And you?" He surfed the listings.

A deep breath. "I took your advice."

"What advice is that?" He was preoccupied with the screen.

I sat and leaned on him. "Out and about."

"What?" He finally faced me. Then quickly away.

"Hi." I kissed him. How could I not want him?

"Hi." Unfocused. Nervous.

I put my hand on his. He didn't respond, like he wasn't even there. Confusing. "I went to Minneapolis today."

"What!"

"You would have been proud of me." I did feel stronger. At least I'd tried.

"Okay." His eyes uncertain.

"You know who Matthew Deere is?"

He nodded. "The actor."

"The very attractive actor. He has a new book out. I went to his book signing."

"That's terrific." His smile, broad for Harold, felt forced.

"Well, almost." I needed a place to put my hands. My lap. "It didn't go well." *Breathe.*

"I wouldn't feel too sorry for a rich actor who makes foolish movies and gets paid obscenely for them."

"I wanted to interview him, you know, on the subject of beauty. Get real first-hand information for my research."

He drummed the remote fretfully, like I'd been caught stealing. "What have you done?"

"Shouldn't I do whatever I can to achieve my vision?"

"Don't drag me into it."

Heat ran up my back. "It was your idea."

"To hassle some . . . pretty boy?"

"It's my work."

"Eunis, really."

It sounded condescending. Suddenly I didn't like him so much.

"What would you expect?" he continued. "This beauty *thing.* It's subjective. Did you make a fool of yourself?"

Shame flooded over me, again. "I frightened him, knocked him down." I wanted Harold to corral me, tell me it was okay, that I had taken an important step, even if the results weren't there.

"Oh god, no, we don't need to show up in one of your brainless celebrity magazines."

It took me a minute to find air. "Your privacy is safe."

Pressure built on my jaw and my teeth hurt. He was no friend. He was like the others. He was going to be in the way. I wanted to lash out at him. But I punched the couch, stood up, and disappeared into the bedroom. When he finally came to bed I kept my back to him. He did the same to me. But the next morning he kissed the back of my neck and said, "I'm sorry." I wasn't so sure.

⟫⟫⟫

"Harold Cloonis?!" Momma pushed aside her Star magazine, stubbed out the Lucky Strike, and twisted her mouth in distaste. "He's a loner, a creep. You're not gonna *marry* the creep! I thought you'd outgrow this." She'd dressed in pineapple yellow Capri pants, a cherry red tunic, and her signature carrot orange dyed hair.

"Momma the fruit cocktail."

"What'd you say?"

"Nothing."

Momma reached for the cigarette pack, but it was done. "Carton," she commanded, directing me to the hall closet with a stiff wave.

"Momma, no." My resistance was pathetically sheepish, scarcely audible.

"Carton." She repeated with exasperation and a sandy cough that echoed off the tired hospital-green kitchen cabinets. I moved dutifully to the hall closet, the lightless sanctuary where I'd first felt atoms at play.

"No friends," Momma called out. "He ain't got a friend. At forty? What's that about?"

I searched my memory for friends. Hidden away, there had been few . . .

"Do you hear me?"

. . . There was Nemo, the mutt, of course. Maybe he wasn't the best-looking, but he could make me laugh. He was a friend. I felt love in my chest, at least I thought it was love, like I thought it was love with Harold.

"You and your weird hunches," continued Momma from the kitchen. "Can you trust them? I don't think so; it's not reality. It's just weather in your head. This is another one of your experiments, like the time you put henna in your hair. Remember that?"

I remembered Momma's cosmetic experiment. I remembered appearing closer to death.

There was silence, then her tone softened. "It was a nice try, Eunis Marie, but this is much more serious. You are what you are."

I brought her the carton. Momma picked it up and slammed

it down on the kitchen table, careful to make noise but not damage the cigarettes. "He wants your body."

"So?"

"You think that's funny?"

I must have smirked; Harold had already been a man and an animal and an uncontrollable electric storm. All new. Cleansing. Our milky smell lingered and moistened my memory.

"This is an ungodly union." Her unequivocal statement of fact. "You'll wanta kill him before he kills you, you'll see." Momma reminiscing her past. "And what about me? Who's gonna take care a me?" She squinted, eyes seeping.

To my own surprise I stared straight back. "He loves me," I said, still unsure why.

A grin spread in stages across my mother's large, lined face and mouth, the first time in a long time. Her gray jowls bobbed a few times and a coarse private laugh cracked out. She stripped open the carton and the next pack, then pointed the Lucky Strike at me. "You don't fuckin' know how good you got it here."

That night after my swim I met Harold at the apartment. When he opened the door his face opened to mine, that all-encompassing smile of his, twisted and ingenuous and completely at my disposal. He breathed me in. "God, I've missed you," he said, cupping his hands strategically to the right and left of my breasts.

We'd been less than a day apart and he chased my uncertainty as if it was just a bad dream.

"I accept," I said touching his face.

Eighteen days later, after the clerk pronounced, "You are now Mr. and Mrs. . . ." —pausing to read and confirm the certificate— ". . . Cloonis," and the dappled light in the Cloquet honeymoon cabin made me believe that I was the luckiest woman in the world, Missy Bassert, the cleaning lady with the palsied left hand and the soiled calico apron, found Harold in his office, above his oak desk, hanging from a 12x12 beam.

The darkness was comforting, even with the freezing wind whipping at me, and I approached the floodlit stone building with caution. I still hadn't completely settled in. At the threshold of its centerpiece, a domed rotunda faced in split layers of blue-gray rock, I hesitated. I'd rather have watched my breath rise in the frigid air curling up the structure's grand Victorian lines than enter. Numb felt good, the cold reminding me of my flesh. But I really had to sleep, if I could.

Even well past midnight, light burned brightly from the lobby. Peeking through the glass into the entrance hall he was there, in the corner, headphones on, rather lumpy and overweight, waxing the floor. I pulled back. I'd learned by now. I waited and watched from the shadows.

Then remembering, I dug into my coat pocket and smoothing out the clipping as best I could in the wind, I held it to the light and re-read it:

<u>England's Daily Mail</u>
"Superhumans could become a reality in 30 years thanks to advances in gene science

A generation of genetically modified 'X-Men' superhumans could be among us by 2045, a Ministry of Defence think tank has said.

Advancements in gene technology could help humans gain mutant powers such as the likes of Wolverine, Cyclops and Storm in the popular comic book and movie series, it has been reported.

The MoD's Development Concepts and Doctrine Centre

warn however that 'genetic inequality' could result from advancements in biology being unequally shared across society."

Marginally fortified, I slipped the clipping back into my pocket. The concierge retreated to a back room.

I stole across the grand lobby and scurried the last few yards into the elevator. All sound was sealed away as I rose through space to the thirteenth floor, as if ascending from the ocean bottom. The smoked-glass panels flickered by. "I'm still gathering," I muttered. The empty elevator continued upward, reflecting fragments of me, circling me. I dropped my head but I reminded myself, despite my fatigue, that I was doing just fine. Quite well, really, considering Harold and his parents and the questioning.

ͻͻͻ

I went around the back of the gray cinderblock building. I wanted to see Harold's face one last time. Maybe it would put an end to the questions, mine as well as the others. A young man, probably no older than fifteen and wearing a raggedy brown Abercrombie & Fitch t-shirt and a dust mask, sorted through some ashes in a small rectangular tub. He waved a large magnet over them and tossing whatever came up in a small pile on the table top, next to chunks of white coals, similar to what you'd find after a barbeque. I watched him for a few minutes, sensing the ungodly dryness of his sifting, before he noticed me and startled, then pulled off his mask and composed himself.

"Can I help you?" He wore latex gloves and dusted them off. "You shouldn't be here."

"There was no one up front."

"Come back when my uncle's in the office."

"I was hoping to see my husband before he's cremated."

"That's not my responsibility."

"Do you know when it will be?"

"You can come with the rest of the family. Talk to my uncle."

"His name was Harold, Harold Cloonis."

His face took on the color of the powder.

"I know I'm not supposed to ask, but you see, my father-in-law won't let me . . . Well, anyway, do you know when it will be?"

He examined the pile of ash and picked up one of the white coals. Now I saw that it wasn't coal; it was a piece of bone.

And then later that week, the cop. "Please tell me again where you were that afternoon?" He was middle-aged, part Asian, abnormally laconic. Not as aggressive as the last time. With a name like Sullivan and a largemouth bass mounted on his wall.

Truth was, I couldn't remember. I knew it was damning, not knowing where I was when my new husband coiled a rope around his neck and broke it . . . "I think I was at the apartment studying, but I just don't know."

"Between two and six, six-thirty?" The detective was emotionless. Not like Columbo or Sonya Cross; more like someone pulled his spark plugs and he was waiting for his pension.

I shrugged.

"No enemies?"

"I told you, I don't know any of his friends. Ask his folks."

He pursed his thin lips. It could have been worse; he could have considered me a suspect.

"It's odd." The way he said it and turned his focus to an open file in his hands, especially with his show-nothing face, felt *accusatory* for the first time.

"Isn't suicide that way?" *Odd.* I was being brave. Like Freyja.

"No, I meant his fractured vertebrae. His neck. It's unusual except when the body drops. But you must know that because of your studies. It's the collapsed carotid artery blocking blood to the brain that usually kills people." A rush of nausea swept over me. He looked up. "You ever fight? You were newlyweds."

"Yes. *Ever* fight, of course."

"Physical?"

"No."

"You'd think he'd be happy."

"He was never a dance-in-the street kind of guy."

"Well, I suppose you'll need to find a silver lining. I understand this opens some opportunities for you. I'm glad to see you've adjusted, Mrs. Cloonis."

"I don't think I've adjusted, Detective."

)))

I watched the elevator numbers climb. *Please let tonight settle more easily than the last.* I was missing something. Harold. I closed my eyes. "You . . . How could you? *You* who was so sure about *me*, and then . . ."

I saw him swinging by the neck, watching me. My eyes bolted open. I hung onto the elevator's brass railing.

"It seemed right at the time. Do whatever it takes. You said so."

I'd been so sure that genetics were the answer, that I could help being in a lab while I learned and prepared for the next stage of my research, that the New York lab was the place. The next grand experiment. The pursuit of ideal beauty was exciting and exhausting.

The elevator whirred upward.

I could be loved. Logically, Harold had ended that debate, *hadn't he?* Once would be enough, on to more important things. Things I promised Nemo, things I promised myself.

I snuck a peek at my face and was repelled as always. Beyond my albinism, more evident than ever as I'd aged, lay my flattened nose, bulging to the sides like sewer culverts; broad volcanic stone-chiseled lips —*natural on Easter Island*; a humped brow; straight ghost-white hair. The years had been no kinder to my birthmark, dog-shit brown and sinister, creeping across my left cheek and down my neck like some horror film mutation.

Love? Who could love a face like that? Who could take on the peril? I ran my finger above my right eye, along my snowbound eyebrow, Harold's fetish. White-white. The only color I possess. *I will please him,* that's what I thought. But maybe I was pleasing myself, maybe because he was something I could control.

The elevator pinged. The doors slid open with a whisper. No one would be in the hallway. I investigated anyway, in both directions.

The corridor, less chrome than the elevator, still existed as an abstract; not at all Victorian like the building's façade. I could have been anywhere, maybe even Minneapolis, but not likely Bemidji. Not a scent of balsam or cedar anywhere. Still. It was Harold's gift, apartment 13-F, part of what they called The Penthouse, my lease-to-buy the benefit of his modest estate.

In his odd accountant's way, Harold had given me freedom to expand yet be invisible, to come to New York and try again at the top of the world, or close to it. Yes, his death was opportune; it kept my dream alive, his sacrifice. I thanked him. But I wished he would go away, that all of the coroner's and detective's questions would go away, though no one could reasonably expect relief so soon after a death. *A suicide.*

I listened, even for the murmur of a TV set, but by then I should have known that The Octagon condominiums were built for discretionary income and privacy. Nothing escaped. Privacy at least tranquilized.

My key slipped fluently into the tumbler. It snapped with authority. I was in.

In the darkness I moved effortlessly, keys to the table.

It was just as I'd wanted and as the brochure had promised: "Floor-to-ceiling windows, where the East Side skyline hangs in your living room like a colossal urban fresco . . . Easy to reach, yet possessing a secluded character all its own."

I readjusted to the welcoming shadows. No need for light; I knew the studio confines edge by edge. Airtight. All atoms in place.

Even in the shadows it had the sheen of a model apartment. No extra fuss. It had none of the flaws that those older apartments bore, none of the snoopy, small building managers or superintendents.

Here, organized entirely by me, the walls were barren but for my college diploma, which reminded me I could do anything. All reflective surfaces, except for the windows, I'd covered or removed. Little stood on the counters — a few unlit candles, my small TV, my laptop, a textbook, the next stage of my education: *Data Mining for Genomics and Proteomics: Analysis of Gene and Protein Expression Data;* and a celebrity magazine or two, part of the ongoing steam-driven sector of my research, a habit I knew I'd inherited from Momma.

Even the magazines were neatly fanned. And the simple triangular table by the high-backed chair on which my diary sat. All hygienic. Except. That damned box, the large cardboard box, still unopened. It sat to the left of the two kitchen stools. *Harold's box.*

And then there it was again, barely audible. The apartment bristled with high frequency white noise, a deep kinetic turbulence that seldom went away. No reason to be anxious. A radio tower? The city? *Never mind.*

Except for my tower apartment, I'd been judicious. I'd stayed under the radar in every way. My overcoat: secondhand. A muted pickup intended to reflect cosmopolitan New York but not bring attention, bought Day One, then aged a month or had it been six weeks?

It slipped from my shoulders to the bamboo floor, which was as tightly woven as my chest. The buttons scratched the silence. I quickly retrieved the coat and hung it up. Everything in its place.

Too late. Particles began to move, and all the spaces between them too. As if I was slipping under water, numinescence enveloping me, my ears feeling it first, just as they always had, then those vibrations around my heart. Knowing there was a rational explanation, and rather than resist, I slid past the unopened box of Harold's books, almost as heavy as Harold himself, and settled into the wing chair.

I followed my breath. I focused on the diffused gemstone light radiating from my floor-to-ceiling cityscape. I ran my left palm across the chair's scarred high back, reminding myself of my persistent intention to correct its imperfection.

A chill in the dark apartment distracted me though every window was hermetically sealed; nothing stirred on The Octagon's 13th floor, *did it?* At best I was a motionless nebulous reflection surrounded by New York's skyline. What moved? *A vardøger!*

"Ridiculous," I said aloud. "Momma and the old witch and Sarah Pooley telling their damn spook stories. And I think of myself as a scientist!" I cracked my jaw, trying to clear my ears.

Mist played around my eyes.

But then a whirring hollow sound, possibly a man's measured voice. Composed but taut, and garbled as if underwater: *Come with me. Build the watchtower. Protect our independence.* That's what it sounded like. Blood pumping faster.

This was not the first time I thought I'd heard or felt something in the apartment. I covered my ears. I didn't want to breathe. But the pumping, I felt it too. Hands off ears.

"Harold?"

I knew it wasn't Harold. Sounded nothing like Harold.

That set off groaning from where my small kitchen met the living area. I waited. A cold dampness seemed to rise off the floor. I directed an ear to the pipes under the kitchen sink. The cool filtered moonlight blanketed the angles. The spaces inside the atoms appeared to rest.

I caught my breath. I waited.

I thought: *someone needs help.*

Then, *stop trying to make sense of nothing.*

I turned my head left and right. My ears began to unclog. When nothing more was spoken and nothing more converged on me, I stood and paused for a moment, waiting for my breath to fully stabilize.

A logical explanation would reveal itself when I least expected it. Or my cursed 'gift' had returned. *Never mind.*

Carefully I assembled the rest of my clothes as always, neatly creased in the right places and settled over the chair. I watched my naked specter move along the glass, directly to the bed and then into it. In thirty-seven minutes the extended silence reassured me, and I drifted into a steady sleep.

☽☽☽

The next morning I referred to research. "La Trobe University (Australia) study, 2010: Heavy coffee consumption and high stress linked to auditory hallucinations. Could also be Parkinson's, temporal-lobe epilepsy, or hyperthyroidism." Doubtful.

CHAPTER NINE

The 4 PM to midnight shift was an advantage. I was lucky. In the early New York rush hour the people jockeying the streets and subways had been early to rise and therefore were empty from a full day. The winter was also an ally, as it was in Minnesota, when everyone wore hoods and stayed close to home.

In the dusk, the restless New Yorkers, smelling mysteriously of curry, cigar or bubblegum, *some of them talking to themselves,* wanted only to be home or to finish their Christmas shopping. They had no interest in making eye contact with anybody. If I wore my hood, and if I was very careful not to be seen, I moved transparently through the crowds, through the rising steam, down the stairs into the bottled subway chambers, and out, with hardly a second glance from anyone.

My legs preferred water, but maneuvering through crowds was a challenge my body could still handle because —as Harold was frequently pleased to remark— *you're so supple.* So I flowed through tight places like those.

Passing through a street vendor's cloud of sweet warm chestnuts, I arrived, undetected and relieved, at the side entrance. I slid my security card through the slot, scrubbed my hands with hand sanitizer, and climbed the narrow, dimly-lit back staircase without touching the railings, two flights to the hallway and lab 18. Another small victory.

I'd avoided the day staff; most left via the elevator. The second shift was sparse —me and Elizabeth and maybe Ruchika, with her irritating disorganized space and her perpetually stained lab coats. We each had our chores and tests and privacy.

The mice in lab 18 and the rats in lab 19 were restless until I switched off the overhead fluorescents. The glow of the under-cabinet lights seemed to relieve their agitation but I still felt it in my ears, a string of low tremors that came every night when I entered the lab. *Ineffectual.* Elizabeth suggested Xanax, but after all, I had a job —even if it wasn't the one I studied for and had been promised— before they saw me that first day.

"I'm here to see the Lab Manager, Mrs. Warring."

"I'm Mrs. Warring, and you are . . . ?"

I held out my hand. "I'm Eunis, your new Research Coordinating Assistant. Good to finally meet you."

"You're Eunis? From Minnesota?"

"Yes. Is there something wrong?"

"Aah, no. No, of course not, dear. I only wasn't expecting you so...can you give me a minute?"

The room immobilized. Time suspended. *She's going to take my work away!*

"I see," I said nodding to the placard on the wall before Mrs. Warring could quit the room, "that you adhere to the state's non-discrimination policy."

"Yes." A lost look deepened in her eyes. "Yes, we do."

Anyway, that was then. I was moving forward, that's what counted, and in one of the world's greatest cities. "I have work to do," I said aloud before catching myself. I had to stop doing that.

Most of the racks of cages sat silent with expectation. In each cage an inbred *Mus musculus* or *Rattus norvegicus* awaited the lab's next scheme, hoping that the night would pass them untouched, at least that's what I suspected. *But I had my orders.* Twenty generations of mating brother and sister and parent until they could be regarded for most purposes as being genetically identical. Each implanted with a chip to identify them and minimize human error. All in the pursuit of health and beauty.

My employers were studying health as a portal to beauty, which was fine for a pharmaceutical company like mine poking around for a marketing edge. But to me, one couldn't dismiss the view that symmetric faces were preferred because symmetric stimuli of any kind were more easily processed by the visual system than their asymmetric counterparts. In other words, there was still strong evidence that beauty was, in fact, objective, and that if I could define that standard, then one day we might be able to create transcendent beauty genes.

The lab's husbandry staff would be in around 4AM to clean the cages, so until then I inhaled the mildly aromatic rodent urine that filled both hermetically-sealed, air-circulated rooms. I regarded the codes on my ELN, my electronic lab notebook. Cradling it, I paced back and forth between the two small connected labs.

"Everything seems in place."

Without really thinking, I translated the codes of a few residents into the individual personalized names Elizabeth and I had bestowed: Stonewall Jackson, he came from the Jackson labs. Mit Romney, from MIT. Emperor Sushi, from Kyoto University. And my personal project: Sam the Shadow, the rat formerly known as 68148:

"Wistar albino rat selected for low ambulation in a bright runway out of a dark starting box (high emotionality) (Tsukuba, 1984); shows more burrowing activity, less aggression. Breeding is difficult because of filial cannibalism."

Above my ELN drawer I noticed a pink note taped to the cabinet. "Sydney *infirmus per* measles. Need to watch her. Told David. He ok'd. Gone home. You're on your own tonight. Maybe tomorrow too. – Eliz."

By 6:57 PM I had administered shots, monitored activity, and inputted the data of Elizabeth's flock. Two of Elizabeth's subjects raced around the perimeters of their cages squeaking hysterically —or so it seemed to me. I'd never seen them respond to the medication that way. I wished I could console them, but I had my schedule. I marked "hyperactive, disturbed" under comments and lay down the ELN, but neither subject abated until I covered each cage in the black perforated canvass that I discovered could mitigate such hyperactivity. This also relaxed me, a little.

By 11:03 PM I'd administered to my group. I took another chew on my vending machine ham and Swiss. The lettuce was soft and didn't tear easily.

"Sammy," I said to my star, now that we could have some

alone time, "this is your night." Sam the Shadow stood on his hind legs and twirled like a dog reaching for a treat. His glassy pink eyes appeared emotionless, but I knew better. I knew that research demonstrated that rats have empathy for each other, that they will go to the aid of one trapped and work to free him.

Sam was two —almost two and a half really— old for a rat. This was his last chance. His head was particularly long, longer than the multipurpose breed Sprague Dawleys, which gave him an Edvard Munch morbidity that drew me to him in the first place.

I checked the clock. I checked his chart. "I'll be back and then we've got to go, so gather your things."

In the lab 18 Mouse Room the drone of the refrigerator was more apparent in the gently broken gloom. No brains needed to be cut or kept that night, no new bodies preserved. *An easier night.* I opened the freezer and pulled the body bag. There were a meager fourteen or fifteen, but this was the once-a-week disposal ritual.

The dead mice clustered around each other, their carcasses frosted. Through the icy glaze their eyes opened forever.

Elizabeth said life is one disaster after another until it isn't. Yet she laughed and said, "Let's go get a drink."

I deferred as usual.

In the time it took to strike a match, I was angry again. There was no note, and so much of my own blank space. *How could I have missed Harold's pain?*

But I knew that I hadn't missed it; I'd missed the depth of it. I'd been distracted, luxuriating in his adoration. Not fully believing it, but indulging in it. Perhaps denying the inevitable catastrophe that Elizabeth embraced and that Momma prophesized.

Did he realize that I was a terrible mistake? His disturbing moods, his death, because of me? And the police with their retracted stares, though there was nothing unusual in that. Their questioning tapered off. Mine remained. The murderess Pamela Ann Wojas inhabiting a remote place in my mind.

I carried the zip-locked bodies into the Rat Room, lay the slab of mice on the counter, and pulled the rat carcasses from their freezer. It was a heavier lot, not just because the bodies were bigger, but also because there were more of them —almost fifty that had passed their usefulness. *But they* had *been useful.* I'd covered my tracks, registered Sam as dead, "found; age determinant," so he was mythologically a part of the coagulum.

I pulled the cardboard bio waste box from the second shelf cabinet, unfolded it, lay both species into their disposable coffin, sealed it, and place it in the lab 19 Biological Waste freezer, to be taken off site and incinerated by a crew of which I had no knowledge. Not unlike Harold's cremation, which, as I said, I wasn't allowed to attend, and which, despite the Bemidji police's conclusions, Harold's father labeled 'that zombie's fault'.

☽☽☽

With Sam safely tucked in the locker, the chlorine attacked my eyes before I even made it to the pool. The narrow hallways, the decaying locker room with its two plastic Christmas wreaths dangling from orphaned nails, even the urine-colored light, did not alter my mindset that in coming here three times a week, I was stripping myself of accumulated weight, like barnacles, and at the same time opening myself to possibilities. Anything that dragged on me had to be constantly cut or washed away. *Like pickling myself in Carver's brine.*

Christmas was like that; something to be scrubbed away and, by all accounts, a manufactured fairytale not at all related to Jesus or his birth. Harold would not be deterred; he was naturally enthralled with Dickens' *Christmas Carol.* Still, Harold hung from a rope.

So despite its lack of charm I was grateful for Natatorium Ondine, the only club that side of town open twenty-four hours with a swimming pool. Well after midnight it was always deserted except for an occasional sighting of the thin little man with the oblong head who ostensibly removed the rubber mats and squeegied the paint-blistered poolside concrete.

The natatorium echoed and plopped, even without life. Diving in, I watched the tiny white hexagon tiles, the order and beauty below the surface. Those hexagons helped me sort the day's discoveries, settle my thoughts and free my body; my *oth-*

er world. *I'm okay. I will be okay. I'll contribute someday. Be grateful, no reason to be angry. Or guilty?* My mind spilled the condemnations into the pool, dispersing them.

With long strokes, I tested myself to reach the far side without air. It was meditative, a place where I could reconfigure the salient lab data to my own work. For instance, mice and humans shared virtually the same set of genes; 3.1 billion base pairs. Though the DNA coding and switches are vast, I already saw certain pharmaceutical combinations affect skin and hair. I noticed effects on eyes and teeth. I watched our computers synthesize the genetic data, and the pool allowed me to savor those small insights and store them. I was on the right track.

Yet as the water streamed across my shoulders, my torso, my legs, I questioned if the harmonious face, rather than being purely genetic code, was also due to a lack of stressors during development. If that was so, it rendered my work useless. I'd assumed there was a quantifiable nexus.

I stroked. I glided. I accepted the benefits of my lab work. I reminded myself that the only straight line was the one I swam, and forgave and forgave and forgave.

☽☽☽

My key slipped fluently into the tumbler. In the shadows I moved effortlessly, keys to the table. The view, as ever, was magnificent.

I lifted Sam into his cage by the kitchen sink and the apartment door latched shut. Like so many other late nights coming from the lab, exhaustion crept back into my bones. A gauzy gibbering began —at first almost indiscernible— perhaps from the refrigerator or the entryway, perhaps next door, I wasn't sure. The sound plugged my ears and pulsed sluggishly through my chest. All I wanted was to sleep.

When I placed my ear along the neighbor's wall, the sound moved farther into my apartment, progressively filling *me. Not again.* Blood flowing more quickly. I scrubbed my palms with sanitizer, very thoroughly, then every finger. There was a practical explanation for what I was hearing, something in the structure of the building perhaps.

I want out, a man with a thin distant voice said. He laughed hysterically, a rippling laugh. Chilling.

I pulled my coat tighter hoping it would calm the flow of blood in and out of my heart. My clinched transparent hand was almost the same color as the coat's muted purple. *Shake it out.* I would breathe him away, purge him, some errant neighbor or radio wave. Something.

He tightened inside me. Like my heart valves couldn't keep up. I sought shelter in the high-backed cabriole-legged chair and, still gripping the bottle of disinfectant, settled into it. The bottle went back into my coat pocket and my legs pulled up under me, legs as bleached as the fragments of Harold's incinerated bones. *Stop.* I lit a candle and pulled my journal from the small red cedar box on the triangular table. Tugging my pen from the fold in the journal, I began to write:

"Harold . . ."

I got no further, the apex beat hauling away my breath. The damned unopened carton of his books, all that I had left of him, sat a mere ten feet away. It was as if he, too, wanted to be set free to clutter my mind and squirrel into my chest, to point out my lack of tangible results. Or was it something more incriminating?

Since arriving at The Octagon, the voices traveling through me had been brief though increasing. The man's tinny voice resumed, gurgling in and out of me as if I was plugged into the walls. The candle flickered. If they were the prophetic voices of 'my gift,' I couldn't decipher any kinship.

"No," I announced to the dark apartment though I retreated deeper into the chair. "Please." I lowered my right leg to the floor and stomped it very hard three times. "Just stop!"

Stomping only heightened the obsession in the man's hushed voice: *Come with me. Get out while you can.* The journal sat untouched in my lap. I held my chest. A panic attack. His voice had the quality of cracking ice. He rattled a contaminated wheeze, fought for a full breath. It was *my* breath, without my voice or consent. Underwater, thumping.

A guttural whimper accelerated maniacally to a shriek, like a colossal lobster thrown into scalding water. Sam scurried around the cage.

"Sammy, did you hear that?" His metal cage tinkled.

I took a slow deep breath. *Hypothalamus, pituitary, adrenals. Between stimulus and response is a space. It's my power to choose.* But it was all bottled air, and not much of it.

"Please. This is stupid. Something I ate." I trembled. I was losing myself. I pulled the cuffs of my sleeves over my fingers, anything to grab onto. Who could I call? *No one. And whose fault was that?*

Soon I'd be spinning. I turned to the Manhattan skyline: real, teeming with life. A reasonable account would be revealed. I'd laugh at myself. *These voices are in my head, not here, not real, please stop. I'll turn on the light.* The candle wax had more chance of moving than I did.

My thoughts seemed to prompt a response, two women groaning from the corner where my small bed was once refuge, yet the moans also seemed to come out of me. Chaotic. Choking. Wearying. I ached for water. I heaved.

Turn on the light! Yes! screeched the young one.

I rubbed the chair's embroidered arms. *Ground me.* I couldn't find my own voice. *Breathe.*

Yes, be useful for once, said the older one. *No more tests.*

Dry sounds exploded from my mouth, I was drowning in sand. So many ways to suffocate: a pillow, a fire, a noose.

Then above the gagging, she added, *Mr. Dickens was here. He wasn't fooled by what he saw. Trust him, if not yourself. He will tell.*

I hugged myself as hard as I could. *Dumbass superstition. I should be free of this crap. Wake up!*

I slapped my face. *There was a perfectly simple explanation.* I was underwater, yet everything came too fast. The heavy wallop of my heart escalating. The candle went out. The skyline disappeared. I couldn't bear my own reflection or my constantly darting eyes, could not raise my voice. My throat, drawn and knotted, hardly took in air. *My chest will explode.*

A shaking hand —*my* shaking hand— fell to the armrest, and I lifted myself, only to slip to the cold, damp floor, cold and damp like wet concrete. *Piss on concrete.* I was beached. Scavengers soon to descend upon my body. The infected smell and wetness seeped under my fingernails, through my palms and coursed up my arms, towards my chest with a tucking sound. *Contaminated. I'll die contaminated.* If I could only get to the sink to wash my hands.

Oh please. I'll wake up. I'm capable, I'm powerful, I can control—.

The voices and my thudding heart filled the room and my body all at once, like hot ricocheting wires cutting across the space at every angle. *Awkward. Unacceptable. Impotent. Worthless.* I saw my keys. I reached for them. Once in hand, I stared at them unable to recall their purpose. Tools of some type? Weapons?

Oh, Mr. Dickens . . . I am lovely . . . said the young woman coquettishly *. . . I'm beautiful to the bone . . . don't forget me.*

I strained for air and lunged for the door handle. Dragging my legs like a fallen paraplegic, I pulled myself through the door, over the threshold, and crawled out of the apartment, terrified. The door latched behind me. The hallway still existed as a stage set without life. Tidy, but not comforting. The voices muffled, dissipating from my body or buried below my clanging heart, but debris still swirled through my head. I needed air, real air, to sort out the mounting bedlam.

CHAPTER TEN

Out of the Octagon rotunda, away from its lights, I headed across the brittle snow for the turbulent waters and the small lighthouse at the end of the island. I passed the anonymous machinery and vacant six-wheel semis parked behind the neighboring "specialty rehabilitation" hospital. More damaged people. More pain.

I considered my impotence. Maybe I *was* just taking up space, unable to help, just as I was unable to help Harold. I quickened my pace.

Scarcely 100 yards from the Octagon's stone steps, the edge of the narrow island summoned me. Thirty-seven years of empirical evidence was damning: I was unqualified as a scientist, everything I'd studied passionately was without result, and everyone I'd embraced ardently was now lifeless. A soiled existence. Like Momma said, my face reflected my estrangement from god.

I drew the hair from my face; frost had formed in it. Maybe the best way to end the steady contradictions erupting in my mind and body —the daily tremors in the lab; the surges impaling me on the streets; the currents breeding in my own apartment— was to cleanse the planet of my stain. Baptism. Salvation.

I'd never imagined life would be so hard. Or beauty so elusive. *But hadn't it always been?* Hadn't Harold tried to alert me before he himself succumbed . . . to what? To his voices? To life's insatiable equations? To his constant weakness? To me?

I longed in that moment to feel the protection of the water, to slip into the lakes and be released, to feel beautiful. No one could take those away from me, those moments of my own. In that moment . . . to slip into the river . . . to freeze permanently the miry drone in my ears, the feelings in my chest, my fractured DNA . . . and disappear. To be absolved. That could be peaceful.

The frigid air emboldened me. I stepped over the chain with the sign forbidding my presence after dark.

The park lamps, mid-nineteenth century reproductions, tall black hanging figures with decoratively cast lights in each hand, led the way to the shore. *Not Bemidji.* Those lamps that were functioning at all strained in the night's steel mist.

I opened and closed my jaw attempting to clear my ears. My heart still beat heavy and fast, my chest sore from the seizure. Weary, I shambled toward the water's edge. Where was the science in this? The predictability? The reality? If I couldn't help myself, if my judgment was always shifting to the whims of momentary experience, how could I ever hope to help others? How could I ever dissect beauty?

A good scientist unlearns her feelings if she hopes to cleanly navigate her data. I was apparently unable to do so. Momma infused me with spooks even though I didn't believe in them. Was the world really always taking away like Momma said?

And Harold. Harold. Full of unseen traps and missing parts.

I was ready to sleep. *Nemo. How Nemo died. Maybe it's simple, lovely . . . to drift away, unnoticed. The way his owners tossed him in the lake, to chill, to drown, to slumber.*

A step through a fallen oval of light and I snickered at my pitying self. "I'm pathetic." And dry. My lips covered in paste. I wet them again and again, but it wasn't enough. I stuck out my tongue so the charred New York winter sat exposed, prickly on it. Gritty, as if I'd dipped it into Harold's ashes and savored them. *An acquired taste? You have to get used to things, Eunis. Create certainty.*

I drew another breath and cross-referenced the night's expectant moisture with those in Minnesota, when —as I stood in Momma's small back entryway— I could tell Carly exactly when the snow would start falling and for how long, solely from a sound in my ears and the frequency in my chest. It had seemed so natural.

At the base of the desolate stone lighthouse I gazed upward, past two dark cell-like window slits, the watchtower clearly long deserted. Yet leaning against the gothic building, my fingertips stuck to the coarse measured stone, the same layered blocks of DNA as The Octagon. I pulled away.

Sultry clouds dragged along the underbelly of the night sky, accentuating the empty lighthouse parapet. When briefly the moon revealed and beamed momentarily down, I stared up at it; no doubt my face reflected the pallor of the moon, cold, leached, colorless. The de novo mutant. I couldn't be sure if the intervening clouds were natural or from the smokestacks out past the treacherous Hell's Gate waters along FDR Drive. But I was mesmerized by the violent brine and filled with calm.

And then there was light in the lighthouse.

"Nelly? Is that you?"

I shuddered. "Oh, shoot."

"Is that you?" He opened the metal door of the lighthouse.

Patina rippled in the moonlight. My atoms slowed as I turned to granite. The restless waters called to me again, stronger and impatient: sleep forever without feeling.

I'm reaching for hell, like you said, Momma. Now comes The Devil, germ line cut.

Below his hulking dark silhouette, a candle sat on the floor next to a sleeping bag. Shadow obscured his face.

The Dark Man and I stood there for an eternity, without a word. No sensible explanations came. I was immobilized.

The end might be painful; I did not want to die.

His body swayed. The wind whistled and passed away, just as atoms had stalled in my Minnesota room when the worst was about to strike. His breath steamed out into the winter air and I conjured it rank and nauseating, smelling of earthly demons – alcohol, tobacco, junk food —partially chewed, unwashed; the imperfections of life.

I grasped for logic, correcting myself aloud, "It's the damn vending machine food. Mycotoxins. I'm hallucinating. Get a grip."

"Banshee, Angel of Death," he broke his silence, "you are not my dear Ellen, you are not my eternal beauty. You have come to take me. I see your eyes flying around me, but I am not ready to go to your darkness. I have more to see, more to tell."

"You're not real," I said. "None of this crap is. I'm having some sort of a breakdown, but it won't last."

"Nothing lasts." He stretched the 's' until it drifted out and over the churning water. He staggered a bit backward as wind curled around us. "Nothing lasts . . . babies, marriages, beauty, dreams, 'that mysterious condition to which we are all tending —the stopped life, the broken threads of yesterday, the deserted seat, the closed book, the unfinished but abandoned occupation, all are images of Death.' Death is coming. Let's dance while we can." He held out a ragged glove hand.

I'd heard this passage before, from Harold! *Fucking Harold.*

Backing away, I stumbled into a snow bank, falling on icy crust. I floundered but the ice on my fingertips grounded me. I rubbed frost over my face.

He stepped forward, loomed over me. "Not a dancer? Oh, but you should. It is all that is left and what we can do together. It will be beautiful. Like my Nelly." He lurched to and fro.

He came around me. In the dim flickering glow of the light-house candle, I saw his face: mid-fifties, graying sideburns tangled and unkempt. His nose came to a point above and be-yond his nostrils. Devilish. His eyes, overcast and twitching, and his pupils, deep pits of despair, were conspicuously unmatched.

He pitched forward, let out a ghastly gagging sound and, with a liquid stream the color of fleshy tissue filled with red chunks, vomited to the ground. Drunk.

He wiped the excess with his sleeve. "Do not want to dance with me? *You* are scared? Of me?" He appeared surprised and sobered. "'I can't get anything that unites reason with beauty.'"

"I'm going now." I straightened up but I couldn't stand with-out touching him. The thought repulsed me.

"Do not be scared." His soiled right arm stabbed at me, just like Momma would. "Your saturnine face . . . there is infection in your mind. What is your sickness? You look like a ghost."

"What?"

"Everyone has infection. What has become of your face?"

"*Your* infection is liquor. Let me pass."

His eyes changed direction, wandered beyond me, over my shoulder. "Liquor?" he said, almost wistfully, while turning to the New York skyline, as if we were suddenly having cocktails on an east side terrace, the party in full swing.

"Yes." I took a generous swig of cold air and considered his dementia, his drunkenness, probably both. Even with his extra five or six inches, I might have been able to take him. He seemed chastened.

"Liquor has got you." I stood. I couldn't imagine what else to say. Where to run? Snow piled up everywhere around us. Even if I screamed, who would hear, my voice merging with the wind?

"Liquor . . ." he repeated, wobbling two steps back and offering me a free path out, ". . . not so perceptive. No, the doctors say it's PSP. I'm sick but not ready to die. You are no banshee. You are but a sad heart, a dark hallucination blinded of your instinct and intuition. You are from that mad, avoided house over there." He pointed to the cluster of buildings edging the park. "I am often confused. I apologize."

His offer of freedom and his unexpected tenderness surprised and unnerved me, as if I had any ballast left.

"But," he grumbled, "who are you to say I am not real? I am as real as you. Touch me."

I recoiled.

Then louder he said, "Test your perceptions, madam. I am your witness, I give you voice. My writing is for you particularly."

The freeze in my shoulders evaporated. "For me?"

"You and the others. Dickens," he stated with some humility. "Charles Dickens." Again he extended the "s" and almost fell over.

I considered steadying him, but no. The man needed help, and I wanted to give it. But whether due to my weariness or my fear of his volatility and his filth, I did not. "Ah, Mr. Dickens . . . are you from the 'mad house,' the hospital over there?"

"The mad house? No, no. I am an outpatient at the hospital. But dear woman, I understand your confusion. 'I cannot say that I derived much comfort from the inspection of this charity in which you live. Everything had a lounging, listless, madhouse air, which was very painful. The moping idiot, cowering down with long disheveled hair; the gibbering maniac, with his hideous laugh and pointed finger; the vacant eye, the fierce, wild face, the gloomy picking of the hands and lips, and munching of the nails: there they were all, without disguise, in naked ugliness and horror. The terrible crowd with which these halls and galleries were filled, so shocked me, that I abridged my stay within the shortest limits.' But you—"

I forced myself. "Mr. Dickens, maybe I can help."

"No, I cannot be saved. But as you have apparently survived that dark place, I will re-imagine you as inherently free and capable of following your own presentiments. Feed the light. Remember you are only a visitor there." He shuddered and turned to the lighthouse. "It is far too cold out here. Do you wish to come in?"

"What?"

"No, you cannot yet imagine that. Very well, do as you wish. But remember, you are only a visitor there." He turned and wobbled the four steps to the lighthouse, then ratcheted closed the thick studded-metal door.

I stood in darkness, unsure whether I was relieved to be set free or disappointed that I'd been abandoned. "Who needs to be saved?" I said into the wind, then turned in a complete circle, as if the answer might be across the river in Queens, or on the path back to The Octagon, or across the quarter mile to New York's east side.

The feral waters broke on three sides of me in a wet pitch-black language that I couldn't organize. My chest ached from exhaustion but told me nothing more. I gaped one last time at the splinter of unsteady light from the lighthouse window-slits. Then they, too, went dark.

CHAPTER ELEVEN

I finally found the front entrance to the Metzinger, the rehabilitation hospital, and to my relief the corridor lights had been dimmed to a blue hue. It was four in the morning. Out of the wind I had to ask myself if I had been listening to Harold too long, all that Dickens stuff? But if Charles was real I had to do something or I'd add regret to my unrest.

No one was at the front desk. Quick action from the hospital staff was required. I didn't think Charles could survive the night.

But that clinic, it was such an open, public place, with an uneasy smell of floor wax and rubbing alcohol. Atoms recoiled. I stepped forward.

Along one passageway after the next, a steady wind came at me —full tilt dread. What could be the worst, they'd gasp. Then I'd feel . . . embarrassed. Ugly. Out of my element. All of the above. Angry.

Occasionally a door clicked open or slammed closed. I flinched, but no bodies appeared. Murmuring voices. I listened closely. *Real or in my head?* "That poor man in the cold." The anonymous walls smothered my voice, absorbed it, and again I was alone.

I followed a maze of hallways until I came to a smaller, brightly lit lobby with an admitting desk. *Finally.* I hated the light, I hated being exposed.

"One of your patients is out there, in the cold!"

A pretty Filipina nurse juggled a clipboard and low bleating hospital phones, *and* she filled out a form being dictated to her over the intercom. She slid the clipboard under her arm and held up her hand to silence me. Rings adorned every finger.

Please don't do that!

"Yes," said the nurse into the intercom, "I got it." She smiled distractedly at me. "Yes, Dr. Saverino, yes, I understand."

Hurry up.

We were both in our thirties, but above the admitting desk hung a mirror and my large convex reflection. We appeared twenty years apart. Bundled with my large dark glasses I looked like a latter-day Greta Garbo, intent on anonymity.

Please, just get off the phone! Skip the bureaucracy. Stop effing wasting time! "One of your patients is out there. You've got to go, now!" *Set the rescue in motion so I can disappear.*

The nurse *still* didn't seem to understand. She lifted her cutesy bureaucratic little head. I followed it. Over my shoulder and across the lobby, I glimpsed a clumpy security guard dressed in a blue gray uniform.

"One of our patients?" the nurse asked, politely clicking off the intercom but still preoccupied with the form.

"Is this an asylum?" I took a breath and immediately corrected myself. "A psychiatric hospital?"

The nurse rested her pen and faced me, alarmed. It was about time. "Not usually. Is this for you? You need a recommendation?" Though charitable, she apparently didn't understand.

"Out at the lighthouse." His boots. "He may be military, a vet."

"We got a lot of those, but we're not missing anybody tonight." The phone rang.

The nurse took the call.

Aw, come on.

She went sideways to me. And I waited. I rubbed my arms. I paced in a small circle, breathing hard, watching the nurse.

What's with these people!

When she eventually turned back to me —breathe, I told myself— I dropped my shoulders and, in an attempt to show the nurse the importance of her attention, I removed my sunglasses. No doubt my eyes darted randomly in the fluorescent light, but she didn't react except to glance once more, barely a head feint, to the security guard.

"You sure you don't need help?" she asked.

"He said he was Charles Dickens, I'm not making this up. He talked about the madhouse. I thought maybe here. One of your patients."

A gaunt man in blue hospital garb came out of nowhere and watched us intently as he crossed the lobby pushing a cart.

"I don't know about that," said the nurse, and I felt aggression. She was too slow to comprehend what she needed to do. Then she added, "Did you take anything tonight?"

"Take?"

"Drugs. A combination of things? Perhaps you were distraught over something at home or—"

"What?" *Why do people always assume?* "Listen, I'm trying to save somebody out there! Out there! A man needs help. It's killer cold *out there*. You need to effing help." I was shouting, it's true, and waving my hands, maybe even hyperventilating, but what the hell did it take to get these folks' attention?!

The nurse must have been on Valium. "I'm not the police, I'm not trying to bust you. I merely want to help." She effing smiled. *Smiled!*

"It's not me. I don't need your effing help. There's a guy out there, Charles Dickens; *he* needs help."

"What kind of help?"

Oh, for god's sake. "Where's the madhouse? He talked about a madhouse."

"I'm Doctor Elias," said a young intern appearing next to me. He wore scrubs and looked to be in his mid-twenties and clearly uncomfortable. He said nothing more, so the Filipina nurse filled in for him.

"Dr. Elias is the Admitting Physician on duty tonight."

The security guard stepped to my other side.

"What is this?" Surrounded, I shrugged them off. I gave them my cornered badger look. Not a blink. "Charles Dickens, he talked about a madhouse."

The two men closed back in.

Really!

The Filipina nurse continued calmly. "There's no 'madhouse' on this island anymore. The only *asylum* on this island was next door, long ago. 1830s-40s, I think. Infamous but long gone. If you wait you can talk privately to Dr. Elias, can't she, doctor?" *She* was giving the young doctor guidance.

"Yes, I—"

I interrupted. "Next door, here on Roosevelt Island?"

"What?"

"The madhouse, the asylum? You said—"

"Yes, ma'am." *Ma'am*. She pointed to the building next door, *my* building. "But it was long ago, it was Blackwell Island then. It's all rebuilt, at least on the inside. Fancy now, upscale condos. The Octagon. I should make that kind of money. Let the resident discuss this with you. Dr. Elias—"

"No!" I was off balance, my eyes spun. I tried to step away but the security guard took my arm, silently, firmly. The young intern stepped behind me, blocking my escape.

"We'll just make sure you're okay," said the Filipina.

Something pricked my neck, warm, spreading. I immersed in immaculate water.

🌙🌙🌙

The squeaking of . . . wheels? A chair perhaps or . . .

"Aah, there we are." A smiling doctor leaned over me. *Not* the young intern; it was an older woman. Horrible breath. Momma's mouth. Whiskers and, despite her smile, trenches of disapproval radiating across her cheeks.

"What?" I tried lifting myself up but I was strapped! To a gurney. The room reverberated white hot with light. I squinted. The straps pulled tight.

"Are you feeling better?" The doctor broadcasted the same plastic grin to the female orderlies on either side of me. "I'm Doctor Saverino. This is nurse assistant—"

"What are you doing?" I was groggy. "Turn off the light."

"We were afraid you might hurt yourself so we gave you a sedative. A gentle one and, boy, it really knocked you out. You're *very* sensitive."

"A what? There are laws, you can't—"

"Well, you're fine now, I imagine. Dr. Elias was doing his best. Shall we let you up so you can answer more questions?"

"*More* questions? Look—"

"Shall we let you up or not?"

"Yes, yes. And turn down the light, please."

"You'll remain calm?"

I was gooey soft around the edges. "Yes, I'm calm."

The doctor gave permission. The orderlies unbuckled the straps and helped me sit up, and as the older orderly went to lower the light, the younger female deliberately glanced her palm over my left breast. "Hey."

On auto-control, the doctor and the other orderly didn't notice.

"Under sedation, you admitted you had considered suicide tonight." The doctor was apathetic.

My forehead and cheeks prickled with shame. I felt nauseous. "You had no right."

"Under the law, we may have saved your life. It was Dr. Elias' call, not mine, mind you."

Unsteady, I slipped backward. The young orderly caught me and ran her hands around the curves of my waist. *Hey!* I'm sure I mustered disapproval.

Instead of contrition the orderly raised her eyebrows, widened her deep-water eyes, and pursed her lips, offering a subtle invitation. *Huh.* Then I noticed the entwined blue serpent and green mermaid tattooed on her neck.

The doctor continued. "Eunis Cloonis, is that correct?"

"Uh, yes, and I'm not suicidal, so you can let me go now."

"Age?"

"Thirty-seven. I thought you already —you probed me while I was sedated? A complete invasion of my privacy."

"Ya were going to harm that beautiful body of yours," said the younger orderly. This time the room cooled —even the doctor turned to censure the orderly.

"Mrs. Cloonis, where do you live?"

My arms took poor direction; eventually they folded in front of me. I listed to the right and had to rest one arm on the gurney to steady myself. I remained silent.

"Do you have family?"

I grunted a laugh.

"A husband?"

A husband? Yes, that. The hard answer would put a stop to their questions. "He's dead."

The doctor slipped a quick peek at the older intern. "And was that recent?"

"Recent enough. Listen, am I under arrest, because—?"

"How recent?"

"I'm not legally obliged to answer your questions and," I started to clear my head, "if you hold me here any longer, I'm likely to sue you and your damn hospital."

The doctor seemed to consider. "How did he die?"

I let him down. And developed a blank spot in my memory, a spot I couldn't or didn't want to retrieve. "None of your business. Do you know the law firm of Stryver, Jaggers and Vholes?"

"No."

"It's my father's firm." *A complete lie*; lawyers created by Dickens and read to me by Harold, with Dickens' clear characterization —and Harold's tacit agreement— that attorneys were venal manipulators, yet here they were to save me. "I'm not your specimen. Shall I call my attorneys?"

"Very well." Dr. Saverino stepped back. "But if you would like some medication under the circumstances we could assign a permanent doctor to your case."

"I don't have a case." Though still groggy I found a handhold of control. "Just give me back my jacket and dark glasses."

"We're only trying to help you, dear."

"Right."

"We'll keep you on file."

"Elizabeth?"

"Yes . . . Eunis?"

"Am I waking you? Because . . ."

"No, no. Sydney's been up for an hour. How nice for you to call."

Curled in my high-backed chair, Sam in my palm, stroking his little head with my thumb, I stared out my thirteenth floor window, through sheets of gray morning sleet, the New York skyline barely visible.

"Is everything alright?" asked Elizabeth.

"I don't know. Yes. Yes, sure. I only wanted to say, well, is Sydney okay?"

"Much better. You know how kids are."

"Not really, but I think I'd like to have that drink with you sometime and find out." I lifted Sam to my shoulder.

"I'd love that." Elizabeth waited for me to continue, but it was a moment before I knew what to say.

"Elizabeth?"

"Yes? You sure you're okay?"

I was glad she couldn't see me, holding my head in my hands. "You seem to go away," Elizabeth had once said, so I did my best to hide those moments. The dark glasses helped. They always had. But those moments away were not flights of fantasy or moments of reflection, they were blanks, spaces of lost time. Something I didn't want to see. Another embarrassment. And they were coming more frequently.

"I don't know," I whispered. I'd made the bed, washed the cup and spoon, straightened the furniture three times. I started to whimper.

"Eunis, what's wrong?"

I wiped away the tears.

"*Eunis?*"

"I'm sorry I bothered you. This is your weekend, your time with Sydney. It's very selfish of me."

"Actually Roddy will be here in an hour; it's *his* weekend to be with Syd. How bout we get that drink?"

"It's not even ten AM."

"You don't know me very well." Elizabeth playful. "How bout coffee?"

"I'm not very good with being outside."

"Well, certainly not today."

"I meant in public."

"Oh."

"Never mind. I'll be fine, really."

"Where *would* you be comfortable?"

☽☽☽

Two hours later, there was a buzz from the concierge, followed minutes later by a knock at my door. I hadn't moved from my chair except to put Sam back in his cage and page listlessly through my new textbook. Developmental biology before molecular: standards for evaluating the FLK, the Funny Looking Kid. Dysmorphology. Maybe I was crazy, but there *was* objective normative data for what a person *should* look like. I'd give it another try.

I straightened up and pushed through the leaden room to the door. A check through the peephole guaranteed that it was Elizabeth. *But who else would it be.* I set myself before opening it.

"Hi." Elizabeth held brown paper bags in each hand. Not a beauty, but normative: plain, thin, in her early forties. Her overcoat dripped. Her short blonde hair, with a streak of fluorescent purple front to back, was matted and flattened.

"Hi." I wasn't sure why I'd invited her.

"Can I come in?" Elizabeth roughed her damp hair.

"Oh, yes, of course. Sorry."

First thing, Elizabeth surveyed the apartment. Inviting her was a mistake. "I brought bagels." She peeled off her coat and hung it in the hall closet without an offer from me. "Kinda dark in here. I know your eyes . . . would you mind if we turn on a light? Light a candle?"

"Sure, I'm sorry."

She glanced around, lifted and put down a couple of my celebrity magazines and inspected the genetics textbook, rubbed her arms. Disapproving? "Diverse reading."

"Sorry." I moved to the thermostat and turned it up. "I keep it fairly cold."

"You don't need to keep apologizing."

Switching on a lamp here and there softened the atmosphere. "Sorry."

"Hey!"

We both chuckled. *Compose yourself.* Except for Harold and my Minnesota family, this was the first time I'd ever had a visitor in my home. Home?

I offered Elizabeth a seat before realizing I only had the one easy chair in the apartment. "You sit here. I'll sit on the floor."

"How bout we both sit at the counter?" She pulled out warm bagels and a small container of cream cheese, and without prompting, found the knife drawer, sliced the bagels, and spread the cream cheese. She handed one to me. I turned it over; I guess I studied it.

"You haven't had a bagel before?"

"Not like this. They're usually spongy."

"Frauds. That's a Minnesota bagel. *This* is a New York bagel. Fresh out of Morrie's oven. Go on."

I took a bite as Elizabeth spied Sam the Shadow in the kitchen corner. "Sammy! Your momma freed you." She went over to the cage and stuck her finger in. She offered him a small piece of bagel. Sam accepted.

"Well, this is cozy. And what a view!"

Mouth full of bagel, a good excuse to mutter.

"This is deluxe. Aren't you happy here?"

"Looks are deceiving." I wiped cream cheese off my hands.

"Eunis, what's the matter?"

I shook my head. *What's there to say?*

Elizabeth reached out and touched my arm. "Tell me . . . please."

I turned to the window.

"Please."

Compose yourself. "What's in the other bag?" I pointed to the second brown bag on the counter.

"Oh, I thought you'd never ask. Where're your glasses?" She was up and pulling down two glasses before I could even point to the cupboard. "The cure for a cold winter day." Elizabeth revealed a bottle of Southern Comfort and poured two healthy shots.

"I don't know. I don't really drink."

"Because?"

I stiffened.

"I came all the way across town. Let's have a little holiday cheer." She handed me a glass, then grabbed her own and clinked the glasses. "Merry Christmas."

Merry. That's a myth. I sensed the sadness buried behind Elizabeth's cheerful eyes. *You asked her to come.* I took a tentative sip. The sweet burn opened my eyes.

"You'll get used to it, you'll see. Take another nip."

☽☽☽

Within twenty minutes, the room had loosened up. Atoms warmed in my chest. *Putting my atoms in order.*

"What's going on?" Elizabeth finally asked.

I closed my eyes. "You're gonna think I'm . . ." I couldn't finish the sentence.

"One thing I know about you, even working with you these few months, is that you're smart and responsible. That's what I know."

"Look at me, I'm hideous. I've always been hideous."

"You're unique."

"So I trip over a curb, you say it's interpretive dance?"

Elizabeth smiled. "Your hair's gorgeous. Effervescent. Your skin is like alabaster. I wish I had your body. And your face is exotic, one of a kind."

"One of a kind. I scare the crap out of people." I actually laughed.

"Not everyone. Not those who really see you. Like your husband. Didn't you say you were married?"

"He's dead."

"Oh, I'm so sorry."

"The point is . . . by all objective data I'm an outlier, worse than a FLK."

"What's that?"

"Doesn't matter. Do you think I'm unbalanced?"

"Unbalanced? Why unbalanced?"

"I have blank spaces . . .places in my memory that are just . . . empty."

Elizabeth laughed. "Join the club."

Tell her. "And sometimes I hear things, feel things."

"What kind of things?"

The closet, the shed. "When I was a child, I started hearing things, feeling and knowing things in advance. I'm not even sure what came first."

"Prophecies?"

"Or maybe it's that I'm nuts. Delusional. I imagine."

"All kids think they're mystical. They are, in a way."

"No. I *knew* things. I could predict the near future and feel the past." I cast an eye over the apartment. Was I going to set off the voices? "You know, like crickets."

Elizabeth shook her head. Didn't understand.

"See, you already think I'm crazy."

"No. I just don't get what you're saying."

"Crickets. They predict temperature. If you count the number of chirps they make. They accurately predict. There's a scientific equation for their predictions. It's called The Dolbear formula. And low-flying birds, they can predict weather. The point is, so can I. I think."

"Well, I guess . . ."

"See, I knew it."

"No, no. I'm just thinking about it. Can you predict other things or only weather?"

"Well, I can *feel* things. In my chest, in my heart. Like when I get next to certain people. If I'm in a small enclosed space —if it's highly-charged."

"Highly charged?"

"Like I feel atoms, frequencies."

"Can you feel me?"

I wanted her to know that I felt her sadness, that she wasn't alone. I wanted to hug her to set the sadness free. But I was afraid I was being intrusive and interfering. And maybe it wasn't very safe for her to get close to me.

"Well, can you?"

I took a small step. "I can sense you, yes."

"And?"

"I don't want to meddle."

She laughed. "Come on, I want to know." She beamed.

"Well, you're sad, I can feel that."

Her face tumbled but she said, "No, I'm fine."

"Okay."

"Really." She rehung her smile.

"See, my electromagnetic field is unreliable." Her face snapped taught like a rope; she wanted me to change the subject. *Let it go.* "Anyway, do you think I'm schitzo?"

She relaxed her shoulders thankful I'd moved on in the conversation. "I don't think so."

"Because my family thinks so." *Harold's father thinks so; maybe the Bemidji police too.* "And there have been some other things."

"Like?"

I hesitated. Elizabeth filled her glass again. "Go on," she said, weaving a bit on the stool.

It was so absurd. "Okay, okay, you asked for it. Here in this apartment."

"What?"

"I've heard noises. Voices. Or I *sense* them."

"Voices? Do you hear them now?" Elizabeth scanned the room.

"No, not now."

"Me neither. What kind of voices?"

"Voices." What the hell, I drained the glass of sweet whiskey.

"Your neighbors."

"Not in this building."

"What kind of voices then?"

"Crazy people. From the past, I think, so I know it makes no sense." I felt gooey again. I straightened my neck. "It doesn't *sound* scientific."

"We're all kinda crazy."

"No." I took a breath and started over. "These are lunatics, asylum lunatics. Depraved. Pitiful. What's *that* got to do with the future? And, and I've even seen one." I pointed to the edge of the island. "Out there."

"You've *seen* one. Did he have a name?" She grinned.

Okay, here goes . . . "Charles Dickens."

Elizabeth snorted. I snorted. She tittered. I tittered. She started laughing. I started laughing.

We both cracked up, and in a series of giggles and shrieks that went on for minutes, rising and falling and rising again, we ended up in tears, barely able to contain ourselves or remain on our stools. I'd never experienced such laughter. Ever.

"Oh my god." The realization grabbed my guts and knotted them tight. "Oh my god." I started to cry, to sob. I was overwhelmed with tears. Of release. Escape. Liberation. Like a hole ripped open and I was imploding. Some perverse progress.

I sagged off the stool to the floor in a fetal position. I guess Elizabeth followed me down, because she held me as I wailed hysterically.

CHAPTER THIRTEEN

The sleet let up, leaving a thick mist hovering over Roosevelt Island and Manhattan. Inside the apartment the shadows reached Sam's cage. Elizabeth had been holding me for a long time, maybe half an hour, maybe more.

"I wanted everything to be like in a book," said Elizabeth interrupting the hush that had finally settled over me. She sat up and downed another hit directly off the Southern Comfort.

"What?" I also sat up, wiped my nose, and leaned against the bottom of the kitchen counter. I refused the bottle from Elizabeth.

"Like changing everything in an instant; like you read in books, in fairytales."

"I don't believe in fairytales!"

"No, of course not. It doesn't happen that way. But it does happen. Only slower. Things change."

"Not this face." I brushed my hair off it.

"It's not what you think. What did your husband think? He obviously loved you."

"Obviously? I'm not so sure."

"Well what did he think?"

"That I had some magical gift, that I could help people."

"You're helping with the research, you know, in the lab."

I didn't want to undervalue her work with my exaggerated mission. "It's more like a curse. I'm oversensitive."

"What else did he think?"

"It's probably all in there —or a lot of it." I pointed to the unopened box of Harold's books. Why had I even bothered to bring it with me? It was an affliction.

"That box?"

"My husband didn't get out much. But he read: Dickinson, Dickens, Poe. Mostly Dickens. Dark stuff. He quoted it *a lot.*

Dickens was like a god to him. He said it was like Dickens understood the world and understood him." I considered mentioning my experience in the hospital, how I'd used Dickens' characters to ward off the doctors. No.

"Has that helped you?"

It's like she read my mind. "Sometimes."

"So the guy you met out there was Charles Dickens?"

"He looked real, but maybe I imagined—"

"Let's imagine that you met a guy named Charles Dickens."

"Don't you see how absurd—"

"You'd better stop this or you're gonna piss me off." She lost her balance and grabbed for the floor. "Damn it."

I put up both hands to appease her.

She settled, but she'd clearly had enough to drink. "Okay," she said. "You talked to Charles Dickens, and . . . ?"

"He quoted Dickens. He wore a Victorian-style coat. You know, calf-length, formal. Mid-1800s, like Dickens would. Except for his boots."

"D'you touch him?"

"God, no."

"Was he *worth* touching?" Elizabeth could be lascivious.

"He was gross."

She pouted, disappointed. "A celebrity, but not one of your beautiful celebrities." She motioned to the magazines above her. "And what did he say?"

"He thought I was ghost."

"And you thought *he* was a ghost?"

"At first."

"Aah, so you started to believe he was real."

"I guess so."

"What did he say besides 'you're a ghost?'"

"He called me a banshee."

"Whatever. Besides the ghosty stuff?"

"He talked like Dickens. I mean, kind of, I don't know, some of it sounded familiar."

"Familiar like what?"

"Stuff my husband read me."

"Stuff from your husband —what was his name?"

"Harold." I saw Harold's face. I saw him wagging a finger at me, just like Momma. I saw him hanging. I saw the ragged v's the noose had furrowed across his neck. And there was something more, something just out of my reach . . .

"Yeah, Harold, the guy in the box." She waved at the cardboard box of his books. "Let's have a look."

She crawled over to the box, tugging the Southern Comfort with her. Using keys from her jeans, she ran one of them along the taped seam and opened it. "You kept a lot of his stuff."

"Actually no, this is all I have. His books. His dad hates my guts. Thinks I caused his son's death."

"I don't understand."

"My husband committed suicide." *That's what the police determined.*

"Oh shit. I'm sorry."

"How come you're allowed to say 'sorry'?"

"You're right." Elizabeth paused. "No. I am sorry. That's heavy. Why?"

I shrugged.

"You don't know?"

"No one knows. His family cut me off. They think I caused it."

"That's terrible."

"Maybe I did, I don't know."

"No, I'm sure you didn't."

My history of causing pain —from Momma on— was quite extensive.

"Don't you want to know?"

"I can't go back. Let's drop it, okay?" My face tightened.

"Okay." With rheumy eyes Elizabeth hung over the lip of the big box and started combing through the books on the top. "Dickens . . . Dickens . . . Dickens. Geez, there's lots of Dickens."

"I told you."

"What did Charlie Dickens say?"

"He talked about an asylum —all sorts of stuff."

"What asylum?"

"I thought it was the hospital next door, but it was here, this building. In the 1800s."

"That same period as Dickens? But he was English, right?"

"Harold said he visited here and wrote about his travels."

"In New York?"

"Yeah, I think so."

"Fuck, I wish I knew more about lit-ra-ture," Elizabeth swayed. She took another hit off the bottle. "Drink this," she said, but I resisted.

Elizabeth fished around in the box, lifting books out, waving them over her head. "You tell me which books might be a journal." She pulled up *A Tale of Two Cities*.

"I don't think so," I said.

"*David Copperfield*?"

"That's a novel."

"*Bleak House? Hard Times?*"

"Not sure."

"*Tell-Tale Heart & Other Stories by Edgar Allan Poe*?"

"That's Poe."

"Right. How about *American Notes for General Circulation*?"

"That could be it."

Fuzzy, Elizabeth had a little trouble opening the book. "1842. Sounds about right. Go on, take another swig. Harold may have a message for us."

"That's not funny." I pictured him holding out his hand to me. It made me queasy.

"Oh shit, yes it is." Cross-legged on the floor, Elizabeth scanned the book. "What am I looking for again? Oh, right, an asylum. Depravity."

I was reduced to a dull spectator. Elizabeth methodically turned pages for ten minutes, maybe a tad more, before her eyelids got heavy and her hand suddenly stopped moving in the fold of the book.

"Eliz?" I said gently. No reply. She'd passed out or fallen asleep.

I pried the Southern Comfort out of her left hand, lowered her carefully to the floor, pulled a small blanket off the high-backed chair, and covered her. Elizabeth snuggled in.

I whispered, "Okay Harold, I'm still gathering." With a steady hand I lifted the book off Elizabeth's lap and held it up to the light. She had reached Chapter VI. I rose to the high-backed chair and let my fingers glide effortlessly over this passage:

> *1842. Blackwell Island. "During my stay in New York . . . a Lunatic Asylum. The building is handsome; and is remarkable for a spacious and elegant staircase . . . I cannot say that I derived much comfort from the inspection of this charity . . . everything had a lounging, listless, madhouse air, which was very painful . . . the moping idiot . . . the gibbering maniac . . .the terrible crowd with which these halls and galleries were filled, so shocked me, that I abridged my stay within the shortest limits . . ."*

The very words the sickly Charles Dickens had spoken. "Harold, is that you?"

My well-organized apartment was mute. I wrapped my arms around my shoulders. I closed my eyes. It was all so untidy.

CHAPTER FOURTEEN

When I opened my eyes Elizabeth was on her feet, stumbling around at the freezer.

"What do you need?" I rose from the chair.

"Ice." The Southern Comfort was back in her hand. "I need fuckin' ice." She struggled opening the freezer door and grappled with the ice trays. "Shit."

"You've probably had enough." I reached for the bottle.

"Who the fuck are you to tell me what to do?" She held tight and wrestled it from me, the bottle leaping upward, slamming me in the face. Hard. My lip bled and a welt formed on my right cheek opposite my birthmark.

"See what you've done," she said. "A drink is a drink."

I tasted blood and touched my stinging lip. I licked my mouth, tried to play down my reaction. "Eliz, you've had enough." But it was Momma all over again; the same disgust with myself for practiced forbearance and my co-dependent pissant lack of fortitude. I wanted to slap her back.

"I'm a big girl. I didn't come from some podunk town in the tundra."

Remember, she's hurting. "No, of course not. But I can help." *Compassion.*

"I don't need help, and I don't think you can help anyone." She made a big show of taking another belt from the bottle. "Aaah. But it would be better with ice."

"Let's get you home, okay?" *Out of my space.*

"Yeah, I got ice at home." She eyeballed down the neck of the almost empty bottle. She lowered it to her lips and finished it. "We'll pick up a bottle on the way home."

〉〉〉

We pulled up to an older brownstone on West 78th Street. With Elizabeth draped over my shoulder I paid the cab driver. He said something derogatory under his breath as he pulled away.

At Elizabeth's apartment door I fumbled with the keys while keeping her standing. The door swung open and an athletic man stood before me, skin the color of well-creamed coffee, late-forties or so.

"Who are—? Elizabeth, are you okay?" He reached for her.

"Oh, I'm really good. This my friend Eunis, from the lab."

He took Elizabeth from me and walked her into the apartment. He seated her on the couch.

"Daddy, I found my homework!" Sydney trotted into the room, her plumplitude bouncing a little. She drew back when she saw me.

My face! Aching from jaw to temple, it was even more distorted thanks to the impact of Elizabeth's bottle.

"Mommy!" The seven-year-old saw her drunken mother strewn over the couch. She ran to her. I remembered similar encounters.

"Your face," he said, a gentle quality in the midst of pandemonium. "You okay?"

I put my hands up. "I'm fine."

"I'm Jerrod Bloomfield, Sydney's dad. What happened?"

I had no response, I just wanted out of the apartment.

"It was Elizabeth, wasn't it?"

"I thought you were in New Jersey." Eyes to the floor.

"Syd forgot her homework. We turned around. First grade. Gotta start right."

"Will you look after Elizabeth?" I inched to the door.

"Of course. But can't we—"

"Thanks." I was out the door, down the narrow staircase, onto the street, into the dusk. The street was raw, damp, cloaked in darkness, everyone doing whatever he or she could to get off the pavement. I wanted someplace to wash my hands. I was overdue.

I followed West End Avenue down to 57th Street where I'd pick up the subway home. I wasn't really in a rush to return to the apartment, but where else would I go? Then once again, the winter nightfall began to mute my feelings, familiar and reassuring. Maybe a small adventure, something I could control, something to divert a mounting anger.

"Eunis!" I heard his voice. "Eunis," he repeated and ran up behind me. "Are you okay?" Jerrod.

Severe cracks in the pavement had forced a slab to heave. "I'm fine."

Before I could even react he reached for my cheek and raised my face to his, a Chinese laundry sign illuminating me.

"Excuse me!" I jerked away. He lacked boundaries.

"Please let me see. I'm so sorry. Your lip. Your cheek."

"I'm fine." I stood out of the light, heat still rising at the incursion. I could've punched *his* face he was so presumptuous.

"Won't you let me help?"

"I've got to go. They're just bruises."

"She doesn't mean to. She's . . ."

"I know."

"Thank you for bringing her home." He placed his hand lightly on my shoulder —another invasion— still surveying my face.

Swallows and peacocks with matching tail feathers are particularly healthy and preferred by potential mates.

I opened and closed my mouth once. "You're welcome." I walked away. Considering my tone I should have said *sorry*, but I hadn't learned how to do that yet. On the other hand, I'd actually noticed myself in action.

The oddest part was how I felt. Turning south on West End, the anger had ebbed and my body felt hugged, hugged in the moist, warm Minnesota hillside, much like it had with Nemo. Head to toe. Restful. I turned back to Jerrod. He was more than a block away and, in the twilight, no more than my imagination. Stupid stuff.

I walked. I thought about the friends I'd had in my life —all three of them: a dog, a dead man, and now a drunk. Every one of them in pain. That's who was attracted to me. Or maybe I was attracted to them. Someday, if I was successful, beautiful people would come from a lab, much of the pain built out of them. Then I'd have no friends.

I laughed at myself. I hadn't done that in a while.

A gentle woman's voice leaked out of the mist, droplets of

delight in her words, though they were nothing more than murmurs to me. A couple in their thirties came toward me, arm-in-arm, and even in the shadowed light I could see the woman touch the man's face. He pulled her closer. Nothing special, but together they were . . . fine. They passed by without noticing me.

I thought again about Elizabeth. It had been good to talk to her —like with Harold— but maybe like Harold she wasn't what she seemed. She didn't want to talk about her unhappiness. I guess I wasn't one to pass judgment. But she was unreliable. Unstable. I touched my swollen cheek: dangerous. Unreliable was the worst.

I stopped. There it was, tingling at my heart, *that* feeling. I searched the low steel wool sky, nothing but dark trouble visible above me. The sky was agitated. I could feel the moisture coming. Within seconds the snowflakes broke the ceiling, dropping, not drifting, pelting my raw face. Big icy ones. *180 billion molecules each, no two the same.* Pressing me for answers. *You recognize us, remember, you and your sister?* they seemed to say. *This can't continue.* Then just as hastily they fell away, turning to water the instant they landed, spilling over my cheeks like a creek. I know it sounds crazy, but for a split second I missed her, my sister. I missed the Bemidji woods. I missed Harold. The flakes blurred my vision but they weren't tears. No self-pity. Just snowflakes, like those I'd predicted for Carly. A useless talent, but it made the most sense of all the things that didn't make sense.

"It's beautiful, ay sistah?" Standing in a brightly lit doorway, a mass of Jamaican woman smoked a cigarette, her head wrapped in splashy yellow, black and orange. Then she called to someone inside, over the steel drum music that spiked the air like icicles falling rhythmically to the pavement. She got a shout in return. She turned back to me.

"C'mon inside, sistah. Good stuff, truss me." She waved me into the buttery light. She tossed the cigarette into the street and rubbernecked into the deli. "C'mon. Jerk sandy? We got it. Curry goat, yes m'am. Squash cake. Patties. Oh the coco bread! All is good. C'mon now."

The woman looked right at me. Smiling. She was . . . *albino!* "Well, sistah?"

I wanted no part of her and yet . . .

"Viva Cuba!" yelled a voice. And with a steady thud of the space, a young, dark cabbage-faced man bolted by and between us, swinging a boom box, breaking our connection. Propeller strobes of blue, white, red and purple revolved over the boom box; a walking carnival! The music loud, not exactly rap, not exactly reggae.

"El Yonki!" the Cubano yelled to the night, fist to the sky.

I waved off the Jamaican woman and moved on. She trotted after me, bosoms bouncing, and placed a box of matches in my palm. I kept moving. She called after me, "Next time, sistah doondoos. Disya place."

Sister. She'd looked right at me. Didn't flinch. The albino sisterhood? More than I wanted to deal with at the moment.

The small matchbox was inscribed with the name and address of the deli:

Ruthie's Roti

Food • Fortunes • Fabrics

"For the community."

I'd never thought of community in the city, or really anywhere. She'd called me sister. My own sister would avoid that. The steady thumping of the boom box, the propeller lights and its human disappeared down the street. Happy.

Carly. My sister. Very much like a propeller. Once she started moving you knew she was there but you couldn't see her. Moving so fast.

Who was she, really? I know, just a half-sister, but *nothing, no connection?* Discouraging, in a way that went deeper than most. And in the few moments when she stopped moving —like the time with the candlesticks, where she wasn't sure if she'd gone too far with Momma or if she'd won— in that moment she was like an electron. You could know her position but you couldn't know where she was headed.

Like Harold. Like Elizabeth. Maybe like everyone. This too, disappointing.

Searching for the sanitizer, my hand landed on my cellphone. Seldom used. Like I said, who would I call? I removed it from my coat and stared at it for a moment. I pressed the faceplate once, twice, a third time. Held the phone to my ear. It was afternoon in Mexico or Washington.

"Hell, yayes!" answered Carly in mid-sentence to someone else. "Who is this?"

"Carly?"

"Well, shit yes! Who were you expecting, Wayne Gretsky? Hello?"

"Carly, it's Eunis."

"Who?"

"Your sister, Eunis." Suddenly I was afraid. I'd opened myself to more grief.

"My sister? Eunis?"

"Yes."

"Well damn, it's been over a year. More. What dya want? You in New York, is that what Mom told me? She's pissed at you. But good for you."

"Can I ask you something?"

"Sure, but make it quick, I'm kinda in the middle of something."

"You still in Mexico?"

"No, back in Spokane. Is that all you wanted to know?"

I didn't want her to go. "Are you happy?"

"What?"

"Are you happy? You always seemed so happy. Most people don't seem to be."

"Of course." The wind roared over Carly's phone, a wall of air. Then, "Eunis, you think too much. I gotta go. I'll call you in a few days, okay?"

"It's just that—"

"We've got a really bad connection. Catch you next week. Glad you're doin' okay in the big city."

I was left surrounded by blotted sidewalk and bus fumes. Okay, nothing new, I was on my own.

CHAPTER FIFTEEN

A woman brushed past me laden with presents. Church carillons drifted from several blocks away. I looked up into the steady snowfall. If they were stellar, sectored, or dendrites, I couldn't tell. They were cells in motion; their shapes vanished as soon as they met my skin, much like the rest of the world.

But as I said, I wasn't going to feel sorry for myself and I wasn't going to subscribe to Harold's storybook Christmas, the one he'd read aloud, sanctifying Dickens's mythic three spirits —Scrooge and all that nonsense— because both he and I knew — though we never discussed it— that there was nothing more pervasive than loneliness at the holidays, *fueled* by the myth of family. Nevertheless I could get behind the idea that people *wanted* to see beauty in each other. Even my homeless Charles Dickens left me with that impression. Whether that desire was biological or some randomly scattered instinct, I couldn't be sure, because it apparently had no roots in my family.

I did know all things were energy. That C.P. Snow's law of thermodynamics applied. And that pain, like happiness or hunger or hysteria, could be described as a set of atoms, moving at a certain speed, bouncing in a certain way. And I admitted to myself that I was embarrassed by my mental battles.

Antidote: a trauma-free childhood; really, it's in the research. Good attachment to parents. *Crap.* Problem solving. *Check.* Moderation in needs and desires. *I was giving it a good try.* Control over emotions. *To be determined.* Optimism. Optimism? *Just make rational decisions.*

Stepping off the curb a horn blared and a taxi shook the air, narrowly missing me. The most sensible thing to do was to continue to cross, to isolate factors and keep going in one methodical direction. There was objective normative data for ear length, palm length, canthal and philtrum distances. There *would* be for facial beauty.

))))

"Sam," I said as soon as I was in the apartment, "you know I'd set you free if I could."

I raised him out of his cage and stroked him. Any minute the shadows would erupt with inmates' voices, trying to tell me something. Sam gave me a steady blank stare.

"I mean *really* free. But rationally, you wouldn't survive. Even in Central Park. There are predators everywhere. You'd be a fish out of water. You wouldn't last twenty-four hours. I'm sorry."

I lowered him back into his cage. I lit a few candles. Sam got his food pellet, half the size of a checker, and a carrot. For me, tomato soup from a can. Crackers. No voices. A clear view across to the East Side. The evening was uneventful. Beautiful.

"Thank you." I shut my eyes, acknowledging goddess Freyja, goddess of beauty and sexuality, magic . . . and death.

"Enough of that."

I opened the Life & Style Weekly to Jennifer Anniston, an expose of a *real* goddess. I felt sorry for her. She was probably a nice woman. And stunning. *Why don't they leave her alone?*

Momma was doubtless reading the same article. Put. The magazine. Down.

So I wrote in my journal:

> "Harold,
>
> I've had an experiment in mind. If I use the normative data for 25-year-old male and female facial structure (for instance skull length 22.410±0.197, height 9.673±0.106 and width 10.513±0.115), as well as the other norms, and I use the computer software and printer at work, I can create a 3D normative face (or pretty darn close) for each sex. Then, using the lab staff as respondents, I can isolate preferences (by offering different hair color, eye color, lip options, etc. on those normative

faces). I'll have to be careful because I doubt Warring will authorize it, but . . .
What do you think?"

Harold. The stack of books Eliz had pulled from his box
waited on the counter. I placed them there, neatly, with the intention of reading: *David Copperfield, Bleak House, Hard Times,*
Poe's *Tell-Tale Heart & Other Short Stories, American Notes.*

But I was indifferent. No, I was resistant. Because, Harold, I'd
given you too much credit for having the answers. You'd only
cause me more pain. But okay, I picked up *American Notes for
General Circulation.* I re-read the passages from Dickens:

> *"One day, during my stay in New York, I paid a visit
> to the different public institutions . . . One of them is
> a Lunatic Asylum . . . capable of accommodating a
> very large number of patients.*
>
> *. . . In the dining room, a bare, dull dreary
> place . . . a woman was locked up alone. She was
> bent, they told me, on committing suicide. If any-
> thing could have strengthened her resolution, it
> would certainly have been the insupportable monot-
> ony of such an existence.*
>
> *. . . The terrible crowd with which these halls
> and galleries were filled, so shocked me that I
> abridged my stay . . . and declined to see that portion
> of the building in which the refractory and violent
> were under closer restraint.*
>
> *. . . this sad refuge of afflicted and degraded
> humanity . . ."*

Atoms are ageless; they're forever, until they're not. Inside it
was modern, but the container was more than 150 years old.
Could a beautiful molecular structure like The Octagon maintain
ancestral scars? Walls weren't supposed to breathe, but if I focused . . . I could imagine them exorcising me. And I knew
Harold had read those sections to me.

Coincidence or mathematical probability? Either was plausi-
ble. Too many choices. The hand sanitizer wasn't in reach. Nor
would Elizabeth be. *Stop.* Fatigue washed over me. I closed the

book; its draft wafted past my chin and cheek. I snuffed out the candles. I slipped into bed. I tossed and turned.

I found myself walking into the lab. Someone had already lowered the lights. Every cage was open. Every cage empty. Where were the inmates?

The door to the lab closed behind me. I hung up my coat. I peered into the first row of empty cages and walked deeper into the room. Heart rate up. *Adrenalin energizes the body. Leave. Make rational decisions.*

Growing quickly but indistinguishable from my heartbeat, was a rumble. Mechanized. No, on closer attention, small feet. Millions and millions of small feet. A shrilling. Like locusts billowing up over the countertops, a gray wave of rodents of all sizes climbed my legs, ran up my arms, dropped from the ceiling into my hair, screeching, tearing at my flesh. Eating me alive.

I woke in a sweat. Sheets adhered to my skin, an unwanted cocoon. It wasn't yet sunrise.

"Sam! Sam, what do you want me to do?"

I switched on the light next to my bed, unglued the bedding from my arms and thighs. Naked across the room, I turned on the light in the kitchen illuminating Sam's cage. He lay motionless in the center —on his back, capsized, tiny claws curled. I'd done it again.

"Sammy!" I flung open his cage. Nothing. I held him in my palm. Rigor mortis. "Oh no, no, no, please no. Sam, what have I done now?" I propped myself against the counter, numb, but not the way I liked.

My phone buzzed. It buzzed again, a message. I stared at Sam, much as he did at me. Vacantly. I tapped the phone and retrieved the voice message:

"Eunis. Carol Warring. I'm sorry to call you so late. I need you to come in tomorrow morning. I know you don't work till the evening, but we need to discuss some things. This is mandatory. Promptly at 9:45 AM, please."

There was something in Warring's voice, an edge that made me stretch my shoulders. Me being oversensitive.

"I let you down, I let you down, Sam. I'm sorry, Sam, I'm so sorry." The apartment grew smaller, that slow almost imperceptible breathing. Pacing from one wall to the next, around the circumference, it was a quick trip, fussing with my fingers. Disinfectant didn't protect those *I* touched.

"You deserved at least one day of freedom, Sam, even if it would have killed you." I caught my own thin reflection in the window, fiddling nervously. I clasped my fingers, held them tightly. I squeezed them until they throbbed, until no blood moved.

Okay. Too much noradrenalin means panic. *Breathe.*

They were going to try to take me down at work. They knew about Sam. Maybe Elizabeth said something. Maybe the hospital tracked me down and Warring heard what I'd done, what I'd *thought* about doing. I wasn't going to hurt myself. It was just a thought, like so many others. I was responsible. I was self-reliant. Sam was only a dead rat, after all. He would've been dead soon anyway. He stared at me from the countertop.

I poured through the kitchen cabinets, one after another, pulling out several plastic containers, sizing them up for Sam's burial. *Not right.* I put it back. *No, not that one either. No, wrong effing size, damn it! No! No! No!* I watched myself hurl the last one against the cabinet, where it ricocheted into the glass by the sink, shattering it.

"Shoot! Shit! Fuck!"

I barreled to the high-backed chair and flopped into it, pissed out of proportion with myself. Even as I knew I was overreacting, I couldn't pull myself out of it. I couldn't seem to do anything right. I sat for almost half an hour, until the pale morning sun reached across the East River, extinguishing the city lights and eventually fetching me back to the surface.

The red cedar box sat on the triangular table to my right. I removed my journal. Cupping the box in both hands, I ran my fingers slowly over it and raised it to my nose, drew in the rich cedar aroma. It further relaxed me.

"Harold, forgive me. I can do better. I *will* do better. Starting now."

"This is where you will rest Sam. Harold gave it to me. It's precious." But again, I questioned myself. "Or would you prefer simple earth around you?"

There were so many answers. I needed to find those that fit.

)))

I walked out of the elevator holding the cedar box. I wore my dark glasses but not the hood. I marched, head up, through the Octagon rotunda, past other congregating tenants jiggling their baby strollers and sorting through their mail. Seeing me for the first time, they gaped. I tossed my hair. What the hell. *At least one day of freedom.*

Down the steps and into the park, the morning chill roused me. "Well," I said aloud, "I feel better already." Two women on a bench turned in response and then continued their conversation. It wasn't so bad.

Just before the cobblestones surrounding the lighthouse, a tree stood in a patch of open ground that wasn't deep in snow. Kneeling, I placed the box to my side and began digging, bare hands. A few passersby noticed.

An elegant older woman with a walking cane stopped to watch me. "Did you lose something, dear?"

"No, I'm fine." I turned to acknowledge the woman and startled her.

"Oh my." She moved on as quickly as possible. And that, I realized again, was how it was going to be.

The ground was simply too hard. My fingernails were caked in brown and broken, my hands raw. I leaned against the tree. "Okay, Sam, I'll find you another burial plot. Better."

With the cedar box back in my arms, I moved toward the lighthouse, thinking aloud as I went, scattering the few passersby. Not my problem.

I tugged on the heavy metal lighthouse door. Padlocked, it didn't budge. I banged on the door. "Charles, Charles are you in there?" No reply but the morning wind which had become kinder around the island's rocky point. Too many locked doors. It was my job to open them.

I removed my dark glasses. The few remaining spectators scuttled briskly away.

I don't know if it was the clean air or the sun turning the

horizon sapphire blue that inspired me, but I took it all in. Right there, I decided Warring wasn't the enemy; that I was grateful for my job, my apartment and the chance to start anew. Turning in a complete circle, across the river to Queens, across the quarter mile to New York's east side and then to the path back to The Octagon. I kept spinning in circles, again and again, until I was dizzy dancing. The giggle in Momma's hallway closet came to mind. *Was it the joy of hiding or the anticipation of being found?* I thanked Sam for what he had taught me: at least one day of freedom.

"You seen somebody?" said a city sanitation guy, coming from behind the lighthouse. "Cause somebody been in there, somebody been foolin' with the locks."

Elizabeth was leaving Mrs. Warring's office just as I arrived.

"I'm sorry." Eliz brushed by, awkward and hushed, as Warring checked her watch, hustled me into her office, and closed the door. I'd decided to replace my large dark glasses with the gray tinted ones the optometrist gave me before leaving Bemidji. *Head up.*

"Sit, please, you're almost late." Warring had a particular guise when she was afraid or angry —they were almost the same— and she had it this time. "What's in the box?"

The cedar box! I was still cradling it. *Shit.* "Aah . . . something I intended to drop off before coming here. I'm not used to the early mornings." *Already excuses.*

"Eunis, please take off your sunglasses."

"It's the light."

"Yes, I know." Warring closed the blinds. "Does it affect your writing?"

"Excuse me? No."

She motioned to me again, with more impatience. "Your glasses, please."

"Sorry." I removed them clumsily and the cedar box fell off my lap with a clatter to the floor. I dropped to the ground, all fours. The box hadn't opened. *Thank god.*

Warring dwelled on my face, the split lip, my swollen cheek, then studied my filthy chipped fingernails. "Please sit." Her irritation filled the air.

I sat, leaving the box at my feet. *Breathe.*

"Okay, well let's get to the point." Warring remained standing. She patrolled, then anchored herself, a straight arm on her thick oak desk, the same type of desk my teachers perched on in elementary school as they lectured, the same sort from which Harold threw himself off. "There are anomalies in your lab's results."

"Anomalies?"

"Yes, a number of irregularities." She opened a small drawer and shuffled through it, then gave up and slid it closed.

It unsettled me, perhaps because the teacher's desk was wrong in this room. Incongruous. Annoying. "Enzyme reports? Hormones skewed?" I asked.

"I'd rather not say until the Lab Supervisor finishes his investigation. Is there any way you can explain what happened here?"

"Well, if I knew what—"

"I told you that's not possible. I just thought you might remember having trouble reading data correctly —perhaps because of your eyesight or—"

"No, no. My eyes are okay. It's only the light. I see up close."

"Yes, we've already gone over that."

"None of the rats have gained weight. I haven't seen any itching." I nudged the cedar box at my feet.

"Hmm."

"Could be valid data shifts."

"Could be, but doubtful. You're using clean syringes? Sure of the doses?"

"Of course."

"Of course."

"I understand that you've been overseeing some of Elizabeth's colonies."

"Yes." *Elizabeth!*

"Do you treat them with the same care as your own colonies?"

"Of course."

"Of course." Warring studied my bruised purple face. "You know you're still on probation for another two months or so."

"I love this job," I said. But I wasn't sure that was still true.

"But you have *other* goals, I understand. Lab work is merely a beginning."

"Well, I—"

"What happened to your face?"

My first reaction was to cover myself but I let my hand drop. "Slipped outside of Macy's."

Warring gazed at the ceiling; didn't appear convinced. "Are there any colleagues you might suspect of being sloppy?"

"No."

"No drugs?" Warring stood her ground. "No one drinking or otherwise compromised?"

Elizabeth's warped, drunken face. "No."

"No. Well, let's let the investigation play out. Just be mindful of the details, okay?"

"Always."

"That'll be all. Thanks for coming in."

I walked to the door.

"Don't forget your box," said Warring picking it up off the floor as the lid began to open.

I turned in terror and grabbed it from her with both hands, sealing it shut. "Thank you."

Suddenly I was bone dry and suffocating.

"You're welcome." Warring's gaze was suggestive of Dr. Saverino's at the hospital. Dubious.

)))

At that mid-morning hour, quite a few more people filled the streets. The sun lingered for the first time in days, peeking from behind skinny stratus clouds. Even with my new gray sunglasses I attracted a few stares before heading into the subway, only to find that I'd have to route through Times Square due to a stalled train.

A litany of Elizabeth's potential remarks to Warring filled my head. I knew then I couldn't poll my lab mates; too risky. I couldn't afford to lose my job. I couldn't afford to change apartments. And I couldn't trust Elizabeth. Lacking control, a straightjacket of options. I slammed the red cedar box, then felt guilty for battering Sam's lifeless body.

"Are you getting off or not?" asked the large black woman shoving past me. "Let's go."

My first reaction was to shove back but instead I welcomed the flow. "Ah, thanks." 42nd Street.

I tagged behind her, no choice as the crowd herded me up the stairs. At the top she disappeared into a mass of heaving bodies.

"C'mon, c'mon," a man behind me said, and before I knew it I'd been jettisoned into Times Square. I'd never been there, not above ground. I stood in awe as the crowds pummeled me left and right. The smell of burnt chestnuts, recycled steam, bus exhaust swirled the air, but it was the lights, everywhere! Huge images flashed all around me.

" . . . And it looks like quite a few days of in-and-out sunshine," read the scrolling caption below the four-story high weatherman, identified below his waist as Gordon Mingle, Meteorologist.

I squinted. It *was* the same Gordon Mingle. Not as geeky. Not as stiff. Taller. Well, *much* taller. I went to high school with him, as much as I'd gone to high school with anyone. Gordon Mingle. On TV, sixty feet tall.

That's when I got the idea.

☽☽☽

"Eunis?"

"Couldn't miss me, right?"

Zoe was a young twenty-something, with large-rimmed glasses and a lazy eye. "What do you do to it?"

"What?"

"Your hair, it's an incredible color, and so lustrous. I just love it."

"It's just . . . me. Thanks. Please." I offered her the seat, still unsure how she'd accept my proposal. "I took the liberty of ordering you that latte." I blew across my cup, the size of a small swimming pool.

"Thank you." She took a sip and assessed me over the rim. She'd almost be attractive if not for that distracting amblyopia. Think Marty Feldman. Eyes going in different directions.

I removed my shades for a moment, so she could see my eyes stutter, so she knew we had something in common. I'd requisitioned a table, thankfully, in the corner by the window so I could still sit mesmerized by Time's Square's vibrating lights and color, the magnitude of it exploding all around me.

"You found me through Hunter College?"

"Yes, through a series of inquiries and investigations, I hope that wasn't too intrusive, and thanks for coming so quickly."

"I work round the corner. I take lunch early."

"Yes, I know."

"And *intrusive*, no, I'm intrigued. Besides, there's no privacy anymore."

"Good. So what exactly is computer science?"

"Anything we can now do or might do with computers in the future. Social media, of course, but also psychology, biology, geography." She glanced out the window too, toward the kaleidoscope of light. "It's something, isn't it? Wallscapes, sky murals, LED ribbons."

"Branding."

"Yes."

"I gather you know quite a bit about this. Computers run most of those signs out there."

"They do."

On the sidewalk, despite all the movement, people pointed and stared at the overwhelming messages. "Four stories high."

"Ten thousand square feet or more on some, yup. Digital billboards, six square blocks of them, twenty-four hours a day. They're called 'spectaculars.'"

"You've studied this." I pointed to an undulating image of Kate Upton.

"Yes." She snickered. "I work it, part-time. Helps with tuition. I'm learning a lot. The psychology interests me."

"Well, that's why I called you. These 'spectaculars,' do they run off basic video files, like After Effects animations?"

"They do, most of them."

"And roughly speaking, how many people see one of these messages a day?"

"Up to one point five million."

"No," I rephrased, running my fingers over Sammy's cedar box, "a day."

"Yes, one point five million. A day."

"And tomorrow night, say for approximately an hour?"

"Christmas Eve, that's a lot of eyeballs. Maybe a hundred thousand."

A hundred thousand!

☽☽☽

At my stop I ascended the unusually long escalator. Opposite me, on the way down the other escalator, presumably coming from her night shift at the rehabilitation hospital, was the young tattooed orderly who assisted Dr. Saverino, the one who'd groped me. She recognized me, looked at me with *those* eyes. A thick, damp heat coated me.

I turned away and, reaching the top of the escalator, walked into the sunlight. It's what Momma and the teachers and even the doctors told me never to do. *Sunlight will kill you.* I stood there for an instant, experiencing it. I'd rarely been in the island's daylight and never when the sun shone. My choice. My skin breathed. A fine day.

I walked the mile to The Octagon, stopping occasionally to window shop —at a clothing boutique, a chocolate shop, though I've never liked chocolate, and a small art gallery— something I'd never done before.

As I neared The Octagon, a familiar voice hailed me. "Eunis." Jerrod sat on the bench at the bus stop.

Suck it in and move past him.

Not possible. He stood in front of me before I'd made it halfway to the Octagon steps.

"Now what?" I said, keeping my head low.

"Can we sit for a few minutes?" He motioned to the bench.

"I've got a lot on my plate today."

"Maybe, but this is important."

"More important than my schedule?"

"Please. Just five minutes."

"I thought you lived in New Jersey."

"I brought Syd back this morning. Please." He ushered me to the bench in the soft morning shadow of The Octagon.

"Jerrod—"

"Roddy. My friends call me Roddy."

"Okay."

"I —we— want to make it up to you, for what happened the other night."

"No need."

"How's your face?" He touched my cheek again.

Inappropriate! I looked up at him, fiercely. He was a bit taller than I'd remembered. Broad shoulders. Kind eyes. Symmetrical features? I'd lingered too long. I focused on the cold stone Octagon over his shoulder. I saw a lot more with my new shades. "I heal quickly."

"She has a problem," he said.

"Apparently."

"She knows it."

"Then she should do something about it."

"I agree. It's one of the reasons she and I aren't together anymore."

"Does she take it out on Sydney? Kids can get the worst of it."

"No. Not that I know of. Not that Syd has ever said. I've asked her."

"Good."

"You were very generous under the circumstances."

"Anyone would do that."

"They would not. Please look at me," he said, his voice plaintive.

The Octagon's shadow couldn't prevent the brush of wild blue sky, the unseasonable warmth of the sun or the benevolence of his mouth, which seemed to smile without actually doing so, a crooked smile. Like he bit down too hard on a sweet cherry and met the pit. Rugged without knowing.

"I'm a lawyer, I see people acting out all the time. It's not pretty. What you did was kind."

"They're hurt. People hurt." *And your soon-to-be ex-wife is among them.*

His face became soft and generous. His eyebrows and cheeks met midway, folding his eyes into miniature pocket smiles. "Exactly," he said. "You understand. Would you take off your sunglasses?"

"No. Are we done?"

"No, we are not. I insist that you let me do something for you."

"You *insist*? I don't need anything."

"You're sure?"

"I'm sure." I evaded his scrutiny. Along the path that led behind the rehabilitation hospital to the lighthouse, the tattooed orderly leaned on the railing. Watching us?

I turned back.

Roddy studied me, appeared to deliberate. "Then dinner?" He handed me his business card.

"What?"

"Dinner. It's the least I can do."

"I've got a busy day." I stood and walked away. In my hand, his business card and Sam in the cedar box, rigid. But it was the sun that preoccupied me, anchored on my cheek where Roddy's finger left an imprint.

Entering the lab I measured my steps, quietly, defensively. I held the door, sensed stillness, a hushed conversation, and with it, fatigue and the urge to walk right out.

I heard Elizabeth, around the corner behind a set of cages. *Whispering like Harold on the phone.* A low tremor began in my chest.

"She may be a problem, maybe she's not. We can handle her."

The main door slipped out of my hand, clicked shut. The conversation stopped. For a static eternity it felt like the electron cloud prepared to rupture. Elizabeth and Ruchika emerged from behind the cages, headed in different directions. Elizabeth barely made eye contact and moved to the other lab. Just as well.

Ruchika sauntered after me, but it was uneasy and false, releasing censorious particles in my head even before our eyes met. She was a young East Indian woman in her mid-twenties, younger than both Elizabeth and me, with a frenzied nest of russet hair and guarded eyes. "Did Warring call you in this morning?"

It was exactly this kind of disingenuous nonsense that marked her from our very first meeting. "Well, if you talked to Elizabeth, you know she did." I rested my hands on my hips.

"What did she ask you?"

"Probably the same things she asked you."

"Which were?"

"If I've noticed anything . . ."

"Anything . . .?" Ruchika poked fingers into her unkempt bramble.

"Like drugs or alcohol or anything."

She squinted, indignant. "I don't do those things."

"I didn't say that you did."

"*I* haven't noticed anything. I don't know what the problem is." She pressed against the counter waiting for me to respond, her lab coat improperly buttoned. *So Ruchika.*

"I just do my job." I started to turn away from her.

"Yes, but you have bigger plans."

Elizabeth had been flapping her mouth. "Yes, I do. So what?" A rush of enmity welled up, surprised me.

"This job's important to me. I worked hard. My family expects me . . ." She let despair escape. "I can't go back."

I could've slapped her. She wasn't the only one who couldn't go back. "You've got the most seniority. You'll be fine." I collected my ELN and pulled my lab coat off the hook. "The whole thing will probably blow over."

"Yeah, probably. I guess." Ruchika hesitated, as if she'd ask something more, but all that came out was an unenthusiastic "Thanks."

Suddenly she was an unworthy opponent. *And when had she become an adversary?* We headed to our respective stations.

𝔇𝔇𝔇

Elizabeth avoided me most of the evening, which suited me fine, allowing me to concentrate on the unequivocal tasks, though the legions of rodents now seemed less comrades in research than marginalized flotsam. We're all connected, I reminded myself. Think of what Sam taught you.

Around eleven o'clock I snuck into the small computer closet where we housed the server and connected to the database with my ELN. I wasn't about to breach security with my laptop. I copied my normative facial data to a disc —it was after all not classified— then translated the data into 3D male and female images using the company software. My plan in motion.

"Eunis!" Ruchika was almost upon me, startling me. But I'd frightened her too. "What're you doing?"

The disc went discreetly into my lab coat. "Just re-checking last week's results off the server. Looking for anomalies in my reports." Did she catch me? I tried to look sanguine.

"Oh. Just your reports?"

"Do I look like a cop? Yes, just *my* reports. And you?"

She rotated around the small room, alighted on a charger; snatched it off the shelf. "Left my charger. My head must've been somewhere else."

We both forced smiles and almost tripped over each other leaving.

"Goodnight."

"Goodnight."

The whole process had taken me less than twenty minutes, and as far as I could tell no rules had been broken nor any trail for detection left. Except for Ruchika. If she went to Warring what would she say? How would I respond?

I was relieved when the shift was over, but as I hung up my lab coat Elizabeth approached me.

"Yes?" I did my best to exude a chill.

"I'm sorry, really," she said.

"About what?" I pulled on my overcoat.

"What do you mean?"

"You're sorry for what?"

"My drinking. The bottle. I don't remember, you know . . . " She waved a hand at my bruised face. "We were having such a good time. Are you okay?"

"Yes. You and Roddy can stop worrying."

"*Roddy*?"

"Yes." *That wasn't very smart.*

"You mean Jerrod? What does he have to do with this?"

"I just thought, since he was there . . ."

"I'm sure he's moved on. He's very pragmatic about my drinking, about most things."

"Okay, well, then I accept your apology. Let's move on too."

"Would you have dinner with us on Christmas?"

Warmth rose in my chest. I *wanted* to excuse her actions. But Elizabeth had left more than marks on my face. She'd left new doubt. Plus I had work to do, with Zoe set to meet me the following evening . . . too important. "You know what, no thanks."

"Please, it's Christmas."

I shook my head. "I don't think so." I walked away.

On the way home, surrounded by holiday lights and pagan

wishful thinking, I dissected other myths surrounding me, like marriage, family, friends, happiness. I'd make my own. I'd always made the most progress on my own. I should've been used to it by then.

Christmas Eve day I spent keeping surfaces in focus: reviewing the research and my notes on beauty, preparing the questions, and cleaning the already spotless apartment. I avoided calling Elizabeth back. I avoided Sam's coffin, relegated to a corner in the kitchen, though Sam was beginning to reek.

☽☽☽

Even in Times Square Christmas Eve had shadows. It was just past 7:30 PM, and if I'd read Zoe's directions correctly my destination was an alley around the block from the coffee shop where we'd met, about halfway down. I spotted an unlikely entrance, seedy, that triggered more edginess.

A single light bulb at the far end of the alley silhouetted garbage stacked high above me along each wall. Grit drifted through the shaft of light, which charted a small, otherworldly pathway. If I was careful I could navigate without touching the discarded waste. The smell, even encased in the large plastic bags, cloyed at my throat and made me gag. Those mounds had been forgotten for a long time.

Time was running out. Even as I moved through the fetid trench it occurred to me that the filth and smell were the least of my worries. I could be mugged, or worse, I could fail.

I didn't see her. She'd said halfway down, look for stairs into a basement. I wasn't early; numerous Times Square clocks had dispelled that. The solitary bulb was a warning, but I'd already burned what was behind me, so I moved forward till I saw the steps. Zoe ascended from the shadows wearing a dark green jacket.

"You made it!" I couldn't have been tighter inside, breezier out.

She wasn't. "Eunis, I've been thinking . . ."

"Zoe, please."

"It's just that I . . . we could be in a lot of trouble. Security's tight."

"First off, you said it's light tonight; skeleton crews."

"It is."

"We'll be in and out in an hour, we'll be gone before it's even monitored, and I'll have the only record." I held up the disc.

She was dour.

My heart quickened. "I've set up blind phone numbers. Untraceable. You thought it was a grand psychological experiment."

"It is."

"So?" Out on the street dark bodies passed left and right. "This is a chance to do really exciting research. With some luck, to change things."

"Luck."

"No one gets hurt, there's nothing illegal."

"Except that *I'm* giving you access to a proprietary four-story high billboard, in Times Square. Let's not kid ourselves."

"Replacing Kate Upton for sixty minutes. She'll be back up doing her stuff before they miss her." I gave Zoe a moment. "You're not even scheduled tonight. You said the board's on remote."

"But if they ever find out . . ."

There was still a little of Harold's money in the bank. "I'll pay you."

Her face shifted, almost indecipherable.

"What's a semester's tuition? Three thousand? That's more than they'll pay you in a couple months, right?"

"With fees, more like five thousand. But I don't know . . ."

That would effectively finish me off. But time was slipping away. "I'll pay you eight thousand, cash. It's all I've got."

"How do I know you'll pay?"

"Because if you lead the cops to me, I'll lose my job and any hope of getting a doctorate. An education in genetics will be gone. You'll lose your job; I'll lose my life. Look at me, what else can I do looking like this? Please."

"You could market your story. Isn't that the way? Your fifteen minutes of fame, with me as your expendable?"

"What do you think they'd do with me? Pay me a little, then turn me into a sideshow freak?"

Her eyes were down, distant, not really seeing the pavement.

"Zoe." I knew I'd almost lost her. "What would your life have been like if what I'm proposing had been possible for your folks?"

Her one good eye met mine, a well of disappointment. With barely a nod we descended the steps through a non-descript metal door, into a narrow, scarcely lit basement hallway with a strangling steamy odor and large sewage pipes running along each concrete wall. An old building.

"Careful," she said as we ducked under a pipe and, farther down, over a series of tattered ventilation ducts. Bodies — rodent and human— could've been secreted away there. The air, claustrophobic like a tomb. Atoms on alert.

We turned left and went down another five or six concrete steps till we came to an unmarked door sheathed in dented metal. Zoe pulled her keys, then wavered. Water rushed to my ears. No time to measure. "It'd be easier to hack the system remotely," I whispered. "No one would even know this is here."

"I don't know why I'm doing this."

"Yes you do." I signaled for her to unlock the door. She took a deep breath and held it, like she was going to dive. She opened it.

I stared into a tiny server room, like the one at the lab except that it was much, much older, with more servers.

"This is just for that one billboard?"

"Give me the disc." Her voice harried, constricted. She fumbled with the disk and, hand shaking, inserted it into the drive and checked her watch. "7:46 PM. You have thirty minutes."

"Hey! We agreed an hour."

"You want your disc back?" Panic twitched around her mouth.

"Okay. Go!"

She pushed PLAY, and the tiny monitor dissolved from Kate Upton's micro bathing suit and ample flesh to a split screen with my normative male and female heads. I could almost hear men in Times Square moaning at their loss, but no, it was deep water amassing around me. *Stay focused.*

My normative faces had skins so perfectly pigmented they

could be Caucasian, African-American or Hispanic. My headline:

"You choose the most beautiful"

Each male and female head animated every eight seconds through the four choices, then repeated itself:

- Blonde hair/blue eyes
- Blonde hair/green eyes
- Dark brown hair/blue eyes
- Dark brown hair/green eyes

A series of numbers —one set for male voters and another for female— scrolled along the bottom, with instructions to text only once. Zoe alternately watched the monitor and a series of digital numbers and lights on the server panel. "This is live on Times Square now?" I could hardly believe my good fortune or the pressure.

"Yes." Tense as ever, chewing her fingernail.

As I stood there wishing I could be on the street watching, Zoe suddenly said, "You know what, get out of here. If security shows up, I can say I was in the square and detected a problem, so I came here. Just get out!"

"What?"

"I'll destroy the disc as soon as I'm out of here. Get out!"

"Are you sure?"

"Bring the cash to the coffee shop on the twenty-sixth at noon. Don't mess with me."

"If you say so."

"Don't screw me, I've done my part. Now get out of here!"

As quickly as I could steer through the hurdles of the passageway, I was out the door, up the steps, and out of the alleyway into the lights. Coming up for air, I ran to the other end of the block. And there it was: magnificent, sixty feet high, my images, my research, and a crowd of people watching and texting.

☽☽☽

The match ignited. I lit the candle. The matchbox given to me by the albino Jamaican woman went back in my pocket. Christmas Eve atop the world, and I could enjoy the colors. At last something to celebrate!

The numbers on my laptop had stopped spinning. Zoe hadn't given me the full thirty minutes, but I had feedback from close to 20,000 respondents! 20,000! My heart swelled, my eyes tingled with . . . dare I say it, joy. On the TV there was no mention of anyone hacking into Times Square. By then Zoe should've been safely at home and the only evidence destroyed.

Data partied in my head like drunken sugar plum fairies. I was consumed with corralling and evaluating it, but as I settled into the high-backed chair and watched the flickering light dance across my apartment, the stench emitting from the red cedar box on the kitchen counter distracted me, the dirty, proliferating stench. It reminded me of how I'd failed him —of my many failures, really— and I wanted to be rid of them. But the seed of freedom that Sam had planted was strong too.

"Sammy." I walked over to him. "I'm sorry. I can't bury you properly. I wanted something beautiful for you. I don't want to incinerate you . . . like the others." *Like Harold.*

It was the practical way, the antiseptic way, bleaching out all impurities but . . . I was going to have to do something soon. The pong of Sam's rotting carcass spread into the air and forced my head to jerk away. *Tonight, of all nights, let me do something right.*

A proper burial, Momma would warn . . . or else. To me it became a simple matter: basic cleanliness demanded it. I pulled on my overcoat and, keeping the box at arm's length, I left the apartment.

I pressed 'down.' The doors closed and the elevator descended. But at the eleventh floor it glided to a stop, surprising me. I questioned the floor indicator. The doors slid open and, despite the late-late hour, a well-dressed older woman wearing expensive jewelry, a red and white Santa hat, and carrying a laundry basket, stepped in. Of course my face jolted her, but the smell collapsed her expression and immediately repelled her.

"My god!" the woman said angrily. "You're disgusting!"

The woman bolted. The elevator door slid shut. I smothered my laugh. The elevator started down again. I *did* feel free.

Once I was out of The Octagon's glare I removed my tinted glasses and appraised the darkened path to the lighthouse. The day's warmth had contracted the mounds of snow, but the earth, lampposts and railings were frosted with crystals as the post-midnight temperatures again plummeted and bewitched the landscape. Momma, unable to see crystals as the multi-dimensional ordering of atoms, saw them as sprites and nixies, members of her unpredictable family of spooks. Notwithstanding her foolishness, I was oddly revitalized by their familiarity and by their certain return, drop-by-drop, to the rivers and oceans. That night they would honor Sam the Shadow.

As I approached the lighthouse at the end of the island, I wondered about Charles Dickens —the writer who traveled that island of outcasts, who saw that very lighthouse almost 200 years earlier, and who was unafraid to speak out concerning the inhumanity he saw there. *Yet he was also an imperialist.* I'd asked Harold about this contradiction when he read it to me. He shrugged, that annoying shrug.

Wasn't it Dickens who wanted to eradicate the East Indians? Conquerors take the vanquished.

He nodded.

"Where's the humanity?" I'd asked.

He had no answer.

And where was my humanity? Ahead in the dark watchtower, I envisioned the destitute Charles Dickens and how I'd failed the poor man. But I still had time to make good on my other promises and I was grateful for that.

My fingers ran along Sam's red cedar coffin. Best to go by water. With so little light I still saw remarkably well. At the tip of the island, behind the lighthouse, where once I'd considered slipping into the water —*you* did *consider killing yourself, Eunis, stop pretending*— I climbed over the railing, careful to keep a grip on the cedar box. Perhaps due to the heady response in Times Square, I felt nimble as I climbed deliberately over the rocks to the choppy water's edge.

"Stop," said a voice above me. "Don't!" The man was clumsy, scampering down the slope to me before I could even respond. It was Charles Dickens.

"Take my hand," he said.

"I'm okay." *And he was alive!*

"Take my hand." He was a bit shaky but seemed more lucid.

"Charles, it's me, I'm okay."

"Who?"

"Charles Dickens. That's you right?"

"No. My name is Malcolm. Let's talk about this up there away from the water. C'mon"

"You don't remember me?"

"I do not."

"It's not what you think."

"Then come up there with me." He pointed to the base of the tower.

"Not before I bury my friend."

"In the box?"

"Sammy." I pulled the matches from my pocket and, holding the flame steady, lit the top of the cedar box on fire. Fire *and* water, complete purification.

"Oh," said Malcolm. "I'm sorry."

"Don't be."

"Do you want me to go?"

"No, please stay. He was a rat among many. But I knew him better than most." The box held the flame. The sweet cedar smoke consoled me. I placed it on the water, gave it a shove.

"Sammy?" he asked.

"Sam, Sammy."

"How old?"

"About two and a half."

Reverence rose in Malcolm's eyes. "This is grand, like the Vikings; a burial ship. May your soul be peaceful, move on, and return. See you soon, Sam."

It was stately, even if it was only legend. "Thank you." I nodded at him. "That was very nice."

The cedar box bobbed in the choppy waters but stayed afloat and on fire. We stood on the shore watching the blazing box drift into open sea. All connected: Sam, Harold's gift, Malcolm, the water and me.

CHAPTER EIGHTEEN

Sam's funeral pyre finally disappeared into the charcoal mist. I turned to Malcolm who had not taken his eyes off the flaming box. I climbed the rocky slope to the lighthouse.

"My hand," he said leaning over the railing, arm extended, his stained brown overcoat riffling in the night breeze and his shin-high military boots partially laced and firmly planted. "Take my hand." I did, then considered where I could wash it.

Back on solid ground I asked again, "You don't remember me?"

"Should I?"

"We met a few nights ago."

"Same place, same time?" He smiled. His teeth needed work. He'd been discarded too long.

"Yes, almost." I returned the smile. "Are you in the light-house?"

His eyes widened. "How did you know?"

"Do you like Charles Dickens?"

"I do, very much."

"When I met you the other night, you quoted him."

His grin folded. "Did I say something wrong? Dickens . . ." He scratched his grimy head, his eyes heavy. "Sometimes . . . I don't know where it comes from. Sorry."

"No, no. What you said to me was important." Perhaps he was an emissary, a connection, someone who could point me more clearly to Dickens, to Harold, and —given his comment regarding *reason and beauty* —even to Dickens's principles or codes of beauty.

"It was?" His face lightened a little.

"Yes." How would I explain it all? I couldn't. "Why do you stay in the lighthouse?"

"I'm good with my hands." He grinned proudly, referring to

the jimmied lock with a twist of his wrist. "Don't need to sleep on the streets. And here I am, ready for my morning intake at the hospital. Most people spend a small fortune to live on this island. I'm gentry, don't you think?"

"Yes, I guess you are. But isn't it cold?"

"Sometimes. Don't you like the cold?"

"I do."

"So there. It makes me feel alive. As long as it doesn't kill me. *That* will come soon enough without my help."

"You could crash at my apartment. It's warmer." *Had I offered that?* To a man who almost frightened me to death a few nights earlier? "At least for tonight."

"I told you, I like the cold."

But he had saved me, *hadn't he?* "Just tonight. For a few hours."

He deliberated. "You're not afraid of me? What I might do?"

"What would you do?"

"I'm not always clearheaded."

"No, neither am I. Come on. I live over there."

"You're sure? Just tonight."

"Sure." I wasn't. But it was time.

☽☽☽

Once more I lit candles. Would Malcolm hear the voices I heard? How exactly could I fashion questions around Harold's death and my hope that the Dickens books held answers? It was unreasonable of course. Yet at this point, why not.

At the same time, I dwelled on my idle laptop and itched to start tallying and correlating the data from my grand experiment. Consensus —particularly consensus from 40,000-50,000 people— could be the means toward finding beauty's coordinates.

I offered Malcolm the old chair but he crossed his legs and sat against the bottom of the kitchen counter, as Elizabeth and I had done only a day or so earlier. In a way, I was glad. He was filthy.

"Would you like some food?"

"Water, please."

When I brought it to him his smell overwhelmed me; worse

than the alleyway garbage. Much worse. He needed a bath. "Would you like to take a shower?"

"That bad, huh?"

"Well . . ."

"I used to be respectable, you know." He finished the water. Set the glass down slowly, unsure where the air met the floor.

"I'll get it warmed up. Get you a towel." In the small bathroom I put away my toothbrush and toothpaste and water cup. My washcloth too. Otherwise, as I scouted around, it was tidy as should be, and safer this way.

I pulled a towel from the small linen closet and turned on the shower. My ears started reverberating. "Oh god, it's starting again."

I held onto the washbasin and waited for the voices. But instead a lustral sensation overtook me. I had no desire to push against it. It held me for only a minute or two, then passed. One breath and I returned to the living room. Malcolm slept against the counter, snoring loudly. The canyons on his face had softened. If not for his clothes, he could have been a contented family member sleeping off holiday festivities. I touched my heart where his calm had surfaced in me.

I turned off the water and carefully stepping over him I grabbed my laptop and organized myself on the bed. The anticipation made me giddy; a rising elation, not unlike the afternoon I knew I'd consummate my relationship with Harold. Or anytime I was about to slip into water. The results were easily parsed and by a little after 2 AM the results were finally in. They were disappointing.

Experiment & Observation: comparing normative male and female faces for attraction variables.

Total Respondents [18,668]:
72% women [13,441]
28% men [5,227]

Female respondents (most attractive male):
Blonde hair/blue eyes [23%]
Blonde hair/green eyes [27%]

Dark brown hair/blue eyes [28%]
Dark brown hair/green eyes [22%]

Male respondents (most attractive female):
Blonde hair/blue eyes [26%]
Blonde hair/green eyes [27%]
Dark brown hair/blue eyes [22%]
Dark brown hair/green eyes [25%]

Even calculating for standard margin of error, it was a wash. *A wash!* Back to square one. I fell asleep on my computer.

☽☽☽

"Where am I? My god, my levo!"

I woke on my bed, wrinkled, still in my clothes.

Malcolm disoriented, draped in the same blanket I'd wrapped around Elizabeth, stumbled to the door. "What have you done? What about my levo?"

"Malcolm, it's okay." I tried to calm him but he struggled with the door, unable to open it. Panic set in.

"If I'm not there, I won't get my meds. They'll cut me off, they'll cut me off." He made croaking other-worldly sounds and started to cry.

"I'll get you there. When do you need to be there?"

He blubbered. I couldn't understand but one word in four. "The Metzinger?" I asked and he nodded as mucous poured out of his nose, spittle from his mouth. I didn't want to touch him but I had to. "Take my hand. I'll get you there."

"It'z too late," he moaned. "Too late." He bent over, disintegrating.

"No, Malcolm. C'mon." I stood him up and towed him through the door to the elevator. On the eleventh floor, it stopped.

"Damn it!" I propped him up *and* pounded the buttons to keep it moving. He drooled and keened and then, with the sound of wet rubber flapping against a wall, he shit himself.

"Oh no." The stench of diarrhea rose quickly, overtaking the space. The elevator doors opened and the same well-dressed, older woman started to get on. She gagged, clutched her mouth and started retching, then stumbled out. I pounded the buttons. The doors closed.

He was much heavier than I'd imagined and I could barely hold up under his weight. Alternately I held my breath and sucked in the nauseating stink sagging and saturating his pants. As we exited the elevator, past the usual gaggle of mothers and babies, we left a slippery trail of yellowed excrement across the rotunda floor.

I dragged him out the door and down the steps, toward the hospital across the way.

"They tried. They tried," he sniveled.

I moved him as quickly as I could but it was like pulling a cadaver. "What did they try, Malcolm? What did they try?"

"Tri, trihexy. Phenidyl, and now without, oh my god, without . . ." He collapsed at my feet, soiling my legs and shoes in his shit.

"We're almost there. C'mon Malcolm, you can do this." I helped him to his feet, turned him around in the right direction. "C'mon." We started again.

"Tell me," I said trying to sober him as we moved and hoping that he'd remove some of his weight off my shoulders and back. "Tell me about your family. Do you have family nearby? Anyone I can call?"

"I'll never die."

"What?"

"Never die. Never on the street." He waved his arms in ballet arcs. His right hand covered in his own shit. "Die with family."

"We're here. Malcolm, see." We busted through the hospital doors into the lobby. I screamed for help. Malcolm skated on the excrement still oozing from his pants to his boots, and as he did he collapsed on top of me, knocking me over. I fell like a freshly cut pine, twice cracking my head on the lobby floor. I was a rag dolly of jaw jolting, teeth rattling timber. The room spun, turned taffy. Malcolm covered me in warm vomit, and I swallowed it.

☽☽☽

First my tongue. Metallic. Throbbing. Gums swollen. Teeth vibrating . . . in waves. Feces, feces stinging . . . my eyes. Dry.

Caked. Binding the skin, my knuckles. A curdled mouthful. His puke, his grit. I passed out again.

CHAPTER NINETEEN

Perfection. "She was at her most attractive when the space between her pupils was just under half, or 46 percent, of the width of her face from ear to ear. The other perfect dimension was when the distance between her eyes and mouth was just over a third, or 36 percent, of the overall length of her face from hairline to chin."

In foam, drifting.

"A University of Toronto study found that the facial proportions of Jessica Alba were close to the average of all female profiles."

Faces. Roddy, Elizabeth, Momma, Harold. What was it that last time with Harold? Before.

I saw him swinging by his neck, eyes open, motionless and dull, though they had cut him down before I got there. Yet I saw him so clearly. What they told me made no sense, broken clusters of words. Sorry. Gone. Dead. Suicide. Disbelief. Disorder. Still disorder. Blank spaces.

I let him down.

A void.

Then questions from the police.

No, the last time . . . with him. Where was it? What had he said? *Forgive me.* No, after that. He'd carried trouble around the house. As usual. No, this was different. Tense. Distracted. Afraid. He was sinking, a man caught in a mire. Wearing my thin camisole, he could see my areola. He loved that. He hardly noticed.

He'd been reading about Dickens, the train crash Dickens had survived. Harold re-read the pages, not as if he'd lost concentration but rather to confirm his disbelief. I asked him why. *I'm gathering,* he said, but there wasn't a hint of joy in the exploration or that his hero had survived, no explanation of what he was gathering or why.

Eventually he came to me as I read. As he passed I saw the

doubt, just as you can see rings on the water's surface and know a rock lies below. The way he looked at me.

But he would deny anything of the sort. Doubt like mine. Not quite. Like he'd been fooled. Deeply. I couldn't tell by *what* because he came behind me and grabbed my shoulders, rather stiffly. I was frightened to see his face so I didn't turn around.

But he loosened. His ache closed around me. I wanted to run from it. It made me angry. *He* made me angry. He rubbed my shoulders, softer gentler. Then my arms, brushing my breasts as he moved past them. Like he was apologizing.

His hands, running along my arms . . .

Feeling his hands. I opened my eyes. A small room, though the walls were out of focus, with bluewhite bright light. It hurt. I closed my eyes.

"I'll turn down the light." A woman's voice.

Even with my eyelids shut I saw darkness descend.

"Is that better?"

Slowly, very slowly, I adjusted to the darkened room and the woman standing over me. "Ya took quite a fall." A mermaid and serpent tattooed on her neck. Cat eyes! The young female orderly! The urge to bolt, but I couldn't move. Couldn't speak.

"I've cleaned ya up the best I could, but when ya a bit better I can wash ya hair."

Dull in my sight, she was late-twenties with large jade aquamarine eyes and thick black eyebrows. Long, lavish ebony hair pulled back. Full lips not needing cosmetic support. Something exotic drew down her cheeks, hard and smooth like carved rocks sculpted by water. She stroked my arm again . . . soothing, even stimulating.

"They want to keep ya a few more days for evaluation, then they want to send you to Bellevue CPEP. You stirred it up, even more than the first time. There's still some talk, but in a hospital like this you'll be quickly forgotten. You're gonna feel disoriented, maybe even nauseous for a while, but they think your concussion isn't that serious." Her touch was tender, consoling.

"I'm not supposed to tell ya this," she went on, "but I don't think you should go to Bellevue. They want to do an EOU, an Extended Observation. For up to seventy-two hours. It's a different evaluation. Psychiatric."

I organized a few bits of the floating debris in my head and wrung out the words. "How many?"

"How many what?"

"Days. Been. Here?" I was ready to revisit the galaxy.

"Two, two days. Is it okay if I rub your head?"

Electrons scattered. I closed and opened my eyes affirmatively. "Work?"

The orderly began massaging my temples and eyebrows. Back to darkness, savoring the orderly's touch. *It's been so long.* This once I would let go of Harold. I wouldn't resist.

"No one knows where you work. Would you like me to call?"

"I can't miss . . ." But I couldn't finish. Exhaustion flooded over me. *Please don't stop.* But the orderly did stop. I wanted more.

"I can call for you. They must be wondering where you disappeared, huh? But you won't be able to return to work for a few more days."

Warring! What would Warring say? Not showing up.

"Do you want to go to Bellevue?"

Psychiatric evaluation. *If Warring finds out* . . . "No, I . . ."

"Listen, I think I can get you out of it."

Opening my eyes was like lifting weights. The orderly parted those full lips; she smiled sweetly. I could've swum in those green eyes. "You can call me Nan. I'm a Nurse Assistant. I can get access to records. If I'm careful, you know, I could do that for you."

The weight prevailed and I went willingly into darkness, Nan's hands applying exactly the right amount of pressure. *Why not. The hell with this.* "Yes," I said. Yes.

)))

The hospital's lobby doors slid open. "Thank you," I said to Nan. The nurse, nurse assistant, had been appropriate. Nice, actually.

I tried to count the days I'd lost, three or four. This one felt crisp, the sun setting. I attempted to lift myself out of the wheelchair but my weight and the oscillating buildings around me dragged me back down.

Nan reset me, tapping me on the shoulder and bending over me. "Let me take you home."

By any measure she was a beauty, exotic, maybe one of the most beautiful women I'd ever seen.

"No, no. You're on duty."

"Not anymore."

"Well, I live a ways from here so— "

"You live right over there." Nan pointed to The Octagon and began wheeling me that way.

"How'd you know?"

"Clairvoyant."

I couldn't turn to see her expression and I was too drained to make sense of her comment. Perhaps she was like me, perhaps she had a special gift, if such things existed.

Nan pushed the wheelchair forward. "Sit, relax."

All I could think of was lying in bed with Nan stroking me, the beauty of it. *Her* beauty, and how it might somehow be a link in my investigations. She seemed to be deep in thought as well, because neither of us spoke again until we reached The Octagon's entrance.

"I'm sure that was degrading." Nan interrupted my trance. "Depraved, really."

"What? I can make it from here, thanks."

"Some Christmas. I guess you were trying to help that poor man, but you end up paying for it instead of being thanked. Let's everyone just keep the system flowing. Check the boxes. Next. Everyone keeping themselves out of harm's way. 'I am sending you out like sheep among wolves. Therefore be as shrewd as snakes and as innocent as doves.'"

"Matthew something-something." With effort I raised myself out of the wheelchair. "'Therefore do not worry about tomorrow, for tomorrow will worry about itself. Each day has enough troubles of its own.' I've heard it all before. Momma's a Lutheran, though probably not like many other Lutherans, thank goodness."

"Hmm. Okay. So can my husband and I lend you a hand?"

"A hand? I'll be fine. I may not look like much but I'm pretty capable."

Nan tore a piece of thin cardboard from the Kleenex box in the basket behind my head and pulled a pen from her pocket. It clicked. I heard her scribbling on the cardboard. "Maybe you'll need someone, you know, to lean on." She handed me the paper and a phone number. "We've gone back to the basics."

"I'm not much on religion."

"We're not born again." She laughed. "Well, maybe we are. But in a *very* different way. Like I said, back to basics. The things that *naturally* drive us. Anyway, all of us can use a hand from time to time. Maybe you could help me."

"Well I do appreciate you getting me out of that place, Nan."

"I hope to see you again. Call that number."

The Octagon tenants filtered in from their day. On went my shaded glasses and hood. I made my way into the building.

☽☽☽

In the elevator up I was lucky enough to encounter only one man, older, probably in his sixties and distinguished, wearing a dark blue striped suit and carrying a newspaper. *Cufflinks!* He stood to my left. I could read the headline:

"Times Square hacked. Police narrow search."

"Good evening." He surprised me.

"Good evening." I stood slightly behind him. I must've appeared odd, covered in my hood and shaded glasses. Nonchalantly, I removed them both.

Almost immediately the elevator seemed to speed up. In my ears and chest. The man stared straight ahead. It wasn't just my hospital hangover. Atoms ricocheted, the pressure a bit unpleasant, a bit arousing. Very physical, absolutely sexual. If I'd acknowledged the fragments of myself dancing in the elevator glass, I would've passed out, I'm sure.

I bowed my head, put my shaded glasses back on. The elevator settled at the eleventh floor. The man got out.

"Good evening," he said again as the doors slid closed.

The atoms disassembled. Maybe it *was* hospital hangover.

☽☽☽

This was an unusual time for me to be in my hallway, early evening, when I was usually at work or, on the weekends, locked in. The final beams of daylight at each end of the hallway softened the sand-colored carpet. I was still pleasantly medicated as I approached my apartment. Until a chill passed through me. Something wasn't right.

Posted on my door in cobalt blue ink was the notice:

MANDATORY MEETING
Tonight 7:15 PM
Homeowners' Association Meeting Room
EVICTION HEARING
HOA Members only are asked to attend and provide a
quorum for discussion regarding the possible eviction of
<u>Penthouse Studio B owner/tenant.</u>

The Lease-to-Own Tenant will be expected to attend and
speak to the HOA Members.
(signed Helen Dorward, President,
Homeowners Association)

Like I said, I was a little slow. But a pall was breeding in me, what Momma called *svingete ark*. I re-read the notice posted on the door. *My* door. P-Studio B. "Oh god, they're evicting me."

I unlatched the door and held onto the table as I put down my keys. My phone, the one I'd left more than three days earlier on the counter, buzzed frantically.

The first message: "Eunis. It's Elizabeth. Where are you? I'm going to have to call someone if you're not here soon. Call me." I closed my eyes.

I listened to the second message. Again Elizabeth. "Where are you? What am I supposed to put in my report? I'm worried that you're okay. And this won't look good with what's going on here. Please call." *Oh geez.* I rubbed my temples.

Third call. "Came by your place this morning. No answer. Please call me. The cops won't do anything for forty-eight hours." *Cops!* I saw a shroud undulating around my heart.

Fourth call. "Damn you, Eunis, if you're trying to stiff me on the eight grand, I'll call the cops. You were supposed to meet me at the coffee shop. Call me and make this right. I'm not kidding." *Oh no. No!*

Fifth call. "Eunis, this is Carol Warring. Why didn't you show up for work? Are you okay? Have you quit because of the investigation? Please call and give some explanation." Then as she hung up, I heard her say, "Highly irregular. I don't need this bullshit." A winding sheet constricted around my heart.

The clock hit 7:15 PM. I opened my eyes. I needed to get to the homeowners meeting.

CHAPTER TWENTY

The basement. According to Dickens I was descending into the asylum's cage for the criminally insane. The HOA meeting was in session. But I could make this right. Once the neighbors understood they were only seeing a fragment of the situation, this would all be behind me and I could get back to my work. But neither my hand on my chest nor deep, deep breaths stopped my growing dread.

Out of the elevator, the buzz of voices and the rapping of a gavel dropped a dank apprehension around me. My breath came in short, fast hitches. A muffled voice addressed the room and the crowd quieted down. I stood at the door. I could hear the speaker clear enough.

"This is the most disgusting, depraved tenant we've ever had. And I've seen it with my own eyes and smelled it with my own nose." More rumble from the crowd.

"It's in our bylaws. Capital improvements will benefit. We get to keep the deposit as well as the security deposit. Most important, our membership can safely walk the halls and lobby, day or night. This tenant must vacate. It's all there in our contract. God knows we have enough witnesses to this degenerate."

A pause.

"I don't see Mrs. Cloonis anywhere to defend herself, though I can't see what she'd have to say under the circumstances. So I guess we can vote or have some discussion."

How often had I ever spoken to strangers? Now to a roomful . . . But all that I'd worked toward would be lost. Harold's sacrifice, for nothing. *I'd* be left with nothing. Penniless. My job, my career. My pledge to Harold —his death wasted. The oaths I'd made to myself reduced to the same ashes, with nowhere but Momma and the farmhouse in my future. Plus all the witches, goblins and ghosts that she'd promised.

I opened the door. A tidal wave of light engulfed me in the windowless room. My ears began to clog. Forty or so people turned to look at me. Some gasped. My hand shook securing my shaded glasses. I hung my head. *No, head up.*

"Mrs. Cloonis, how nice of you to grace us with your presence. Don't bother sitting. You can speak first, if you have anything to say."

It was a restless crowd. As I passed them the undertow dragged on my thighs and feet. My chest wavered between panic and primitive hostility, as if I moved through currents of warm and cold water, trying to balance between benign and beast. But I *wanted* to lose myself in the savage.

Somehow I kept moving toward the lectern. The energy inside and out was uncontrollable, *that worst possible feeling,* tossing me in waves, this way and that. To steady myself I grabbed for a chair and a shoulder. I was slapped away and cursed.

The woman at the lectern was the woman from the elevator, the one with the Santa hat and the expensive jewelry and the laundry basket in the middle of the night. She'd inhaled Sam rotting and Malcolm shitting himself.

"I'm Helen Dorward, President of the Homeowners Association," I heard the woman say, though I couldn't see her mouth move. "I'm glad you took the time to come here. Perhaps there is something about your behavior and the behavior of your friends that we don't understand."

A few in the audience chortled.

"Please, please come up here, Mrs. Cloonis. Tell us why allowing you into our home was not a terrible mistake."

I stumbled up the platform to the lectern, my legs slack, my usual physical strength missing. My eyes burned with dull, dry heat; a fish out of water, curling in the sun. Inside, a voice taunted me. *Where's the beauty now, bitch?*

A dry heave soured my throat and tongue. I blinked hard hoping I could steady myself, make sense of it. I thought of swimming in the lakes, but the room had its hold on me. It rippled in and out of focus. I lowered my head. *So many eyes.*

The wet, diluted sounds didn't match the audience. Grunts. Hissing. The clank and thud of heavy chains dragging around me. *Dickinson would say you're not waiting for Eternity; you're close to it.* A cough. The blur that must have been Helen Dorward moved quickly away and to the side, eventually inching her way off the platform.

Through a scorching weariness, I stared at the floor, at the shoes in the front row.

"Say something, you freak," yelled a man.

More rumble.

I was so tired and so dry. I could barely lift the words. "I . . . I was trying to help . . ." There was laughter. Derisive.

Eyes on the lectern. I searched for strength, anything that would return moisture to my body, to my spirit. I imagined myself in Minnesota, in the lake, swimming. Then I just let it fly . . .

"I don't know if any of you have ever been in the water with someone who's drowning."

A shrill female voice. "You're gonna give a lecture? What's your point?"

I lifted my eyes and turned her way but couldn't pick out a single face in the crowd. They *all* looked up at me with disgust. Men, women, mostly white, East Indian, a few blacks and Asians. Afflicted with the same . . . *anger.*

I took a breath. Eyes returned to the lectern. *You're swimming.* "I know this sounds wild coming from someone who looks like me, but a lot of faces scare me."

A little laughter. It sounded like a few in the crowd were *with* me.

"Yeah. But one of the scariest was of a man who lived 150 yards from you/us, in that old tower." I swung my head in that direction. "That's not a legend. Perhaps you've seen him, often dressed in a calf-length mid-Victorian frock coat. Have any of you looked?"

"Again, what's your point?!"

I gathered myself. "That man was drowning, and he was only 150 yards away. Did any of you know he was calling for help?" I waited. "Did any of you know and look away?"

Another voice in the crowd, gravely and deep for a woman.

"What's this got to do with you smearing excrement over our elevator and lobby?"

The crowd swelled, guttural and agreeing.

"And smelling like a rotted corpse." Added a new voice.

My gaze again on the front row feet. I continued, "Well, I looked away from that drowning man once, and I felt like shit."

"Ooh."

"Oh come on, you've heard that word before. It's the same as *'excrement.'*" Another breath. "So the second chance I had, I offered him a shower and shelter for the night. One night. But without his meds he was in trouble, which is when you saw me taking him to the Metzinger next door."

"You shouldn't have brought him into our building."

"One night. One night out of the killer cold. He was drowning and that's what I did."

"Jeopardizing the whole building."

"The building?" A dark storm wailed out of my chest, a force I couldn't suppress. "You don't know how fucking lucky you got it here." Silence.

I left the room and the voices erupted behind me.

I traveled up the elevator. Shards of my face circled me. The moment had been disastrous, but it had also been beautiful. Harold was with me, quoting Dickens, something about the safety of the simple truth.

Into the apartment, I was on the phone:

"Elizabeth, I'm okay. I'll be at work tomorrow night. I'll explain. Tell Warring I'll explain." What did that mean?

I staggered to my bed, curled onto it. The drugs continued to dissipate. The reality of what had just happened began to sink in. Tiny tremors started vibrating, circulating, through my body, intensifying, treacherous currents in an endless sea, no land in sight, nothing to hold on to. *Keep swimming. Keep swimming. Keep swimming.* And when I could no longer stay above the waves, I plunged into sleep.

꒰꒰꒰

"Eunis, would you like to explain, because I think I know what's going on." Carol Warring leaned back in her chair, sliding her fingers over the temples of her glasses the way you'd sharpen a blade. She'd drawn the blinds to ward off the morning light that would spread across me, but still I stood motionless, coat folded over my arm, unable to look Warring in the eye.

I'd rehearsed different explanations, including the simple truth, but I was loath to mention the hospital, loath to offer any link to the psychiatric notes that might reveal my rash but documented suicidal thoughts. Loath to pull Elizabeth into it. And perhaps Ruchika had mentioned seeing me in the server closet, or . . .

Warring filled the space. "Are you seeing someone? Because I think he, or she, is battering you."

"What?! No. No." I almost giggled. I was so relieved.

"Your welts, your bruises. Your odd behavior the other day. Now this disappearance. Look at your face." I started to cover myself but thought better of it. "More scratches than the other day. I can get you help, but I can't have you in my labs."

Explaining the first bruises would have exposed Elizabeth to serious trouble. And I couldn't explain what happened at the hospital with Charles Dickens . . . Malcolm.

"When I asked around," continued Warring, "one of your lab mates said she didn't know, but that you were often covered up. Quite a bit, actually." She wouldn't release her gaze. "These are all the signs of a battered relationship. I know because a family member had the same issues. You've got to be strong because I'm going to have to put you on temporary leave. It might explain why there are problems in the lab, with the results. But I can't jeopardize my lab, our research. And you will need to seek help."

"But I'm not— "

"That's the standard response. But you disappeared for three days without explanation. Not even a phone call. That alone is sufficient for me to put you on leave. I'm not going to terminate you because you seem to be a nice young woman, and you need help —for whatever is haunting you— but I *will* need to suspend pay until we have an explanation or you can provide proof that you're stable enough to perform. Do you understand?"

I contemplated lying. But what was I going to say? I dropped chin to chest and started for the door.

"Can I offer you a thought?"

I turned and nodded.

"Our work here, finding ways to impact beauty with our products, it's premised on beauty's finite coordinates."

"Yes."

"But there are infinite possibilities, and we shouldn't lose sight of them."

I felt her support, even if I couldn't process her words. "It's complex, but it's not what you think."

"Then what is it?"

I waved my hands in futility. "You're making a mistake about me. My numbers are good. Just because I can't explain every-thing . . . Anyway, I appreciate your concern."

As the door of Warring's office closed behind me, with all the ramifications of my suspension not yet even clear, my heart was oddly lighter.

)))

On the way to the apartment, Warring's words rolled over and over in my head. If beauty was agreeable to most because of its determinate qualities, wasn't ugliness, with all its possibilities, a genus of bedlam? Warring may have meant it as a salve, but in-stead I reconsidered the enormity of my task and how emphatically I was failing. It would take a cocktail of DNA genes from the swamp to create beauty and I hadn't even isolated one ingredient. Not one!

In something of a daze I met Zoe at the coffee shop. We stood in the coffee line without looking at each other. I slipped her the money.

"Well I hope it was worth it, the research," she said looking straight ahead, pocketing the envelope, now a bit more taciturn.

"Disappointing. Nothing clear cut."

"With that large sampling? Maybe it's simply eye of the be-holder and all that. Subjective."

"That's always been one of the arguments. But there's plenty of contradictory data, a 2008 Tel Aviv University study—"

"I gotta go. Don't call me again. Good luck." She headed uptown through the heavy pedestrian traffic. I guess we would never be friends.

Without work I felt aimless. I tarried at a large newsstand, searching newspaper headlines for an update on the hunt for the notorious Times Square Hacker. I scanned cover photos on the rack of celebrity magazines. I stopped for more coffee, and by the time I got to The Octagon it was late, and all I remembered of the trip was that some idiot left a wad of gum for me to sit on in the subway.

Agitated, I couldn't make the damn key work in the lobby door. I was sure they'd changed the lock until I realized I was forcing one of my lab keys into it. Then I spilled the remaining hot coffee over my blouse.

Once in the apartment, I switched on my small TV as a distraction. Stupid sitcom reruns, a cooking show, a cop show, and the nightly news.

". . . What's so frightening about this breach," said the female executive pointing to the massive billboard above her, "is that if hackers could stop Kate Upton, terrorist hackers could do much more serious harm."

The caption showed the woman speaking as a Vice President of A.C.E. Media. She looked earnestly at the reporter holding the mike. The frame cut to two in-studio news anchors, one male and one female, a static photo inserted to the upper left of the female.

"Well," said the female anchor, an Asian woman in her forties, as the camera returned to the two-shot, "it seems a long way from Kate Upton to terrorists."

"Does it?" said the male anchor, a man in his fifties, merriment circling his mouth.

"Paul."

The male anchor made an attempt at seriousness, speaking to the camera. "Police have asked anyone who was in Times Square Christmas Eve between 7:30 and 9:30, and who saw anything suspicious, to please call this number. Also . . ."

The image over the anchorwoman's shoulder flew to full screen.

". . . anyone with knowledge of any of these three suspects

caught by various security cameras should also call."

He described the blurry photos. "A Caucasian woman, twenty five to thirty-five, five-three to five-six, brown hair, wearing a dark green or charcoal jacket."

The frame changed. "An African American man, thirty-five to forty-five, possibly six feet or taller, wearing an embroidered brown dashiki pant suit . . ."

The frame cut once more. "And an albino woman, also thirty-five to forty-five, although possibly younger, five-six or so, white hair, wearing dark clothing."

"Shit." The photo, a high-angle shot from above, could have been me, was probably me. My face had betrayed me again.

He shuffled papers. "When we come back . . ."

I switched off the TV but my reflection stared back from the vacated screen. "Shit!" There, hanging on the wall, was my friggin' reflection in my framed diploma, its smug inviolability leering back at me. I went over to it and hurled the friggin' thing across the room, where it hit the front door and splintered, spraying the floor with crystals and shards. It felt good!

Rage overtook me. Storming across my *fucking impeccable little space*, I pulled the small tube TV with me, off the counter, out of its socket, releasing a muffled implosion as it hit the floor. Success! Turning to the large plate glass window and, *again*, my reflection, I picked up a kitchen stool and, with more strength than I knew I had, heaved the friggin' stool at the floor-to-ceiling window. It refused to shatter, barely budged, it mocked me.

I collected the stool again. Thinking of all the abuses my face had engendered, I rammed that damn stool hard against the window. Pain blossomed through my ribs and drove me back to the floor. I slid across like a child playing water Twister, my palms and face drawing daggers of glass. But as I closed my eyes, that friggin' window: nothing, nothing but a little crackle!

🌓🌓🌓

Lying on the floor of splintered glass, looking up at the array of blues that met New York's silver and gray skyline, I was oddly peaceful, like lying in the Bemidji sunshine, on that grassy hillside. No need to move, no need to struggle.

Like Papa Karl in the hospital, in his vegetative state, following the rail yard accident. I held on to him —no one else cared to— and those few hours each week cradling his powerless hand . . . somehow he knew I was there, and being there with him made his slow journey to the sky more —more orderly. More complete. Unconditional. No need to struggle. Like the Kris Kristofferson song Lyle sang, *nothing left to lose.*

Perhaps the building or its inhabitants had released me.

Something poked into my waist. I reached into my pant pocket. Not glass, a piece of thin, stiff cardboard. I turned it over: Nan's phone number.

Nan's touch, her pitch-black hair, trailing along my cheek. Most of all, those jade eyes, those generous natural pools drawing me in to that stunning face, that perfect skin, those miraculous genes. Nan. And her husband. Spectacular too? DNA worthy of my search?

Perhaps the answers lay in my bloody hand, shards of crystal rising out of it. Disappearing for a while seemed like a good idea. *What did I have to lose?*

CHAPTER TWENTY-ONE

Down five steps from street level, I arrived at Nan's apartment with nothing more than my laptop and genetics textbook in hand. I rang the bell marked only as "Basement." Nan came immediately to the door, arms and eyes wide open, like she was ready to assimilate me. "Welcome, sweet Eunis," she said before I stepped closer and she noticed the remnants of my recent encounters with glass. "Oh no, come in. It's worse than you said."

She snuck a look to the street and closed the door. She stroked my shoulders and made me sit on the wide burgundy sofa while she rounded up medical supplies.

"I'm fine," I called to her.

"I'm sure you are," she called back. "But we're going to take care of you anyway."

The apartment was dark despite the glorious sunshine outside. Larger than one would expect in the city, it had a grand L-shaped room rolling out in almost every direction, minimized only by its low nineteenth-century hammered-tin ceiling.

The room was festooned in Utrecht velvet and thick fabrics, the sort Momma coveted but could never afford.

"What d'ya think?" Nan arrived with an aluminum bowl of warm water and a washcloth. She sat on the settee opposite me.

"Pretty big."

"I know, we're lucky. We have supporters."

"Supporters? You mean benefactors?"

"Sure." Nan started to say more but stopped.

I didn't pry. Watching her beauty, I was hopeful. "Thank you so much for having me here. Just for a few days."

"Well, we'll see." She attended to my cuts and a few remaining splinters, carefully picking each one out, dropping them all into a large cobalt blue ashtray, and running the warm washcloth over my face in comforting circles. I shut my eyes.

Whatever residual rage I may have had was washed away. I had no desire to open my eyes. Her touch was better than the cold on my skin, which had been my only option since Harold's death. *Go away, Harold.*

Next, she tenderly manipulated my palms, then a finger at a time. I reopened my eyes, made sure I wasn't dreaming. I soaked up the splendor of the apartment —scrollwork and mahogany and braided sashes framing the archway into the dining room. Muscular framed, deep-cushioned chairs embroidered in indigo and saffron. A side table covered in scarlet taffeta. I'd never seen a room like it except in drawings and a few old photographs.

"It's beautiful." *A palace.*

Nan paused, a consoling smile. "I'm glad you like it. It's your new home."

"Well, for a few days anyhow. Till I figure out what to do." *Till things cool down.* "I'm very grateful, of course, but why are you being so kind? You hardly know me."

"Do I have to know you to be kind? Did you know that man, the one you brought to the hospital?"

"No, not really."

"So?"

My hand went to my heart. "You're very beautiful."

She smiled and bowed her head. "Besides, I'm sure you'll find a way to thank us."

I couldn't imagine what I could do for her or her husband that would repay such generosity.

After Nan showed me to my room and I told her it was the biggest I'd ever seen, she assured me that she and Levi each had their own room —puzzling me— and that each had an equally large bed. "We spend so much time in it, might as well have room to roam, right? Closets are a bit small, though."

Cream and crimson swag framed my bed, a bed fit for royalty. I was entranced.

"We can find you more space if the closet is a problem," she offered.

In leaving The Octagon hastily I hadn't considered packing clothes, but Nan pointed out that we were not that different in size. "I have plenty of clothes for you to wear."

It was true although I worried I had a bit more breast and thigh than she.

"Perhaps I'll go tomorrow." But the thought of returning to the Octagon hellhole —though fashionable, modern, luxurious— was abhorrent and perhaps risky with the cops poking around. I'd probably be locked out anyway. Besides, The Octagon wasn't luxurious like Nan and Levi's, it wasn't elegant. And it didn't offer friendship.

)))

Levi didn't come home after work.

"He had to go out of town," said Nan, though earlier she said the three of us would have dinner together at the apartment.

"What does he do?"

She set a plate of linguine in front of me. "I hope pasta and clams is okay with you. I shoulda asked. One of Levi's favorites."

"I'm not used to anyone making anything for me. Yes, it's fine —more than fine— and in the future let me help."

"Once you settle in, but right now you need to heal. You've been through a lot."

Being cared for! Even Harold hadn't gone to those extremes. There I was, sitting at a real dining room table, having a real conversation. Not with some broken person but with a strikingly exotic, bright woman. Great genes. "Do you have a picture of him?" I scanned the tabletops, shelves and walls for a clue.

"Who?"

"Levi."

"No, I keep him here." She pointed to her head.

Not in her heart? "It must be tough him having to travel so much."

"It works okay for us. Everyone needs a little space, don't ya think? Space to study."

"Study! What do you like to study?"

"People." She poured us both a glass of wine.

"Me too. Have you ever considered . . ." *Careful!* ". . . people's genes?"

"No, not particularly." She yawned.

"So what does he do?"

"Who?"

"Levi."

"Oh . . . Levi . . . He's sort of a goodwill ambassador." Nan took a moment, then spoke carefully. "He's a distributor. Sort of a salesman, I guess, but more like he smoothes the way, an advance man."

"I never heard that term before."

"Yeah, well, he goes ahead to see that things go smoothly. He coordinates." Her fingernails clicked on the tabletop.

I was asking too many questions but I had to ask one more. "What does he distribute?"

Nan picked up her fork, twirled her linguine and slowly sucked it in, licking her generous lips in conclusion. "Films. Documentaries." She looked over me, uninterested, around the room.

"Oh." *Enough questions.* I started on my linguine. "I'd like to see one sometime."

She returned to me. "Yes, I'm sure you will."

CHAPTER TWENTY-TWO

The next morning imprints of my dreams swam with me in the imperial bed: men and women of all sizes and colors moving over and under each other. I'd had a few erotic dreams before but none so vivid. I ran my hands over my belly before deciding I should get up and make a plan for myself.

Nan had already left for the hospital, as she said she would, so I slipped on the kimono she left for me, a silky pink three-quarter-length robe that caressed my every move down the maze-like hallway, through the living room and dining room to the kitchen. There I found a carafe of coffee brewing and Nan's note reminding me to make myself comfortable. She'd return in the early evening.

Is it silly to say I felt . . . regal? And when had I ever been able to say that? Everything in the apartment, the dimmed lighting, the sumptuous furniture, the venerable carpeting, the subdued colors, even the smell of aged wood, made me comfortable. In some ways the place felt incongruent with Nan, and perhaps it was Levi's design touch. But the courtly beauty matched Nan's and her supreme claim to sit at the head of it.

It was an underground palace. And it made me comfortable. Make note, I thought, comfort could be a universal quality of beauty. Did it have that effect on everyone?

The kitchen was not as posh as the rest nor as spacious, and like most of the apartment, it lacked windows. The floors appeared to be antique ship grates of dark mahogany, varnished and shiny and placed side-by-side, wall-to-wall encased in a clear thin lacquered surface. The way every kitchen object was hooked or locked down or put away, gave it the feel of a ship's galley.

Time to explore. Rather than retrace my steps, I passed to the other door at the end of the kitchen, into a smaller, darker hallway. I fumbled for a light switch, only to bang against one locked door on my left. Slowly, I slid to the next available sliver of light coming from under a door.

Maybe it was the coffee, maybe it was the new possibilities this environment offered, but I giggled. A rush of optimism. 'Curiosity killed the cat,' said Momma. 'It will cause you pain.' But after all, Nan said to make myself comfortable, and it was best to understand my coordinates.

The handle turned, opening to a small dark turquoise room with a spacious bed, covered in a violet quilted comforter and large magenta pillows. The bed filled almost every inch of the room. A small round window —a porthole really— hung over the bed and reflected meager light onto the immense mirror opposite it. If I'd taken two steps into the room I'd have been onto the bed, and I was tempted —it was that inviting. But I was a visitor.

In addition to the enormous mirror reflecting the bed and me, which I avoided, I saw a tiny bathroom and a small cluster of photographs on the wall, framed in weathered life preservers, the vessel's name obliterated by sun, salt and sand. At first the photos appeared to be landscapes, perhaps of desert dunes, a place where a ship might find itself aground. But on closer review they may have been the lines and curves of human bodies.

"Wow." I wasn't sure what to make of the space. Small tremors began in my chest, *someone crying perhaps. And laughter.*

As the energy built, I withdrew, absorbing one last delectable round. It reminded me of cotton candy, which reminded me of Harold's unshakable preference for bright pastel shirts. *The Cotton Candy Room*, I named it, though it could easily have been called The Shipwreck Room.

The room's door clicked shut and I slid my hands along the wall to the end. Coolness streamed past my palms and fingertips into yet another larger hallway, and I found a switch that revealed brown tongue and groove walls created out of salvaged ship doors, some with their own portholes. I peered through one but there was nothing but blackness.

These walls were hung with nautical rope bumpers and primitive wooden and clay masks —African, I guessed. The mouths grinned and inhaled. The eyes opened wide in voracity or closed in ecstasy. Occasionally a tongue protruded in search of taste. I fell deeper and deeper into the ship's magic.

Halfway down this hall on the right were two functioning doors. The first was locked but the second I entered easily. Completely dark until I found the switch, light illuminated an ornate metal and stained glass lantern with arabesque apertures suspended above another immense bed, the biggest one I'd ever seen anywhere. Bigger even than the custom-made bed in the magazine spotlighting Kim Kardashian. Or was it Paris Hilton?

The room lacked any windows along its fabric-covered walls, a desert oven; heat that the other rooms did not emit. Against the backdrop of sand-colored fabric, the ceiling was hung with brilliant red, purple and brown material that splayed outward from the center to the four corners and down to the floor creating a Moroccan tent effect.

The heat. I considered loosening my robe, even throwing it off, but the wide bed distracted me again, with its dark blue patterned spread, and the brightly colored pillows of striped maroon, royal and plum scattered over it. The pervasive masculinity was inescapable. I was enticed to crawl upon this bed too, *to tumble with its beauty*, but again I thought better of it. I was a guest.

But I couldn't leave. The room had such a powerful beauty — historic and Byzantine and virile— that I wasn't sure if I was *thinking* its beauty or *feeling* it. Was it my eyes or my limbic system reacting to it? Were my enzymes, my biological molecules, being set in motion? I shook my head in wonder. I would need to ask Nan about this room. Or Levi.

There was but one small door along the left wall, a closet framed by copper-strapped lifeboat oars, and inside, a few men's casual shirts, slacks and sports jackets. A violin case. On the shelf above sat bundled shrimp nets, a jar of small bird feathers and a distressed iron and wood brush of some sort. With rigid four-inch bristles it looked like a child's miniature rake, probably for grooming a horse or scraping mud off shoes or perhaps some nautical function. I'd never seen anything like it, not even in the encyclopedia. I stepped on an ottoman to get a closer look. It gave off an iron smell, a kind of body odor, which from my studies I knew to be the result of human touch against the iron, so I didn't reach for it.

Across the room, to the right of the bed was a door that connected to an unusually substantial bathroom. Sparse, nothing unusual except for a white ivory cup on the basin that might have been rather valuable; a very large oval soaking tub, which seemed to clog my ears as I got closer; and in the mirrored cabinet, where I did my best to avoid my reflection, some ibuprofen and a child's plastic battleship-blue X-Men Wolverine comb, like something Lyle would have played with circa 1990. I returned it to the shelf. An odd collection. I cleared the obstruction from my ears and rinsed my hands, though I didn't touch the towels; I air dried them then walked across the tiled, sand-colored floor, and out.

The place was . . . *intoxicating*, certainly erotic. I inhaled deeply. More to explore!

Yet another corner, this time to the right. I walked along the dimly lit hallway hung with floor-to-ceiling tapestries from an undetermined time period. The first: a mermaid beneath the ocean, seaweed flowing from her scalp, summoning wild-eyed sailors to jump from their ship and join her. The second: Poseidon or Neptune or Bythos, a king of the sea, half man and half fish with his mermaid queen. I ran my fingers over the thick material then stepped back to take in the entire image. I longed to swim, to surrender to the rapture of the water.

As I looked more closely I saw the sea king's genital erect and the sea queen seemingly offering her triangle to a small cluster of humans swimming after her. Below them on the ocean floor lay the bones and carcasses of those who had come before. And yet I was spellbound.

No judgment. Don't be Momma.

Quickly away from the tapestried hallway and back to my bedroom, I stood panting in the doorway and realized I'd gone in a circle. I collected myself. Cotton Candy Hallway to African Hallway to Tapestries Hallway. Three bedrooms including mine. *Mine!* Cotton Candy Room, Moroccan Room and mine. And possibly a fourth, the locked room around the corner from The Cotton Candy Room.

But en route to the living room I'd passed one other room on my left, and my overriding sense of the apartment was that it was palatial and labyrinthian, like some great ship.

I followed the hallway from my bedroom and just before the living room I found a door marked "Cinema." Locked.

So much room for two, *and* they were so generous to share it with me. Lodging on a ship! The best of both worlds and beauty everywhere! I had so many questions. They had gathered so many beautiful things. Where and why? But I had to measure my nosiness. I didn't want to upset them. I didn't want their generosity to be a burden. I didn't want to be an unwelcomed guest. I'd never been a guest anywhere before.

I twirled the silk kimono left and right with delight. *Maybe, just maybe, my luck was changing.*

CHAPTER TWENTY-THREE

After showering I peeked out Nan's front door. Unlike Roosevelt Island, a stream of trucks and bodies crisscrossed on the street above me. Only five steps, the garbage can, and the wrought iron railing, between me and the traffic. The whole block shook —a bus over the metal plate in the street eight feet away, a trash can turned over, the deep and repetitive thud and piercing screech of concrete being drilled down the street. Nighttime would be better for picking up my things at The Octagon.

I tried calling Elizabeth several times for an update on work. The cell service in the basement apartment was non-existent.

Except for the violin case and the collectible X-Men Wolverine comb I'd found in the Moroccan Room, the only things I came across in their immaculate apartment were occasional artifacts of elaborate bronze, ceramic or alabaster placed strategically apart —a pitcher, a small cuneiform, an urn, a small primitive sculpture with large eyes, little else, and an odd earthenware and skin-like figurine of a mermaid, no more than eighteen inches high. Even during the day, with so little natural light, the tiffany lamps glowed seductively. Beauty everywhere. Everything shipshape. Everything orderly.

It kind of made me crazy, *so* much order, and I can't tell you why. But I liked it too.

By late in the afternoon, waiting for darkness to fall, I lay in bed staring at the ornate hammered-tin ceiling, contemplating my next moves. I ran a series of lists through my head then realized I was absentmindedly exploring my own body. Something I'd never before given myself permission to do. My breathing accelerated. I shut my eyes. *Beyond the pleasure of the winter cold or the water . . .*

Nan's keys were in the front door and she called out, "Eunis, it's me, I'm home."

"I'll be right there." Heartbeat intercepted, I removed my fingers from the undiscovered mystery. *Breathe.*

I tugged on the sheath dress Nan had left for me, straightened myself up, decided I'd broach the subject of beauty with her, and met her in the kitchen where she unloaded groceries.

"Hi," she said, put down a bottle of red wine, and gave me a big hug and a kiss on the mouth.

"Oh, huh, hi." My voice cracked, finger to my lip. I wasn't sure if I should wipe it off.

Nan resumed organizing the groceries as if we were an old couple with thousands of homecomings like this, except my spine vibrated. She pulled a Star magazine out of the brown bag and shoved it toward me on the counter.

"You like celebrities." Her voice had a flat nasal quality I hadn't noticed before.

"Not celebrities exactly. But thank you," I said tapping the magazine. "How did you know?"

"At the hospital."

"A bad habit."

"A guilty pleasure. But if not celebrities, then what?" A tinge of blue collar, but it had an unremarkable quality that didn't fit her exquisite face. She was tired.

It was as good a time as any to explore her willingness to lend her beauty to my research. "My work is around beauty?"

"That's always nice."

"No, that's not what I meant." I fidgeted with the bottle of wine. Nan put away jars of elegantly labeled gourmet items I'd never heard of.

"What do you think it is?" I said scraping on the wine label.

"What?" She glanced at me.

"Beauty. Like you. You're beautiful, exotic. People can agree on that, just like they can agree on Jennifer Lawrence, even though you two look nothing alike."

Nan stopped and turned to me. She let the light bless her sculpted cheek and let her eyes go soft and deep. She held that light as if she'd been born with it. "Thanks, Eunis. Not everyone thinks so."

I swallowed. "But most do. Like most find me unattractive and frightening."

"That's not true."

"Of course it is. What do you think beauty is? How do *you* measure it? I'm not talking about attraction, that could be body type, physical, sentimental. Any number of things."

"Yeah." She perked up.

"I'm searching for the quintessential components of *facial* beauty, the ideal. It's what I do. But I don't seem to get any closer to the answer."

"Why not just enjoy it?"

"I do."

"But that's not enough?"

"Beauty has no practical use." As soon as I said it, I knew it was received wrong, her face flattened out. I stammered, bubbled with positivity. "It's what makes us all go, and it makes some people money, but couldn't we also put it to a shared practical use?"

Anger started to fill her eyes. I'd made it worse. *How*, I didn't understand.

"What the hell does *shared* mean?"

Tell her the truth. "Your beauty . . . if others looked even vaguely like you, we would be seeing beauty in everyone."

She shook her head as if as if I was stealing something from her. "What do you mean, if they looked vaguely like me? What the hell does *that* mean?"

"I'm sorry, I'm going too fast." I put up my hands and hung my head. "I'm sorry."

She looked at me, questioning.

I lifted my head. "Listen Nan, I really appreciate what you and Levi have done for me—"

Her face turned years younger, childlike, almost pleading. "You don't like the place!"

"No, no it's not that, it's . . . well, I'm used to spending most of my time alone."

"Do you want me to leave?" Nan took a step toward the door.

"Oh my god, no, this is your place. I would never . . ." I

moved toward the door.

She put up her hands. "Because if you do, I'll get out for a few more hours."

"No, no." I reached for her, but she was just out of reach.

"Levi would be very unhappy with me if you left." She put her arms to her sides. "We want you to be comfortable."

"I am. I'm sorry, I didn't mean . . ."

"Good." Nan came around the table, rubbed my shoulders and kissed the back of my head. "Good." She reverted to stacking jars of olives on the shelf.

❱❱❱

Levi didn't come home that night either, and Nan convinced me to watch television with her on the couch rather than go to The Octagon. That suited me fine since I was more interested in learning about her. I was very offhand. "Where'd you grow up?"

"Upstate." The sitcom chattered on.

"What got you into nursing?"

"A means to an end."

"How so?"

"It gave me access." Nan changed the channel.

"To helping people?"

She sat upright. "Are you grilling me again?" But this time instead of anger she smiled sweetly. She let out an exaggerated sigh, turned down the volume, and faced me. "I knew early on — probably high school— that I wanted different things than my folks and most of my friends. Was that true about you too?" She took my hands in hers.

"Actually, I *wanted* what most people wanted." I let her hold them.

"Oh."

"Looking like this kind of limited my opportunities."

"You look great." She put her hand on my shoulder.

"Thanks, but that's not how my momma saw things."

"My mom was a cunt too."

It took me a moment to regroup. "That's not what I meant."

"No, really? Because if your mother didn't treat you like the incredible woman that I see in front of me —sexy, vibrant, unique, a magnet— then she was a cunt. Mine was. She wanted me to go to church and lie. It wasn't even her religion."

Nan was opening up.

She continued. "Muslim. My mom wanted to keep me —the whole family— as far away from the myth as possible, to clean up our public image, the *American* version. So we —I— was told to go Christian. The sacrificial lamb. But with religion you're just trading one myth for another. The message was the same: sit on feelings, abstain till the next life, whenever that is. It wasn't until I met up with Levi that I realized I could feel whatever I wanted, whenever I wanted, without guilt."

Without guilt? I couldn't remember a time when I wasn't wearing it. Often multi-layers. I understood the concept of no guilt, but I didn't know anyone like that. Maybe my sister Carly.

"Where'd you meet him?"

She looked surprised, even ambivalent. "I met Levi at a party. They were showing movies."

"What was it about his face that you found handsome?"

"Look, I don't know." She fiddled with the remote again, surfed the channels.

I took a deep breath. *Tread lightly.* "How long have you been together?"

"Enough about me. Tell me about yourself." She flashed a congealed smile.

"What do you want to know?" I sat back. If I was going to expect her to be forthright I guess it was fair to offer the same.

"Do you have email so we can notify your family where you are?"

"I don't do email." *Who would I email?*

"Do you have any family locally?"

"No."

"Wherever they are, you're not close with them, are you?" A small, empathic tilt of her head.

"No."

"We'll be your new family." She casually stroked my arm.

I drew it away. "I've got a friend here in the city."

Nan's eyes flickered. "You do?"

"A woman I work with. But I'm not sure . . ."

"Not sure of what?"

Time to admit. "That she's my friend."

"Be careful then. Those are the ones that can kill you."

"She may already have."

"I'm so sorry." Sympathy rose in her beautiful lake green eyes. "If you don't feel comfortable talking about this I'll understand."

I shook my head and went on to tell her the story about work. "But I think," I said realizing it for the first time, "that I may get an attorney involved if I can pull together the money. They can't just take my job away."

"I don't know about attorneys." She sat up, teased her fingers through her abundant midnight hair. "They're a greedy bunch, pretty much out for themselves. I'd be careful. Besides, sometimes it's better to take care of things your own way, more direct." Her eyes unfathomable, reminiscing a vision. Whatever it was, a small smile emerged on her lips. They curled back showing her eyeteeth.

Where were we? Attorneys. Greedy? I didn't feel that way about Roddy. Maybe it was his skin. Or that foolish smile.

"Anyway," continued Nan, "Levi has a friend who's an attorney, if it comes to that. But for now it sounds like your best option is to lay low."

"I guess so, but I hate to be wasting my time, doing nothing."

"You're not wasting anything. You can read your textbook, keep studying, work on your research. We can play. What else do you want to be doing?"

"Make money, I have a job —well, I thought I did—"

"I told you, you don't need to worry around money just yet."

"I'm restless when I'm not doing enough."

"Not doing enough? Well, we'll see, you've only just arrived."

I was so tired. "It's nothing, it's stupid." I picked up the TV remote. "How does this thing work?"

Nan sat back and met my eyes, as if she divined my fatigue. "I think you're gonna like it here."

CHAPTER TWENTY-FOUR

"The primary control point for gene expression is usually at the very beginning of the protein production process."

I kept reading and re-reading the same text, waiting for Nan to go to sleep. When I finally remarked that I was going to the apartment to get my things and to see if I'd been formally evicted, Nan insisted on accompanying me. Even though it was after midnight. "You'll need extra hands." She wouldn't take no for an answer.

The empty subway car lurched and clacked like the Bemidji hockey rink. We settled into our seats, my head down and hooded, Nan with her head held high and imperial in a strobe of showering black and white light.

Especially on my late night trips from work I'd fancied being packed among people but didn't have to experience it. Illogical: a place where I could be near people but must not. Nan patted my knee.

As we pulled into the Lexington Avenue station, a clean-cut guy in his late twenties stood alone on the platform. He peered into our car, looked both ways down the station, and stepped in. Something wild in his eyes. He sat right next to me, even though our car was empty. I didn't look up.

"There's plenty of space," said Nan pointing at the empty seats. "Why don't you give my friend a little breathing room?"

"I like it here. This is my favorite seat." He shuffled closer to me. He was sweating. He smelled musty. He placed his left hand on my thigh. His jacket fell open. His pants were unbuttoned.

"Please move away," I said heart accelerating. I knocked at his arm but he'd braced himself for that and actually ran his hand to my crotch.

"You did hear my friend, didn't you?" Nan leaned forward to make eye contact with him.

"Who wants to be first?" he said. "The ugly one with the great tits or you?"

I shoved him and he stumbled getting up. "Okay, then it's you," he said to me, releasing his stiff member. "And you," he said turning to Nan and revealing a letter opener, "do not make a sound or I will hurt her." He began to pull at my pants.

I kicked at him but he stepped back and laughed. "Let's make this pleasant for everyone."

She was on her feet and showing him her neck. "You see this?" She pointed to her tattoo.

He turned. "You want to be first?"

And from nowhere she had a knife in her hand and the blade swept across his face. Deep. High cheek to mouth.

He screamed. The right side of his face peeled open. Before the blood started flowing I could see inside his cheek, his tongue spasm. He grabbed the flap, his fingers inexplicably in his mouth without resistance. He moaned, "You bitch!"

"Want more?" She raised her knife above his left eye, ready to plunge it in. "Or maybe I should cut this off." She reached for his cock.

He stumbled backwards, catching a pole and leaving a handprint of blood on it.

She turned to me with the same hellbound look I'd seen on the Johanson's dog when it attacked Nemo. "Should I finish him off?" She grinned. "I can be quick. No one will ever know."

"No," I stammered.

He looked in disbelief at his hands, then at his reflection in the dark window. "You fucking bitch!"

Another strobe of light as we crossed under the Queensboro Bridge and East River. He stumbled out of our car leaving his bloody handprint on every surface he touched.

She looked as if she'd go after him.

I laid a hand on her arm. "Our stop," I said.

And once we started traveling up the long escalator, I started shaking then crying.

"Are you okay? We're okay, right?" she said.

"It's not that." I turned to her rising just above me on the next step. "No one's ever stood up for me like that."

She pulled me to her, my head at her waist, and she stroked my hair. I caught a glimpse of the violence that had just passed. A series of shudders jolted my body. And she held tighter. If we hadn't eventually reached the top of the escalator, I might have been there still, holding on to her.

"I don't really want to call the cops," I said feeling guilty. But I couldn't meet with them, not with that blurry photo of me on all their corkboards and desks.

She didn't ask why. She seemed to understand and nodded.

))))

When we arrived at The Octagon I'd gathered myself and cautioned her that there could be a confrontation. If it was the police I wasn't sure what explanation would suffice to ensure she wasn't snared in the same net.

"We've already had ours for the night," she said as we rose in the elevator. "Besides, it's the night before New Year's Eve. People will be resting up for the big parties tomorrow evening." She took my hand and kissed my hair, an affection I was starting to get used to. "We'll be in and out in no time, and you can put this place behind you forever."

But this was my life. I'd created this . . . with Harold's help. His sacrifice. Now I'd destroyed it. She watched herself in the elevator glass. I was grateful for her, for the calm of her safe harbor.

My apartment door was still plastered with the original meeting notice but nothing more. Would the inmates attack? The HOA? The police? I flipped on the light.

"Oh geez," she said.

The tangle of broken glass, scattered books and toppled stools reminded me how disorderly my life had become. I didn't know my humiliation could run deeper; I didn't know what to say. "Come on," she said crushing my wrecked diploma under her foot and moving with purpose toward the small bureau. "Let's put this all behind you."

))))

When Levi arrived late in the afternoon he wasn't what I expected. I'd envisioned the DNA of a handsome blonde blue-eyed Adonis to perfectly counterbalance Nan's dark exotic Aphrodite. But he wasn't blonde, he was swarthy. He wasn't handsome, he was melon-faced with a four o'clock shadow, and adding his slight paunch and shaved dome, his head-to-toe appearance was that of Mr. Peanut. A violin player. He did have a princely tan, magnificent, really. Nan draped herself around his taller frame and he around her like teenagers in heat.

I stood awkwardly in the living room, believing that at any moment they'd tear each other's clothes off. *What if?!* I considered taking the long way around the apartment to my bedroom but Levi finally looked over Nan's shoulder to acknowledge me.

"You must be Eunis," he said with a smile and a sonorous voice, a voice that could command a ship or lead legions, completely incongruous with his physical appearance. And in that way he and Nan were a matched set, complimenting each other's shortfall.

He moved forward, measured me up and down. "Superb. You are quite the specimen indeed. You are . . . superb." Without warning he took me in his arms and united my body with his. He kissed my mouth and neck. I pushed him away.

"Levi!" Nan said sharply. "Eunis is just getting used to being part of our family."

"Of course." But he was barely able to bottle his enthusiasm nor mask the delight in his eyes. His inventory continued, his hands opening and closing as if hoping to put physical dimension to his words.

I explored the carpet pattern. I rearranged myself. *Harold! What do I do?* Yet there was something I liked being so desired and having a body next to mine.

He stood back, giving me a little air. "I'm sorry, Eunis. We're just so happy to have you here. And on New Year's Eve. How perfect."

Perfection, apparently the word of the day. They were certainly an affectionate couple. Still, I didn't like being referred to as a specimen. A rebuke almost slipped out before I controlled myself. "Thank you for having me."

"We wouldn't have it any other way."

"Levi . . .?" she said.

He hadn't taken his eyes off me. My face flushed. *Oh god.*

"Leviathan!" she said again, this time with edge.

"Oh, yeah, right." He nodded to her.

"Let's get ready to celebrate Eunis's freedom." She sounded cheery, absolving the reckless atoms, though mine still bubbled. "We cleared out her apartment last night so she's *here.*"

"That's great," he said.

But most of my life was still at The Octagon, scattered across my once perfectly constructed asylum.

Levi swept up his briefcase and small suitcase. "I'll put my things away, take a shower, and we can let the party begin. I'm in the Moroccan, right?"

That's what I called it!

"Of course." Nan set off behind him, I suppose to tell him what had happened in the subway.

For the first time in my life I had real, functioning, allies. If I took my time, if I explained my work *to them both*, I was sure Nan would consent. But I had to show them that I cared too, that I appreciated their friendship.

☽☽☽

The evening began around 7:30 with a light meal of wild salmon, *petit pois* —a small sweet French pea, Levi informed me, something I must have missed in the encyclopedia's volumes— and a mixed green salad with vinaigrette. If Nan had told him about the subway, I couldn't tell. Perhaps he didn't want to upset me. The subject never came up again.

"We don't want to start too heavy." Levi was a bit more subdued now. He poured more wine.

Worldly, or maybe it was that the dining room was resplendent with candles glowing all around. I felt . . . *relaxed*. And admired.

"One glass is probably enough for me." I held my hand over the glass. The luminous first one was already upon me.

"We like our drinks," he said, looking a bit like I'd slapped him.

"Oh, no, I didn't mean there's anything wrong . . ."

"You do drink?"

"A little."

"Well, you won't join us in this toast?" A small wound clouded his eyes.

This isn't about Momma or Lyle or Elizabeth. "Okay. Sure."

Levi raised his glass in salute. "A new year, the beginning of new adventures. A time to celebrate."

After dinner the opulent mood, and the three glasses of wine, turned me liquid. Nan put on lush music and my body absorbed it as we moved to the living room. Levi lay out on the wide chaise and to my surprise Nan sat next to *me* on what Levi called the chesterfield —a luxurious couch.

"Nan tells me you're a geneticist."

"I work in a lab."

"And your work involves beauty." His mouth tightened, smothering *something* as he glanced at Nan.

I shifted in my chair, not sure what I'd seen. "Well, they wouldn't say so —the research facility— they're interested in developing drugs with positive side effects, mostly for marketing purposes. I probably shouldn't talk too much about it. I'm already in enough trouble."

"But you, you have a more specific purpose?"

That was kind of him, not to push. "I do." I felt unusually compliant. And after all, he was opening the conversation *for* me.

"And it is . . . ?"

I glanced at Nan. She put her arms around me and kneaded my shoulder supportively.

"Beauty. I have to know the archetype of facial beauty." I laughed self-consciously.

"Because?" He smiled warmly.

"I don't want anyone to go through what I've gone through." There, I'd said it. "Science can make it better; I know it can. We've already made great strides. Think of children with cleft palates or people with excessive facial warts or Proteus, Elephant Man syndrome. Any type of deformity or abnormality.

Even the plain would have a better life if we were genetically adapted. Everyone loves beauty, people wouldn't be lonely."

"She's had a tough time," said Nan.

I sagged.

"Don't do that," Levi said rather sharply.

"What?"

"Undervalue yourself."

"You sound like my husband."

"Husband?" Levi sat up, alarmed.

"He's dead." Nan pressed a hand to her cheek. "Suicide."

"Oh." Levi sat back. "Oh, I'm sorry."

I shrugged. But I could see he was on my side.

He lifted himself out of the chaise and walked over to the grand bar where he materialized a bucket of ice, three stubby thickly-cut glasses, and a bottle of tequila. When he returned he confidently dropped two cubes of ice in each glass. I admired his self-assurance and noticed how Nan also watched him with admiration. He'd help me convince Nan.

"Tequila all right? Or would you prefer something else? Scotch, perhaps?"

My first thought was of Elizabeth. "I'm already pretty good. Maybe I shouldn't. I've never tried tequila."

Ever courteous, he smiled and raised his glass. Urbane. His mellifluous voice rained down around me. "Let's toast to exploring beauty."

☽☽☽

Sometime after that my skin began to mesh with the air around me, breathing from every pore, turning my body receptive, my mind swimming happily in the same way it did in the Minnesota lakes —*free!* I felt Nan's fingers running through my hair, my body weight gone, floating. Her mouth found the nape of my neck and, following a bestial tear at my left ear that electrified me, her tongue licked and probed mine.

What? Please her. It feels so . . . yes.

My body was vivid and my eyes closed, but I easily found Nan's mouth and moved luxuriously around in it, my tongue attacking exploring and tasting everything —teeth, roof, gums, lips— all at once, *none of it enough,* thick and warm, bitter —*even more addicting*— and tugging me into submission. *I'm willing. Bliss?* Her touch was at once *tender*, then *harsh, clawing at me,* and *in command*, a tight *wonderful* grip over my shoulders, pulling down the front of my dress, *without hesitation, without concern for tearing the dress, without concern for anything.*

Nan lifted me up, cupping my breasts, licking my nipples, sucking them *hard. My belly. Share! Please her. Whatever she wants.* I wanted *my* mouth *anywhere on Nan's body.*

"Come," said Nan, the only sound I heard.

She pulled off her own clothes and directed me to the immense chaise lounge where Levi brought me *safely down to his body*, now *naked too. The three of us. Pressed against each other.* Hands moved along ridgelines and into caverns, *tropical and sticky and smelling dangerous.* I wanted my *tongue traveling there, tasting along animal, redolent landscapes.*

They too! One of them ran nails across my back. *Yours, to do as you wish.* Someone sucked my nipples *stiff.* A hand probing, opening my thighs, *I accept.* I spread. Levi's warm fleshy head in my lap, *pleading*, his tongue lavishing *inside me. Yes.* Nan offering —no, *forcing!*— her *magnificent vulva. Yes. My tongue penetrating her magnificence, my tongue acknowledging her magnificence. Viscous. Exquisite brine. Unsafe, complex, sweet. Breath away, somewhere. Nowhere. Levi! Levi!* And then Levi, his member *in my mouth, rigid.* Nan both hands on my mound, elbows forcing me open, *no resistance, no resistance.* In my bush, *sucking my lips, engorging* them, *plunging deeper.* I arched. Fingers *ruling my perineum. Nan! Cries. All of us.* My mouth full of *whatever Levi wanted to give me. Please.* And then it came, *his gift*, a stream *of chalky otherworld velvet.* And my own body *climbing*, climbing to places I could never have imagined or I'd put away, an ecstatic kingdom, Freyja's kingdom that I'd almost believed and now knew existed. Freyja! I shook violently —*luminescence*— *emptying, emptying, emptying*, in cascading spasms; exquisite emptying.

CHAPTER TWENTY-FIVE

"Another?" Levi handed me the next shot of tequila. "It's good, isn't it?"

"Yes." Dreamy, exhausted, like I'd been washed clean from the inside out. "That was . . ."

"Recherché. You liked that, didn't you? Welcome to the family." He sat across from me on the chaise, completely naked, Mr. Peanut, his own glass in hand, his cock still glistening with victory. Nan stood naked, beatific, above him, holding his dark satin robe.

The velvet sofa teased along my spine and thighs and brushed against my wet vulva. Someone had draped the silky pink kimono over my shoulders, with me half-draped over the sofa's armrest.

"Drink in celebration," he said as Nan joined him to cuddle on the chaise, both beaming at me.

"I've never had a night like that." I took another sip.

"You're happy?" he asked.

"Yes, I guess I am." I'm sure my crescents were showing.

"Good, because the night is young."

"Really? I think I'll be going to sleep; it's almost midnight. I'm pretty loaded." *The most loaded I'd ever been or even knew I could be.* I snorted.

"We've invited some friends over."

"You'll like them," injected Nan. Her unwrapped body was as magnificent as her face. Whoever's genes combined to make her . . .

"Friends? I'm not used to being with a bunch of people. This was . . ." I arced my arm over them and the room, ". . . wonderful. I had no idea . . .but I, I'll be self-conscious and . . . I don't really want to get dressed." A contrite smile.

Nan looked at Levi and sat back to hear his answer.

"Isn't being naked beautiful?" he asked.

"Yes, I guess it is." I remembered being naked with Harold.

"Then cheers. Consider it research." He sipped from his glass and passed it to Nan. He tilted his head playfully at me.

"Maybe just one more before I go to bed." I took another sip.

There was a knock at the door.

"Oh, I better—" I tried to raise myself off the couch.

"You *stay*," commanded Levi, throwing his robe on and heading for the door.

Anyway, I was too spongy to move. A deep sigh. *Don't let these people down. They're your friends; please them.* I did feel good. *You won't fail them like you failed Harold.* I plucked at the kimono.

"If it makes you more comfortable," said Nan, completely naked and making no effort to cover herself. "But it's really not necessary."

"Eunis," said Levi as if we're meeting a friend on the street, *as if I were a normal-looking person meeting a friend on the street, fully dressed*, "this is Marguerite." Marguerite stood like a statue, a thin woman, probably sixty or older, with a face-lift that accentuated her age, orange-like-a-first-aid-kit-dyed hair, and especially large, perfectly sculpted breasts revealed despite her full-length fox coat. She leaned over and kissed Nan on the lips and Nan ran her hand under the coat and appropriated Marguerite's ass. I was astounded but also agreeable to it, as if it all made sense, as if I wanted some too.

"Aah," said Marguerite. "So nice to feel you again . . . *Nan*."

Yes, mimed Nan reciprocating.

Marguerite turned to me. "And to meet you too, Eunis. We've heard so much about you." Suspended in a gentle wet solution I felt no need to respond. Levi took Marguerite's coat revealing her ample chest and a simple but obviously expensive lace slip. He waited for instruction.

"Where will Eunis be?" Marguerite asked.

"Not yet sure." Levi waited patiently.

"Then throw it anywhere," said Marguerite. She turned back to me in my pink kimono. "You certainly are unique." An appreciative eye blink to Nan. "But that kimono hides the beauty beneath it. Why bother? And I would say that pink is not your color. I'd like to see you in black. Do you have anything like that, Nan?"

"Happy New Year, Marguerite," said Nan.

"Oh, and Happy New Year," added Marguerite, smiling at me. *Salvador Dali* flashed through my mind; a fragment from the encyclopedia and reading to Nemo.

"What's your pleasure? Let's let Eunis settle in a bit."

"Of course," said Marguerite. "I brought some goodies to share." She opened her left hand revealing six small capsules of blue and green, the same colors as Nan's tattoo.

"Levi," called Nan, "please bring Marguerite some liquid. Party's about to begin." Marguerite sat next to me on the sofa and smiled. Teeth as white as an egg.

"Aah," said Levi, quickly arriving with another glass. As he handed it to Marguerite I spotted the entwined blue serpent and green mermaid tattooed on Levi's shoulder and spine. Then he bent and kissed me, his tongue in my mouth. I could smell myself on his lips; I could taste myself on his tongue. I found myself freely responding. He stroked my hair. I leaned into the sofa, *the magnificent sofa.*

The doorbell chimed. *Heavenly.* More visitors. This time a twenty-something named Maurice with a trim body, a shock of prematurely alabaster hair, and the face of a rare bird. Spectacular beryl green eyes. With him Roberto, a smaller, broad chested, thickly muscled black man, probably in his thirties — hard to say— but handsome.

"Welcome." I heard Levi through my blissful fog.

"Here, dear." Marguerite placed the blue/green capsule on my tongue and brought the tequila to my lips. "Things only get better."

When I opened my eyes Freyja had touched the entire room. It glowed edgelessly, and it rippled as certainly as the Minnesota ponds and the florescent green corridor of pines leading to Lake Itasca. The walls whispered to me to rise up, to explore their tactility, and I found myself in the Tapestries Hallway pressing my body against the mermaid tapestry, hoping to enter it.

"You must be Eunis," said an eye-catching strawberry blonde in her forties, naked from the waist down. She smelled of oranges. "I'm Cherry."

I laughed. "It's wonderful to see you, Cherry."

"Come with me." She put her hand in mine and, as we ran down the hallway laughing, away from the living room, a voice in my head repeated *come with me*, and then many voices, *outside my head (?)* gathered in the apartment. Cherry and I sped through the African Hallway where primitive faces blurred as we passed, her legs equal to mine.

"Here" said Cherry. It was The Cotton Candy Room.

"Oooo." I was breathless. "I like this room."

"Me too." Cherry hauled me into the lowly lit room. A man and a woman already in the bed sat up —indistinguishable, like twins; monozygotic divided. They hooted and rolled to the left to make room for Cherry and me. The woman fell out of the bed with a thud and laughed in a high-pitched titter as her companion helped her up.

"C'mon." Cherry led me onto the massive bed, and as the gleeful lookalikes undulated out of the room, Cherry snatched the pink kimono off me and flung it to the floor, revealing me to myself in the mirror. She kissed me all over and I watched myself being kissed. My body *was* quite attractive.

Cherry worked down my belly, her body from behind reflected in the mirror. Her body was lovely too. Flawless skin. Big thighs. Full fleshy buttocks. From her reddish blonde patch, Cherry's labia hung like fruit.

All together, we were watery. Shimmering. Colors everywhere. Perfection. *Let's see all the loveliness.* I pulled Cherry's top off but she resisted fully exposing herself, staying pressed down on me.

"Let me see you." I seized Cherry by her thick strawberry blond mane. "Let's see all of you, dear Freyja." She had a twisted, childlike expression and shy, which turned diffident, remorseful. I looked down. She had scars but no breasts.

"Oh." My stomach dropped. Cherry's face contracted in panic. "Oh," I said again, and gently stroking her, I began licking her and smothering her chest in kisses. I had entered a world where I was used and useful, where I could sample beauty without re-crimination. *This was joy.*

CHAPTER TWENTY-SIX

Laughter. Opening my eyes told me nothing about the time of day. Parched, I got a whiff of burnt candle wax. My room. My body vibrated. *Wow.* Exhaustion prevented me from sitting up yet my body, despite my thirst, was sinuous, like I was still submersed. I stretched among the tangled sheets.

A man's shirt hung at the end of the bed —an elegant cowboy shirt, embroidered black and white with a light blue yoke and purple piping, which reminded me of my half-brother, Lyle. I pushed him from my mind and slipped it on. When I got to my feet I was unsteady but relieved that the shirt covered my thighs midway. *Reflexive modesty.* I snapped the buttons closed and, following friendly laughter, made my way gingerly through the empty but war-torn living room to the kitchen.

"Ah." Nan spotted me and lifted a cup of coffee. "Happy New Year."

"New Year," I repeated dazed, shy. Beside Nan in her emerald robe was the small black hunky one. And spread out on the table, my 15 years of scrapbook celebrity clippings, organized by body part.

"Roberto," he reminded me. "We met last night."

"Yes." I was hazy, regarding again my photos.

"Good, you remember me."

"Did we . . . ?"

"No, we didn't. Marguerite's such a hog. But I hope so the next time."

Next?

He crossed the kitchen, put down his cup, kissed my hand. *Chivalrous, thank goodness.* He turned to Nan. "I'd better get going." She stooped, he pecked her on the cheek. "As always, the perfect evening. Everything," he acknowledged me, "so perfect."

Be appreciative. I returned his smile. *A whole new world. But different* —I smiled to myself— *than Disney's Little Mermaid.*

As he closed the door I turned pointedly to Nan who returned a sullen stare. "What are my research photos doing here?"

"Research?" She laughed.

"They were in my room."

"Oh, I thought they'd be fun to look at."

"So you're willing to give me feedback?"

"On what?"

I handed Nan her coffee cup to allow for more space on the tabletop. I spread the clippings more evenly.

"Okay," I said grounding myself. "Pick your most beautiful and tell me why. What part of their face does it for you?"

"They're all pretty cute."

"Not cute. Beautiful. Forget as much as possible their movie roles. I get that this isn't *uber* scientific, but just do it."

"Right." She raised her eyebrows, seeing that I was serious. "Okay."

When she finished creating her Beautiful pile, I asked, "Is there a common characteristic of the beauties? Is it Jennifer Lawrence's hair? Her eyes? Her mouth?"

"Her innocence."

"Hmm, okay. But that's not a facial feature."

Nan shrugged, gazed into the living room.

Heat kindled in my belly. "You didn't claim Leonardo DiCaprio. What's wrong with his face?"

"Shit, I dunno. I'd sleep with him." She swung her head in mock weariness between the pile and me. I stood my ground. "Too much baby face." She rubbed the back of her neck, aggravated too.

"Specific part."

"Chin. Put a beard on it."

"Why do you like Penelope Cruz?"

"Fuck! I'd sleep with her too!"

"Because?"

"Her lips! And I'd also take Maggie Q . . ."

"She's not in this group!"

" . . .for her legs. Give me good body parts!" Then swiping the photos off the table, she said, "I'm done!"

I wet my lips. I ran teeth over tongue. *Breathe.* One by one I retrieved the photos off the floor. "Alright, okay." *Breathe.* "But some of them are less beautiful than others."

"Not really. You can see even from Roberto that *anyone* can be perfect." Her deep pool eyes were frozen solid.

Really? "Oh come on, he was just being kind."

The brooding slipped away from her face restoring *its* perfection, as if a tide had reanimated a beach. "Did you enjoy yourself?"

"What?"

"Last night."

"I think so. But it was a bit much." I reached for mooring, the coffee pot.

She reached her arm across, obstructing me. "A bit much?"

Part of me wanted to grab the pot and smash it across her spectacular face. *Where did that come from?* "Well, for me, a country girl."

"Did you learn something about beauty?"

I detected sarcasm. "I'm not sure, I think I did, maybe."

"Do you still think I'm beautiful?"

My tongue moved along the inside of my cheek. "Yes, of course."

"Which part? Of my face?"

Be the scientist, not the adversary. "Your eyes. Your lips. Your eyebrows. The way your hair frames it all."

"Okay." She removed her arm from the pot. "Okay."

"Can I ask you a question?"

"Sure." Just that quickly, she was childlike again.

"Did I meet Atara?"

Nan wagged her head, smiled. But she'd stiffened, almost imperceptibly. "Atara?"

"Yes, Marguerite seemed to think I knew her. I think so, so much drifted in and out last night."

"There was no Atara here. Marguerite was fucked up like the rest of us, like you. I'm sure you imagined many things. And I hope you'll keep imagining. We love having you here."

I felt unsure and it must have shown.

"Really," she said. "I'm sorry if I was short." She looked at the clock. "I'm going to take a shower, okay? It's almost six o'clock."

"Six! Six at night?" Having no windows was disorienting. Experimenting was disorienting.

"Yes." Her eyes heavy, embraced me. "Drink a lot of water this evening." She patted my shoulder as she exited the kitchen.

I cradled the coffee cup in both hands. She was a peculiar one. But hadn't that been the case with every person I'd gotten to know? And I shouldn't forget, I reminded myself, how considerate she'd been to me.

I wandered to the living room. It was still enchanting although after the last twenty-four hours it was terribly messy and disorganized with ashtrays spilling over, pillows askew, and glasses and bottles left on shelves and the floor. I started to pick up a pillow.

"Quite a party." Levi entered the room dressed in casual business slacks, a dress shirt, and holding his briefcase. "You were a hit! I guess you're not as shy as you made out."

A hit? "Well, you certainly made me feel comfortable."

"Mmm, yes."

"Luckily, New Years comes just once a year."

"Not in this house." He walked over to me. "May I kiss you?"

After last night that seemed appropriate. "Sure."

He leaned over and, running his fingers up my left thigh, kissed me, rather tenderly. "You're quite a woman."

I couldn't pull away —I'd spill the coffee. I spoke into his chest. "We should talk, don't you think? That was very intimate. I've never done anything like that. I want to get to know who you are, what you do, what's important to you."

He removed his hand. "I think you already know. It's the same as you. Anyhow, I've got to go." He checked his wristwatch.

"It's New Year's Day."

"Got to be somewhere in the morning."

"On January second?"

"Actually a very busy season; new product coming in all the time. Gotta go. Nan'll take care of you until I get back. Bye." He put his free arm around me and gave me a gentle squeeze. "See you soon. You're a sweet woman and delicious and don't you forget it."

He was quite a man. I'd never dreamed of such a relationship, but who was I to know? And on his return I would ask for his support.

))))

While Nan was in the shower I slipped quietly out of the apartment, hood drawn, imagining a cleansing swim at the Ondine. I left a note saying I'd be back. I didn't want a chaperone, I needed to get out, alone. I needed time to think.

So many people, so many looking at me. The way they looked at me. It *felt* good. I was blushing. And Levi and Nan had been great but . . . but what? *Couldn't I just be happy? For once!*

A block away from their apartment I began phoning Elizabeth. The line was consistently busy and dumping to a message: the mailbox was full. I kept walking, invigorated by the crisp New Year's air. After the fifth or sixth try at reaching Elizabeth, I resolved to walk all the way to her place after my swim, checking the entire time to see if anyone followed me.

Forty laps completed the delicious unbottling of my body and the maintenance on my psyche that had started at Nan's the night before, a grand way to start the New Year! Reinvigorated by my frolic in the pool, and with almost no one on the street, I found the walk to Elizabeth's that much sweeter, dreaming of DNA samples, extracted efficiently from the swamp. There had been many attractive people at Levi and Nan's —most of them actually.

Was there something universally beautiful about them? *Their touch.* But even those weren't homogenous. And what about the alcohol and the pills? Definitely tainted research. Nonetheless, beauty in everything. That couldn't be bad, could it?

And the sex . . . that was —if not beautiful— cathartic. Was it dangerous? Sharing carnal liquids, possibly incubating disease? It certainly wasn't reasonable. *I'm gathering, shameful as you may see it, Harold. You didn't expect me to stop what you started, did you?*

I sighed. It'd been days since I'd even thought about Harold, or about the blank, lost spaces that came with him. I could appreciate that too.

"Post, lady?" The guy shoved the headline in my face:

Mother gives birth to frog child

And below it:

Cops close in on Times Square Hacker

I bought the paper but there was nothing really new. No mention of Zoe. Yet it started my head blathering again. As I approached Elizabeth's the flurry of usual questions had regained mass and velocity. Real world decisions couldn't be put off indefinitely. I needed my job, I'd needed to confront Warring.

I rang Elizabeth's bell. Nothing. Then again. Nothing. I started down the brownstone steps. The door cracked open. I turned at the sound.

"Eunis?" It was Roddy.

"I'm sorry, I was —I've been trying to call but—"

"Elizabeth isn't taking calls right now."

"I'm sorry, this was a bad idea." I continued down the steps.

"Wait!" He dashed after me. "Come in, please."

Look at him. "I'm intruding."

"No you are not. Just stay for a few minutes."

Elizabeth's couch, with its rough, uneven grain and rather worn and drab shade of coral, compared unfavorably to the refined sofa at Levi and Nan's. Roddy brought me a glass of water, welcomed as the previous evening's drugs had begun to reduce me to one of Carver's dehydrated mountings. Roddy sat across from me, attentive, his eyes —I saw for the first time without my shaded glasses— cerulean, with green-tinted opal; a Minnesota morning sky reflecting off the water. Moist.

"Where's Elizabeth?"

The focus in his eyes evaporated. "She . . . She went into rehab this morning."

"I'm sorry."

"No, it's best for her and for Syd."

"Is Syd okay?"

"She's in the bedroom, asleep. She's fine, but seeing her mom like that —again— it's tough on a kid."

We sat uncomfortably in silence, me nodding like a donkey, not sure what to say next. I noticed the even texture of his skin, like distressed well-worn leather. Pliable. Skin texture was a cue to fertility and health. But that was a study of women. Thornhill again. And then there was that book, *Love At First Sight*, "a ground-breaking theory of attraction" using celebrity couples as case studies. Jennifer Aniston and Brad Pitt were on the cover. Enough said.

"You don't have any kids, do you?" he finally asked.

"No."

"Not yet."

"No, never."

"You don't know that."

"I made sure of it."

"How do you mean?"

"I made sure of it. I took care of it years ago."

"But you'd be a great mom. Why would you do that?"

"I'm not giving birth to a monster."

"Eunis, whatever someone said to you in the past is not everyone's viewpoint. I know; I'm an attorney."

"Yes, I know you're an attorney. It's irrelevant."

"Nothing is irrelevant. I thought you, as a scientist, knew that."

I crossed my arms.

"You're impatient with this line of reasoning."

"I am." I met his eyes. They were patient.

"As an attorney I can't discount anything. Every possibility, every potential argument, needs to be vetted. I better be sure that I'm never blindsided by an argument. Because if I am, I've failed my clients."

"Okay." I saw the logic. "But I'm not your client."

"Thoreau said 'It's not what you look at that matters, it's what you see.'"

"Thoreau?"

"Henry David."

"The philosopher." I let my words dropped like ingots, without enthusiasm.

"Yes. Is philosopher a dirty job?"

"Not very practical. Kind of a fairytale storyteller. Making up myths."

"I guess that's *one* way of looking at it. Perhaps arguing a point might be more accurate. You're pretty hard on yourself. People have been debating attraction forever."

"Like a lawyer."

"I suppose. It's a discussion. And what's wrong with myths anyway?

"Are you schooling me?"

"Don't we all school each other? Isn't that what the ancient myths are all about? Anyhow, the point is that I don't see what you see."

"No?"

"Your husband found you attractive. I'm sure there have been others."

I thought of the past twenty-four hours. "Perhaps." I felt my crescent dimples emerging. "But attraction is different than beauty."

Aah." He also smiled. "I'm not the only one."

His eyes jumped back. He realized what he'd said.

I flushed.

He gave a little cough. "What I mean is . . . there's a lot of data out there and we attempt to organize and translate it so it makes sense to us. But each one of us has peculiar filters. Information gets jumbled. You appreciate that, working in the lab."

"In the lab we have control groups, we're objective. Personal opinions don't count."

"Objective? You like thinking everything's under control." He sounded a little smug to me.

"That's not what I said!" My jaw clenched. "What's relevant to me is that, *according to qualified research,* even the relative length of the second to fourth finger may reveal developmental facial imbalances, which could be addressed prenatally. *That's* vetting it, not winging it. Down to the digit." I raised my pinky and rubbed it in front of him.

"Why do you do the work you do?"

"I'm studying." I grew restless on the couch. "I'm learning to narrow down, to isolate factors, to find answers, to help people."

"Narrow down? And is everything research? Is everything work?"

"Yes, narrow down!" I got to my feet. "Time for me to go. If you need any help with Syd or Elizabeth, let me know." I softened ever-so-slightly, just for a moment. "Please."

"Why not sit down and consider broader factors. Maybe things can't always be isolated."

"I think they can. Please tell Elizabeth I'm pulling for her."

"A good scientist doesn't turn her back on an argument."

"That's an attorney," I said rising and grabbing my swim bag. "Scientists don't argue, we measure. Happy New Year." I walked out.

"So nice for you to stop by," he yelled after me. The sarcasm stung my ears.

CHAPTER TWENTY-SEVEN

Roddy was a pompous ass. Down West End Avenue, irritated and walking in cadence to that irritation, my stomach churned. *No wonder Elizabeth drank. No wonder!*

When I re-focused on the street, I discovered security gates —grids of metal everywhere. Not a storefront open. Except . . . light poured onto the sidewalk a block and a half down. Closer, music tempered the air, lilting, warming the concrete. Not as loud as the last time I'd passed Ruthie's Roti.

"Sistah doondoos, you come back." This time the albino Jamaican woman's head was bound in a simple-but-elegant avocado green turban. She lit a cigarette from the ember of the previous one, swatted ashes off her ample bosom, and tossed the used butt away. She had a big expansive face, even friendlier than I'd remembered.

"All is good. C'mon now. Disya place, I told you." She sized me up and down then broke into a broad smile, "I see you been ah-gone-ee since I see you, sistah. Good thing."

"Agony?"

"No, sistah. The good stuff. Sex, right? C'mon, sit in my place, we talk."

Heat struck at my temples. I felt exposed, like the Jamaican woman could see me, inside and out. Impossible.

She waited, one meaty arm on her hip, the other waving the cigarette in a slow figure eight as if conjuring the night, as if there was nothing unusual about her comment; as if she'd already moved on. Up and down the street, darkness. The light was buttery as before, an oasis.

As I stepped into the shop I noticed the sign in the window:

Spiritual Readings & Conjure
Miss Ruthie Bluestone

> Help in all matters of life, love, health &
> reuniting with loved ones.
> - Remove evil influences
> - Improve financial status
> - Interpret dreams
> - Read bone

Oh! But I was already in. She beckoned me to sit in a corner where shelves of disorderly white linens rose to the ceiling flanked by two wooden chairs. On the other side of the store, slow cooking food wisped out of chafing dishes. A tantalizing aroma —clove, garlic— I couldn't place it.

"Sit, please. You want drink?"

"No, thank you." I lowered my swim bag to the floor.

"Okay." She sat next to me and blew smoke in my face. I waved it away. "So," she said, "what you think?"

I don't know why this struck me as comical, maybe I just felt good for a change, my annoyance with Roddy aside. I tried not to smirk. "I'm not interested in fortune telling, and I'm not paying for it."

"Okay. What you think?"

"What do I think about what?"

"Every thing; the duppy; every thing."

What the heck?

"You not only won who see." Her arms flapped like curd buntings on a clothesline. "You understand?"

"No, not really." I was doing my best not to laugh, but I *felt* cheerful. I liked her.

"Okay. You understand *duppy*?"

"No."

"He's your ghost."

"Ghost?"

"You carry him round. You better put him way sometime. There's no other way, okay?"

"Sure, okay." Whatever.

She wasn't annoyed. "Okay, let's try the water. You and me, we like the water." She pointed to the swim bag at my feet.

"Yes?"

"Yes."

"You see things, yes, without your eyes."

"I guess I do, sometimes. But how—?"

"I see different, but okay. Like water. Hmm, it's different. For you," she pantomimed a swimming stroke and a large circle motion.

I filled in. "Lakes, ponds."

"Yes, that. Me, the ribba. You understand ribba?"

"River, yes."

"You want to go in water. I understand. Me too, when I was a little girl. But water can be dangerous, you know. My daughter Vinnette, she can tell you, water can be dangerous. You be careful. There's a Jamaican legend, "Ribba Mumma," okay?"

I was amused. "Please."

"Ribba Mumma, she's a mermaid, very beautiful. Black hair, okay? Long. For hair, she have, you say golden, golden comb." She moved her fingers above her head to demonstrate. "Comb."

"Yes, I understand. Ribba Mumma has a gold comb."

"Good. If she show up don't look at her. Don't look at Ribba Mumma. Not with your eyes. She very dangerous." She wagged her finger, took another drag off her cigarette. "Be careful when you swim. Stay away from Ribba Mumma."

"This is the legend?"

"Shush." She shut her eyes and tilted her head back for a moment. She reached out her hand searching for mine and I instinctively took it. She held it and spoke with her eyes closed. "When you leave water, look around, pick up Ribba Mumma comb. Don't look at her after you take comb. Understand? You be rich!" She settled in, opened her eyes, satisfied with a huge grin, her face glistening, as if all problems had been resolved.

"Okay." Folktales and superstition everywhere. "You see my face?"

"Mmm."

"Ugly. What would make it beautiful?"

"No, no. Oh no. Never say baby beautiful; makes her grow ugly. You say she ugly, she grows beautiful. That's the way. Nothing to do."

"That simple?"

"Could be, yup. Could be."

"Well, thank you . . ." I peeped at my watch. Nan was probably worrying about me. *Someone worrying about me!* New, reassuring, and disquieting at the same time. *Why me?*

"You need place? Could be upstairs, you wanta see?"

"An apartment here?"

"Could be, wanta see? Cheap."

"Thank you . . . what's your name?"

"Miss Ruttie."

"Thank you, Miss Ruthie. I already have two homes." There was irony in that.

"No, I don think so." Ruthie crushed the cigarette under her considerable weight. "When ready, you come. You live in Ruttie place." Her smile revealed large yellowed teeth and darkened gums. "This your place."

☽☽☽

When I arrived at Levi and Nan's, Nan was waiting up for me, sitting in a dark corner of the living room wrapped in an expensive looking turquoise negligee. "Where've ya been?"

"I told you I was going out."

"You could be robbed or raped or both on the streets at this hour. Didn't the other night give you a taste of that?"

"I'm okay." I hung my overcoat in the closet.

"About the other night . . . " She remained in the shadows.

"I am so grateful. You were amazing."

"Yes, but why do you suppose he chose you first?"

"What?"

She lifted out of the chair and into the meager light. "Nothing. It's just . . . nothing. I was hoping you'd take a tub with me." She saw my resistance. "Just a short one. I've already filled it. C'mon, just for a few minutes. It'll help you sleep."

What was she getting at?

"It's waiting for us." She touched my shoulder and cheek as she walked by.

Water, steeping in a warm tub . . . "Okay, but just a few minutes."

The perimeter of the large Moroccan Room tub was circled in candles, the walls suggesting a sleepy grotto. Nan soaked in it, her majestic face cameoed in a regal mist, her eyelids closed in trance; her lips parted in . . . anticipation? Perhaps carnal, though I wasn't interested. Not this evening. Yet I couldn't resist the water. It stirred as I slipped in.

"You're still healing. You need to pace yourself." Nan didn't open her eyes. "Haven't we been taking good care of you?"

"You have, but I'm pretty capable." Light perspiration beaded on my forehead, serenity snaked into my bones. I started to unwind.

She rolled her neck, that serpentine neck. Still, her eyes remained closed. "You said that before. I should go with you the next time. Where'd you go tonight?"

"To see a friend."

"I thought you didn't have any friends here."

"I guess I was wrong. Listen, I'm tired. I'm going to bed."

She opened her eyes. They were glassy. "Let me rinse your back before you go."

Well, I was already in. "Okay, but then I've got to get some sleep." I turned my back to her. My eyes drifted closed, anticipating her touch.

"Maybe wash your hair too, your beautiful effervescent hair."

"No, I'm too —"

She yanked my hair down into the water, steadily bringing me backward and under until the bathwater closed in around me, covered my face, invaded my throat, plugged it, stole my breath. My eyes flashed opened. My hands went up, everything moving and formless in the short light. She kept tugging. Hair hot-wrenched from scalp.

She didn't realize. Let me up! No stored air. I tried to lift but nothing was solid; there was nothing to leverage. Pinned under.

I thrashed. Thunder in my ears. My throat knotted and cramping. My chest an iron slab, hauling me down. Deep, irrevocable sleep moments away. I kicked back, hard, against her, slamming her against the end of the tub. She let go. I surfaced coughing, my throat raw, the air precious, my chest pounding.

"Oh, I'm sorry," she said before I could turn. "I thought you'd like it."

It took another moment before a space opened in my lungs and the spasms in my chest subsided. When I finally focused on her she exuded a soft worried aura.

"Are you okay?"

"I think so." I reached for the rim.

"Good."

I lifted myself out, took hold of my robe and turned to her one last time. I savored several full breaths. "Are you angry with me?"

"Angry? No. I guess I wasn't thinking. But you're okay?"

I wrapped the robe around me. "I'm okay."

Those aqueous eyes studied me, those voluptuous lips wet with appetite. A sense of buried hunger, maybe even delight. "Good." She reclined in the tub and reclosed her eyes.

I backed out of the room. I hoped Levi would come home soon.

Nan sat at the end of my bed with a cup of coffee. "D'ya sleep well?"

The sheets were tucked tightly and I was trapped under them, like the first time I'd met her. I was on alert, trying to embrace her generosity, but uneasy. "I did, thank you. How long have you been watching me?"

"What do you mean?"

"While I slept."

"Oh," she said, "not long." She handed me the coffee, rubbed the blanket and my foot beneath it then stood. "I'm sorry about last night. I think I scared you."

"It's okay."

"Really?" She was contrite, eyes hooded, a teenager who'd overstepped. Vulnerable. "Thanks. Maybe sometime you'll let me wash your hair, but I'll ask first, I promise. I promise."

Remorseful. I could relate. I recognized those genes as part of her beauty. And her anger . . . I wasn't without my own anger. But I didn't know *why* she was angry, not with her beauty and all her comforts. "That sounds nice. And thank you for the coffee." I lifted the cup.

"Ya know why I offered you our place?" She paused, eyes wide. "Because I saw something in you . . ." Her voice tripped. She cleared her throat. "You remind me of someone."

"Me?" I laughed.

She began to cry. Tiny rivulets cascaded slowly down her face.

I sat up in the bed. "Are you okay?"

"It's-it's nothing, I'm just easily . . ."

"What?"

". . . Family stuff, we can talk about it some other time. Sorry." She pulled the water from her eyes with languorous strokes, like a magician.

I leaned forward. "I'd be happy to talk to you about it. How about now?" A few clues about her might relax me.

"Can't," she sighed. "Hospital." She rubbed her eyes dry with her forearms. "Oh, ya, I almost forgot. I've planned something special for you this evening." She waved. "I'll be back by then."

"Nan, I really appreciate everything but—"

"You've said that before." Her jawbone shifted, she ran her tongue over her teeth. "I'm suffocating you, aren't I? Sorry. I just wanted to do something nice for you."

"No, no, it's very sweet of you." *Keep her on your side.* "It's my stuff. I've got a lot of *stuff.* What did you have in mind?"

The desert color came back to her cheeks and her eyes bloomed turquoise green. "It's a surprise, and it begins this evening at seven o'clock."

I wasn't ready for any more surprises. But I smiled. With her I'd keep smiling, and vigilant.

🌙🌙🌙

Notwithstanding her charm, I waited to leave the apartment shortly after Nan, not to cause a fuss, and I managed the early morning commute better than I'd anticipated, occasionally returning people's stares. They always looked away.

"Mrs. Warring wasn't expecting you," said the secretary, "but she'll see you for five minutes." She ushered me into Warring's office.

"Eunis." Warring, rigid, didn't get up from her desk. "I see that your bruises are healing."

"I want to explain." Maybe it was the coffee, I was jittery, and I really hated that effing desk of hers. *Stay focused.*

"An explanation would be welcomed." She leaned back in her chair, flexing a pencil up and down.

Swim, one stroke at a time. "Now you understand about Elizabeth, and maybe that answers some of your questions concerning the lab. I think she does her job very well, but the bruises, well some of them were an accident, with Elizabeth. She didn't mean to, of course, but she was . . .well, you know, she lost control."

"Of course. Control." Warring put the pencil down without a sound.

"Yes."

"She's been a good worker." Warring hinted a smile.

"She wasn't right. Muddled, disordered. You can imagine. Now that she's in rehab I guess you can understand why I didn't want to tell you about the cuts and bruises. She didn't mean to. She isn't a violent person. She's really very responsible. It was an accident."

"Yes." Warring went silent, her mouth tighter, less merciful.

My heart thumped. "You *do* know about the rehab?"

Warring smacked her lips. "I was told Elizabeth was taking vacation days."

My supraorbital ridge started banging. "Oh god."

"Anything else?" She looked at her watch.

I'd done it again. "Elizabeth is good at her work. She would never jeopardize—"

"Please spare me the testimonials. Our investigation continues." She stood up and motioned to the door.

"I wasn't covering for myself, I just thought—"

Her jaw flexed. She pointed again to the door. "Now."

I walked out. I looked for a desk, anything, to hide behind. Everything was brightly lit. The secretary and a waiting lab tech tracked me, stony eyed, their condemnation implied. I was going to have to fix this. I had no idea how.

☽☽☽

On the street, it rang. Searching frantically through my coat pockets for the cell phone, it rang again. Frisking accelerated. "Shit." Like I was slapping attacking hornets. A black kid gave me a *whatthefuck* look.

I answered the phone, heaving and breathing irregularly. "Yes?" I glared back at the kid. He stutter-stepped away, down the street. I hustled to the corner of the building and checked the alleyway. Almost no one had my number. "Yes? Roddy?" Wishful thinking.

"Who? Eunis, Eunis is that you, girl?"

"This is Eunis, who's this?"

"Lyle."

"Lyle?"

"Lyle!"

"Lyle." I went from anxious to stunned. "Lyle. Wow."

"Yes, your long lost baby brother."

"*Baby brother*?"

"Lyle."

"Yes, don't start that again." I finally caught my breath. "Um, okay. I never heard you refer to me as your sister, or you as my baby brother."

"We're family, ain't we?"

I pulled the phone from my ear and studied it at arm's length. I put it back on my ear. "This is Lyle Kindsvatter of Bemidji, Minnesota?"

"Bemidji. Minnesota. Go Beavers. Home of Gary Puckett."

I'd never heard him so chirpy. "Why are you calling?" A loud police siren screamed past. "Lyle, I'm sorry, what did you say?"

"I'm comin' to New York. Just spoke to Carly, and she says you're doin' all great up there."

"Down here."

"Down there, and she said you might have a place for me to stay?"

A place to stay?

"She said she'd heard you got some money from Harold's . . . his what-do-ya-call-it—?"

"—Suicide . . . unless you mean his *estate*."

"Yeah that," said Lyle. "So you'all have a pretty cool condo or somethin' up —down there?"

"I did, and it's small. But you'd be welcome if I was."

"What?"

"Nothing. It's small, and you can stay at my condo *when* I can, but right now I can't."

"I don't understand. Can I live with you or not?"

"Right now . . . well, I'm kind of in the process of moving. Really, if I had a place," I shut my eyes and saw Lyle drunk in the Kiwanis basement, pressing his beloved Martin D-35 to his chest and singing to rows of empty chairs, "you'd be welcome."

"Well, it's okay. I can live wherever you are for a little while until we get to the condo."

I shook my head, like that would make him see. "Lyle, you don't understand. Things aren't going so well right now."

"But Carly said—"

"She was wrong."

"I might get a backup gig, so I'm comin'. Ya never know where it could lead. Maybe somebody from a label. Not sure when, got some issues I gotta clear up. But don't worry, I'll find you, and now you've got my cell number. Hey, and do you know anybody in that scene?"

"What scene?"

"My scene."

"What's your scene, Lyle?"

"Same as always, country/western music. It's just meetin' the right people, Eunis."

And then he was gone. "Lyle?" I pressed the phone tighter to my ear. Gone. "Holy shit." Another lightning rod for trouble. Could I hide from him in this city?

Carol Warring exited the building. I took two steps into the alley shadows to avoid her.

She saw me lurking in the alley and stared at me. "I don't need this bullshit."

)))

I left a nervous message for Roddy to call me, admittedly relieved that I didn't reach him. Putting off the inevitable. Scrubbing my hands was no use. The burden followed me back to Nan and Levi's apartment.

At the apartment, still restless and searching for an excuse to make it *all* go away, I examined the new wardrobe Levi and Nan had provided: lacey and sheer and low cut; more provocative than anything I would have chosen; yet so generous and so flattering. Perhaps I could fill in with a few things more demure the next time I visited The Octagon.

I flipped absently through a People magazine.

X-Men Auction Draws Millionaire Bidders
"Those trinkets you bought when you were young
may be worth something. Paraphernalia from the

> *first two X-Men films, as well as early X-Men collec-*
> *tor items, are drawing advanced bids of up to*
> *$12,000 for an auction in Toronto. The curiosities*
> *are garnering attention from collectors around the*
> *world including . . ."*

I continued paging through it. I fidgeted. I put the magazine down. On the bookshelf I found an old encyclopedia, probably Levi's. I searched for Freyja but found nothing except a reference to Aphrodite:

> *"Aphrodite: Goddess of beauty, love, desire, and*
> *pleasure. Although married, she had many lovers.*
> *She was depicted as a beautiful woman and, of all*
> *the goddesses, most likely to appear nude or semi-*
> *nude. (also see: Venus, Atargatis & Ashtarte*
> *[Syrian])"*

Nan walked in. "Hi."

I closed the book. "Can we talk? I've done something terrible. I don't know what to do."

Nan put down her things and motioned for me to sit on the sofa. She was immediately supportive and listened patiently as I retold how I'd outed Elizabeth.

"They'll fire her because of me."

"Sounds like a mistake, but you've called her husband." Her face had the color and consistency of soft, tan clay, almost edible and absolutely perfect. "What else can you do?" She put her hand on mine. "What did your boss say? Is she going to reinstate you?"

"Never got that far. I'm so ashamed. I may have destroyed her career."

"I think you've done the right thing. Until he calls why don't you relax? A drink maybe? I've got some pot."

"Maybe a drink, a glass of wine." *Think things out.*

After we'd both sipped a couple of glasses of pinot, and Frey-ja had transformed the room into a lagoon, and Nan had reminded me that I was safe there with nothing to struggle against, I acquiesced to her deep green pools. A realization broke the surface of those pools and rippled outward.

"Your surprise. I forgot to tell you about your surprise." She checked her watch. "Geez, it's almost seven." Nan got up. "I'll be going out."

"That's my surprise?" I wanted to keep swimming with her, wanted her to see my disappointment and that I'd forgiven her, or that at least I was working on it, that I appreciated her friendship, like a beautiful sister I almost had. We could talk about her family. Maybe I'd tell her about the upcoming genetics conference at The New York Academy of Sciences.

"No." Nan was amused. "I just want you to have the space all to yourself, to use in any way you see fit. And no hair-washing necessary."

"Huh, okay. But I'd *like* you to stay."

"We'll have plenty of time, you're sweet."

Within minutes, she gave me a big hug and a peck on the lips, and was out the door. "You may want to slip into something more comfortable."

Instead of relaxing me, my antennae went up. I just wanted a cocoon.

CHAPTER TWENTY-NINE

A little past seven o'clock the blissful doorbell chimed and I answered it. Perhaps Nan had forgotten her keys. It was Roberto, Mr. Pectoralis of the Biceps Brachi, still as stubby and well built as on New Year's morning in the kitchen. I pictured my "Faces" scrapbook spread out for ridicule. *Let it go.*

"This should be fun." He brushed past me into the living room. "How about some candles?"

"I'm afraid I don't understand."

"Roberto. You remember me?"

"I do, but Nan's not here."

"What did Nan tell you?"

"She said there was a surprise."

"That's me. Where would you like to do it?"

"What?!"

"Your massage. Which room would you like? No, never mind." He went to a dark blue and orange vase, lifted it at an angle, and slipped a key from under it. I'd never considered *under* the vase. "The table's already in there. C'mon." He took my hand and directed me to the room marked "Cinema."

He glanced over his shoulder at me. "You do like massage?"

"I've never really—"

"But it seems like something you'd enjoy. I'm a masseur." He unlocked the door with his right hand and wiggled his left. "Angels in my fingers, you'll see." He flipped on a light that rimmed the entire room in a soft glow where the ceiling curves met the wall.

The room had none of the theatrics or nautical themes of the rest of the kingdom, but had, as its centerpiece, a large massage table surrounded by calming sand-colored walls and large same-colored pillows propped against them. Even the floor was a light tan. Very soothing.

"You can hang your clothes there." He pointed to a row of hooks. "I'll get you some water. You can slip under the sheet, on your stomach, forehead in that head rest." He departed.

A massage. I had my questions. *Could be worth exploring.* I called to him, "I don't know you very well." Apparently he hadn't heard me. I stood there foolish for a minute, then *what the hell*, stripped, hung my clothes, and crawled under the cool sheet. It felt good. When he entered I asked, "This is just a massage, right?"

"My massage is not *just* a massage. And you can ask me to stop whenever, okay?"

"Okay." *Okay.*

"Do you mind if I take a hit of something?"

"I guess not. I already had two glasses of wine."

He lit a small pipe from his pocket, inhaled, and ducking under my headrest, put his lips close to mine and blew the smoke into my mouth and nose.

"Hey!" I coughed. "You should've asked. Maybe you got the wrong idea the other night."

"Sorry. Do you want me to leave?"

"No, it's okay." I lay my forehead on the headrest. "But please ask me the next time. I'm not sure pot even does anything for me."

I heard Roberto flip a couple of switches. I heard rustling. Music began, low, sparse, calming. Then his hands were on my shoulders and neck, stretching, tugging, manipulating, and sliding down my rib cage and spine. His fingers were strong and deep but not painful. He explored each bone, each muscle, deliberately. No rush. He flowed over me, freeing one tension after another, unknown knots and nubs, sea spray lifting off from the ocean surface but not returning.

"I'm not hurting you am I?"

I could barely respond. "No," I whispered.

"Breathe," he said. "Breathe deeply. Release through my fingers." He folded the sheet painstakingly from the left side of my body. The air cooled ever-so-slightly. He ran his hand over my hips and down both sides of my left thigh, so that he lightly grazed the hair flanking my vulva.

"I'm going to use my elbow." He ran his fingers the length of my hair and drew it back from my ear and came close to it. "Let me know if it's too much." Then he leaned his elbow into the space just below my waist and above my left butt and applied pressure. His command, the exact right amount of pressure, surprised me again.

Space opening between atoms.

He re-covered the left side and applied the same release on my right.

I breathed *with him.*

"Yes," he said, as if he'd heard me. "Exhale, breathe through the muscles."

I drifted in transcendent foam, just above the water's surface, a cleansing mist that left no trace. *The pot. Was that pot? Ooh.* I skimmed through the waves, the Chippewa Forest all around me, the vegetation delicate, fluorescent, and alive. Hallucinogenic.

It breathed, slowly, extravagantly. Hypnotically. The forest's greens pulsed off the earth in patient hoops, meeting my floating body and passing it. I, the willing porpoise suspended, arching through the hoop waves without fear, without consequence. Timeless.

A zephyr passed over me, cooling me, toes to waist. His right hand, like an extension of me, lay on my buttock. I wanted his left hand too.

"You're uncovered," he said, "and I can't wait much longer, Aphrodite. May I enter you?"

I couldn't imagine anything else. I heard myself answer "Yes."

He was on me, from behind, finding his way into me. I gasped. He went deeper.

"Are you okay," he asked.

"Yes," I said. *Yes.*

He kissed the nape of my neck and went deeper still, until I was sure we couldn't be any closer. Though I'd welcome it. We rode the skies above the oceans and forests together. "I can feel you all around me, Aphrodite. You're perfect. Perfect. Perfect."

And with that he unleashed his stream into me, the cool then warm fluid reaching my deepest pool, triggering my flood of cries and orgasms and tears. Blissful tears.

He knelt between me and lay delicately on my back, still inside me. "Perfection," he whispered.

"Yes." I pulled him closer.

〉〉〉

When we lay against the pillows I was still traveling through the spring Minnesota forests and over and beneath its wetlands. "A magic kingdom," I heard myself telling Roberto. "Colors everywhere."

He stroked my hair, all the way to my shoulders and back up. "Iridescent," he said.

I cuddled to his chest. His sweat smelled of soap. *Disappointing.* I'd rather have had the smell of dark loam and edaphon, or the clarity of a muddy mossy lake. But no matter.

"In here," Roberto called out, a deep godly voice because my ear was still to his chest. Others entered the room. *How long had we been lying there?* The others disrobed and discovered each other. It was luxurious to watch.

When Roberto let go of me someone else took his place. An older man, I think. He knelt above me. He had wolf gray eyes. They were afraid.

"Shush, shush," I said to the man. His eyes widened; his face loosened. Like me, he simply wanted safety.

"I've never done this before," he said. "The drugs, I mean. So it's not you. You have the most beautiful body I have ever seen. Are you the woman they promised? Your hair is magic. Your lips . . ."

"Jonah." An elegant gray-haired black woman squatted to our level. "Stop talking. You don't need to talk. Just *be*." She kissed the top of his head and raised her round naked body up. Her ample hips dissolved into the rolling silhouettes. *She must be the queen.*

"Are you the king?" I asked.

"Yes."

In that instant I could read his mind. We could serve each other. We could both be in the cocoon. "Then you may taste me." I spread my legs. And he went down on me while I slowly stroked his hair.

ꙮ ꙮ ꙮ

I was pacing the top step of Elizabeth's brownstone when Roddy arrived, his gait steady, his ascent *up* the steps molten. So natural. He placed his arm on my waist and escorted me inside, but not before I noticed two neighbor-women fixing us with disapproving stares. I could be done with this and back in my protective shell in little more than an hour.

Once inside he offered me water, which I accepted. We sat facing each other. The midday light over his shoulder blinded me. He noticed, got up and closed the window shade.

I removed my shadowed glasses and hung my head. "At the lab, I thought Carol Warring knew."

"Knew what?"

"About Elizabeth's rehab."

"Oh shit." He rubbed his forehead.

"What have I done?"

He reached for me. Took my hand. His mouth, even then kind, prompted a not-unpleasant intoxication, perhaps re-stimulating a recent drug. I pushed his hand aside. After a drink of water, I slid a coaster under it and set it down on the well-worn coffee table.

"It was bound to come out. You couldn't have known."

"I was trying to save myself. I should never have assumed. I'm *the* most selfish—!"

"Stop. You couldn't have known. Will Warring reconsider your job?"

"Not sure. Besides, I don't even know if I want the damn job anymore. I need it, but I'm so confused. What're we going to do about Eliz?"

"They can't fire Elizabeth for going to rehab."

"You don't know that."

"Of course I do. I'm an employment attorney."

"They can't fire her?"

"They can fire her for screwing up lab results if she was drunk. They can't fire her for going to rehab."

I straightened up. "I never saw her drunk at work. She's pretty happy there."

"That's useful but of course it's only one point of view. How about the other woman, the East Indian girl? What's her name?"

"Ruchika."

"I'll talk to her. I can't imagine Eliz going to work drunk or even drinking on the job. So stop worrying."

"I'm just not meant for . . . anyplace."

"Where are you from?"

I studied him, wondering why he cared. "Bemidji, Minnesota. Actually, just north of there, between Puposky and Nebish. I'm sure you're familiar with the area." I tried to grin.

"I'm not."

"Because they don't exist anymore. They're legend now, nothing more. That's where *I'm* from: nowhere."

"And your family?"

"What good is this?" Like Momma was poking at me. I wanted to get back to my safe, dark ship, to Nan and Levi, where I'd be held and stroked and appreciated. He must've heard my exasperation.

"Your mother? Your father?"

"My mother is a bitter, superstitious woman who believes in myths and spooky goblins and spirits. I never knew my real father, and my step-father is dead."

"Brothers? Sisters?"

"One wants to be a star. The other thinks she is. Maybe she is."

"You sound bitter."

"They don't relate to me." I ran my hand along my face. "Who can blame them?"

He took a big breath, exhaled. "My mother was black, a sweet woman with a speech impediment from a family of six. She was the oldest and the one who was worked the hardest. She met my father, a dance instructor, Portuguese and Jewish, during the civil rights movement in Alabama. They traveled to Memphis together where they were both involved in advance logistics for Martin Luther King. They got married. They were in dreamland, I'm told —a few days, maybe a week. Shortly after that Martin

Luther King was assassinated, and shortly after that it came out that my father had had a passing acquaintance with James Earl Ray. Do you know who that is?"

"The guy who shot King."

"The guy who *allegedly* shot King. He was a thief, a pornographer and a racist. My father was beaten to death by my mother's own brother. My mother's been in a mental facility ever since. She will die there, probably very soon. Even King's family is pretty sure James Earl Ray wasn't the assassin."

I didn't know what to say. Like I'd been carved out.

"*Saudade*," he said. "It's a Portuguese word. Hard to translate. Life's lingering melancholy."

"It's always there, isn't it?"

A small nod in agreement. "For everyone. Even for Ray. His father was always on the run, a forger, a criminal, dragging the family around, and Ray's younger sister caught fire and died playing with matches. Tragedy is everywhere, all the time. But you don't strike me as someone who will give in."

I managed another sip of water. "I never intended to."

"Good, then don't." He paused. "And if your family doesn't fit, find family that does."

"What about you and Elizabeth? Aren't you giving in?" I put down the glass of water making sure it was centered on the coaster.

"There are many ways to map the arc of a relationship. One of ours was by the way we spoke to each other. At first I called her Eliz. Then Lizzy. Then Lizzy Plum Garden. Then Plumby. Then asshole."

I laughed. "Oh, I'm sorry."

"No, it *is* funny. Sad but funny." He frowned then shook it off. "I like seeing you smile."

I took a deep breath. I had no good place to rest my gaze.

"But when contempt takes over," he said smoothing over the awkward air, "it's time to shake hands and go your separate ways. You can do a lot worse. You, you were married. What did you call your husband?"

"Harold."

"And then?"

"Dead."

"Right." Regret tinged his voice and for a moment his eyes were apologetic. "Do you mind?" He reached for my glass of water.

I didn't share water glasses, not even with Harold. "Sure."

He took a swig. "Will you have dinner with me?"

"No."

The water glass stopped, suspended halfway to the table. Trace disappointment in his eyes. "Why not?"

My stomach tightened. It seemed to do that a lot with him. But now more than ever I'd impinged on Elizabeth. The right thing to do was to leave them alone, to accept my new lifestyle. It hurt all out of proportion.

"Just not interested." I slipped my shades back on. "Let me know what I can do to repair the mess I've made for Eliz."

CHAPTER THIRTY

I'd struggled through the darting and lumbering, smoking and coughing bodies of the city's afternoon sidewalks, purchased a faux twill briefcase from a Rastafarian street vendor, and navigated the subways. I was thankful to be home. Nan and Levi's home.

Settling in with a glass of red wine and opening my laptop, I studied the speakers attending the Genetics & Genomics Conference at the Academy of Sciences, an impressive list; all potential research mentors, then turned to the newest Life & Style Weekly an arm's length away. It tempted me with headlines about Jennifer Anniston's new beau and the final trials for the state Miss USA competitions that would soon begin. I tossed the spectra of personal questions out of my mind and gave in.

I was surprised but happy to have company when, hours later, the apartment door finally opened. Levi, beat up, stepped inside, his peanut head furrowed.

"Hi." Relieved, I went to help him with his luggage and overcoat.

He brightened. "Hi to you. Nan home?"

"Not yet."

He surprised me again by taking me in his arms. He smelled metallic, flat, like stale in-flight air. "D'ya miss me?"

"Uh, sure. Yes." I was still pleased and confused by his approval.

He cocked a worn comprehending grin and put space between us. "Too busy, I'm sure, to think of your main man." Without energy, he stretched out his thick manicured fingers and tussled my hair. "I'm not gonna let you forget me. I'm home now, at least for a couple of days."

He glimpsed the wine bottle and glass sitting on the side table next to the couch. "Would you consider new glasses and the bottle of Don Julio for us? Maybe a couple ice cubes, hey Euni? I'll be out of the shower in no time." He disappeared down the hallway.

Euni? No one had ever called me that. *I guess*, it sounded endearing. And it was an opportunity for just the two of us to get to know one another. Perhaps time to ask for his support.

When he returned, Levi and I relaxed on the couch, the bottle of Don Julio on the table in front of us. Levi, in his midnight blue satin robe and an inharmonious pair of black sweats, had his arm ready to descend upon my shoulders. That part of the evening was beginning to feel habitual, no longer an exploration but a ritual. I wanted to tell him about the conference, but for the time being it would be my secret.

"You and Nan have been wonderful to me. Thank you again. I can see why you two are so compatible."

"You can?"

"She's beautiful —beyond beautiful— and you're obviously a well-traveled, well-informed man."

He thought about it. "Yes, it works, definitely. We have our agreements, and we abide by them." He ran his thumb around the lip of his glass.

"Agreements?"

"Every couple has them, don't you think?"

"I'm not one to ask. I don't have a lot of experience in those things."

He fell silent and seemed to lose his way; it made me awkward. "Do you know anything about Charles Dickens?"

His neck tilted back, examining me. "The writer?"

"You seem . . . well read."

"Well, thank you." He smiled, but the shower hadn't cleansed his fatigue. "I'm not so sure of that."

"So?"

"Dickens. *The Old Curiosity Shop*; I'm sure I read it, long ago." Again he fingered his glass. "Probably others. Wasn't he bi-polar or depressed or something? Brilliant but not happy. Why the interest in Dickens? Would you like some of his books? I can make that happen." He had the air of a different man, less self-assured, more likeable.

"No, I have plenty of those, thanks."

"Then what?" He took a good belt and savored it returning the glass to the table. "He have something to do with beauty?"

"No." I didn't really know what I was searching for in those books. How was I going to explain to Levi?

When I remained mute he continued. "Tell me something about yourself. How have you studied beauty?" He seemed genuinely interested. "Objects d'art?"

"Not exactly."

"Well," he said getting up and walking over to the earthenware mermaid figurine and returning with it to the sofa. "What do you think of some of our art? You've probably noticed it around the apartment." He placed the figurine in front of me. "You can pick it up, just be careful."

I hesitated.

"Please, go ahead."

As soon as I did my fingertips prickled with its tactility.

He smiled. "Almost vibrissa-like, isn't it?" He pointed at the mermaid. "The bottom part is actual fish scales, very old and perfectly preserved."

"How old?"

"Very old." He took the figurine from me and placed it back on the shelf.

"A type of taxidermy," I said.

"Yes. Why, do you know anything about it?"

So I explained about my years at Carver's and how it was my first hands-on experience with beauty.

"And why didn't you continue with that? It sounds like you had enough skill and experience to open your own shop."

"Not my passion." As soon as it was out I wanted to retract it. It sounded so woo-woo and new age.

"Well," he said, "you're certainly a passionate person and you should be able to express that, whatever that is for you."

"You play the violin."

His eyes registered surprise.

"I saw it in your closet."

"Haven't played it much lately."

"Are you passionate about that? Would you play for me?"

"Sure, if you want."

"Now?"

"Yes, sure." Something brightened in him because he was up and back quickly, violin case in hand. "It's a good idea." He reached into his pocket. Here." He handed me a small rufous brown feather barred with streaks of grey.

"What's this?"

"Keep it. It's a wren's feather. Clever is better than strength. Think of it as a good luck charm."

I studied it, nonplussed.

"Go on." He laid his violin case on the couch.

A gift is a gift. I slipped it into my skirt pocket. He clicked open the case and tightened the strings until he smiled rather sweetly at me. "Turkey in the Straw?" His grin widened.

"What?"

"I'm joking." His fingers paused above the strings. He pulled the tawny instrument to his chin and chest, and then his fingers dropped and the bow began to sweep. Classical or gypsy, I don't know these things, but it was slow and weeping from the very first note, emptying unimaginable sorrow into the room. I could barely breathe, the grief was physical, tides rolling in, pulling away.

His half-closed eyes were on me the whole time so I shut mine. I couldn't handle the undertow. Me. He took me to sea. At moments he was vast and barely audible, but he held me afloat delicately, a last rite, as if I was adrift with no chance of return. All hope lost. Nothing to struggle against. My beautiful water had come to take me. Forever.

He slid his arm behind me and stroked down my side. I wasn't even aware that the music had stopped, that he had put down the bow and violin.

I could hardly speak. "That was beautiful." His hand moved to my breast on the way to loosening my blouse. I opened my eyes. *He* was beautiful. His other hand traveled inside my skirt to the cleft above my ass.

"Levi, I'm not sure what's —"

His mouth moved to my neck. The front door snapped open.

Nan. Carrying a small plastic bag.

She fixed me with a smoldering stare. "Couldn't wait, Leviathan?" She turned to him.

He made no attempt to remove his hand. In fact he held me more firmly. I didn't resist. I couldn't and I didn't want to.

"Come join us, baby." He tapped the space next to him with his free hand. "C'mon, all's fair."

Nan didn't budge, and I was lost at sea.

"What's in the bag?" he asked.

"Present for Eunis. Now that you've come home you can join us."

〉〉〉

Nan changed out of her hospital blues and herded us into the Cinema room where she'd moved the massage table to the side, made a large pile of pillows for the three of us to rest against, and flipping a switch, lowered a large movie screen down the wall.

"Ah," said Levi not wanting to look at me, nor I at him, "I love movies." Bottle in hand, eyes mushy.

"Eunis," Nan said. "I thought you'd find this interesting, seeing how you're studying beauty. That whole thing about sexy faces being equal."

"Beautiful and symmetrical," I corrected her. "And that's not all. Space *between* features counts too. A 'Golden Ratio,' what the Greeks called the 'divine proportion.'"

"Whatever." She opened a small cabinet in the wall, placed a DVD into the player, and lowered the lights.

"No, seriously, there are studies—"

Nan hovered over the Play button. "How bout me? How do I rate?"

"You? Beautiful. I've told you that."

Levi drummed his fingers, rolled his eyes to the ceiling.

"Okay, but no one would put me in their class, your scrapbook team."

"Maybe not. But that doesn't mean you're not. You're exotic. You've got spectacular genes."

"Syrian," Levi injected, a blasé sigh.

This might have been a good time to mention the DNA sample.

"Would I be beautiful if I was, say, fat? Or if my teeth were crooked?"

"You would be, I'm sure. Your face is that perfect."

"But maybe not for everyone."

"Maybe not, but for most."

Levi got up. "Call me when this shit is over and we get to the good stuff."

What was she hunting for? Whatever it was, it was draining.

"Okay, that's enough." Before he was more than a few strides out of the room she called him back. "Levi, get your ass in here. And bring the tequila!"

He quickly returned, scowling. "C'mon girls." He handed Nan the bottle without looking at her. He leaned against the wall. "What are we gonna watch *now*? Something *new*, perhaps?" He raised an eyebrow to her.

"Not quite yet, Levi. Give it some time."

"Okay, okay, just roll it, damn it."

She lowered the lights. Levi tumbled in between Nan and me, wrapping his arm around me and nuzzling her.

"That's a good boy." She ran her fingers across his shaven skull and rested on him, all the weight now falling on me.

It wasn't comfortable, those two bodies lumped on me, but I wasn't about to toss a match into the combustible air. *Just support them.*

Nan reached behind him and ran a single finger across my naked shoulder. Then pushed the remote. "I know you like Dickens."

I couldn't recall saying anything like that to her. "Is this a documentary on Dickens?" I straightened up, encouraged.

"No, something more fun."

)))

Whatever we drank, it was more than just tequila. I remember the film starting. An older film: *Olivia Twisted,* about a young women who is mercilessly misused by her gang and society, until a kindhearted prostitute makes love to her and sexually emancipates Olivia before nobly sacrificing her own life for her.

A lot of nude bodies and an amalgam of assorted sexual encounters. Not much else. My first porn film: it didn't titillate me. Was that Nan's purpose in showing it to me? Or was it the characters? Were they supposed to be me and Nan?

I surfaced from sleep, in bed, in the Moroccan Room, covers thrown aside, with Levi on his flank, back to me and snoring, and Nan asleep, spread-eagled, next to him.

"What happened?" I whispered, but I knew. It'd happened again. Seeing no clothes of mine anywhere, I slipped silently from the bed and the room, down the hall, naked, to my room, though the air barely parted as I advanced.

⟩⟩⟩

It's not like I didn't try. I ordered the Buccal DNA sampling kit. I weighed the most tactical methods to approach targeted speakers at the conference, which was my best chance to move my work forward, even if most everything else collapsed.

I saw nothing in the papers or on TV about the Times Square Hacker. I waited for a call from Warring. I wrote query letters to a couple research facilities in the city but I knew that once they spoke to Warring, I was toast, so I didn't send them. I was treading water but as Harold would chide me, "Patience: an idea, like a ghost, must be spoken to a little before it will explain itself."

Then one night, with no party planned, when Nan had a day-shift and returned around 8 PM, she caught me with my swim bag ready to go out.

"Can I come?" Her eyes bordered in fatigue.

My nights at Natatorium Ondine, alone, were precious. "I thought you didn't swim."

"I have to get over that." She rushed off to get her things. "It'll only take me a few minutes, I promise."

In the taxi, streetlights coasted across her face and returned her to darkness, over and over. Her fatigue smothered any conversation, even as we slipped on our bathing suits. As my one-time guest she could swim free, and though I could see that the chemical smell of the place displeased her as it did me, once she was in the water she matched me lap for lap until I pulled out, sat on the pool's edge, and watched her swim another twenty.

The woman was strong.

"I needed that," she said pulling herself next to me on the edge, obviously revitalized. "Thank you for letting me tag along."

I handed her a towel.

"You're thinking of leaving, aren't you?" Teenage vulnerability returned to her eyes.

"Yes."

"Remember, about three months ago, I said you reminded me of someone?"

"Someone in your family."

"My sister, the only one I got along with. She was very beautiful. Some said *too beautiful.*"

"Too beautiful?"

"So beautiful, my parents said, that no one would be worthy of her. But that didn't stop the men from trying."

"Your parents must have both been pretty gorgeous to have the two of you."

"Well, she drowned." Nan stared into the pool's viridian depths. "She went swimming, a river we both loved. She'd been swimming there a lot with a boy she'd been seeing. One evening, she didn't come back."

"I'm so sorry."

"That's why having you around has been so special to me. It's not just the physical—"

"No."

"It's you. The companionship, especially with Levi gone so often."

I took her hand. "How do I remind you of her?"

"Quiet. Magnetic." She stopped short. "Please don't leave, not for a while. I don't have many friends."

I had never thought of her exactly as a *friend.* And there hadn't been a lot of companionship, the little I knew about that. I was just a familiar, though intimate, tenant. One who was staying comfortably low profile from the cops. But the loss of family resounded deep beneath my heart. She was sore, and I was touched. "What about all those people who come to the parties —Marguerite, Maurice, all of them?"

"They're toys. You need to have plenty of toys so everyone can play with something." She quickly closed down. "Come on," she said, helping me up. "Let's go home and open some wine."

I wouldn't be able to stay —not much longer— even with my concerns about the police. But I could be her friend, maybe even be a surrogate sister. And I loved the idea of us being confidantes.

》》》

On the evenings when the television was off, two or three nights a week, I roamed the shipboard palace until the nightly festivities began. I was taken care of. Often pampered, like a favored pet. Nan didn't offer to wash my hair, but I was baptized nightly in the large Moroccan tub in sweet smelling emollients of almond and clove or cardamom. Washed anew with bricks of laurel soap, Aleppo, Nan called them, and finished by ointments of rose or cinnamon or light vanilla, fit for Amphitrite. Then wrapped in a thick, oversized Turkish towel to marinate. No more chest tremors, no more voices. I wondered if that was evolution.

"You got a package." Nan turned the small carton over several times.

"Yes, I ordered it. I was hoping you could help me out."

"What does that mean?"

"I want you to be my standard for beauty."

Her eyes flickered with confusion. "You're kidding."

"I'm not."

"You want to take photos of me?"

"I want your DNA. I want to inspect your code. It could be the basis for generations of beautiful children."

"What's in this box?" It was as much a challenge as a question.

"A sampling kit. Painless."

"Show me." She handed me the box. I hadn't lost her yet.

I spread out the kit. It was pretty benign: an untreated cotton paper swab with plastic handle, a transport pouch with desiccant to keep it dry, sealing tape, gloves, ink strip, alcohol pad, and forms.

"I'm not giving you my fingerprint."

"No, no. That's for suspected criminals. I don't need your prints."

"I'm not sure about this coding thing."

"Your beauty could become the standard. You could be the mother of all beauty."

Her mouth fell open, ever more sumptuous mystified. "I like being unique. I need to think about this."

So, week after week, I waited for her answer. I studied. I put my thesis down on paper. I tore it up and started again. I asked her, "What about your sample?"

"Still considering."

Forbearance. Not my best quality.

Checking the Internet for new research had become dull labor, a task lacking results. I counted the days to the conference. I was almost always slow to wake, the thickness of the air lulling away anticipation. I swam more and allowed myself the luxury of touching and being touched. I was something of a celebrity, although occasionally I'd catch Nan watching me with what appeared to be disapproval, her mouth hard, her eyes frozen. But I could have been imagining.

"Are we okay?" I asked her after one evening encounter and the apartment had cleared out. "You seem unhappy with me."

"No, don't be silly. What did he say to you?" She straightened a few things on the coffee table and cuddled next to me on the sofa.

"The doctor?"

"Yes."

"I don't remember exactly."

"You know he was with me too?"

"I didn't, but I have no special rights." The attachments wonderful but temporary.

"No, you don't." She smiled. "But what did he say?"

"He was pleasant. Smart. Not a great lover. But pleasant."

"Well, he was very taken with you, and I just thought maybe he said something to you."

"About what? What would he say? We talked briefly about why he got into medicine. I told him about my research. What did he say to you?"

She picked her teeth. She huffed. "He thought you were a beautiful person."

"He said that?"

"I just said so, didn't I?"

I shrugged. "So what? You're a *really* beautiful person." I put my arm around her.

She stiffened. "Yeah," she said without enthusiasm and reached for the TV remote.

"Now stop," I said grabbing the remote before she could. "What's this about?"

"Nothing."

"Bull."

She lunged for it. "Give me the fucking remote."

I pulled back. "You've given me shelter, food, friendship. You've let me do my research. You've asked very little in return. I'm grateful to you. And to Levi, he's a great guy."

"Yes, I see you two are *pals*. Give me the remote." She opened her right hand.

"Don't twist this. I'm trying to let you know that you're . . ." I waved the wand aimlessly. I searched for the word but the best I could come up with was " . . . astonishing."

She laughed, a blend of consent and lingering anger.

"Really," I said and took her hand. "Really."

She wriggled free. Her tongue snapped, a little like leather. "The remote." Her hand open and waiting. Her smile distant.

"There's a lot of buttons on these things, aren't there?" I passed her the clicker, a familiar weariness settling along my chest. "You're not going to give me your DNA sample, are you?"

"Probably not." She pointed the wand and the screen surged to life.

I grew more excited about the upcoming conference.

One more extended weekend. I lifted the glass, and through its upturned bottom and its amber liquid I saw the newest crowd rippling in. Someone kissed my right cheek, clear of the birthmark.

"And this is our Eunis." Levi's strong gentle hands caressed my neck, drawing my hair away from my nape.

"Andy will take good care of her," said Nan prying Levi's hands off me and threading her own in my tresses. She gave my locks a sharp, painful tug. Touch no longer brought the exhilarating coolness of the Minnesota waters or Roddy's warm hillside. No, now I was simply indulging Nan and Levi, preserving myself, with nothing more than a loss of feeling and a series of blind spots. Not sustainable.

CHAPTER THIRTY-ONE

It was one of those days when everything spills. Maybe because I'd never been in a space with 200 roaming *anything*, it made me extra nervous to think about being surrounded by 200 experts and interested genetastics. So I dropped my soap in the shower, I knocked my laptop off the bed, I splattered coffee over the kitchen floor. "Shoot!"

"*We're* up early." Nan said unfazed by the dark expanding puddle.

I crouched over my clumsiness with a towel. "I'm going out today." I didn't like being on my knees in her presence.

"Out? Where?"

"A conference."

"A conference?"

"Genetics. New investigations, protocol, ethics, that sort of thing."

"You seem nervous."

"I am. I think you'd find some of it interesting."

"I'm expected at the hospital."

"I didn't mean—"

"I wish you'd mentioned it to us."

"I did."

"I don't remember."

"Well, it's been almost a month."

"Time goes fast here, doesn't it?"

"Actually . . ." I wanted to be careful how I phrased this. "I'm not making the kind of progress I need to make." I braced for incriminations.

"I can see that."

"You can?" I never thought she noticed.

"Maybe *too* comfortable."

Levi ambled in. "What's too comfortable?" He assessed my

ass. I looked back to her. She assessed him. I stood and rinsed the towel.

"Eunis is going to a genetics conference today."

"Really."

"I think it will be good for her. Time for her to get out, have other interests."

"But you'll still live here," he said.

"I'm just going to a conference, hoping to find someone who might help take my research to the next level. But soon, I'll need to—"

"Levi, it's time to let the little girl fly."

He gave her a sour glance. "Well," he said turning to me as I inched to the door, "I like having you here."

"You've both been great." I checked my watch, slipped on my shades. "I've got to go."

☽☽☽

After verifying my pre-registration and clipping on my nametag, I put my head down and did my best to cut through the thicket of people, an aisle seat in mind. No such luck; only middle row seats available. I sat in the rear. Careful not to step on his feet, I acknowledged the guy to my left, studied the syllabus for the umpteenth time, and anchored my eyes on the empty lectern.

A young woman gave the welcoming introduction. She was easily ten years my junior. I contemplated leaving. I was in over my head. But wedged in left and right, I waited.

She reminded us of the closing keynote speaker and drew enthusiastic applause. Some in the auditorium scattered to other presentations. I didn't move. Rolf Lund was speaking on Genome Integrity and the Healthy 46. I needed to learn all I could about those forty-six separate chromosome sequences in the human genome.

My main target, Lund was an expert in epigenetics, and a square man: head, nose, shoulders —all tall and square like a stack of children's building blocks with a widow's peak and crew cut.

"Professor Lund?" My heart pulsed; a series of dull heavy blows, someone striking an anvil. I'd waited till the rest of the admirers dispersed for coffee break prior to the next breakout sessions.

"Yes."

"Like everyone else here I'm excited by your research. Really excited."

"That's very kind of you."

"And I'm wondering . . ."

"Yes?"

"I'm wondering . . . I've been researching the coordinates of human beauty for a long time. I'm working in a research facility that's tangentially studying attractiveness."

"Different things, attraction and beauty."

"Yes, precisely. I want to find the code, the Facial Beauty Code, whatever that mix is, and eventually make it available to the general population."

He whistled, a long low one. "That's quite formidable. And the sequencing . . ."

I nodded. "I'm wondering if someone like you would be willing to take me under your wing and help me work to the next level. Be my molecular research mentor?"

"Well . . ." He pursed his lips and studied me, no doubt considering the enormity of such a project and the potential public scrutiny it might bring. "Do you have a background paper on this?"

I gulped. He was interested! "I do." I shuffled clumsily through my briefcase.

"Eunis Cloonis?"

Professor Lund looked over my shoulder and up.

"Eunis Cloonis?"

Past her midsection, tilting my head up, up, she was the tallest woman I'd ever seen, maybe five inches short of seven foot. She stood much taller than Lund, with a forehead rising more than half her long face.

"Yes."

"Detective Gergis, NYPD." She showed me her credentials. "We need to talk."

Professor Lund promptly excused himself.

"Sir? Professor . . . !"

He didn't look back. A whirlpool sucked me down, consuming me.

𝄞𝄞𝄞

On the way to the precinct Detective Gergis told me how she'd been to my apartment, left notes, had been calling for weeks. I lost much of her early babble, still fixed on Professor Lund's square shoulders as he wandered away from me.

She was a neophyte vegan, distrustful of her building's new superintendent, allergic to almonds, a big Mets fan. "You know Zoe Lowenstein."

"A little." It was one of those older precincts, reminded me of elementary school. Her desk, like Harold's, was oak, but unlike his, was cluttered with papers, a Mr. Met bobble head, and three mostly-completed Royal Crowns.

"They have bone marrow, you know." I pointed to the colas.

"Oh." She gathered the bottles and dropped them into her wastebasket. "I'm not sure about this vegan thing." She shuffled through some papers; picked up none. "An administrator at Hunter College says she spoke to you; you were asking about Zoe. Why?"

"She's interested in some of the things I'm interested in."

"Like?"

"Social science."

"You tracked her down because she's one of a million people in this city interested in social science?" She unclipped a pen from her shirt pocket.

"No, because of these." Off came my shades then I replaced them. "If you've met her you know she's very self-conscious about her lazy eye."

Detective Gergis' shoulder dipped, more of a spasm. Hang a basket around her neck and you could've used her forehead as a backboard. She waited for an explanation, pen suspended. She clicked it open. I was only seconds ahead of her.

"Why me and Zoe? I'd seen her and, if you must know, I thought she was cute. What did Zoe say?"

"That's between me and Miss Lowenstein. You're aware that someone hijacked a Times Square billboard."

"I'd heard something like that. Saw the headlines. Didn't

sound too important."

"Important to the billboard company. Twenty-seven minutes of Kate Upton interrupted."

"Really." I didn't hide my disdain.

"It's amazing what's worth $5,000 today." The detective hinting at accord.

"Five K for twenty-seven minutes of Kate Upton?"

"She's more expensive. This was just for the lost media time." She fixated on the Royal Crowns in the wastebasket. "You're sure about the bone marrow?"

"Pretty sure."

"Zoe Lowenstein."

"What I know of Zoe, she's a very nice person. I don't think she was attracted to me. It's not the first time." I waited as she slid more papers around her desk. "Anything else?"

"Where were you that evening?"

"What evening?"

"Christmas Eve."

"In my apartment."

"Anybody with you? Anybody who can corroborate where you were?"

I had to think a moment. "Actually," I said, marveling, "yes, the president of my homeowner's association, a woman named Helen Dorward. I'm afraid she doesn't think very highly of me. Also a man named Malcolm, a patient at the Metzinger Clinic."

"Really, *two* alibis?" She jotted something on the back of her hand.

"Do you need anything else?" *Get me out of here.*

"Why would they need bone marrow?"

"Not my field of study."

"What is your field of study?"

Now I'd done it! "Lab technician, pharmaceuticals. Anything else?"

A woman in uniform dropped a new stack of papers on her shale-shifting desktop. "Not for the time being. Answer your phone next time."

She ushered me into the lobby; I didn't look back, eyes

straight ahead. I reached the street and began walking —not clear in what direction, *just get away*. My phone buzzed. My first thought: *she wants me to come back in. They found another link to me.* I considered letting the phone buzz —at least until I was several blocks away and could offer to come in *tomorrow*, while I sorted things out. But it was buzzing against my chest. "Shit."

I stopped. People pushed past me in both directions.

"Yes?" I answered without even looking.

"Eunis, damn am I glad I found you girl. I need your help."

"Who is this?"

"It's Lyle. Look, I can't talk long, they said I only have three minutes. You're my one call."

"What?"

"I need a lawyer and I need you to bail me out. It's bullshit. My dick boss thinks I took some cash, but I didn't. I only borrowed it. I was gonna give it back next shift."

"Your boss?

"I've been delivering pizza. Here in the city. Ya gotta bail me out. I'm at the 82nd Street precinct. Eunis?"

From one precinct to the next, venues I could do without. "Yes?"

"You gotta get me outta here."

CHAPTER THIRTY-TWO

Roddy exited the holding area. "He's out, Eunis. Bail covered. They're releasing him."

"Thanks, I didn't know who else to call."

"I'm glad you did. My chance to make it up to you."

Lyle brushed himself off as he slammed open the door into the lobby. "Complete bullshit."

"Let's get you both home." Roddy held open the door to the street.

Home? Not even in my own body was I home anymore. I hadn't considered the next stop. Had barely taken a breath. The others halted with me, as if I was somehow in control.

"Bloomfield, that's a Jewish name, huh?" Lyle shoved a bright yellow and black-striped "Hollywood Pizza" hat into his back pocket. "I guess most lawyers are."

Roddy responded with a generous smile. "So you're Eunis's brother."

I came to the surface. "Half-brother."

"Not only a Jew," Roddy said placing his hand firmly on Lyle's shoulder, "but half black too."

"Go on!" said Lyle. "You are not—"

"I can make it home on my own, thanks." I hoped they both noticed my uncompromising tone. I wanted them out of my sight, both of them, until I could figure something. *Figure* what, *believe* what? Was I going to believe anything my kinetic brain told me? It wasn't like my kidney was acting up. There were treatments for that. Pills. *But curing my thoughts?*

"You're very kind, Roddy. I don't know how to properly thank you." Actually, I did . . . *Eunis! Not everything is carnal. Yes, but gratitude could be sensual.* "Lyle would thank you too, if he thought about it. Wouldn't you, Lyle?"

"Well, sure." Lyle seemed bewildered.

Roddy leaned in front of him, looked directly at me. "Have dinner with me. Let's talk."

"I'm pretty hungry myself." Lyle scanned us, back and forth. "But ahh, I'm a little tight on cash . . ."

"I can't."

"Why not?" Roddy's arms hung to his sides. No armor, no pretense.

"Course if I could borrow something from you, Sis, I could pay you back."

"Sis?!" I fixed Lyle with bemusement; he closed his mouth. I turned to Roddy, his aging yet enduring face. *Don't look away.* "I don't know who you are . . . " I explored his terrain: the vibrancy of his slightly rucked skin, a light tan, the color of fall flame grass plumes.

"I'm not so hard to understand." Even then whimsy teetered on his lips, like he was appreciating my obstinance.

"Well, I'm grateful for what you've done."

His eyes offered an unhurried mutability, like the waterways that freed my body, frictionless and searching me.

"You keep showing up and I really appreciate it."

"You would do the same."

"How 'bout the dinner we was talkin' about?" Lyle clueless.

"It's been a long day, Lyle." I turned to Roddy. "Please understand, and tell Elizabeth, hi." I started down the street.

"You're always walking away," he called.

I waved my arm above my head.

Roddy told Lyle, "Go take care of your sister."

"We have time for dinner?"

"Go!"

Where to head next, The Octagon or Levi and Nan's? Unfortunately Roddy's hillside was the only destination that appealed to me.

"Somethin's wrong with your phone." Lyle hustled up to me. "I been tryin' for more an a week. It's blocked or somethin'. Finally gave up."

Like it was my fault he was in town and already in trouble.

"Anyways, what do ya think about some dinner?"

I just kept walking, still wasn't sure where. Maybe I hoped

he'd fall away, like an ionized atom. But he kept tagging along.

"I'm powerful hungry, Sis."

Rolf Lund liked my idea. How to get back to him? Or had that possibility been lost? I pulled my hair away from my neck. Maybe the evening air would revive me.

"After some food can I stay with you because—"

"No." I finally looked at him.

"My boss threw me out."

"Mine too," I said. "Your boss, you live with your boss?"

"Cheryl. A woman. She's holding my Martin ransom."

I considered the inference. I decided I was in no position to judge. "You'll have to pay off your bail. You're not sticking Roddy with it."

"Course not. He'll get his money. Jews always do."

"You ungrateful son of a bitch!" I slapped him full palm, wasn't sorry at all. In fact, I *hoped* it hurt. He was stunned, but probably not the first time for Lyle.

"Same bitch raised you." He rubbed his cheek. "So, okay, this guy's your friend, sorry, but I gotta find a place to stay tonight. And I'm *real* hungry."

This ass was actually related to me. *What next?* Focus. Down the street was . . . the oasis! "I've got just the place. But you'll have to put up with black people. You think you can handle that?"

"O' course. I ain't got nothin' against black people. They're some of the best musicians in the world."

"Come on." Half way down the block we stepped into Ruthie's Roti. Around my heart frequencies started percolating.

"Welcome." He was tall, African, in his thirties. The veins in his forehead bulged. "What is your pleasure?"

It wasn't just that he spoke crisply, almost like an Englishman, but the *quality* of his voice was . . . cultured. I gave a head feint in Lyle's direction. "He's hungry." Not, *my brother's* hungry.

"Sir?" he said to Lyle, revealing broad, unattractive gums. His hair was close-cropped with stunted dreds. A short black beard set off wide lips. "What can we get you?" He was freshly scrubbed, and on the way to the food I caught a hint of soap as I passed him. A pleasant face —almost handsome if he refrained from smiling.

"Sistah doon-doos, you back!" A sudden gust, Ruthie chugged into the room. "Anthony, what they need?"

"She and this gentleman just walked in."

"What's that stuff over there?" Lyle pointed to the steaming chaffing dishes.

"Curried goat," said Anthony.

"Thanks." Lyle waved it off. "I can wait."

"What *is* your name, sistah?" Ruthie offered me a seat and patted my knee. "Good you back."

"Eunis."

Ruthie checked me, then Lyle. He was hoping for a place to rest his eyes but it wasn't on this large albino woman.

"I'm with her." Lyle, still the little lost boy I remembered.

"Yes," Ruthie said disapprovingly, then returned to me. "What you think? Ready for room?" Her boulder-of-a head tipped skyward then back. She stood and held out her hand. "Come, c'mon. Just look."

"I'm not really—"

"I'll be heading to the museum in about ten minutes," said Anthony puttering with the chafing dishes. "You okay here?"

"Love you." Ruthie threw him a kiss, her large arm flapping.

"Love you." He returned the kiss.

She lifted me out of the chair and shuttled me toward a white flickering light around the corner. "You too," she said nodding to Lyle.

The beaded curtain bounced off my face and shoulders, sounding like rain as we moved through it. I questioned the cleanliness of those beads. The tempo around my heart escalated.

"This Eunis, everyone," announced Ruthie to the three women and the little boy seated around the oval Formica table. A TV was on in the background, the volume turned low, thankfully.

Lyle shifted uncomfortably, head down.

"Your name again?" Ruthie asked him.

"Lyle. I'm her brother."

"Half-brother." For the first time I noticed that Lyle's cowboy shirt was streaked in sweat. Embarrassing.

"Lyle," repeated Ruthie to the group that had stopped gabbing and looked up at us intruders —except the little boy, who grunted and whacked his mound of rice with a large spoon.

"Anthony Junior," said the teenage girl next to the boy, ostensibly his very young mother, "you stop that." The boy glanced at her and, as she looked back to me, went back to hammering his food. The mother needed to be firmer with her son.

"Sorry." She grabbed the spoon from her four-year-old.

"Ow!" The TV threw a beige cast on the little fella's skin.

"This Simone." Ruthie introduced the teenage mother. "And Vinnette and Brytney."

"What's wrong with her face?" asked the little boy pointing at me. "Is she a duppy?"

"No," said Ruthie. "She our friend. She our sistah. But she carry a duppy with her."

"No such things as a duppy, Granma." Simone put down her fork. "Don't scare Junior."

"You don't be so sure. When you grow, you see." Ruthie faced the woman in the pink workout suit. "Vinnette understands, don't you, child?" Vinnette's thin spectacular face turned into the light, her sable hair pulled tight in a ponytail.

I swallowed. She was that beautiful. It was a face you'd see in fashion advertising, except her neck had several unnatural lumps along it.

Anthony Junior again grasped at the spoon and Simone caught his hand.

"Ow! Ow!" cried the little boy and burst into tears. "Ow!"

"What's the matter with him?" asked Ruthie.

"He says his hand's been hurting." Simone passed him the spoon but he kept crying.

I leaned forward. "Can I see?"

"You a doctor?" Brytney looked up from her food, searched for the glasses perched on her head.

"No, but can I see?"

Simone made sure with Ruthie, who affirmed with the slightest tip of her head. Anthony Junior wanted no part of me and leaned against his mother. "Let the lady look at your hands."

He stuck his free hand out, staying close to Simone.

Carefully, I touched his hand and he winced. "That hurts?"

He nodded.

"And this?"

"Ow."

His skin. He didn't share skin tone with his mother or with Anthony, his dad, who I'd met in the outer room. "How old?"

"Four and a couple months," offered Simone. "Why?"

"Have his hands always been this swollen?"

"He's been playing outside in the cold."

"And then in here where it's pretty warm."

Junior pulled his hand away from me.

"Yes, so what? What's wrong?" Simone was quickly anxious.

"Well, I could be wrong, of course, but—"

"But what?" asked Ruthie.

I faced Simone. *Be gentle.* "Have you or Anthony been tested for the HbS gene?"

"I don't know what that is."

"I could be wrong."

"Wrong about what?"

Don't overly alarm them. "There's a chance he has dactylitis, a form of sickle cell anemia. His hands are puffy, and look at his skin." I reached for Anthony Junior's face. Again he drew away from me. "It's yellowish, can you see? Has it always been like that?"

"No." Simone began to well up.

Brytney clutched Simone's arm and pulled the glasses off her head, fixing me with anger. Ruthie came across the room, stood behind Simone, squeezing her shoulders. "Shush, shush," she said. She'd lost her carefree demeanor.

"No, it's okay." *Don't scare Anthony Junior.* "There are two tests, a DNA test for you and Anthony Sr. and another —it's called electrophoresis— for Anthony Jr. It tests hemoglobin, blood. If you and Anthony Sr. both have the HbS cell, there's a chance Anthony Jr. has the—" The little boy and his mother both looked terrified. "It's manageable, more now than ever."

"He's sick, oh lord." Ruthie slumped.

"Even if he has it," I tried to make eye contact with each of them, "he should be fine with treatment. And the tests are mostly painless."

"Oh my god." Simone hugged her child, fought back tears. Brytney covered her mouth.

"Are the tests expensive?" Vinnette put an arm around Simone.

Ruthie set doleful eyes on her great grandson. "We don have insurance." She looked up. So many distraught faces, all watching me.

"There's equipment at the lab." *What was I saying!*

Brytney squinted. "You have the equipment?"

"Could you?" asked Simone. "Please."

What had I just done? They were all mute yet pleading. "It'll take a few days. I'll do what I can." But I knew that if I was right, I'd be unleashing financial problems that would cripple them — the whole family. And I thought of Momma's admonition and how —*tussers* or not— I continued to bring trouble to everyone.

"Eunis," interrupted Lyle, "can we get goin'?"

Even Ruthie could see my irritation, my rush of anger. "You can't come with me, Lyle. That's it."

"No," Ruthie shook her head. "You right, bad idea."

He gave her a dirty look then thought better of it.

"You stay here," she said to Lyle. "We got room upstairs. Couple nights."

He was speechless.

"He has no money," I said.

"Who has?" Ruthie motioned Lyle to come closer. "It be okay, trust me." She pat me on the shoulder and escorted me to the door. "But that room be yours when you come back, sistah."

"He's trouble," I said aside, guilty for saying it. But I'd have felt worse if I hadn't warned her.

"Don't you worry. You think careful. Loud up di ting."

My mouth went slack, I didn't understand.

"You clean up your business, okay?"

"Yes."

"And thank you. I knew you special, and not just cuz you special like me."

CHAPTER THIRTY-THREE

It was closing in on midnight. Something fresh infused the evening, something I couldn't quite taste, a tide that lifted me up, reminded me of bounding rhythmically around in The Beaver, with no history to burden me. Being useful. I saw it in Ruthie's eyes. I was being useful and that made a difference. It made me lighter.

Across the open Octagon lobby, shoulders back, I resolved not to change course, regardless of who appeared. As I got into the elevator a hand reached in to stop the doors from closing. *Cufflinks.*

"Sorry," he said before I even saw his face. It was the distinguished sixty-something gentleman, wearing the same blue striped suit and still carrying a newspaper tucked under his arm. "Oh, it's you."

"Yes." I focused on the floor display above. I shoved my hand into my skirt pocket to ground myself, surprised to find the feather Levi had given me still wedged in there. Even as the elevator doors closed, atoms bounced around the elevator cage. I removed the feather and looked at it again.

"A wren feather?" he asked.

"Why yes." Again I was puzzled. But I hardly glanced at him.

"Good if you're a sailor. It'll keep you from shipwreck or drowning."

"Oh, okay." He didn't look like the superstitious type.

I stuck it back in my pocket. We rose silently and I felt our mutual discomfort, which is why I suppose he offered more small talk.

"You see the latest news on that Times Square caper?" He tapped his paper, eyes also on the LCD display.

"No, too busy in the lab."

"A lab? What kind?"

"Pharmaceuticals. What about Times Square?"

"They say they have several suspects. Personally I think it's interesting what they did, quantifying facial beauty or something like that, wasn't it?"

The day's encounters with Ruthie's family and Rolf Lund must have reorganized my matter because I heard myself pushing the conversation. "I'm not sure, but can I ask you something?" I took my eyes off the indicator and turned to him. *Breathe.*

"Yes." He turned to me, as if it were a normal request from a normal person.

"Working in a lab," *and as isolated as my rats,* "I'm something of a research junkie, and as you can see from my appearance, not the most attractive person in the world . . ."

He clicked his tongue and shook his head, demurring.

". . . But what elements of the face might someone like you find beautiful?"

"Someone like me?"

Attractive, like in GQ. "You're obviously successful and probably well-educated, if that isn't a rude generalization."

He laughed. "It's not rude, but why does it make a difference?"

"I'm not sure that it does, but you just happened to get stuck in here with me, so . . . what do you find most beautiful in a face?"

"Don't you think that's subjective? One man's opinion?"

"Okay, maybe. But there must be something. Some *things* you look for in a face."

"Lots of things, I guess." He chuckled. "Never thought about it much."

"Tell me one." I kept eye contact.

"One. Very well. That you faced that mob, that you stood up to them." He stretched out his hand and I took it hesitantly. "James Dorward, Jim. I live on the eleventh floor." His hand was cool, not cold, and quite pleasant. He let go, reluctantly, it seemed. "I'm Helen Dorward's husband."

"Dorward." The pressure inside the elevator and in my chest and throat was still rising.

"Yes."

I exhaled deeply. "Your wife is the President."

"Only of the Homeowners Association." He smiled. "Although she often thinks of her position and domain as grander, without, of course, the *noblesse oblige.*"

"I don't understand."

"It doesn't matter really. But you were treated badly. You didn't deserve that, although your response to the HOA was a bit—"

"Terse."

"Yes." He shook his head. "But I would probably have said the same thing. Anyway, if you've been to your apartment you know that your key still works. Your lease-to-buy option does not allow you to be formally evicted if you've paid the first half year in advance, which apparently you did."

He was really quite attractive. I'd like to have quantified him.

"And the HOA cannot keep your deposit unless you've been legally evicted, which they cannot do for another thirteen days when your advance rents will be used up." He touched the side of his nose. "You know the saga: The Ides of March, the assassination of Caesar. *Se défaire.* Chase out the old. It's an opportunity."

"Thirteen days?"

"Lucky thirteen."

A superstitious GQ. Still, the fundamental forces holding my atoms and molecules together were clearly shifting, I couldn't deny that. I had thirteen days to embrace the change or be blown apart.

He stretched his neck and I heard it click. "Something else."

"What's that?"

"Your hair."

"My hair?"

"It's like white lightning, hypnotic. And this . . ." he said, stepping out of the elevator door and siphoning with him the unmistakable energy, "is my floor. Goodnight."

)))

The splendor of New York's skyline twinkled before me, the

high back chair a throne. I'd resurrected two candles and their light illuminated the rubble surrounding me. *Hypnotic hair.* I ran my fingers through it, pulled it forward and studied it. Just my usual achromatic hair.

Clean up the business. Harold's box of books reached out for me. I stared back at it. Somewhere in there was that Dickens quote that Harold so often repeated, now so annoying and so damn prescient: "An idea, like a ghost ..."

Outside, the wind buffeted my windows. I heard it wailing. Harold had quoted Dickens so many times. I searched my memory for just the right one, the one that might offer an answer, a way out. Words fluttered around my head like moths, but nothing alighted. On the floor, jumbled amongst the detritus: *Hard Times* and *Bleak House* and Poe's *Tell-Tale Heart.*

I *did* have a duppy. Admitting it drew an inkling of fear and relief. Momma would have been pleased; she always thought I needed an exorcism. How I would do it was another question, but I could start by cleaning up the mess I'd allowed to amass around me.

"I can fix this." I lifted myself up and began to collect the debris scattered throughout the apartment. One dish. A mug. Both chipped. A spoon, bent. They went into the large plastic trash container from under the sink. I picked up a torn Life & Style Weekly, considered it, and tossed it into the bin. I righted the two kitchen stools. My shoe crackled over glass. My diploma, wrenched from its frame, tattered but salvageable. I folded it and put it in my pocket, admittedly a prideful act signifying some misbegotten vanity. I re-stacked *Bleak House,* the Poe short stories, and the other Dickens books that Elizabeth had removed from Harold's box. They went into a grocery bag, determined this time to actually read them.

I wiped the counters; I swept up. I straightened the high-backed chair, the triangular table, and the stools one last time. Candles snuffed and discarded with the rest. All but the bag of liberated books and Harold's large box of books went down the incinerator shaft.

Next step: Nan and Levi.

CHAPTER THIRTY-FOUR

"Did you know," I whispered loudly to the sleeping Nan, pulling off my clothes and snuggling in between her and Levi, "that a 1995 study by Thornhill found that women have more orgasms when their men have balanced facial features and bodies, regardless of their romantic attachment or the guys' sexual experience? Is that nuts?"

Levi snorted and rolled over. "Wha, what?"

Nan, groggy, peeked over to the bedside clock. "It's not even five AM."

I was in Nan's face, pulling back her ebony hair. "What is it exactly that drew you to Levi? That first thing? What made him beautiful, handsome to you?"

"It's late. Go back to sleep." Her eyes already closed again.

"No, come on. First thing."

"Are you crazy?" Nan waved me off.

"What does a perfectly beautiful woman like you find enticing, what was the first thing?" My lips purred close to her ear. "First thing?"

"Ah . . ." She was disoriented, eyes still closed. "I don't know . . ."

"Come on."

"Probably his tattoo. Go to sleep."

"His snake and mermaid?"

"What? It's a serpent. Yes."

"Why?"

Nan opened her eyes. "Listen, where were you—?"

"Why?" I persisted.

"I don't know. The tattoo, the serpent, and Atargatis together, they made him look . . . dangerous."

"You liked that."

"Yes."

"Why'd you get your tattoo? Did you want to look danger-ous too?"

"I *am* dangerous, that's why I got mine." She crooked her head back.

"Okay, move over, I want to fuck your husband." I climbed over Nan, spooned around Levi, and reached to fondle his dick.

"Damn it, get away from him!" Nan began to clear.

Levi started to awaken.

"You know what else is crazy?" I continued over my shoul-der to Nan as I brought Levi to life. "They have machines that rank facial features and create algorithms of desirable elements of attractiveness. And according to some, it's stress that deter-mines how the face develops. Stress, we all got that. So what was it about *their* story —the attractive ones— that made their lives less stressful?"

Levi moaned.

"Get your hands off him, his body's mine! I say *when*. I *own* him."

"Or was it that they were less stressful in their lives simply because they were attractive?"

"Mmmm." Levi reached behind for me. "You're so good, Eunis. It's beautiful what you do."

"Get the fuck out of our bed!" screamed Nan, now fully awake and thrashing the pillow. She readied to strike me before Levi reached up and stopped her fist mid arc.

"Okay." I let go of him.

"No. Nooo!" groaned Levi. "Why the fuck did you do that, Atara? Eunis, come back here."

"Maybe tomorrow," I said exiting the room. "Maybe." Over my shoulder I heard Levi continue his rant. "What the fuck is the matter with you?"

"She's a bitch. And fucking ugly too," Nan shrieked.

"I think that depends on who she's fucking."

"Asshole."

☽☽☽

The next morning, around fifteen minutes after I heard the front door slam behind Levi, Nan came into my room. "I think you better leave."

I stretched lazily on the big bed. "Why? I like it here." I yawned expansively and prepared for her attack.

"We don't need you anymore."

"You needed me?"

"We tried to help you out but you obviously don't know your limits."

"But I like Levi, Leviathan. I like his dick, and he likes my—"

"I said get out."

"But we were having so much fun."

"The fun is over. Besides, I've got someone else coming in. You're taking up space."

"There's so much I still need to study. I want to take measurements of your face. You're so, so beautiful."

"Well, ya can't." Nan threw her head skyward, as if taking a mental snapshot of herself.

"Hmm. Will Levi be happy that you're throwing me out?"

"He'll like your replacement. He always does. He likes freaks."

"I see, and you so beautiful, so perfect. Well, let's make a deal."

"Just get out." Nan advanced toward me.

No blade in her hand. Could I take her in a fight? Maybe in a *fair* fight. Maybe if I had clothes on; *ridiculous.* "I don't think so." *Breathe.* "I'll be here when Levi returns and we'll see what he says."

Nan went no farther. "You know that brown shit you have on your face?" She stabbed a finger at me.

"Congenital melanocytic nevus."

"Yeah, that shit. Well the lore behind that that . . ." Nan circled her hand in the air unable to restate the technical name.

"It's a birthmark."

"Yeah, well you got it because when your mother was pregnant she never got what she wanted. And you won't either. So take your favorite dress and get the fuck out." Her face was taut, her eyes flaming. She showed teeth. *A demon.*

Never get what I want. I continued to luxuriate in the bed, for Nan's sake, slipping the sheets over and around me, taunting her without a word. As I did, her face softened. Just like that, the flow reversed, water tugged around my feet, coursed between my toes. As if the tide had shifted to her command.

My thighs quivered to the rhythm of the sheets. I was swimming in them. My belly tingled. My chest opened. My nipples became erect. I was aroused. I'd lost control. My resistance siphoned off with the surf.

"What kind of deal?" As if her munificent current swept away all hostility, she bowed to me. "Maybe we should take a nice warm tub together and talk this out."

An accord? Nan's strong hands rubbing down my shoulders, the loofah on my spine; our bodies touching each other, then separating, then slipping together again, folding in to each other. *Her hair, those aquamarine eyes, so pleasing . . . even when she was angry.* Especially *when she was angry.* Desire engulfed me: bathe away the hurtful words, return to pleasure.

"Come." Nan undid the tie from her raven hair and shook it out, the strands falling like satin around her bronze shoulders and flawless neck.

I ceased moving among the sheets. Ruthie wagged her finger at me. *Fight, fight back.*

"No," I said sitting up rubbing my shins. "No tub. The deal is: a patient at the hospital. I want you to check how he's doing. Where he is. Malcolm somebody, has PSP. You've heard of the guy. Thinks he's Charles Dickens part of the time."

"That's it? That's what you want?"

Clean up my mess. "For now."

Nan dripped sweetly, "How soon will you get your fuck-ugly face out of here?"

She was planning something. "You know, *Atara* —it is Atara, isn't it— that depends on how fast you get me the information. My phone is miraculously working again. Why don't you call me from the hospital and I'll be gone by the time you return."

"Why should I do anything for you?"

"Levi. I think he likes me."

"You're full of shit. But okay. Then you better be gone."

"And by the way," I didn't miss a beat, combing my fingers through my own mane, "if the information is not complete, I'll be back. I'll come visit Levi. So get it right the first time. I don't want to play detective on this one."

))))

The minute Atara left the room I sprang out of bed, dressed, and collected my few possessions: my laptop, my grocery bag of books; my cell phone. I checked the phone's settings and, sure enough, almost everything had been turned off. *Sonovabitch.*

As I waited for Atara's call, I wandered nervously, distracted. I wanted to remember that place, remember it clearly. I wanted to commit to memory my secret addiction to the physical.

In the Moroccan Room, my phone rang. "Okay, bitch," said Atara, "here's your info: Malcolm Jones was a patient until recently. Delusions of Charles Dickens, etc. etc. But he's gone now. Released almost two months ago. They couldn't do any more for him here."

"Home town?"

"Nothing in the intake forms or in his history. But with *your* history maybe an extended trip to the psych ward would be good for *you.* I can arrange it. Levi and I can't do any more for you, so get the fuck out before I'm home or serious shit is gonna come down on you." She hung up.

There, at the lip of the oval tub, both beckoning and repelling, was the X-Men Wolverine comb. Part of Ruthie's legend. Electromagnetic forces, I guess, I pocketed it and quickly left the apartment.

))))

After a day of searching homeless shelters, calling hospitals and clinics, no one had ever heard of Malcolm, nor of his Charles Dickens alter ego. The police were of no use, and it really wasn't a department I wanted to stir up. I could only hope that Malcolm had found a home or that he had passed peacefully and with some dignity. I'd been of no help.

At Ruthie's, Simone sat at the kitchen table reading a book to Anthony Jr. She made brief eye contact, but I enjoyed a homecoming welcome from Anthony and Vinnette while Lyle, concurrently clinging to and lightly strumming his recovered guitar, mooned over Vinnette.

The family's faith in me was overblown, especially with Warring finalizing my ouster, but I'd purchased the syringes. At least I'd be applying what I'd learned and I'd be useful —*if* I could get in and out of the lab, which I'd have to do quickly once I'd drawn their blood.

After putting down my laptop and the rest of my things, I drew samples from Simone and Anthony. Anthony Jr. was less receptive to me and my needle. "What a brave little boy you are," I said to him, but he had none of it, kicking and screaming that I scared him. "What are you reading to him?" I asked Simone.

"The legend of Jack Mansong." She showed me the cover.

I placed the syringe to the side. "So Anthony, you like Jack Mansong?"

He stopped sniveling. "He was brave and kind."

"What did he do?"

"He was a slave and he freed other slaves. He had magic Obi."

"Is that a picture of him on the cover?"

"Yes."

"He had three fingers."

"Yes."

"Doesn't that scare you?"

"No."

"But my face scares you. You're afraid I'll hurt you with the needle."

"Yes."

"But your great grandma has a face like mine, not dark and black like yours, and you love her."

He nods.

"Well, your mom and dad and grandma and great grandma all trust me, even though I look different. They let me take a sample. Can you be brave like your mom and dad? And see, I have *five* fingers." I wiggled them and tickled his side.

He giggled.

"You have five fingers too, but they hurt sometimes, don't they? I think we can make that pain go away. You just have to be brave like three-fingered Jack Mansong."

He looked at his mother. He looked at his father. They both nodded. He closed his eyes and stuck out his arm. I knew the feeling.

꩜꩜꩜

As I sealed Junior's sample and gathered up his parents' vials, I stared into Jack Mansong's eyes. In my haste I'd missed something important. "Oh no."

The others ceased their small talk.

"My scrapbook, it's back at . . ."

"No big deal," said Lyle putting out a cool vibe for Vinnette to see. She continued ladling soup into the chaffing dish.

"It *is* a big deal." Fifteen years of work and over 600 images quantifying beauty in that scrapbook, at least ten inches thick with *data*. "I have to go back."

"Go back where?" Ruthie walked into the storefront carrying a bolt of lime cloth.

"Back to the apartment where I was staying. And here," I fished through my pocket, "here's something for Junior's medical bills. Maybe you can get something for it, you know, a collector. I've read you can get good money for these things."

"What's this?" Ruthie turned the child's plastic comb over and over.

"You said Ribba Mumma's comb . . . I thought maybe . . ." I'd rationalized that I'd earned it, but I'd been complicit in petty theft.

"Worthless. It's a toy." Ruthie frowned, put the comb down. "You don't take legends seriously. Give it to Junior. Worthless." She brandished her meaty hand above her head like a parent fed up with trying to bring sense to things and turned with the bolt of cloth into the back room.

"You like art objects?" asked Anthony.

"No!" I was pissed at myself but taking it out on him.

"Well, you're always talking about beauty. Where I work we have a lot of beautiful things . . . antiquities, from ancient times. Not cartoon collector items like that." He dismissed the comb.

"I know what antiquities are. I'm not interested in beautiful *things*, but thanks."

"They're *historically* beautiful." Anthony dropped his shoulders and winked at Vinnette.

"Lyle," I said, "you still have your Hollywood Pizza hat? The yellow one?"

"Sure."

"Can you get a couple large pizza boxes?"

"I guess, why?"

"And buy two large frozen." I turned to Anthony and Vinnette. "When I get back can I use your kitchen to heat a couple pizzas?"

Anthony was entertained. "Of course."

"Good." I turned to Lyle. "Are you willing to help me?"

"I guess."

"Yes or no, 'cause it could be dangerous."

He peeked over at Vinnette. "I'm cool with danger." She pretended not to see, rocked her head, leaked a small smile, and continued turning the soup.

Foolhardy was probably more accurate and here I was walking us both into it.

CHAPTER THIRTY-FIVE

The front entrance to the lab was modern, faceless, a glass and brick building twenty floors high, designed by a world-renowned architect I'd never heard of. More than a million square feet, of which my employers leased 33,210 on two floors, and all I needed were five square feet of it, for less than an hour. Without my security passkey, not likely. But I had promised.

I'd entered through the front entrance once, the day I was hired and given my key. Now, having researched my target, I waited in its shadows like a thief, for the four AM bio waste crew to arrive, the paradoxical exit to my career. The March morning wind threaded currents through my hair. I shivered.

"Miss Flores." I greeted the crew chief with a smile. She was a small sturdy woman with quick dark eyes and a no-nonsense mouth. "I feel ridiculous . . ."

She waved the four-person crew through the front door with the swipe of her card and stepped in front of it as it closed. "Do I know you?"

"I work on the seventh, late shift, but I'm usually out before you get in. Lab nineteen."

She looked me over pretty good. "So?"

"There's a test I've got to complete before morning and I spaced it out, then left my card at home. I'm usually in bed by now."

Her mouth was tighter still. "This is my problem?"

"I can show you ID."

"Let's see."

I pulled out my Minnesota driver's license.

"You're the one they call *La Siguanaba*."

What did I say to that? "I've been called all sorts of names. Can you let me in?"

"It's your hair."

"What is?"

"The trap. Men see *Sigua* drawing her golden comb through her long, beautiful hair. They see her by the lakes and rivers, in the moonlight. Her body lures them till she turns and they see her face. She's a shape-shifter. Their souls are not safe."

"Can you let me in?"

"Sure, I *can*. But why?"

"Because you know I work here. I can describe every inch of those labs, and I can leave a mess that will reflect badly on you and your crew."

"Why would you do that?"

"Spirits have bad tempers, even the nice ones." I grinned. "I'm sure you've heard that. All I want is to finish my tests and get some sleep."

"I don't believe in spirits." She grinned back.

I deliberated knocking her down and kicking in her teeth. "What *do* you believe in?"

"*Tres ciegos ratones blancos*; three blind mice, white. My niece wants pet mice. She wants to save them from this place."

"We don't have any blind mice."

"She won't know the difference."

"A win for everyone." I held out my hand.

"Especially the mice." She shook it.

"Especially the mice."

〉〉〉

Think of a simple battery with positive and negative terminals. That was basically my power supply. The cathode and anode of the chamber attracted oppositely charged particles in the casting tray. In that tray the teeth of a comb left small holes in the gel when it cooled, and that's where I placed the blood samples. The equipment did the rest. Opposites attract, and I had my results.

Then to round up the mice and slip out undiscovered. I turned the corner.

"Excuse me," he said, his hulk blinking down at me. "What are you doing?" It was Eddie the large night watchman, sitting on the counter, chopsticks in hand, eating Chinese food out of a container, shoes and socks off, size-18 feet dangling.

"Tests," I said showing him the vials. "Tests I should have finished yesterday."

"Oh. Kinda late for you to be here." Even in the bright fluorescents his stout face was smooth and childlike.

"Yeah," I said. "Mmm, that smells great."

"Pork chow fun."

I looked longingly at his takeout.

"You haven't eaten?"

"Got so wrapped up, just forgot." I let my eyes fall to the floor, but I didn't move.

He looked at his remaining chow fun. "Well . . . "

"I guess you've got to finish your rounds, huh? You're on that silly clock. And I've got to get going."

"Oh, upstairs, yeah." He took one last look at his dinner. "D'ya want the rest?" He reached the box to me.

"Oh, I couldn't." I looked away again. I still didn't move.

"No, please. Take it. I was almost done. Better get to work. You won't mention this?"

"You're allowed to eat."

"No, actually I'm not. Not on duty."

"Well then, I'll just take *my* Chinese food home with me," I said accepting the chow fun.

He gave me a meek smile. "Thanks."

"No, thank you." I held up the box.

He ambled away, shoes and socks in hand. I heard the stairwell door close.

I dumped the remaining Chinese food in one of the bio waste cartons. I appropriated three of the older mice from my cages — no point damaging Elizabeth's reputation any further with mine already in the toilet— and left them in the takeout container on the shelf for Flores, next to the frozen dead who would be reduced to ash. Anthony Junior would require a bit more care.

☽☽☽

"The thing is, Lyle, just do what a pizza guy does. Don't take no for an answer. You can't take them back. Your boss will kill you. Say you'll leave them for free, if that's what it takes to get to the kitchen. Whatever. But they'll pay, so have a price in mind for two large pepperoni and green pepper pizzas plus tax. Bring the pizzas into the kitchen. Only the kitchen. Then I can slip in the front door."

"You're sure you can just waltz in?"

"Kitchen only. They'll be so hammered by eleven PM on a St. Patrick's Day night that you could feed them shit on a platter."

He gaped at me, like I wasn't the goody-two-shoes he'd remembered. And I wasn't.

"They'll still be happy. Numb. *And* fucking everything in sight."

Lyle cocked his head.

"Do not dabble in anything you are offered —drinks, drugs, smoke or sex— because this place is very fucking dangerous."

"How dangerous?"

"Not sure exactly." I swallowed the night air. "But what's going on in there, it's bad."

"What kind of sex? Better than being blown up to a Muslim?"

"Lyle!"

"So let's not go there for a stupid scrapbook of Momma's clippings."

"They're not Momma's clippings, they're mine. More than fifteen years of organizing and cross-referencing. I've got to have that binder back."

I'd looked at that scrapbook of faces and face parts thousands of times, tens of thousands of times. I still didn't see the code. But I knew it must be in there, somewhere. To let that book go would be giving up on my dream.

"So Lyle . . . Lyle! Listen to me. You get in and out. It's a bit of a maze the first time in the apartment. It's like a labyrinth, a ship's belly. Keep it simple: front door to kitchen, kitchen to front door. Goodbye, adios. You're just there to distract them. Once I'm in, I can find the scrapbook —it's not easily hidden— and I can get out on my own. Got it?"

"Just a pizza guy?"

"Just a pizza guy."

"I can do it." He nodded, assuring himself.

"Good."

"Can I bring my guitar?"

I cuffed his arm.

))))

At 11:15 PM Lyle and I had been watching people stream into Atara and Levi's apartment for nearly an hour. Over that time at least seventy-five percent of those entering were in some sort of altered state. It was obvious, the staggering path, the way they leaned on each other, the way they stood and stared at meaningless objects for minutes at a time before entering. I knew the feeling. Once they were in they were only going higher.

I didn't see a familiar face, which was good in case Atara had been bad-mouthing me, making me an outsider. More irony. I just had to hope Atara and Levi —what *was* his real name— had screwed their brains out and were not in the living room.

"You ready, Mr. Pizza?" Even with his thermal delivery box zippered shut I caught a whiff of oregano and pepperoni. *We could stay home and eat it.*

"You're sure this is gonna be okay?" As if this was the first he'd asked the question.

"No."

He smiled weakly. "Okay, then."

The street flowed unevenly with revelers —a leprechaun cocked hat here and there, some yelling or speaking loudly, others running through or dancing or singing. Even a young Chinese man swinging a shillelagh walked by, a cudgel to cure and maim. According to legend.

Lyle crossed the alleyway and jogged across the street. One glimpse over his shoulder and he was down the steps and ringing the basement doorbell. Memory of its angelic chimes reawakened me, and part of my body wished I was already on the other side of the door, merging into the tactile glow. Like the old days. Skin on skin.

Even at a distance Lyle was restless without the guitar in his arms, uneasy in his own hide. Whereas I'd become easy with my own and with others. *Was that true?*

He slouched and primped. Maybe it was the gaudy yellow pizza hat. Maybe it was the number of times he'd rung the doorbell. He looked back to me. Worry clamped around his mouth, soliciting retreat.

The door opened. I sucked air. I should never have gotten Lyle into it.

He talked to a woman I didn't recognize. Then he was in. *Don't turn around!* He pushed his heel against the door, leaving it ajar. *All right, Lyle!*

In seconds I was across the street and into the dimly lit apartment. Thick warmth massaged me. The tinkly piano welcomed me.

> *"You zombie*
> *Be born again my friend*
> *Won't you sign in stranger . . ."*

The lyric came mocking and, as I had hoped, bodies clasped, huddled, fondled, more interested in devouring each other than checking my ship passport. Lyle was in the kitchen accepting a joint from the woman and laughing. *Shit!*

Like my Minnesota woods, I'd mastered this terrain and I moved swiftly toward my old bedroom, the last place I'd left the scrapbook. On route I stepped over two men wrestling amorously in the Tapestries Hallway. Shirtless, white hair, lithe chest, Maurice. He didn't look up.

I skated past them into my bedroom —*my bedroom*— which I was surprised to find empty, though the bed had already been inaugurated judging by the nautical curls of blankets and pillows. In the small closet, a pair of men's Navy white dress pants, a dark blue double-breasted peacoat, but no scrapbook.

Next, the Moroccan Room, the room I'd *most* wanted to avoid, although it was possible Atara hadn't accurately communicated with Levi about my ouster. At its entrance I listened for activity. Voices.

"Aren't these wonderful?" said a woman, and before the answer came I envisioned Marguerite's flaming orange hair.

"Gorgeous," he said. "They feel gorgeous."

"Come," said Marguerite. "Nan has surprises for you too."

Peeking around the door, her naked, trim, re-engineered body and large breasts were silhouetted by the light blazing from the bathroom doorway. Facing her, a young sandy-haired man in his early twenties, easily forty years her junior and naked from the waist down, wore the remainder Naval service dress white t-shirt and a long-sleeved open-collared jumper. A dark blue neckerchief sat undone draped over his neck and chest.

"Come," she said again, taking his hand, pulling the neckerchief from his shoulders and draping it over hers as she led him into the bathroom, leaving the Moroccan Room empty.

I didn't hesitate. Moving stealthily though the room, I scanned for the scrapbook before searching the closet. There, on the shelf where I'd seen the miniature child's rake or brush, sat my binder. *Yes!* The euphoria, the adrenalin, I had to slow it down. *Be smart.*

I picked up a striped ottoman from the main room and placed it gingerly beneath the closet shelf, then pulled down my album. Like long-lost family, I pinned it to my chest and closed my eyes.

"Now you wait right there while I get Nan, okay?" I heard Marguerite tell the young sailor.

I lurked in the closet as Marguerite, humming, swayed unabashedly out of the room and closed the door. I was quickly out of the closet clutching my scrapbook and ready to escape. But I stopped. Frequencies radiated around my heart, leading me by invisible current to the bathroom.

The lights had been dimmed. Essence of sweet turmeric hung in the air. Candles ringed the large oval tub except where the young man sat passively on its lip. Not far from him lay the small brush/rake that I'd originally seen on the closet shelf.

I moved closer. "Are you okay?" I whispered.

The young man —a boy, really, I could now see— was startled. He shifted his head toward me but didn't turn to face me. "I'm waiting for Nan. Are you Nan?"

"No." My chest filled with liquid, the air squeezed out of me. "Maybe you shouldn't be here."

He stared intently across the tub to a bare wall. "I'm not sure. I've never done anything like this before."

I stepped closer to him. "What has Nan promised you?"

"I'm not sure. She said it's what every sailor desires."

I could barely contain my breathing. "I think you should come with me." *Come with me.* He turned, he looked right through me. "You're blind."

"Yes, Libya."

"Will you trust me? You shouldn't be here." I reached for him, like I was pulling him out of a deep well. He reached haphazardly for me.

"I think you're right." His voice shook. He began spinning nervously.

"Take my arm." His flailing knocked the bulky scrapbook to the floor and strewed pages across it. I let go of him and fumbled for my book. A mistake.

"Where are you?"

Just before he tumbled over I caught him and —like a hot poker branding me— heat seared from shoulder to sacrum. I was going to need both arms.

It was him or my scrapbook. All those years . . . all that would be denied me.

"I'm here." I gave him my hand just as Harold gave me his. "Follow me."

The small rake sat on the tub's edge. Fierce frequencies emerged from my heart, scorching rings that pierced my chest and banded me in fire. My right arm trembled, my veins popped, my hand closed to a fist with the pain. A fury took me from the inside, calling for force, anything to protect the young man.

The rake: *that* I could handle. I grabbed it with my free hand. *It could hurt if necessary.* I could kill if I had to.

I led him with certainty, *like Freyja the warrior,* out of the bathroom, out of the Moroccan Room and into the hallway. A very tall couple, draped on each other, came toward us. I let the rake fall to my side.

"Please trust me," I whispered to the young man, fastened my arms around his waist and hauled him to me, planting my lips ferociously on his. His arms flailed for a moment then settled around my head, his mouth opening wider, his tongue welcoming me in.

"A foursome?" wondered the dizzy woman, before her lanky partner yanked her farther down the hallway and I released the young man from our embrace.

"Don't stop." The young Navy man leaned into me for an encore.

I regarded the beautiful young boy with the empty blue eyes. "Let's get your pants back on." I directed him into my old bedroom. I closed the door. I couldn't let go of the rake; it had become part of me.

"I think I've found what I want," he said.

"Not tonight." I handed him his pants, then his peacoat.

He put them on begrudgingly and, as soon as he was done, I steered him back into the claustrophobic hallway. He ran his free hand down my body. "You feel *so* good. I've never felt anyone who felt so . . . complete, so right."

"You're young." I hustled him toward the living room and the front door.

"Hey, Eunis," said Maurice, now untangled from his man friend. "I was hoping I'd see you tonight. Maybe it's our night."

"That's sweet," I said, shoving the boy Adonis in front of me, out of the apartment, and up the steps to the sidewalk. A cab throttled down the street. Shouts and whistles hailed the cab; a rowdy bunch a half block away. I leapt off the curb and stood in front of the oncoming taxi. My hand tightened around the rake handle waiting for impact. The cab screeched to a halt.

"Geez lady," said the cab driver. Then seeing my face, "Oh my god!"

"You got money?" I asked the young sailor, propelling him into the cab.

"Yeah."

"You got an address here in the city besides this one?"

"Yeah, but you and I—"

"Take him home," I said to the cabbie. "And don't cheat him."

"You're beautiful," said the sailor.

"So are you." I tapped the side of the taxi. As it sped off I finally exhaled.

Oh, shit. Lyle.

CHAPTER THIRTY-SIX

Returning to the pleasure boat was madness. *Madness.* At least I could recognize that. I studied the odd child's rake. Its grip on me had loosened but I felt compelled to hold on to it, just in case.

Damn it, Lyle. Whatever happened to him would be my fault.

I checked my cell phone for the time. Jeez! I tried calling him. No answer, mailbox full.

Perpetually drowning, thoughtless, irresponsible and reckless. Always reckless. Heedlessly jumping into waters without measuring to the other shore. He didn't want to be saved. Perhaps a family trait.

I'd been a spectator long enough. I could have done what so many others have done; I could have tried to make a deal with God. But that was lazy. Even in that moment I could have promised God that if he let me safely rescue my brother, I'd give up the scrapbook.

And anyway, maybe it was the scrapbook's extra weight taking me down the vortex. All the hours I'd stared at those faces, tried to decode their common magnetism; it hadn't shown me the answers, it had only created more questions. Maybe it was time to let it go. It was a deal worth contemplating, but it was one I had to make with myself.

The front door finally opened and, child's rake ready, I pushed past two familiar women who greeted me without fanfare as I entered. I'd fully integrated into that society. There, at the bar, the same woman who let Lyle in, who offered the joint, was draped around his neck, a full Old Fashioned glass part of the ensemble. He was trying to break free.

A collective *oooh* issued from the Cinema Room, then applause, and I knew where most of the *benefactors* had congregated. The cinema door opened and the crowd began to file out, lead by Atara surrounded by four men, the most attractive a shirtless, curly-haired man. Atara laughed at something he said. He drew closer to her.

Particles dashed around my chest. I hustled across the room and stood directly behind the woman trying to suck Lyle's face, my back to Atara and her oncoming entourage. I tapped the woman's shoulder. When she turned around the best she could do was a little peeping sound, and her drink dropped to the floor, shattering.

"That hunk over there's been asking about you all night," I said. A head feint to the shirtless guy. "You don't want to miss out on him." As if I was experienced.

She turned and tracked him.

"Congratulations, you're a lucky woman." I grabbed Lyle as the woman gaped at the guy, then forlornly at her lost bourbon, and then back to Lyle.

"This guy, "I patted Lyle's shoulder, "he's a lot kinkier than he looks." I brandished the child's rake at her. "Trust me, he's more than you could handle. I know."

"But—" she said.

I nodded to the shirtless guy. "Delicious."

She took a step toward him.

And with that I marched Lyle to the front door, pushed it open and pressed Lyle through it, my second salvaged man of the night.

⟫⟫⟫

On the ride to Ruthie's we sat quietly in the squeaky cab, which sounded as if bolts were coming loose though neither of us dared mention them. Lyle stared straight ahead. I held the rake in my lap. Even without the scrapbook I was exhilarated.

"It's not like you to turn down an offer of anything, certainly not sex and drugs," I said.

Lyle stared ahead, like he didn't hear me.

"I'm glad you're safe . . . You don't usually follow directions."

He leaned to the side window, watched the street streak by. "I had a few tokes, a couple drinks." His breath fogged the window then disappeared.

"Yeah, but the sex? You looked like you weren't interested."

"Just didn't," is all he said.

So unlike him to show self-restraint, to actually *fight* it. "She wasn't bad looking."

"Wasn't interested, okay? Just drop it."

Maybe it was his lack of success with Vinnette. "Okay."

"D'ya get that all-important scrapbook you had to have?" Teeth in those words, he was angry.

I pictured it strewn across the Moroccan floor mopping up Atara's spillage, being shredded in a venomous fit, lost forever. "Why're you so angry? I thought you were cool with danger."

He sulked in the dark. I didn't push it.

☽☽☽

The next morning I took my place in the kitchen and setting my coffee on the table I addressed Ruthie. "I'm getting rid of the duppy."

She made a grunting sound and went back to skinning a goat, its head dangling, eyes absent. The last of its blood trickled into a large Maxwell House coffee can emblazoned with its ironic slogan.

"What's that?" Anthony gestured at the rake and opened the refrigerator. He poked around until he reemerged with a couple eggs then pecked Ruthie on the cheek.

"Don't know," I said. "Some kid's toy. Another one. A place like that, having kids toys around seems . . . I can't imagine a child being there. You saw the kid's plastic comb, the X-Men comb."

Ruthie grunted, concurring.

"Let me see." Anthony put down the eggs and picked up the rake with some reverence. The longer he inspected it the more contempt rose in his eyes. "Where'd you get this?" He turned it over.

Ruthie grunted again. I watched her. She held the carcass and pelt with her left hand, and making a fist with her right, slid it forward, separating the skin from the body. A large awl and a broad stubby knife lay on the counter to her right. Her neck glistened. Another grunt.

"Where'd you get this?" he asked again.

"A place I was staying. It has a strong strange smell –iron or something. Strange place for a child's rake. Never saw a child there, thank God, and there wasn't a blade of grass within two blocks. Nothing to rake."

"This isn't a rake."

"What do you mean?"

"You know what I do, right?" Anthony barely took his eyes off the rake.

"Something at a museum."

"I inventory for a curator at the Metropolitan. Middle Eastern stuff . . ." he fluttered his hand, "six hundred to twelve hundred." He rotated the rake again, carefully. "One of Muhammad's first converts to Islam —a very young man— was tortured with something like this."

Ruthie turned around. We all stared at the rake.

"It isn't a rake. It's a carding comb," said Anthony.

"Like for combing wool or something." Vinnette stepped into the kitchen and followed our eyes to the comb.

"Originally. Not this one. Observe the size of the teeth. And they're too rigid." He pushed lightly against one of them. It sliced him anyway, blood bloomed from his finger. "Shit! Sorry," he said to me, as if I'd never heard language like that.

I waved him off with a not-to-worry, never taking my eyes off the carding comb.

"The duppy," said Ruthie, alarm warping her face.

I glanced at her. "I don't think so."

"Somehow," she said. "You have more than one."

I refocused on the comb. Anthony carried on. "It could have gold in the handle, but even if it didn't it would be worth a lot of money. A museum piece. Who would want something so horrific in their home?"

"I can think of one woman," I said.

CHAPTER THIRTY-SEVEN

"It's not that weird, Sis. She just needs you." Lyle had gotten comfortable that week at Ruthie's and I hadn't. It wasn't just Ruthie's snoring.

"Please stop calling me sis." I paced, as much as it was possible in Ruthie's kitchen. "It's not like Carly couldn't take care of Momma for a while, Carly's her favorite."

Lyle took it like a punch to the stomach then tried to hide it by standing and walking to the fridge. But he'd just eaten, and left most of his food on his plate. He quickly ran out of room and paused.

"She loves you too," I said. "And why now?" Why when I had two days left on my apartment and serious questions surrounding my job?

"She says she's got real bad arthritis, gettin' to the end. Says she's dyin'." Lyle loitered on the thought. "Carly, ya know, she'll never stop what she's doin' until the funeral; maybe not even then. You're the responsible one."

"Dying? You talked to her doctor?" I shrank from the truth or lie of it, wanted nothing to do with the consequences of Momma's condition, whatever it was.

His eyes drifted across the kitchen to the darkened TV. He fiddled with a cabinet knob. "O' course."

"Hmm. What's the diagnosis?"

"I don't understand that stuff. Listen, the old buzzard needs you. She didn't sound too good."

"What about you?"

His face went deep and lost for a moment. "Ya know I wouldn't be any good at it. I'd forget her pills, or take 'em myself. She'd need me and I'd be out at some bar."

"Or getting laid."

Something stirred across his mouth, a grin gone melancholy,

something I hadn't seen before. I felt it too. Not wiseass as expected. More like he was slowly drowning and knew it. New York had failed him like all the rest.

I rallied past it. "You'd do fine with Momma and you don't have anything here. Might be good for you."

He gave me an are-you-kidding look.

"Sorry," I said. Momma couldn't be good for anybody except maybe Sarah Pooley.

"I'll be goin' too," he sniffed, "but I'm not made up for it. I ain't takin' care of Momma. I just ain't."

"You're going back? To Bemidji?"

"And you gotta come with me." *Come with me* looped around my brain. It sparked anger then resistance in my chest.

"I don't gotta do anything." I wagged my face in his.

He didn't back off, he didn't attack. "Sis—"

"Don't friggin' call me that!"

"You gotta come back." Matter of fact, guile gone from his face —first time I'd seen it in years.

I browsed Ruthie's linoleum. Spoke to the floor. "I have done my part. The woman is not good for me."

"Oh, and it's a fucking picnic for me."

Oh really! "You never did a ficking day of work that I ever saw. Of course you weren't home that much. *Except* the two times we had to bail you out. And now, miraculously, we have the third performance in the fucking series."

"Maybe that's all true. But my venues are gettin' bigger." He laughed at himself. He hung his head. "But she needs you."

"It's bullshit." I threw my glasses on the table.

))))

I circled the lab. Elizabeth was feeding her rat and spoke to me through a row of cages. "I guess it never occurred to Warring that Ruchika would screw up results on purpose, just to keep her contract re-vesting."

"Me neither."

"How'd she take your resignation?"

"She didn't really understand but she seemed sympathetic enough when I told her about my mother. She's happy with her cages and little else."

Elizabeth laughed. "Well, I care."

I rested my hand on her shoulder. She closed the cage and squeezed my hand without looking up. "I'm going to miss you," she said, then turned and gave me a hug. "I'm sorry."

"I'm sorry," I said.

We both got misty.

I patted her shoulder and walked away, ambling down the aisle, zigzagging from one side to the other, my hands a half inch off the mesh of cages —the whole row— listening and feeling for a clue.

At the end of the aisle I entered the lab 18 Mouse Room, the freezer buzzing for more attention. Without stopping I opened and grabbed the bag of frozen mice, breezed through the room and into the Rat Room, where I leaned against the larger freezer. Then opened the door and pulled the bag of frozen rats to the table. Another large haul.

I removed a cardboard bio waste box from the second shelf cabinet, unfolded it, laid first the mice, then the rats into their disposable coffin. Then I drew *Tell-Tale Heart & Other Stories by Edgar Allan Poe* from under my lab coat where I'd tucked it into my waist. Slowly, I opened the book for a final look.

Just like the first time I'd come upon it, I shuddered. It was no normal book. The pages had been mortised out, and in the guts of it lay a mass of mousey brown hair, a full scalp's worth, unclean, even at a glance. Eerie. Just gazing into it, it was a trap door I knew I couldn't enter without consequences.

Along the top layer were two braids of hair, each with the same orange and blue bead, the size of a small walnut. Despite my misgivings I ran my fingers along one of the braids. It was coarse. Oily. The smell. Like it'd been fermented.

My blank spaces propagated. The atoms again, the way my heart reacted to more and more. It was uncomfortable. Not all the time but . . . but I had set something in motion. Or perhaps my time had come. Whatever. A clue: that was progress, even if it scared me. Just doing *something* was better than not. Why Harold had that book, with that hair, panicked me. But I'd brought it from Bemidji and Bemidji had some answers. It was as good a reason as any to go back, since there really weren't any *good* reasons.

I closed the book. I placed the book in the box between the frozen mice and the frozen rats, doing my best to tuck it out of sight. I sealed the box and double-checked the seal. I placed the box into the lab 19 Biological Waste Freezer. The door closed with an irrevocable click. The box would be taken off site and incinerated.

〉〉〉

"Keep this in a safe place." I handed the torture comb to Anthony.

"Do you want me to get it appraised?"

"No, it's insurance." *I hope.*

"That's what I mean. The museum might buy it. Somebody will."

"No. You said it's pretty much one of a kind."

He nodded.

"And if it's that old and that valuable," I went on, "the owner probably had it appraised. And there'll be a record of that somewhere, something that identifies the current owner."

"Probably, yes, but—"

"I'm not the current owner, but I'll bet he —or she— wouldn't want to draw a lot of attention to this thing and themselves. There could even be DNA on it."

"DNA?"

"Keep it in a bag somewhere safe."

Veins in his brow swelled with worry. "If you stole it—"

"I traded for it. Trust me, it's my insurance."

"Insurance?"

"As much as I've got."

There was no trusting Atara. Not with that vindictive streak. And I was pretty sure the torture comb could implicate her in *something.* She'd used it on someone or maybe several people, people who were too frightened or too twisted to tell. Maybe she'd even gone too far on someone. I could see now she was capable of anything. Yes, the comb might be a reach, but it might be my only leverage.

))))

Brytney and Vinnette had taken everything out of my Octagon penthouse except Harold's box of books and a People magazine on the counter. "You're sure you don't want any of it?" asked Bryt. The apartment was barren and very bright.

I slipped my shades on. "Absolutely. Keep what you want, sell the rest, and put the money toward Junior's medical expenses." Not that it would make the slightest dent. That family was in trouble too.

"What about the box?" asked Vinnette.

"Heavy," said Bryt.

Harold's box of books. A burden or part of the solution? Maybe my resistance to scouring through it for clues was that, in some way, Harold and I weren't that different, that in some way we were very much the same. That raised my ire. Maybe Harold's dad would change his mind; maybe he'd take his son's Poe and Dickenson and Dickens. But I knew he wanted nothing to do with them.

"I'm taking it to Minnesota," I said. "They'll pick up in a half hour."

"Optimist." Bryt checked her watch. "One o'clock? I don't think so. Count on four-thirty or five."

"Just leave the door open, Eunis. There's nothing to steal but the books, and they're too heavy." Vinnette started for the door.

"You comin'?" Bryt asked.

"No, I'll meet up with you later."

The women began jabbering and were gone. Alone in the penthouse I sat on the large carton of books facing the New York skyline.

"Well, it was quite an experiment. I'm still not sure of the results. There were times when I almost thought you were helping me, like you knew this was the wrong place, that my future was elsewhere." The farmhouse in Bemidji? I searched each corner for a response, from Harold or the inmates. "I know you're here."

The skyline was marinated in light. "It's spectacular. The building is magnificent." A downdraft. "A lot of pain here."

"Knock, knock." A man's voice. Two United Parcel guys

stood in the doorway. The younger one craned his neck searching for someone else in the apartment. "Wasn't she talking to someone?"

The older guy smacked his shoulder. "United Parcel, lady. You had a pick up?"

"You're early."

"The sooner we're done, the sooner we're done."

I showed them the box. Unconcerned by its size, they lifted it as if it were a box of balloons. "Have a good day, lady," said the older guy.

"Did you see her face?" whispered the younger one as they disappeared out of the apartment.

"Schmuck!" I heard the older guy say.

The elevator pinged and all traces of them disappeared.

"Sam," I said to the empty studio. "I don't know if your soul sailed to heaven in that cedar box like Malcolm said. Maybe you're with him. Or maybe your soul's still here and you're enjoying the view with the inmates. Not many rats get this view."

One last time I inhaled the skyline. *And according to the funeral ritual?* The wife of the deceased man lays on the funeral pyre, alongside her husband.

Yes, but before the fire is lit, she is asked to rise from his side and rejoin the living.

"Hey." Roddy stepped into the penthouse. Then "Wow," as he took in the view.

"Did you know," I said surfacing from my People magazine, "that Donald Trump *owns* the Miss USA pageant?"

"Trump's not surprising."

"According to this he also owns Miss Universe and a bunch of other beauty contests." I let the magazine drop to my lap, like it was diseased, diseased like the past three months. "Fantasy, what we all hope for."

"Hmm. A *proposed* ideal, proposed by someone or something outside of our own imagination." Roddy crouched until he joined me, cross-legged, on the floor by the large window.

"But it's *our* imagination," I countered. "It's still fantasy. It's what we hope for."

He thought about it. I jumped in before he could speak. "Fantasy and imagination are both unreal."

"But are they the same? I don't think so. Take, for instance, your beauty coordinates."

"Here we go."

"No, no, hear me out. Trump's enterprises, your magazines, advertising, porn . . ." He picked up the People and let it tip disdainfully from his fingers and fall back to the floor. "Aren't they all fantasies planted from outside us?"

"And they require outside forces to be fulfilled."

"Exactly."

"So how is imagination different?"

"What do you think?"

"Well, it's inside here." I tapped my head.

"What happens in there?"

"Hard to say, most of the time."

"No, really." He waited as I considered. "Is it cramped in

there?" he asked.

"Sometimes."

"But when you're imagining, *not* fantasizing?"

"It's spacious. It's mine alone."

"You're being creative. And probably sympathetic."

"I'm a scientist."

"Being creative."

"I need to stay within parameters."

"You imagined beauty in Harold. And what I imagine to be beautiful is different from another man's conception. It may be unreal but it's also worthy. It's *my* creation."

He was insinuating. I skirted it. "So you're saying that objective beauty, what society agrees upon, is just marketed and massed produced. I don't believe that."

"Nor do I. But it does seem to arise by imitation, sometimes spread over a long period of time, creating a social agreement, or by a social icon, someone so stunning that society wants to emulate them."

Atara! But I said, "Scarlett Johansen, Halle Berry, George Clooney."

"Take your pick. Maybe even a group like The Beatles. They certainly changed a generation's hair and clothing style in a matter of months."

What a mind! "You've certainly thought a lot about it."

"More since I met you."

He was hard not to like, especially when he kept dipping my heart in possibilities. And I wanted to but . . .

He looked earnestly at me. "Maybe you should stay here and interview him."

"Him?"

"Trump. I'll bet he has many ways to turn fantasized beauty into gold."

"No, I've got to go. Momma needs me." But the idea wasn't so crazy. Trump probably knew all the measures of beauty, especially the ones most admired by the American public.

"I'll bet you could find a way to him."

"I'm not sure why," I said changing the subject, "but I wanted to explain a few things to you before I go." I braced myself.

"If you say so."

"You've been kind to me."

"That's what friends are for."

"I guess. I don't have a lot of history with friends. I don't have much history with anything beyond my life in Bemidji, really, except these past five months here."

"Please stay."

"There's nothing to stay for."

"That's not true."

"Ten more hours in this place, then it's gone. Most people will never see this magnificent skyline; most people in the *world*. But I did. Now it's gone. Luckily, thanks to you, I can leave the lab – at least for now."

"It's not much."

"It'll get me to Minnesota."

"But your work?"

"I'm not sure it's in a lab."

"Can't your brother take care of your mother?"

"No, he really can't. I wouldn't trust him. He doesn't trust himself. My sister wouldn't even consider it. No, it's got to be me. But there's something else."

Roddy reached for my hand.

"No." I withdrew. The rebuke was like a slap across his face and he rubbed it. "I'm not like other people."

"No, you're not."

"Let me finish." I held up my hand and brushed the hair off my face. "There's something not right about me." He started to speak but I closed him down. "It's Harold. He's with me all the time."

"That's natural."

"Maybe, but I have lapses of memory; things I can't remember." *Disturbing things.*

"We all—"

"Roddy, there's truth back there that I have to face. It's not just my extreme sensitivity to small spaces and the things I may or may not feel . . . or hear."

"You hear things too?"

"Something happened to my husband, something that I was unable to see coming with all my supposed prophetic gifts or to prevent or . . ." A corrosive drip was underway in my stomach, vertigo traveled up my chest to my temples.

"Or what?"

"I don't know. I seem to cause heartache for the people I know. Maybe I'm not as nice a person as you think I am."

"I don't think, I *know*."

It was going to happen to Elizabeth, it was going to happen to him too. My neck stiffened. "You and I are never going to be together."

"What makes you think—?"

"Stop." I fought to stay cold to those warm eyes of his. My face tightened. *Tell him so he'll go away.* "I may be just as twisted inside as out. Possibly clinically disturbed. I may have already caused one man's death."

"I'm sure you didn't."

"I may be dangerous —to myself and others. I don't know. It's always been that way. I don't understand so much that most women my age already understand."

"Don't be so sure." He tried to regain some ground. "And stop blaming yourself. Man or woman, I doubt there are many people who truly understand everything that's going on around us. Maybe the Dali Lama or Jesus or some guy in Henderson, North Carolina. But we all gotta be careful of believing what we think."

"No, I'm a freak. I attract freaks."

"I resemble that remark." He flashed a little smile.

I wanted him to hold me; I wanted him to push me away.

"It's a fabrication, that you're not okay."

I shook my head.

"Here's what I know," he said, "though I heard it and read it so many times before I finally *got* it. The greatest trap is living a life based on what other people think. It's one of the *instructive* myths."

"It's not what *other* people think, it's what I've experienced." *Just agree with me and leave.* But my mouth wouldn't stop talking. "What does that mean, instructive myth?"

"We all live by the stories we've been told, legend and myth, some of it —much of it— foolhardy, some of it sound instruction."

I huffed.

He rocked forward. "Look, consider there are two types of myths. One like the politicians throw at us, the one that uses the word myth to mean 'lie.' They use it to bludgeon an idea. Like it was a myth, a lie, that the healthcare system in this country wasn't broken. When we all knew it was terribly broken. Using myth that way is a bastardization of our language, a manipulation, a fabrication. And of course those types of myths get repeated over and over again. Just like false family myths."

I didn't want to encourage him, but I loved watching his mind in motion. "I'm sure you're going to tell me about the other kind of myth."

"The original, ancient meaning of myth is that it's a *truth* that's been passed down through the ages by men and women because of their *experience*. There's a collective truth to it. It's *instructive*. We should hold that myth with reverence, even if we don't believe all of it."

"But how can you trust any of it? How do you know which are the original myths, the handed-down histories, versus the manipulative or biased lies?"

"Well, knowing *the source* is important."

"It's in my head!"

"Okay, if it's spacious in there and you let your imagination play out . . . I'll bet you'll look for a compassionate result. You've got the good luck *charm*. And *feeling* the myth, letting it settle in before raging for or against it, that's what works for me too." He patted his heart. "It goes beyond language."

"Seems like a risky business." I checked my cell phone for the time. Maybe he'd get the hint. One of us had to break out of the eddy.

"Yes, it is."

"Well, whatever. I'm a freak." I slipped the phone into my pocket. "I need to find out what that means and I have to accept it."

"Me too," he said.

I sighed. He was anything but a freak. "Well," I rose off the floor and dusted myself off, "time to say good-bye." I said it as if I was saying good-bye to the apartment and, avoiding Roddy, I bid farewell to every corner.

He got to his feet. "Well," he said awkwardly extending his hand to shake mine, "then I guess it's off to the great north woods."

"Yes." I turned to face him, kept my arms folded in front of me. But then something caved in so deep in my chest that I walked over and gave him a hug, a small one. Our bodies made a low harmonic sound. "I think you're a good man." I pulled away, tearing several nerve endings.

"I'll take that as a compliment. Call me, tell me how it's going up there, okay?"

A small fragment of glass on the floor caught my eye and I stayed glued to it. "If there's time, sure."

"Must be busy-busy up there this time of year, huh?"

"I told you, if there's time."

"Okay, then." He patted his thighs. "Good luck with your past, it was never meant to last." He walked out of the apartment leaving a few small heel clicks in the air, until the door squeaked, swung closed, and latched.

CHAPTER THIRTY-NINE

Three things consumed me that last week in New York: swimming at the Natatorium, trying to recover whatever elements of beauty I imagined in Harold, and connecting to Donald Trump. Buried in one of my now discarded celebrity magazines was a reference to Gordon Mingle, in some way related to the Miss USA pageant, to Trump and Trump's experienced view of capitalism and its correlation to beauty. I emailed Gordon at his office and was shocked to get a quick reply.

"Feel free to call me."

And so I did. "I didn't think you'd remember me."

"Oh, I do. I do. You'd be surprised. But I'm not sure I can be of much help. I'm quite downstream from Mr. Trump. Besides, he's in Beverly Hills now, according to the press."

"But you're a celebrity, he'd respond to you."

"My celebrity is an illusion. You dabble in that sort of thing too, don't you?"

I had no idea what he was talking about and it made me uncomfortable. But if I couldn't get to Trump, I had an alternate plan. "I read you'll be hosting the Minnesota Miss USA trials."

"Going back the end of this week."

"Me too. Any chance we could meet?"

He laughed as if he liked the idea. "Try my cell when you get to Bemidji, or if you're on the Lake Shore Limited next Monday."

I'd make that happen.

〉〉〉

As the Amtrak pulled out of Penn Station for Chicago, the station's dark subterranean passages grinded by and my own distorted reflection sat constant, like a patient jailer. I shut my eyes and rested my head against the window. I fell asleep to the rhythm of the rails, thinking of what my stepfather, Papa Karl, called the dog spikes that secured, with luck, each length of track; an uneven clacking that rushed me back to Momma's farmhouse and the uneasy questions surrounding Harold's death.

I slept all the way to Rochester where boarding passengers quickly jockeyed for empty seats. Lyle was spread across our space, eyes closed clutching his guitar. I maneuvered over him and set out to find Gordon Mingle.

Three cars up, there he was.

"Gordon." I stood over him.

He needed a moment to place me. "Eunis Kindsvatter! You took me up on my invitation." He stood and shook my hand. An unusually pleasing reception.

"I did." I nodded at the empty seat next to him. "May I?"

"For a moment, there's a woman already sitting here."

I maneuvered in next to him and smiled. He sported a small diamond stud in his right ear and still retained a hint of the plank stiffness that helped define him in high school. "So, family in Bemidji?"

"Actually, they're all dead."

My head bobbed in condolence.

"S'okay," he said. "The preliminary trials in Bemidji will keep me busy. Miss USA. Hard to believe someone thinks I'm a celebrity, like I'll draw some attention. Anyway it's a free trip home and my class is having a reunion so . . ."

"Why not?"

"Exactly, why not? Free is a beautiful word in America." His head tilted, appraising me. "You know," he said under his breath, "I'm glad you contacted me. I'm glad we could talk here. Who knows if I'll have time in Bemidji."

"Really?"

"I know something about you that nobody else does. It's pretty *dark*." His smile evaporated with sinister coolness.

My spine arched. *Shit.* Not a clue in his face; nothing more than self-satisfied anticipation. I flashed on Harold swinging from the beam.

"Really?" I was supposed to be the tactician. Nonchalant was the best way to handle it. *The false prom date?* He was two grades above me. *The Valentine flowers planted in shit?*

"Why the train?" Maybe he'd drop whatever he was oozing to tell. "Don't they pay weathermen enough to fly?" *If he knew something about Times Square, he could finger me. Maybe he'd heard about Vic King, the attempted rape. Or he was aware of my exploits with Atara and Levi.*

"I'll share *my* secret if you promise not to pass it along to anyone in Bemidji," he said cool and businesslike. "I'm a hero there now."

"Will you make the same promise to me?" I floated it lightly, hoping to gauge the danger.

"I'm not so sure." His face was blank and serious. "What I know about you could get you in trouble. Like I said, dark."

Twisting the knife. He wanted money. This was a mistake.

His chestnut beard rose up like a curtain starting a new act, a broad smile. "Okay, deal." He held out his hand.

"Deal," I shook it, holding on to his uncommitted grip. I'd wash my hands later.

"Hey, that's my seat!" A freckled-faced black woman in her late fifties motioned me to get out.

"Yes, of course," I said, standing, the aggravation still tacked to her face.

"We'll catch up later," Gordon said to me, "catch up on old times." His face expressionless.

"Yes, definitely." I felt like I'd set my own trap.

☽☽☽

On the way back to my seat I weighed the dangers of involving Gordon in my research and decided that I had to stick with my plan. To distract myself I bought the latest Life & Style Weekly, a photo of a young Daryl Hanna and the current Daryl splashed across the cover. The headline:

Ex-mermaid Daryl Hannah says she left Hollywood because her autism made her 'Terrified' of fame

Which reminded me of Matthew Deere. Which reminded me of the fearful trail I'd left behind me, everywhere I'd gone.

When Lyle finally stirred from his extended siesta, he made no attempt to engage me. He unfolded a Guitar Player magazine and began reading.

"Can I ask you something?" I said.

"Sure," he said. He barely looked up.

"Going back to Bemidji like this, aren't you kind of giving up your music career? That's always been your dream."

He paused and put a hand on the magazine. "Yeah, well, we can't all go to college."

"What's that supposed to mean?"

"You and Carly."

"Me and Carly?!" The gall!

"You know what I mean?"

"You know, I don't."

"Well, don't get all Chivas and Mercedes with me. It's not like you made anythin' with your dream of test-tubbin' Frankensteins."

"So you're bitter."

"Aren't you?"

"Never mind." My lips tightened. "I'm going to wash my hands."

"'Kay." He went back to flipping pages.

ꭰꭰꭰ

As soon as I was far enough from Lyle, I picked up my pace. I slid open the metal door between cars, taking in the roar of the accordion gangway and the passing countryside, then hearing the door latch behind me as I slid open the next.

With the lights low and many passengers asleep, I carefully perused each passenger, with the hope that he or she would not wake and look up at me. Mostly on my mind was what I might have to do with myself if Gordon's secret was as dark as he suggested. Or what I might have to do with him.

I passed through seven or eight cars, and not a few uncomfortable looks, before I found Gordon with the African-American woman, boxing the air above her purple hair, regaling him with a story, loudly, as if the rest of the car was gathered around her rather than trying to sleep.

"Eunis!" he said, glad to have a life preserver.

"I'm not done," said the woman.

"Beatrice, this my friend. Remember? We planned to have dinner together." He started to get up. She pushed him back down.

"I remember. I didn't hear your name called." Beatrice frowned at the sight of me.

"They're using mine," I said. "And it's last call."

"Only heard man's names being called."

"Yes," I said, "I'm a man. I just look like a woman."

"No woman I've ever seen." Beatrice puffed out her eyes.

"Exactly," I said.

"Excuse me." Gordon tried stepping over Beatrice.

"No hurry, I can come with you. I ain't eaten yet either. You'll want to hear the rest of my Michael Jackson story." She started to get up, propelling her bosom into Gordon's left eye.

"It's personal," said Gordon rubbing the eye and straddling Beatrice.

"What, you one of them gay boys? I'm too much woman for you?" She was eyeball to eyeball with him.

Gordon tugged at his sleeves. "It's personal." He lifted his leg over Beatrice, who gave a fake grab for his balls. He balked, almost falling into the aisle.

Beatrice cackled brashly. "Don't stop till you get enough."

"It's personal," I repeated, stabilizing Gordon and helping him over Beatrice.

"I'll finish the story when you get back." Beatrice was miffed.

☽☽☽

"Where can we go for privacy?" I asked.

"It's a train," Gordon said shutting down privacy as an option. "But thank you for that back there."

"You're welcome."

"I should have gotten a sleeper. I figured maybe after we switched trains in Chicago—"

"How about this?" We'd come across a door marked "Powder Lounge," and I opened it to a room almost twice the size of the train's bathrooms. "Okay?"

I drew him in, closed and locked the door behind us, and assigned myself a stool that didn't require that I admire myself in the counter-to-ceiling mirror. He took the other seat. I removed my shades.

"So?" I heard myself sinking into deep water.

"So, what?"

"Why didn't you fly?" My ears wouldn't clear.

"Oh. You're not gonna repeat this, right?"

"Neither one of us." I pointed back and forth. "What you know about me stays secret too. We have a deal. Right? Bemidji buddies." The hollow timbre of the room solidified in my chest.

"I'm scared of flying."

"That's it?" If I could have brushed the hostility away I would have, but it was the room, the atoms in the small lounge. My ears were plugged, 'my gift' overtaking me.

"It doesn't look good for me," continued Gordon, "to have phobias like that. I'm already the center of enough gossip at the station. People have a lot of stories." He stroked his beard.

"If you say so." The tide hadn't crested. It continued to gather in me.

"How about you? Why not fly?" He pulled out a cigarette, stared at it as if it would talk to him, and when it didn't he put it back in the pack and in his pocket.

Patience. "Don't like the attention, airport security, the lines. I just want to be anonymous." *Enough fucking small talk.* I took deep breaths. "Plus I feel safe in trains." I thought of Papa Karlyle, his reassuring way, his commitment to detail. 'Every spike must be checked, every tie plate secured,' he'd say. 'People count on us.'

Gordon nodded.

"So what's this deep dark secret about me?" I simulated a smile.

"It's something that happened in Bemidji."

That let out Times Square, Atara and Levi. "Okay." It was Victor. It was *Harold!* "This going to be a guessing game?" My impatience spiked, a rising torrent of bile.

"Come on, take a guess. Remember, I'm the *only* person besides you who knows this *dark* secret." *Definitely Harold.*

Hostility swelled. I sat on my hands to control them. I couldn't remember being possessed like that —well, maybe the time with the carding comb. The surge strained to break through. I wanted to take him by the neck . . . "Just tell me."

"Ever pretend to be someone else? You were in plain view, but they thought you were someone or something else?"

The sensation was so strong I nearly leapt at him.

"The Beaver. You were The Beaver." He grinned and waited, open-faced.

Consciously I breathed in and out, expelling the fury passing through me.

"You okay?" He reached out.

I signaled him off. "I'm okay, just caught my breath." The possession peaked and began to abate. "It was something . . . in the room."

"What?"

I had mixed two universes. "Nothing."

"You're sure? Because it looked like more than *nothing*. Maybe I shouldn't have kidded you so much."

"About The Beaver." The water ebbed. I regained equilibrium.

"I was Beaver fifty-four, just before you. I never was supposed to know."

"Of course not."

"I ran late. I should've delivered the suit days before. I dropped it off last minute and I saw you. And by the way, I think you were the best Beaver ever, the way you moved. I could tell when it wasn't you anymore because the next Beaver, whoever it was, wasn't very . . . fluid. You were very athletic, moved like you were in water."

"Thank you."

"You still appear to be in great shape."

"Wow." The energy had left me, thank goodness. "Two Beavers in a room together and *knowing* it. That can't have happened before."

"What are the chances?" He slapped his knees.

We beamed at each other.

I sighed in relief.

We traded stories of our experiences inside the suit. He understood, even agreed, with some of what I'd seen from in there: people, a strange bunch. I'm not sure I'd ever had a positive shared experience with *anyone* before, especially as Harold and I did almost everything separately. So Gordon was definitely unique. An ally? Maybe.

Almost an hour later, well after midnight, someone rattled the door. When it didn't immediately open, there was a rapid knock.

"Somebody in there? I need to freshen up."

Gordon unlatched the door.

It was Beatrice. "What in god's name are the two of *you* doin' locked up in this lounge together? Lordy, you be sick people. Get out, get me some privacy, please!"

Gordon and I shared another grin as we were ushered out.

"Don't stop till you get enough," I said.

"Damn!" Beatrice exclaimed, and we stumbled out, snickering.

CHAPTER FORTY

Returning to our seats, we stopped a moment between cars, me with a cup of hot coffee purchased from the snack bar, and he with an unlit cigarette.

"That's illegal," I said as Gordon attempted to light up. "Even out here." The gangway between cars was a funhouse, a moving floor tilting left and right, two chained accordion waffles of thick mesh on either side see-sawing up and down. Above, we could see sky, and below, fast-moving track and blackness.

"Lend me a hand," he said, wanting me to shield the lighter's flame to his cigarette. An hour earlier I'd felt like throwing him off the train. Now I kind of liked him. As I moved closer I realized he was one of the few males I'd met recently who produced no corporeal vibration in me whatsoever. Zero. And apparently he had no attraction to me either because, as the cigarette glowed, he stepped away with ease. A relief.

"Thanks." He slipped the lighter into his jacket. "So you've been studying beauty all these years."

"I have."

"And what have you learned?"

I must have smiled because, before I could answer, he remarked, "Nice dimples."

"Thanks."

"Sorry to interrupt."

"I've learned that there are a number of scientific ways to quantify beauty. But they seem to be even less reliable than predicting the weather."

"Now, now, we do our best."

"Do you know about crickets and low-flying birds?"

"You mean their alleged ability to predict weather?"

"Yes. Do you think a person can have that skill?"

"Skill?"

"Intuition," I said and frowned.

He took a long drag from his cigarette. "Maybe. I've never heard of anyone like that, but if I did I'd keep them close to my desk and feed them caramels. You know, in case the weather service computers went down." He blew a stream of smoke from the side of his mouth. It disappeared, ghost-like, into the night. "I've learned to live with insecurity. You can't imagine the hate calls I get, especially when it comes to people's vacations. Like I control what the good lord doles out."

"I can do it. Or at least I could. And you can keep the caramels for yourself."

"You can make it rain!"

"No, but at certain times, under the right conditions, I can predict with certainty. I did it all the time when I was growing up."

"I see. You haven't grown out of it? Is your talent relegated to Bemidji? Kind of a small market." He popped his lips. My fondness for him compounded, and I felt bad that I'd manipulated him to that point. But it was time to reel in my catch.

"Don't think so. Hey, let's make another deal —Honor of The Beavers: you let me sit in on the Miss USA trials and I'll tune into the weather and feed you whatever I get?"

"Sounds irresistible." He scratched his beard. "Except you get more than I do. Can I pick the ones I want? I'm partial to catastrophic events. You got those? Catastrophe pulls audience. You want me to *look good*, right?"

"I can't promise. But anyway, wouldn't you like my scientific take on the pageant contestants? Sure you would, you're a scientist too."

"We seem to be mixing media."

"It'd be a different way of viewing the girls. Come on." I gave him a playful punch.

"I'll bet the organizers will love your systematic input."

I was learning his trademark sarcasm —and appreciating it. "So?" I asked. "Do we have a deal?"

His cheeks puffed out, then he exhaled. "I guess it could be fun. You'd certainly have a different approach to evaluating the girls. Might be interesting, though you'd have to apply your science to the pageant format."

"I can do that." I cut him off, excited to have found a friend. "And don't forget I might be forecasting some weather for you."

"That'll be a bonus." He stomped on the cigarette. "Let's get some sleep. It's a long ride."

☽☽☽

Our arrival in Chicago's Union Station, wrinkled and grumpy from nineteen hours on the train, had the peculiar stickiness of a dream. While we waited to board The Empire Builder for the additional fourteen hours to Fargo, Lyle disappeared again, leaving me with the luggage, his guitar, and titanic irritation. In some absurd, inexplicable way, he and I were related.

I'd been through the station, briefly, on my way to New York. I'd wrapped myself in my overcoat and had kept my head down that whole time. This time was different; *I* was different.

I watched the cantankerous Beatrice trail-blaze through the crowd, as if —based on her supposed familial relationship to the pop star— she was heir apparent to Michael Jackson's right of way. Gordon suggested that tomorrow she'd be Denzel Washington's ex-mistress or Kerry Washington's aunt, whatever held attention. But I wanted some of that chutzpah, even if it was contrived.

As I waited at the far end of the hard wooden pew in the station's Great Hall, I took inventory. Yes, I'd grown comfortable with my anonymity but not, I decided, attached to it. Progress. I could enjoy the gallery's grandeur. Sharp voices, expectant footsteps, and blurry train announcements bounced off the Great Hall's barrel-vaulted skylight and marble floors. A giant fishbowl.

I laid my head back so it rested on the pew. The cathedral ceiling, more than 100 feet high, was the tallest I'd ever seen. *A palace in a fishbowl.*

I watched the shop lights glitter. I inhaled the confluence of food and people smells, aged and woven into the stone. Strong and pleasing. Yet even in the palace there was unease. Besides Beatrice, I tracked other harried travelers until they noticed me and turned away. I closed my eyes.

Someone tapped me on the shoulder. It was Daryl Hannah, older and grayer than I'd ever seen her, and she held the hand of a sweet, round-faced little black boy, maybe eight years old. "Would you like to join us for tea?" she said.

"Me?" I said.

"You're Eunis, aren't you?"

"Yes."

"Well, come with us." And she led me and the little boy to a small door behind a cart stacked high with luggage.

The door opened into another royal room, with the same cathedral ceilings and nothing but a large table covered in white linen, four chairs, all crowded together in a corner of it, a teapot, four cups and saucers.

"Please," she said offering me a place at the table. The little boy smiled at me and sat to my left as Daryl sat to my right.

"This is lovely," I managed to say, still unsure of my invitation. "Do you like tea?" I asked the little boy.

"I do," he said and I could have sworn his face changed, more hair certainly, an Afro. And it wasn't exactly a smile after all, just his wide eyes unafraid to meet mine.

"Here," said Daryl, lifting her cup in salute, though I hadn't seen her pour from the teapot. "To us."

"To us." I turned to the little boy once more. He'd changed again. Older. Acne skin. Broader nose. He still watched me but his eyes were blank; he could have been one of Carver's stuffings. Daryl didn't seem to notice anything unusual.

"Will you talk to me like my next door neighbor?" asked the young man, now clearly in his early twenties.

"Yes, what would you like to talk about?" I faced him fully. As I did his face changed again, nose thinner, skin lighter, eyebrows, cheekbones —every facet tighter, sculpted.

"Beauty," he said. "What was so beautiful about Harold? You're an expert aren't you?"

"Well, I've—"

"Because if you're not," said the young man, now aged once more, his lips thinner, his nose pointed, even his eyelashes extravagant in their length and thinness, "you have no right being here."

"But I was invited." I looked to Daryl for support but she wagged her left index finger at me to refrain from arguing. She was missing part of the finger.

"I don't understand," I said.

"Precisely," said the black man, now ghoulishly white, bony, and feminine. "And why not?" He sounded belligerent. Then he answered for me. "Because you didn't try."

"Try?"

"You could have put all that money toward surgery."

"There would have been nothing left for my education. I would have been forever in that farmhouse with nothing to give."

"Give?" The black man and Daryl said in unison.

"Yes."

"Then why are you here?" The completely ghost-white black man slammed his hand to the table, overturning the cup and spilling my tea.

"Now look what you've done!" he screamed, expression grotesque.

"I can't sleep like this," Daryl said. "I just can't."

"Am I beautiful?" he asked.

Something brought me to the surface, dragging my constant career failure with it. *"Because you didn't try," he said. "Then why are you here?" he said.* And as passengers streamed by me, I thought I actually saw Daryl. I had to turn completely around to find her again in the crowd. *There!* Just her long blonde curls. Born in Chicago, after all. She wouldn't have wanted to be in a fish bowl —a mermaid— with all those people, and yet . . .

☽☽☽

The hours passed. When I saw Lyle across the colossal open floor of the palace, he appeared more aimless than usual. His head was down, but it was his gait that lacked motivation. If he spent the rest of his life making his way the final seventy yards to my bench, he would not apparently have cared. That he somehow managed to point his way in my direction at all appeared to be the only measureable constant.

"Here." I handed him his guitar. "You'll feel better."

"Thanks." With a wan smile he pulled the D-35 to his chest, but he didn't open the case. He stared across the large hall from whence he'd come.

I put an arm on his shoulder and sat with him without another word.

CHAPTER FORTY-ONE

At 4:30 in the morning Fargo is a desolate town. We wandered the empty streets for a couple of hours, during which Lyle said little except to nod when I reminded him that, "This was the Great Northern Railroad. Your father helped lay rails all the way here." We rented a metallic blue beater Plymouth Neon to drive the final three hours to Bemidji.

"Thank you," I said keeping my eyes mostly on the road, the flat farmland of the lower Red River Valley spreading in every direction along the unseen shoreline of ancient Lake Agassiz. The fields were dry enough by then for the farmers to plow and plant without squandering their tractors to the mud. Mounds of sugar beet, corn, and barley rose from the primal silt.

"For what?" He was curled up in the corner of the seat against the door, hoodie pulled down like a wanted felon avoiding the law.

"For sticking your neck out in New York for me. And for that Carver job, the taxidermist."

"What did Carver have to do with me?"

"You suggested there might be a job for me."

"Yeah, because the guy was creepy, the place was creepy, and the stuffin's were creepy."

"He didn't think of himself as a stuffer. It was art to him."

"But why me?" Lyle asked. "I only worked there a week."

"Thanks to you, I got to go to state."

"No shit. And now you and I are headed back to Momma and that fuckin' hole of a farmhouse. No job, no prospects. One big fuckin' round trip to nowhere." He tugged his hood back a half-inch. "And you're welcome."

I laughed and, reluctantly, so did he.

"Seriously," he straightened up, his eyes widening in recognition. "I never thought of the chemicals, but dya think those fumes every day . . . they might have poisoned your body, your brain?" His eyes were already past my answer, like he considered his own exposure.

"It's never bothered me," I said. "I'm pretty healthy. Maybe someday." *Hydrochloric, Oxalic, Formic, the others. My blank spots?*

He said nothing and gazed dully through the windshield at the newly planted fields.

Row after row of crops, like whitecaps upon the lake, extended to the horizon, hypnotizing me. "Anyhow," I said, my eyes returning to the road, "why are you coming back? I don't get it."

"Yeah, well . . . I guess I should help you a little, specially since that last gig-shit slipped through my fingers."

"Gig-shit. Sounds unappetizing."

"I'm here to help."

"Well, thank you again."

"You're welcome again."

A three-inch giant water bug slammed the windshield, liquefied and glued to it. Lyle asked again, "You know anythin' about those chemicals?"

I shrugged him off. "You were only there a week."

"Yeah." He studied the puréed insect. "I guess."

ꙨꙨꙨ

"Why don't you play something," I said to Lyle as we passed through the village of White Earth and its wreckage of scattered trailer homes reeking of poverty; shutters hanging by a wire, a child's plastic wading pool —spores of black mold overtaking its pink and yellow— windows boarded with plywood and criss-crossed in duct tape, a rusted truck on blocks —*like momma's caboose*— and small droppings of a man's underwear embedded across a muddy side yard.

"Not in the mood." He batted away the invitation, the same wilted energy I'd felt from Harold just before he . . .

"You can't stop singing, whatever's bugging you," I said.

He objected with a grumble.

"You never met Harold, did you?"

"No. He a nice guy? I guess he musta been if you married him."

"Yeah, he was."

From the corner of my eye I saw Lyle study my face, then turn back to the windshield and the advent of gradually rolling hills and simple farmhouses. "How come you always made do?"

"Couldn't depend on my good looks, could I?"

"Guess not." Then he realized how harsh it sounded. "Sorry. But Harold, he thought you were cool."

"He didn't think anything was *cool*, but he had a good heart."

"You two were okay? I mean, you guys didn't fight or anything?"

"Why do you ask?"

"Well ... there was ..."

"What?"

"Talk." He lowered his eyes as we passed a small white church.

"Like?"

"You know, the cops and everything. You've always had that temper."

"Temper?"

"They asked me a lot of questions about you, but I just said . . ."

"What?" I tightened my gripped on the steering wheel.

"That we aren't a very close family and that all I knew is what I'd heard about him."

"Which was?"

"I dunno."

"Yes, you do. Tell me."

"Aw, you know my friends, they're kinda lowlifes. What do they know?"

I slowed the car and put the blinker on, as if I'd pull into the dirt parking lot next to the church and the large cemetery.

"Shall we hang out with the Lutherans till you tell me?" I knew his aversion to graveyards.

"Well," he waved me back onto the road, "he had a weird girlfriend or friend before you, I guess."

"What do you mean weird? What was her name?" This was

the first I'd heard of any girlfriend of Harold's. My jaw tightened. How easy it was to get lost in the marshy wetlands to our right and left.

"Never got a name. Like I said, heard it from a friend."

"She was weird how?"

"Dunno, she was strange, is all's I remember."

"You're strange, I'm strange. We're all strange."

"Can't remember."

"Can't remember or won't tell?"

"I'd tell you. Like I said, it was one of my lowlife friends who mentioned it, ya know, drink talk. Pretty sure before you."

"*Pretty sure!* When we get to Bemidji find him for me, your lowlife friend."

"*Her.* The electrician. You want to meet her, really? Why?"

"Set it up, okay? Just set it up." Another clue, but it frightened me.

I drove through more wetlands, past houses begun but never finished, through dense woodlands and past side roads, rutted, sandy and likely impossible to traverse. Certain traps. We skirted west of Bemidji, through the anachronistic town of Pony Lake with its reassuring quaintness and steeple church, then north past more trailer homes —some derelict, others qualified to be. Finally, we turned onto the Smith Road dirt, past sparsely-flung neighbor shanties, neighbors we mostly avoided and who mostly avoided us, till we reached Momma's dilapidated farmhouse, the old caboose with its cupola still up on timbers, still shredding life particle-by-particle, still laboring against the inevitable.

CHAPTER FORTY-TWO

"You ready?" I asked.

Lyle and I shared a last look of uneasy solidarity, the farmhouse quavering to a silent wind, like it could topple and consume us at any moment.

Seeing his despondence I patted his leg. "It'll be fine."

"Wonder if the spooks will remember us," he said. "Cause Momma don't want no misery."

Even as he made fun of the resident spirits, his apprehension was apparent. I could see and sense them too, in the peeling gunmetal paint, the rotting planks, the intransigent weeds. "Come on." I pulled my luggage from the trunk.

We approached through the rear entryway, the kitchen door the only functioning portal in or out, as far as I could remember, unless one shimmied down the drainpipe, and even then . . . Some might never get out; a flicker of approval for Carly.

Cigarette haze hung in the air, two empty Keystone bottles chaperoned an ashtray brimming with spent Lucky Strikes. Absurdly balanced, like a discontinued museum diorama, the mounted creatures and wax figures already stored away, or destroyed. The room hadn't changed, the sickly pale green cabinets and brown scuffed floral linoleum familiarly dangerous and vaguely welcoming. I had just walked out of that room, *hadn't I?*

Momma straggled into the room carrying a third bottle. "I see you made it. Go put your stuff away." She zigzaged over to Lyle and left a wet kiss on his cheek, which he quickly but surreptitiously wiped away when she finally acknowledged me. "Easy trip?"

"Forty hours, Momma," Lyle answered wearily before I could speak.

"Well maybe Eunis can rustle up some dinner for us. I'll bet you're hungry."

I seethed. I determined that my first project would be to purify the outside, scraping and repainting the house, anything to stay outside.

𝄆𝄆𝄆

When I settled onto my old bed for the first time, pressure clamped my whole head. I started to address the room, then stopped. "No," I said.

I pulled the journal out of my luggage, and finding a comfortable angle between pillow and wall, I wrote:

> "Harold,
>
> "I'm back in the cellar —my old room. Only mustier. More cobwebs. Like Momma always knew I'd return. William Schroeder waiting for me on the wall. What did he have, really? Eighteen days before the strokes and becoming vegetative? What we can do now!
>
> "Anyway, my room: it's even smaller than I remember, though I haven't been gone that long. Maybe I've gotten bigger. Ha! Maybe.
>
> "Otherwise, no changes. Not even Momma. There's nothing wrong with her that wasn't wrong with her when I left six months ago that I can see.
>
> "But there was one surprise: I opened a kitchen cupboard and noticed my stepfather's favorite plate at the bottom of a stack. Sounds silly, a favorite plate. But he'd worked for the railroad his entire life before the accident, and that handmade plate, a large uneven brown plate with the railroad's insignia emblazoned in dark brown and orange in the center, was all he'd eat off of.
>
> "At least once a week, he'd tell me about the plate and the railroad, like he'd never told me before. The rest of them didn't listen. Sometimes Carly would carry on another conversation with Momma, as if Papa Karlyle wasn't even talking. He paid it no mind because he loved telling me about

the railroad.

"Anyhow, the plate reminded me of him, and how kind he was to everyone. Even me. He's probably the only family I ever had before you.

"By the way, was my temper that bad? I don't remember being violent. I need clues. You didn't leave many."

)))

After renting a pressure washer, ordering paint, and grabbing some basic tools in town, I deduced that a phone call to Muriel and Rhoald, Harold's parents, was a poor investigative approach since they would almost certainly tell me to go to hell, or at least Rhoald would. Muriel would be more demure, not that either of them would know what that word meant.

So I gave them no warning and knocked on their door. I glanced nervously around the compulsively clean and organized yard. Already beyond the ravages of winter and early spring, the yard bloomed ground plum and an edge of marsh marigold. In the first week of April!

I turned to the door. Was there a radio playing? I knocked again. *Please, make it Muriel.* The solid black door opened.

"God," he said, "it's you." Rhoald slammed the door in my face.

I closed my eyes, took a breath, knocked again.

The door sprung instantly open. Rhoald's eyes were fevered, his small beet-red face and pate of remaining hair bristled. "Zombie, don't you get the message? You're not welcome. Not ever."

"I need to talk to you about Harold."

"Mean the son you killed? Our *only* son."

"I didn't kill him." But there was so much I couldn't explain. Guilt and the nagging feeling of anger I had for Harold.

"The cops weren't so sure of that, but I guess your good looks got you off." He sneered. "Anyway, we have nothin' to discuss."

You're a scientist, a detective. "Don't you want to know why he killed himself?"

"*My* son wouldn't kill himself."

"Well, who would?"

"If it wasn't by you directly, it was by you indirectly. And he's dead. There's nothin' to talk about."

"Rhoald, who's at the door?" Muriel's voice came from inside the house.

"And don't upset her. You've already done enough." He slammed the door a second time.

〉〉〉

Sarah Pooley's oxidized sedan sat in the farmhouse driveway, burgundy going on gray, and Sarah herself met me as I entered the kitchen. "Your mother's lookin' for you."

"Hello to you too, Sarah."

She curled and tightened her lips —especially her upper lip— so that rigid lines carved away from her ashen mouth. Aging like uncovered guacamole. "Welcome," she said stiffly. "Your mother needs you."

"She seems fine to me. Most of my work's going to be outside."

"She's gettin' older. You can't see all the trouble."

"Momma's what, fifty-seven now? That's not old."

"I'm not gonna argue with you." Sarah pulled on her light jacket. "It's your responsibility and you've got enough strikes against you that I'd think you'd just take care of the one person who took care of you when nobody else gave a shit. Good bye." She pushed past me and out of the farmhouse.

"Hey." Lyle headed sheepishly for the old Frigidaire as if he'd heard nothing.

"She doesn't look sick to me," I said. "Why'd you get me up here?"

"Told you," Lyle talked into the fridge, grabbing white bread and mayo and some luncheon meat. "Momma said she needed you."

"And the doctor?"

He shrugged.

"That's the same answer you gave me the last time, except now here I am."

He started building his sandwich, licking the knife of mayo as he went along, then putting it back in the jar.

"That's disgusting."

"No big deal." He launched into the sandwich as cover.

"When you're done stuffing your face you're going to drive down to town, and you're going to find your friend and that weird woman, the one who was friends with Harold. And you're going to set up a meeting or get her name and an address."

"My friend? She's probably long gone."

"I'll be long gone if you don't help me. You can deal with Momma." But I knew better, even as I said it.

He turned pale. "You'd desert her?"

"I took your word that she needed me."

"She does."

"Yeah, as a housekeeper, delivery service and general punching bag. Until I see or hear proof that she's actually sick, I'm setting my own rules. I've got my own agenda. You understand?"

"Don't be that way."

"Find me a clue."

CHAPTER FORTY-THREE

"What're ya doin'?" asked Momma, "Them's mine."

"Momma," I took hold of a half-finished pint of gin, "you're so sick this alcohol can't be good for you."

"Put those bottles down," she said with a vengeance.

"Let me check with your doctor. What's his name?"

"None of your damn business."

"I'm here to help. You said you needed me up here, right? Or was that something Lyle made up?"

"Lyle's a good boy."

"He's a man, and the good part can be argued. Did you tell him I had to come up?"

"Sorta. Now put down those damn bottles. At my age I gotta right to enjoy myself."

"Seems like that age started around the time I was four."

"You ain't got no idea what it's like bringing up a baby alone."

"You had Karl."

"Only after I made myself available to him . . . for yer sake."

"Papa Karl was a good man."

"Karlyle was a simpleton. A dreamer and a simpleton."

"What's your doctor's name?"

"Not till you put down my bottles." Momma stuck out her chin.

"I got places on this farm you'll never find them. Especially with all my tools and tarps spread across the yard and by the barn. I can wait." I kept gathering additional bottles of schnapps and Yukon Jack from the cupboard.

"Ungrateful little fuck!"

"Doctor's name."

"Hall."

"First name?"

"Doctor."

"There must be twenty doctor Halls in the area. And not one of them will give me any information unless I call him with some assurance."

"Don't know his first name. Give me my fuckin' bottles." Momma charged me.

I stood my ground. "Maybe I'll just drop them here, let you clean them up."

She stopped, shook with anger, looked for something to throw at me. "After all I've done."

It was a familiar anger; I recognized it . . . in myself. "You've taught me well."

She reached for the skillet on the stove. "Gimme my bottles!"

I could look like her. I could rage. I was ashamed. "Or you'll what? You'll throw me out?" And then I even understood the frustration on her face.

My cell phone rang. *Shit!* Hands useless. I *had* to put the bottles down. "You're off the hook for now," I said changing my tone to sweetness, "but I want to make sure you're as healthy as you can be."

I laid the armful of bottles onto the counter and Momma started grabbing them back.

"Yes?" I said to the cell, and listened. "That's good enough, Lyle. Thanks."

☽☽☽

The Drink 'n' Dive, not surprisingly, sat in the only part of Bemidji that hadn't been restored, an anachronism, or worse: an indelible stain. Going back at least fifty years it had been the purlieu for drunks, drugs, hookers, trouble. The stories Momma told. Even the cops avoided it.

I headed there to question Lyle's connection, Sparky. On the way, I imagined her. *She might be the woman whose hair was stashed in Harold's Edgar Allan Poe book.* Its unsavory qualities still with me.

When I arrived, Sparky's gray junker van, "Lightning Electric," was parked outside.

As I stepped into the bar's gloom I almost crashed into Geraldine Mae Scotts, the notorious eighty-something-year-old grand diva who'd been singing bawdy sea shanties at the bar for more than half a century.

"Sparky?" I asked as she moved determinedly past me, a brown muskrat wig sliding off her head. She pointed to the back and headed to the other side of the large room where, to my amazement, Gordon Mingle waited at a small table. He waved at the two of us. I'm sure Gordon was as shocked to see me in such a disreputable place as I was to see him there. But neither of us showed signs of it. I turned to find Sparky.

A sparse Hendrix-like guitar swelled across the room, its waves breaking briefly for a deep-chambered voice, "spellbound," as the bar slowly filled with desperate clientele: a man missing most of his teeth, another dragging an oxygen canister, a chinless woman with more skull than hair. I sighed. It was too early for such a gathering.

Three topless mermaids floated languorously behind the huge bar. Their breasts fell back upon their chests as they rose in rotation to the surface for a breath of air. Their scaled lower bodies and fins fluttered with a variety of marine greens.

The music drifted:

"We were swimming through a daydream
And the sea released our feet
Then the sun laughed on the water
And hid what lay beneath . . . "

I stood alone, unnoticed, at the center of the wooden bar, mermaids flowing above me in the massive tank —two white, one Asian— drawing ravening male attention, as the nymphs beckoned and suggested, and the men nodded in acquiescence. Everyone at the bar and in the large glass aquarium above them would likely be scarred and shredded if the tank were to shatter.

"You must be Eunis," came a sandpaper, high-pitched voice from behind.

I spun around.

"Ow," said the woman when she fully took me in.

"Yes," I said without offering a handshake, which would have been both out of place and hygienically a mistake. "Is there a place we can talk? Back there?"

I walked behind her, not sure what *I'd* just seen. When we slid into the booth, back by the restrooms, the sharp smell of bleach and the broad smell of urine forced me to abandon breathing. Not for long.

"So?" Sparky said. She was very thin; piercings almost completely masked her face. Her eyes were set deep in shadow between sharp objects that threatened to blind. She could've been Asian, she could've been Native American, she could've been white. And almost any age. A well-worn beret pulled low on her shaved head, the stubble insufficient to hide the filth accumulating on her scalp, and no way to ascertain if it was her hair stashed in *The Tell-Tale Heart*. The ridge of her nose — though impaled so savagely I had to look at her sideways not to take on pain— was the only feature that suggested flesh and blood.

"Sparky?"

She rolled up the sleeve of her work shirt and itched at her arm, which surprisingly lacked tattoos of any kind. "I don't have all day, and I'm just doing this 'cause your brother is a fucking saint."

I would've loved to inquire regarding his sainthood, but there were more pressing matters. "Lyle said you knew a woman who knew Harold Cloonis."

"Your husband," she said matter-of-factly.

"You knew him?"

"You mean did I have intercourse with him?"

"No, that's not at all—"

"I never met him, but he must have been some strange dude."

"You found him strange?"

"Not me, lady. I fucking told you, I never met him."

"But?"

"But there was this —not sure what to call her— I guess, friend." She waggled her head. "Acquaintance. Anyway, she dated him. Well, they fucked like bunnies."

"Harold fucked like bunnies." I'd assumed I was the first, though I'd never asked. But then he had never offered. Anger, again.

"*She* said. Never watched them. Nothing wrong with that."

"When was this?"

> "... *We were spellbound*
> *Yes spellbound...*"

Sparky paused as one of the mermaids, a full-figured woman with long red hair flowing like kelp, waved at her. She waved back. "Three, four years ago."

Before me. I relaxed.

Sparky returned to me.

"That her, the one in the tank with the big bosombas?" I asked.

"Sherry? Shit, no. Pammy, Pamela, was tall, thin, short hair. She should have worn her hair longer, more feminine. Whatever she could do."

"Lyle said you thought she was weird."

"I never said that." Sparky's body twitched in obvious discomfort. "She was different, that's all."

"Where is she now? Her last name? How do I find her?"

"Don't know, don't know. Good luck." Sparky began to slide out of the booth.

"Something, *anything,* you remember of what she told you about her time with Harold?"

"You wouldn't hurt her?"

"Me?! Of course not. It's about Harold." Unraveling Harold.

"Well, the Woodland Cabins, down by Kabekona. She mentioned he took her there."

The same place he'd taken me. I was adrift again.

> "...*Who knew we were just creatures*
> *Shipwrecked on a beach*
> *With nothing but each other*
> *And the truth just out of reach*
> *We were spellbound*
> *Spellbound*
> *Yes spellbound*"

CHAPTER FORTY-FOUR

Traveling south on Route 371, the old highway straightened out, the terrain flattened, and the corridor of pine and poplar trees broadened like the sumptuous entrance to a private estate or castle. There was nary a car in either direction. The Chippewa National Forest, that first time with Harold, the revelation at the beauty opening up and surrounding me, and the anticipation of *us*— a couple of discovery.

Leech Lake spread out on my left, and soon I turned onto County Road 38 toward Kabekona Bay. The sign was still weathered, unimposing, but my heart dropped a few notches: "Woodland Cabins" and the arrow. I remembered a sliver of that day, the owner's recognition of Harold as we entered, ever-so-slight. I'd meant to ask him about it, maybe I did, but it had been lost.

The whining of the vacuum cleaner was enough to drive me out, but I stood my ground in the reception cabin. I let the screen door slam and the woman jerked up from her cleaning.

"Oh. Oh! I didn't hear you come in," she stammered. "We're not open for the season for another three weeks."

I'd rehearsed several entrance speeches but they all failed me. "My husband stayed here, before we were married, and I need to find the woman."

The lady switched off the vacuum and pushed the bandana back over her broad forehead to her tangle of brown hair. "What?"

I considered removing my shaded glasses for sincerity. Re-thought it. "I have a photo of my husband . . . my late husband, and it's important for me to find the woman he was with." I pulled the photo from my jean pocket, shuttled closer, holding it out for the woman.

"I'm not sure . . . What is it you want?" She didn't take the photo, her resistance growing.

"I need your help. I'm sorry, I know this is unconventional, but my husband . . . he committed suicide, and so much is unclear, and I thought that this woman —she was with him before me, before my time— she might have some clues, you know, for why he did it."

"Have I seen you before?" The woman came closer.

I wondered if the truth was best. "Well, yes. I was here with him about a year ago. He proposed to me here. We had the cabin at the end."

"Number one, The Tamarack."

"He liked his privacy."

"Look, I'm sorry, but we're not a detective agency, and my guess is that my husband might not approve."

"If you'd just look at my husband's photo. Please."

"Why a woman *before* your time? I've learned to stay away from such things."

"We were barely newlyweds and he killed himself. Can you imagine living with that?"

The woman wiped the sweat away with her arm. She made a low humming sound, almost a growl. "Look, I'm going over to Cabin Number Eleven to patch a wall. Should take me half an hour."

"I really can't wait."

"Be quiet!" snapped the woman. "See those binders?" She pointed to two shelves of binders that strongly resembled my own "Faces" scrapbook. "We keep one photo of every visitor or every couple that spends a week here. You're probably in there with your husband. It's chronological, you understand?"

The idea of photos unsettled me. "I doubt my husband would let you take a picture of us, and I don't remember—"

"It's in our contract and people appreciate it. Marty's an amateur photographer. They're spontaneous; they capture an intimate moment, memories. We've done it since the day we opened. I've got work to do." She heaved brusquely and stepped away. "You're welcome to search for your photo. I'll be back in a half hour."

She pushed past me but released the screen door gradually so it didn't slam. I was left staring at three shelves of binders. Organized: a binder every year or two. But they weren't *that* organized. No names or notations under a single photo, and the scrapbooks didn't break evenly.

When I finally found the previous May, I discovered a photo that most likely was Harold and me, at a distance, out on the small dock, both with our arms up, as if in the midst of a conflagration. The photo cut a swath of pain along my sternum. I tossed the memory.

You're a scientist. Narrow. The handful of pages gave me thickness by year, a skill that Harold had manifested. I took that information.

Calculating back four years to January 4th, I began moving to the present, scanning the pages of photographs, four rows, five photos each. My eye checked the wall clock every few minutes.

I was looking for Harold, but given the photo of Harold and me from only a year earlier, a long shot might be hard to decipher. I was surprised to find that most of the photos were *not* framed long, but loving, tender, probably taken close-up with a telephoto lens. Still, to find Harold . . .

My task was made easier because the winter months were out. May to September, twice to mid-October. I removed my shades, following every frame with my finger, wanting to stop at times to take in the warmth of couples seeing each other, perhaps like they'd never seen each other before or might never see each other again. I suppressed the longing and moved methodically on.

The pages fattened behind me. I was almost within a year of reaching *my* May with Harold, when I flipped back a page, took a second look at a shot of a couple, apparently on the same weathered dock in front of Cabin #1 on which Harold and I had stood. *And fought?* It *was* Harold, despite the shadow across his face, because the gawky fellow wore a dark blue pinstripe suit jacket, and beneath it, a cotton candy coral shirt. At a summer resort, *who else!* A breeze came off the lake, a yearning that swept through the screen door and startled me. I closed my eyes then took another look.

He held the woman at arm's length, taking her in, awe apparently in his eye, the blue green lake behind them. She was older than he, thin, almost as tall, eyes wide in complicitous thrall, her blonde hair cut too short or too long. Pammy.

His arms rested, cupping above her waist and her arms . . . she had no arms! Sprouting from each shoulder was a small nob, then a thin hand, nothing more. Thalidomide, or something like it.

I snapped the scrapbook closed, all wind knocked out of me. I started to cry, my chest ground into fine particles, and all of them slipping away. I couldn't tell exactly why. But the clock was ticking and I had to keep moving.

CHAPTER FORTY-FIVE

Harold's box of books had been delivered and sat open in the kitchen, Momma scavenging through. "What's this crap?" she asked holding a cigarette perilously close to one of the old books.

"It's *my* crap." I pulled *Dickens and the Staplehurst Train Crash* from her and rounded up several others Momma had scattered on the table, one of which, *Great Expectations*, sat in a puddle of beer.

"Touchy, touchy."

I wiped the beer off *Great Expectations* with my jeans and put it in the box. "Lyle!" I called out.

"He's resting."

"Lyle, can you come out here and help me move something?" Momma glowered.

"Whatcha need?" Lyle walked stiffly, more gangly and disoriented than ever.

"She shouldn't a waked you," said Momma. "I told her you was restin'."

"It's okay, Momma, just layin' down." A small wave at me, a small smile.

"You okay?" I asked.

He motioned not to worry. "Whatcha need?"

"This box. Into the cellar."

After a lot of shuffling and grunting, Lyle and I got the box to the cellar steps and down, but not before he had to take multiple breaks along the way. He was pretty pale.

"You sure you're okay?" I asked again.

"Hangover."

I wasn't convinced.

"How'd it go?" He propped himself on the box. "With Sparky? She give you good juice?"

"I guess."

"You learn somethin' about Harold?"

"Can't be sure. I've got very little to measure it against."

"Small sample, huh?"

"Why, yes. You understand sample size?"

"Not really, just somethin' comin' up. Vocabulary. I try to keep learnin'. Makes for good lyrics."

"You're writing again."

He shook his head. "Not really. Maybe thinkin' about it."

"Well, good, that's great."

"You need anythin' else?" He tapped the box of books.

"I'm good. Thanks." I leaned to hug him.

He started, he hesitated, he pulled away, signaled goodbye. "See ya," he said, trudging his way up the groaning stairs.

Alone, my journal and *Bleak House* by my bedside, I paged through *Charles Dickens and the Staplehurst Train Crash*. My phone, suddenly connecting me to people, rang. I settled the book into my lap and reached for the phone. Roddy, *again*. I was ready to disconnect, then decided I'd throw the sailor off the ship, once and for all.

"Roddy," I said flatly.

"Sorry to bother you," he said, "but I got some information I thought you'd want."

"How's that?"

"Your friend Ruthie, the Jamaican lady, her grandson-in-law is looking for you."

"Anthony."

"Anthony. He's gotten calls about the comb, whatever that means, and he's not sure what he should do."

I was speechless.

"Eunis?"

"Yes."

"He said to tell you he hasn't mentioned the comb to anyone. Still, he got a call. He says another curator got a call too. What's all this about a comb?"

"No big deal, just some friends getting dramatic." I imagined Roddy, probably a simper on his lips.

"Over a tool of beauty?" He said with some bite.

I'd never thought of it quite that way. "Yes."

"Anyway," he continued, "Anthony didn't know how to reach you. What should he do?"

"I'll call him. For now tell him to keep doing what he's doing and say he knows nothing. How'd he call you?"

"Lyle gave him my number."

"Lyle? Really?" *Why would Lyle do that?* A not-so-small worm of irritation twisted inside. But I was glad to hear Roddy's voice after all.

"You okay?" he said, softening. "How's it going up there?"

I tugged on my hair. "Fine, fine. Thank you, thanks for calling."

"How are you?" he asked again.

"I'm reading Dickens."

"Children searching for their father."

"What?"

"Dickens, he was always writing about that. Anyway, how are you, really?"

"I'm fine, like I said."

"Could you use some help?"

I laughed. "If I need to get bailed out, you'll be the first I'll call."

"Good, I'll count on it."

The Dickens book beckoned. "Thanks, thanks again for calling."

"Sure."

"Okay, bye." And as soon as I'd hung up I realized I hadn't bothered to ask how he was doing.

I fiddled with *Dickens and the Staplehurst Train Crash*. I even considered calling Roddy back. Then came that recurring dead frame into which Harold swung, vacant eye, by his neck, then out. *Come with me.* "Damn it!" I picked up *Dickens and the Staplehurst Train Crash*. I began reading:

> "On June 9, 1865, the Tidal Train which transported
> cross-channel passengers was making its way to
> London, clattering through Kent at 50 miles per

hour. Between Headcorn and Staplehurst, 50 feet of track had been pulled up for repair, the tracklayers miscalculating the time of the approaching train, a train that carried Charles Dickens and his closely guarded secret, his mistress Nelly.

The train hurtled over a small bridge into a stream. Ten passengers were killed and 40 injured. Dickens, a small man, was able to squeeze through a window and help administer to some of the injured, but not before he helped a beautiful young girl off the train, desperate that the Press and his wife not know his secret."

"Son of a bitch!" I could envision Harold reading those passages, doubt or guilt fixed upon his face, as if he, not his muse, had been discovered. Had I discovered? And every one of the few things that I thought I knew, and I thought I could control, now felt like a violation. My frustration filled the room.

"Harold, you bastard!" I grabbed the journal and threw it across the room, first striking the light bulb then the small washbasin and tearing the yellow suturing fabric off the mirror, as shadows swung back and forth over me, and the muslin marigolds folded to the floor. Through the mirror's corroded surface, I saw my own nebulous rage, slow vapors rising, disappearing in darkness, and rising again. All so unscientific. Until I considered what Lyle said, about inhaling Carver's chemicals and what it might have done to my brain. What it might have caused me to do.

So I steadied myself, opened my laptop and looked it up. The research showed that at high concentrations Formic acid (ant venom) has dangerous fumes potentially causing acidosis — confusion, memory loss, and seizures. What had I done?

Past the sign on Lake Bemidji boasting "Headwaters of the Mississippi," and across the bridge separating it from Lake Irving, Nymore had been assimilated into Bemidji proper. The Hotel Hell area of tree-toppers, catty-mans, rail-setters, and truckers was gone. As well, Lyle's "inspiration connection," leveled clean, and in its place the Stanford Center, a state-of-the-art convention monolith, a curved modern-day coliseum surrounded by acres of empty asphalt parking. In the old days, at least, there were places to hide. No more.

Far to the left of the obligatory building, a small cluster of cars reflected the sun, which drew me closer, though I'd hoped Gordon would call any minute, postponing the Miss USA interviews. But of course he would not. And what good would it have done? Eventually I would've needed to meet the other judges.

Anyway, *here* at Miss USA was a tribute and testament to beauty. I pulled down the car's visor and checked the small mirror: a New York casual dark green blazer, playing down my shape as much as possible, taupe slacks, and my shades. Never enough camouflage.

But I came prepared. Besides assigning a Fischer–Saller scale letter to each of the hair colors —only two genes have been firmly established— and a number to each of the fifteen genes associated with eye color, I'd taken the statistics of every Miss USA winner since 1952 and crunched the numbers to give me the composite ideal:

> Age: 21.5 years
> Height: 5'8"
> Weight: 118.5 lbs.
> Measurements: 34-23-34*
> Hair: Deep Brunette
> Eyes: Green**

Born: April
(Everything but their astrological sign and their shade
of skin, though most were Caucasian)

*Other research suggested her waist should measure
twelve inches smaller than her bust and hips. Close
enough.
** Eye color varies depending on the lighting conditions, especially for lighter-colored eyes. I'd adjust for
the room as best I could

And of course there were trends since 1952 that the composite didn't reflect. I was still most interested in the face and
wanted to see if the standard held, and if not, how symmetry,
eye and hair color played out, and why.

I followed the cardboard signs past the security guard who
didn't check my ID despite the signage:

**"Miss USA candidates and judges ONLY.
Identification required."**

The whole building reverberated as if empty. It felt that way
every step across the mammoth exhibition hall on which my sister Carly would have played hockey —had the hall existed back
then —to "Lake View 7," a small rectangular room blasted in silver light with a panorama of high weeds, untended gravel
berms, and the lake. It was sparsely set with nine folding chairs
in a semi-circle around one solitary chair for the candidate, She
Who Would Be Beauty. Against the wall I noted clipboards,
pens, paper cups, and two coffee urns making ticking noises.

One last wish: that I was dipping into one of my small, cool
lakes rather than exposing myself to nine other sets of eyes and
sharing the enormous responsibility of changing a young woman's life forever.

I'd done my best to arrive just as the interviews were to
begin —10 AM— so I could slip into the rear of the room without fanfare. Unfortunately no one sat in the hot seat and a

number of the judges milled around. Over the shoulder of a tall man in a sport jacket and two well-dressed women, I spotted Gordon, dressed casually, smiling, and holding a brushed aluminum bullet mug.

"Eunis!" he said with a welcoming wave to join. "Come in, meet the other judges."

One woman, perhaps mid sixties with fine platinum hair and a hematite necklace, turned to acknowledge me with a pleasant smile. Very country club, as I had expected. No reaction; she was nice. Perhaps Gordon had forewarned the judges.

The couple in conversation lagged. I drew near to the group, every atom in me urging escape, hearing the man's voice more clearly —deep and assured, chuckling, familiar, alarming. With the other woman, he opened the circle to me. He towered above.

Victor King! I was stunned.

Gordon, showing his best manners, introduced the two women first, though the sound of rushing water obliterated their names. I shook their hands, dazed and unable to meet their eyes. A mistake, I knew. I was a judge, after all.

"Eunis, you know Victor, don't you?" Gordon asked innocently. "He graduated ahead of you a couple of years. Star football, star hockey; well, star everything. He's still here in Bemidji with his beautiful wife, Michelle, herself quite an athlete, and he's our newly-elected mayor, head of the city council."

"Melissa," corrected Victor.

A tunnel of gray genetic matter circled me, wanting to suck me away, but I was on land, I couldn't move.

"I'm not sure we've ever met." Victor extended his hand, taking mine before I could pull it away, and tightened around it — impossible to tell whether he misjudged his own strength or if he was threatening me, but it hurt.

"Aah," said Gordon, putting down his mug and flowing quickly to the door. "Our first young lady and our last judge, thank goodness. Please, please judges, be sure you have a clipboard and a pen. Additional comments and observations can be written on the back of any sheet. Please take your seats."

"Vic! Sisel. I'm so sorry. The kids were just . . . well, you understand, sorry," offered the newest judge, a well-groomed man flushed with stress. Middle-aged with the face of a mature lamb, his eyes and cheeks drooped and the first signs of a gut pushed at his sport jacket.

"Sit, sit, please," instructed Gordon, and the twenty-something Japanese woman who had been talking to Victor took his arm and walked him to the center of the semi-circle, leaving chairs to the right and left of them. Gordon went to the first candidate as the other judges went to the chairs.

I stood immobilized until Gordon noticed and shooed me to my seat. I realized that, to avoid sitting next to Victor, I'd have to slide in to the outside chair. I did so, cutting so close to the lamb-faced judge that he nearly sat on my lap before pulling away, annoyed.

I stared straight ahead. When the young candidate walked nervously to the center of all eyes and then recovered, seating herself demurely, she was an adorable young woman, with rounded cheeks like my sister Carly, but without the attitude.

"Here," whispered Gordon putting the clipboard and pen in my lap. "You'll need these."

By the time I'd composed myself Gordon had introduced the judges, then offered direction and a level of intimidation when he mentioned to the candidate that Minnesota hadn't had a Miss USA winner since Barbara Peterson was crowned in 1976.

"Edina, Minnesota," offered Sisel Overgaard, the pleasant platinum-haired judge.

"Bob Barker and Helen O'Connell," added lamb-face, now identified as Sandy, though he was probably eight at the time. The Japanese woman, striking, herself with requisite fashion model cheekbones, peeked admiringly at Victor. "They were the hosts in seventy-six," Sandy clarified.

"At any rate," continued Gordon, short-circuiting the coffee-klatch atmosphere, "you have sworn that you are between the ages of eighteen and twenty-seven. Is that right, Erin?"

Erin looked barely eighteen. "Yes," said the strawberry blonde. She flashed a practiced smile at every judge. Her freckles glowed. Eyes blue, face symmetrical.

"And you've never competed before, not in any state?"

"No."

"You are not now, or have ever been, married?"

"No, sir." Again that smile.

"And I'm sorry to ask, but it's required: you are not pregnant, nor have ever given birth to a child?"

I would never have considered that as affecting beauty.

"Not yet, but I hope to someday." Erin made sure she achieved eye contact with every judge, even me, though she couldn't fully engage me with my gray shades on. But she tried.

"Finally," said Gordon checking off his list, "I'm sure a beautiful young woman like you has a boyfriend, maybe many, but if you should ascend past these preliminaries to state champion and then to Miss USA, you understand that you are required to remain single throughout the process and throughout your reign."

The reign of a monarch —it raised a burning sensation in me. Outside a wind had kicked up, bouncing light off the young scrub pines.

"I will happily remain single for that privilege." By now Erin was quite unruffled.

"Terrific." Gordon checked off his last directive. Again he read from his clipboard: "This is the first of three equally important areas of the competition: the judges' panel, where we will interview you and the other competitors. Swimsuit and evening gown competition tomorrow."

Erin took a deep breath and smiled while whisking away a pesky coil of honey-colored hair that had fallen over her broad perfect forehead.

"The lucky young woman who will be selected by our judges as the new Minnesota title holder will embark on a magical year of appearances, parades, prizes, and awards, culminating in an all-expense paid trip to the national Miss USA competition," he stopped, "er...pageant, where she will compete with the other forty-nine state title holders. The winners of this division then advance to compete live on the national Miss USA telecast."

Gordon paused for a breath. "It says here that our program is designed to be an excellent vehicle for advancing your career and personal goals." He added a long exhale. "Oh, and congratulations making it beyond the selection committee."

That solicited an acknowledging flutter of her eyelids. All the while I tried to reorganize my thoughts, which included my own intricate numbering system, cross-referencing my research on facial balance and other factors. Perhaps her cheekbones failed her. I felt guilty.

"So, Erin, are you ready for the questions from our panel of judges?"

Erin straightened her neck and flashed the brightest biggest smile yet. "I certainly am." She placed her hands, practiced, in her lap.

Victor jumped in first. "Of course you're quite beautiful, Erin, but this competition is about inner beauty too." Out of the corner of my shades I saw Gordon close his eyes. Victor studied Erin's perfect ankles and calves. Legs, I had read, could 'make or break' a contestant, especially in the swimsuit category.

"So what," he continued, "do you think is the most important characteristic a young woman can bring to her relationship with a man —a young man." This made even Jacqui, the Japanese woman, widen her eyes, but she kept them trained on Erin.

"Truth," said Erin.

"Truth?" said Victor.

"What I mean is honesty." She was visibly upset with her answer.

Sandy, Sisel Overgaard, and another woman far to my right took notes.

"Ahh, honesty," said Victor.

"And I should add," said Erin sitting erect, regaining form, "that it pertains equally to any relationship, man or woman, young or old."

Jacqui logged that comment. As for me, I became obsessed with an unexplained stain on the sleeve of my blazer and a pressure building in my chest.

"Of course," said Victor. "Of course. But can't too much honesty create . . . problems?"

Erin thought a moment. "Well, I suppose it can. There may

be times when discretion is the better part of valor. But if some-one asks me a direct question I'm likely to give them the answer, unless the answer is unnecessarily hurtful. In that case, I might attenuate my answer. It can be a challenge."

"Yes, thank you," said Victor. "You obviously like challenges too." It was an invitation. And then he delivered the requisite public protection for himself. "Well done."

Erin smiled.

"Eunis, do you have a follow-up question?" asked Victor, startling me.

Erin and the other judges turned my way.

"Well, aah, not a follow-up . . . but Erin, being beautiful . . . how would you deal with sexual harassment, or worse, the threat of sexual violence?"

Before Erin could answer, Gordon inserted himself. "I just think—"

"Would you let it go?" I continued. "Or would you be con-cerned that the perpetrator might continue his or her ways if left unchecked?"

"I'm, I'm not sure." Erin shifted uncomfortably. "But I think being pro-active can prevent such situations." She faced the oth-er judges. "I like to set limits."

"Very good," injected Gordon, swiftly passing the next ques-tion to Sisel who accommodated with something domesticated that evaporated from my consciousness.

The morning continued on like that, civil and largely in keep-ing with manners, as one candidate after another revolved through. They were all quite attractive and I applied my facial balance scale to them, quantifying hair, eye, and skin quality and color. I checked lips, brows, even facial posture. The more I cod-ified, the more it felt unfair, even to the girl who forgot to spit out her gum and had to swallow it.

Around 3 PM I began watching the sun splinter on the lake and started drifting like Huck Finn down the Mississippi. Hon-estly, as beautiful as they were, none were as beautiful as Atara, as much as I hated to admit it.

"Eunis?" asked Gordon. "Do you have a question for Lindsay before we wrap up the day?"

She was a petite young woman, early twenties, auburn hair, peach skin, peaceful gray eyes. Dressed in a sensible teal crew neck sweater and a flounce skirt, the color of fawn. "Certainly. Lindsay, what do you find most attractive in others?"

Lindsay thought a moment. "Inquisitive people, people who are excited about whatever: agriculture or fractal patterns or history."

"And you?"

"History. Well, mostly ancestry."

"You consider heritage important?"

"I'm fascinated by it." She was genuinely enthused. "I think we are all-all-all . . ." she struggled and took a breath. "We are all products of our lin-lin-lineage. For instance, my name, Li-Lindsay, is Scottish, English. It means a la-lake or a marsh. And I love to swim. It can also mean an island of linden trees and I can be like that too, like an island. I li-like to be alone sometimes, to be quiet, so I can think. And linden trees, they're lime colored, you may be aware, lightweight but strong. I feel I'm like that."

A subterranean bubble appeared to tickle her mouth then popped her back into the room. "But more than that, it leads to other discoveries. It inspired me to study the impact of the tree in Scotland."

I found myself brimming with Lindsay. "So tell us, what have you discovered?"

"Well," continued Lindsay spiritedly, "Li-linden trees can be measured in centuries. There's one in Gloucestershire estimated to be two thousand years old. The trees create herbal medicines, their sticky nectar so good for bees and creating honey. It's also a great wood for sculpting and, because of its acoustics, great for making guitars."

Victor checked his watch and craned his neck to make contact with Gordon, who pretended not to see.

"Going back to the first recorded history of Scotland, the first century when the Romans tried to conquer 'the painted people,' Scots were hardy, successfully defending themselves with little but stone and linden wood. The myth is that our people were light as the wind, so uncatchable, but hard as stone in a battle, and always stuck to their beliefs."

Jacqui and Sisel gurgled. Sandy scribbled something in his notes.

Lindsay continued. "The Germans associate the tree with justice and peace. Their mythology says to dance around the tree unearths truth. It's the tree of lo-lovers."

"And, of course," interrupted Victor, "there's Lindsay Lohan."

Lindsay suddenly looked disorientated.

"Well," said Gordon jumping in, "our time *is* up. Thank you so much, Lindsay, for your thoughtful answers. I'm sure I speak for all the judges when I say that you've been delightful and we're so glad you're in this competition. We'll see you tomorrow for the swimsuit and evening gown segments."

☽☽☽

"What's the rush?" said Gordon, catching up to me in the parking lot. "I think that went well, don't you?"

I fumbled with my keys, eager to avoid Victor as he ambled out with Jacqui, Sisel, and Sandy strategically circling him. "I guess."

"You sound disappointed. Nothing gained for your research?"

"I'm not sure. Maybe the objective coordinates are too fine for me to see. They all had elements. But I've got to go."

"Okay, but don't forget now, you owe me."

"Owe?"

"If you predict gorgeous weather," Gordon said and breathed in the endless sky and refuge of sunshine, "you're too late. Sometimes I forget how remarkable it can be here. This is uncommonly spectacular for this time of year, don't you think? *I* wouldn't have predicted this."

"Thanks for including me." I touched his sleeve. "And, yes, it's unusual, beautiful, bizarre."

"Tomorrow." Gordon tapped the car hood as he walked away.

"Tomorrow."

There wasn't much to be gained from the next day's evening gown and swimsuit competitions —not from my point of view.

Superfluous. I imagined it was Victor's favorite.

And during a break in the afternoon, I'd walked into the restroom only to find one of the more exquisite participants, a brown-haired, moss-eyed beauty named April... taking a shit. The stall door had swung open. Just that context changed everything, wrung the beauty out of her.

Would that have been true if it had been Roddy? Yes, early on, I think it would have. And what about Harold, where did his beauty reside? I added timing to the growing and troubling subjective contributors to beauty.

Without warning, my atoms reeled. I spun around.

"I figured I'd find ya hanging around a beauty event." Atara glowed with anticipation. I was certain she'd spring at me in the next moment. "With your looks, I'll always find you." Her irresistible mouth opened, she bared teeth.

I fingered my keys. "What do you want?"

"I want my fucking comb, you pathetic excuse of a woman."

"You've come to the wrong place, I don't have any comb." It must have been worth a whole lot more than I'd realized.

She jumped at me and laughed as I launched back against the car, crushing my wrist, shooting pain up my right arm. "You don't want to mess with me," I said. "You don't really want the authorities to know what goes on in your apartment."

This pleased her. "You really are a hick. No one gives a shit what goes on in my ship. We're all consenting adults . . . just like you, you beast. You got what you wanted, and I got you on tape. One look at you, and one at me, and the cops'll see that you're just a jealous bitch twisted by your own ugliness. Now give me the comb before you have an accident. It's mine, just like Levi's mine."

"Victor!" I called across the parking lot, maybe twenty-five yards. "Could you come over here for a moment?"

She shook her head. "Oh really, like this'll make a difference."

"Well, hello, who's this?" Victor was already sizing her up.

I guess I was glad to see him. What tape? "Someone I knew in New York. She and her *husband*." The dare made it more inviting.

"I'm Victor. Welcome to Bemidji." He took both of her hands in his. "I'm the mayor."

She gave me one last look, cold like an executioner, and by the time she'd met Victor's eyes, she was a different woman. Seductive, she'd changed skins in front of me. "Mr. Mayor, a pleasure."

"Vic, call me Vic." There probably wasn't a man alive who wouldn't have flashed the same staggered, open-mouthed surrender. Probably many women too, and she knew it, a dose of her favored drug.

"Vic," she said.

"Did you need something, Eunis?" He barely took his eyes off her.

"Just wanted you to meet Atara. She's just in for a short time."

"Is this the first visit to our town for you and your husband, or has Eunis already shown you around?"

"My husband's not here."

"Oh."

"Is that an invitation?"

"It could be."

"You'd do that for me?"

"Absolutely, if it's okay with Eunis."

Atara answered for me. "Oh, it's okay with Eunis. It will give her time to find a small item I lent her. In fact, Mayor—"

"Vic."

"Vic. You'd be surprised how the two of us met. I'd bet you'd get a chuckle."

I opened the car door and dropped in, placed the key in the ignition.

She knocked on my window. "Looking forward to the next time," she said, her voice muted through the glass and her deep viridian pools awash in pleasure. "*Really* looking forward."

In those eyes, even in the late afternoon light, I couldn't see to the bottom of her malice.

CHAPTER FORTY-SEVEN

Rather than return to the farmhouse to grapple with Momma's demands, the farmhouse rehabilitation project, or Lyle's lethargy, I followed the last sweep of the sun west, a desolate strip of asphalt, toward the scattering of lakes and ponds that might be small and warm enough for a late afternoon dip. I needed something to cleanse me of the day and help still the colliding atoms set off by Victor and Atara, and what Atara had implied. Not just physical harm, but a tape.

Just as I was about to pass Carver's abandoned taxidermy shop, my phone pinged with a text message. I steered into the tall weeds under Carver's weathered sign, his eyes shrouded by the years but still staring down on me. "Preserve beauty forever."

Reaching for the phone my first thought was Roddy. I was eager for his voice, a paradox that I registered with less opposition than usual. But I didn't recognize the number. Just three words: "Try Johnny Ray."

I studied it for a minute, not understanding. Possibly a wrong number. To my right, the shuttered taxidermy shop sat heaped against itself. Almost a decade on and off I'd spent working for Carver, and it'd been almost ten years since I'd set foot in the place. It drew me out of the car and into the unusually warm, moist air, across the clearing to the sagging front steps, to plywood posted "Keep Out," crisscrossed with two-by-two's, riddled with nails barring entrance.

I walked around back. Someone had hung brick-colored muslin over the windows. I wiped the perspiration from my forehead. The wood paneling was hoary and cupping and some had fallen off, leaving the tar underbelly exposed and tearing. *Worse even than Momma's house. Be thankful.*

The rear door was chained but someone or some thing had

pried it partially open. A thin shaft of light fell in. I peeked. I tugged on the door and it flapped open, allowing me to step into the darkness.

Inside, Mr. Carver's precious workspace had been ransacked. By the doorway, puddles of water, I hoped, collected where the rain had overrun the roof's defenses in an attempt to decontaminate the past. I hopped over rusted cans, a few oozing strange yellow or black mucous. A cream and coral mushroom the size of a basketball had sprouted from the foot of his long workbench, enveloping the leg and sending spores onto the surface. They appeared luminous in the dark.

I picked my way to my old workbench, spotted a strainer, forceps, a headless hammer. Two skins of undetermined creatures still decomposed on hooks, quivering. Stillness everywhere, and yet a draft?

Hairs separated from the skins, settling on my face and lips, fouling me before I swiped them away. Something scurried over my foot. I screamed. The room closed in, perhaps invading chemicals, and me immobilized. *Stop breathing.* I'd breathed here for ten years; my madness had an itinerary.

Rushing water. Victor? Harold? Atoms jiggered then started colliding. Something imminent. And I was frozen. A car pulled up, idling. *Be still.* It pulled away.

I turned abruptly, kicking glass and awakening the grieving dust, a choking particulate, then tipped through cobwebs and out, gasping for air in the twilight. I feasted on it till I was in the car, vibrating. I yanked the small bottle of hand purifier from the glove box, rubbed it liberally over my hands, arms, and face before sliding the key in the ignition and accelerating away.

To really breathe, I rolled down the window. The deep rumble of an engine broke the silence. From behind a clump of ragged black spruce, a dark blue car jumped to the roadway and was upon me, surrounding me in dagger-piercing decibels. *Trying to pass? Forcing me to the road's far side, down the small embankment?* I clenched the wheel. The car sped inches from me —if my elbow had been crooked out the window, it would have been ripped from my body. That's how close. Then it was gone, its brattling muffler and blue hulk careening away into the sundown shadows.

I rolled to a stop. My air, *the* air, was thin, my molecules still in motion. I opened the car door and leaned out for a full breath. *Was that a threat or my galloping imagination?*

Standing by the car, not a branch moved. All moisture was gone. I was breathing deep but it was like inhaling fine sand, it was *that* still, suddenly *that* dry. With the feeling of a giant magnet pulling me away from the Mazda to the sky.

I couldn't see above the treetops but they'd stopped moving. Completely. Not a sound. No birds. Everywhere I looked. My hand went to my heart. I closed my eyes and listened.

Then back into the car, I grabbed my phone and Gordon's card. I punched in his number, clumsily, missing one —*shit!*— and starting over. It rang. I started driving. After a few rings: Gordon's languorous voicemail.

"C'mon, c'mon," I yelled at the phone and searched the sky above my windshield. In the rearview mirror, the sky turned charcoal. Mean. Whatever reality I was living had me tethered, pulling me up, pulling me down. His voicemail beeped.

"Gordon," I shouted, "I'm northwest of Bemidji and Route 2, a little past Carver's old place. It's 7:15 or so. I think . . . I think I'm sensing a vortex."

CHAPTER FORTY-EIGHT

By the time I arrived at the farmhouse I was sure I'd made a fool of myself. I sat for a moment in the car, windows rolled down. *If I stuck to science, really thought about it, there'd be an explanation for this without the drama.* The sky was clear. *No more than a punk driver, probably.* There wasn't an appreciable weather pattern that would cause anyone concern.

"Someone drove you off the road?" Lyle was propped up on his bed, watching me march back and forth at the foot of it. "Some drunk?"

"What do you know about Victor King?"

"The pretty boy mayor?"

"Yeah, him."

"We both majored in women, but we didn't exactly travel the same crowd. Plus, he was older."

"Ever see him in the Drink 'n' Dive? I heard he likes to party."

"Yeah, well, he used to come in. A lot. I'd see him. Every fuckin' woman buzzin' around him, but he stopped cold."

"When he started his political push?"

"Nah, way before that. Maybe fifteen years ago, time you were workin' for crazy Carver. Why?"

"So he's stopped drinking?"

"Shit, no. He still drinks like a fish, just don't like 'em."

"What does that mean?"

"Word is he had a nightmare. Join the club, right? Anyways, really scared the bejesus out of him, and I'm glad somethin' slowed the sonuvabitch down because—"

"What kind of a nightmare?"

"Shit, I don't know. All's I hear is that one day he doesn't want to have nothin' to do with the Drink 'n' Dive. Was roarin' drunk one night at The Back Door, you know the place?"

I nodded.

"Friend of mine hears him whimperin' to a couple buddies bout being freaked out by mermaids, 'face the color of the moon, hair bright as the sun, eyes of a rabid wolf.' Scary shit like that. So he ain't goin' back to the Dive, no matter how fine those fishy titties look."

Eyes of rabid wolf!

"You think he tried to run you off the road?"

I kind of snarled. "Don't know." *A dark blue car.*

"Why'd he do that? He barely knows you."

"I told you, I don't know."

"Or," said Lyle salaciously, "you and pretty boy been secretly doin' the humpty? His wife would fuckin' love that, take the kids and every last penny. I hear she's got her own bad temper." A modicum of glee surfaced in his tired eyes. "His royal reputation would go down the toilet, which *would* be kinda nice."

He tossed me a guilty glance. "I don't mean nothin' against you."

"Don't know him. Just saw him today at the Miss USA interviews. He's one of the judges."

"Figures. Got his hands in everything. How'd that go, the beauty thing?"

"Weird. All pretty girls, of course."

"Any phone numbers for me?" The hackneyed line, delivered lifelessly, with no expectation of a response.

I stopped pacing and gave him a small grin. "Why aren't you out there making your own sales calls? It's not like you not to be tailing some attractive woman."

He acted cool. "Not interested right now."

"You don't seem interested in anything."

"Who was your favorite?" Lyle sat up, shifted his weight.

"Favorite?"

"Of the beauty queens?"

"There was one, but you can't say anything. It's top secret until the swimsuit and evening gown competitions, and the judges' vote. And even then . . ."

He zipped his lips closed. Then slumped before he caught

himself.

"A young woman named Lindsay. Very bright, poised, thoughtful. Pretty but not classic. We'll see if the judges pick someone close to the composite."

"No phone number?" He feigned a smile. He looked really tired.

I shook my head, kept the charade going. "No phone number."

"How about you?" He moved to the edge of the bed and put his feet on the floor. "Roddy's in New York and—"

"Yes, about Roddy. You gave Anthony his phone number."

"Because you really like and trust him."

"I never said that."

"Didn't need to. Besides you're *his* barbecue sauce."

"You're smoking weed again."

"Never stopped. Look, you can't keep pinin' over Harold. Not that it's my business, but I never really understood that. He was what Momma called a *tusser*. He was dark, you're not."

"I don't know. Lately . . ."

"Nah, I know dark." He shifted his weight again then smiled, like my little brother.

"She *did* call him that."

"What?"

"A *tusser*." I motioned Lyle over a few inches and sat next to him on the bed. It squeaked. "I saw Harold when he was his most incandescent, shining light over me. I seemed to be his 'on' switch. The rest was Poe and Dickens and the troubling world, and I understood it, still do, but I imagined Freyja —remember her?— golden hair, gliding through water."

"The beauty queen."

"Yes. I breathed better when I did, and it made him happy. Which made me happy. It's not like I've had lots of choices. He was pretty good to me. But . . . "

"But what?"

"Nothing." I pressed my lips together. "There were times I didn't like him."

"Yeah, so?"

"But he was my husband. I think I loved him."

"Right." Lyle tossed it off his shoulders like it was obvious.

"He made me angry. You even said I've got a temper."

"You do."

"A couple times I wanted to hit him."

"Wantin' and doin' are different. But yeah, I know that one." Lyle was pretty much limp except flinching his shoulder like it was all normal. I was taxing him.

I glanced at Lyle's guitar stashed on a chair in the corner. "Anyhow . . . " I pointed to it.

"No. We're finishin' this conversation." He gathered himself up a bit. "Did ya hit him?"

"I don't know. I don't think so."

"Then what's the problem?

"What if I hung him?"

"I think you'd know, Sis, it's not the kinda thing you'd forget." He started to slide off the bed.

"Maybe." I reached out my arm and set him against the headboard. "You're pretty tired." I started to rise.

"No, no. Stay." He pulled me down.

"Okay. Let's talk about happier relationships. What or who besides that D-35 has made you happy?"

He laughed, dove inward, then returned to me. "I don't even know about the guitar anymore. There was a woman."

I leaned forward, pleasantly surprised, still trying to let go of Harold but knowing I couldn't be finished with him.

"She really wasn't much to look at, but she knew how to sit next to me, not a word sometimes." He looked across the room at the blank wall. "Spent half a day in the cabin once, spoke three words between us. Leaned on me is all and I knew she was . . . there. I mean really there, ya understand?"

"Yes. What happened?"

A deep breath and he stood, a little shaky. "I fucked it up: the guitar, bourbon. Just not sure how she'd travel, maybe drag me down. I've always been lookin' over my shoulder, like somethin's gonna weigh me down. I was so sure of the music." His vest hung on the headboard and he slipped it on. "Stupid. I fucked everythin' up."

"You're not done with music."

"I'm done with everythin', Sis."

"Seems a little drastic. You're just down on your luck. It'll pass."

His smile was small and held no hope. "Mom will want dinner soon." He moved to the door cutting off further conversation. He put his arm around my shoulders and walked me out.

)))

The next afternoon, I pulled off my boots, the bib overalls I'd found rolled up under the staircase, and my t-shirt, then took a shower and drove to the Miss USA swimsuit and evening gown competitions. Afterward the judges met privately to discuss our observations of the candidates and make our recommendations. A platter of fresh donuts sat untouched on the counter next to the burning coffee, which breathed life into the sterile room.

"I think the best way," Gordon said after getting everyone to circle their chairs and forcing me to sit directly to the right of Victor, "is for each of us to make a case for our top three candidates. Sisel, why don't you begin."

Victor spread his legs into my space.

Sisel was generous in her assessments, perhaps too generous, I thought, because one of her top candidates was a young woman wearing way too much makeup. But Sisel also ranked Lindsay high, which pleased me since —if I had to choose— Lindsay was my top choice.

Gordon went round the circle and there was some consensus that Lindsay might be one of the top four or so candidates, along with Erin, a Hispanic girl named Emily, which seemed an inappropriate name for a Hispanic, and Ashley, a buxom young woman who *stood out* during both the swimsuit and evening gown competitions, despite mangling the interview portion with a steady stream of *likes* wedged between *ums,* and a lengthy dissertation on Theo James.

I made a strong argument, I thought, for Lindsay: her poise, her natural beauty, her inquisitive mind. "Lindsay is a young woman that is truly beautiful inside and out," I concluded, passing the discussion to Victor.

"Well," said Victor, "I'm afraid I could never vote for Lindsay. She stutters."

And that was that. Within minutes he had eviscerated her and reconfigured the discussion around lesser straw-women candidates before convincing the others that Ashley should wear the crown. She was very close to the composite except for her bust measurements, which put her well ahead of all but two previous winners.

As I walked out with Gordon, the others seemed fine with the resolution, or perhaps just happy to be done with the infringement on their time. I craned my neck, looking to see which vehicle Victor was driving and worried that Atara might reappear.

"You're agitated." Gordon walked me to my car.

"I guess strong character begins and ends with tits. But it was beautiful to see her try."

"Lindsay."

"Yes."

Gordon shrugged. "I'm just *one* of the judges." A car pulled up next to us. I readied myself.

"You finished?" asked the pretty man behind the wheel.

"A moment," said Gordon turning back to me. "About yesterday's call..."

"I'm sorry about that. I thought... I don't know." I removed my shades. "It felt like something atmospheric. Maybe a straight line wind, a blow down."

"It was."

"What?"

"A small tornado. Touched down around twenty minutes after you called. Cut a swath roughly a quarter mile wide, a mile long. Haven't had time to see the area, but apparently it took down some buildings. No one hurt. That area's quite remote, luckily. So I guess we're even."

My mouth fell open. Apparently I *did* have a gift.

"You're surprised?" Gordon said.

"We have reservations," interrupted the pretty man leaning across the front car seat and trying not to be rude. "Charles and

Jason are waiting."

"Let's talk before I leave," Gordon said to me. "I think you have a talent."

"Crickets and low-flying birds," I murmured.

"What? Yes, yes right." Gordon gave me a hug and got in the car. The pretty man kissed him on the cheek. "We'll talk," Gordon said, and the car drove off.

In less than a minute I'd learned something about Gordon and the vagaries of my intuition, but it wasn't until I caught sight of Victor over my shoulder that I started to hone my investigation. He slid into a dark blue or black car, sporty, driven by his wife, the still beautiful Perfect Teeth Melissa. A dark blue or black car.

CHAPTER FORTY-NINE

I sat by the caboose waiting for Lyle, the metal hulk rusted a terra cotta red that absorbed all light. It slept, near dead for years, on sleeper timbers at the front of our driveway. As children, Momma let us crawl around and on and through its weary iron, tin and wood carcass, sharp, blistered edges everywhere. What was Momma thinking? We were crawling a live scorpion! Only the cupola at the top hadn't been completely savaged, where Papa Karl had thrown a now-tattered tarp expecting, I suppose, he'd start rehabilitation one day. His accident changed all that.

It was just a jungle gym for me and Lyle. A dangerous one, I could see now, and one that was primarily his domain. I'd climb it yelling, "Get on board, train leaving for all points east" or "Join me on the rocket." But I scared him and he pushed me away in any way he could. Thankful, I could always tell, when I went off to the shed or later, into the woods. That corroded hack caboose; what was Momma thinking?

Anyway, I wasn't doing much better. Researching Johnny Ray always ended with the fifties 'Cry Guy' singer Johnnie Ray, dearly departed and no longer available for appearances. I needed to track the live one down.

Gordon had never heard of him. Momma didn't have a clue. I even called Victor . . .

"Hello, King residence."

"Is this Mrs. King, Melissa?"

"No, this is her son, Michael. I'll get her."

Before I could explain that I wanted Victor, it was too late.

"Hello, this is Melissa."

"I'm sorry, Mrs. King . . . my name is Eunis, I was a Miss USA judge with Victor."

"Oh . . . right. I think my husband mentioned you. I guess you went out for drinks after the gown competition and the results. I guess you earned it, but boy, Victor doesn't usually stay out that late anymore."

Keep out of it. "Well, yes . . ."

"Victor's not at the office."

"I know."

"And he's not home today either. He's always out and around. Can I leave him a message?"

"No . . . but you wouldn't happen to know a Johnny Ray in the vicinity, would you?"

"Is he? —no, that's, that's someone else. No, no I don't."

"Thanks."

"I'll let Victor know you called." *Oh goodie.*

Yet that simple phone call set so many atoms in motion — attracting, repelling and colliding with one another.

Lyle finally sauntered to the caboose, hands wedged in his jeans.

I looked up at him. "You ever heard of a Johnny Ray around here, not the 1950's singer?"

Lyle slouched against the timber where the creosote had dried. Another unseasonably warm day. He lifted his head. "You mean like Johnny Ray Bardo?"

"Who?"

"My guitar teacher —well, the first real one."

"Around here?"

"Last I heard. He wasn't very mobile."

"Could you introduce me?"

Lyle's mouth twisted a bit. "No."

"Why the heck not?"

"Not a good idea."

"For me or you?"

"Aw shit."

"Well?"

Lyle shook his head. "I kinda still owe him for some lessons and an amp."

"Really?" I sighed. "But you could point me there?"

"I guess, sure, but why?"

"You got me. May be part of the molecular structure."

"What?"

"Never mind. Come on let's go for a ride. The old train gives me the creeps."

"It's our heritage." He patted it, then rubbed the red and orange dust off his palms. "But I ain't goin' to Johnny Ray's with you. I'll show you the trailer park, that's it."

)))

A few minutes later we were on Route 15.

"You heard Momma's throwing a Death & Dying party for herself end of the week."

Lyle stuck his head out the car and let the wind whip at his face. "I heard, invitations an all. 'Life's too short. Bring a bottle.'"

I had to laugh. Momma knew what she wanted. "Maybe we should get her a needlepoint with that on it. She's the cozy type."

"Maybe embroider a bloody hatchet." He burped.

We both laughed.

"You're sure you won't visit Johnny Ray?"

"Positive."

"Then is it okay if we go by old Carver's place?"

"You got some strange habits."

"Always have." As we passed by, a magnolia bush, fluorescent purple, caught my attention, and then a forsythia spiked gold.

"I'm not gonna stay around for no party," said Lyle.

"No need." I glanced at him, my hand relaxed on the steering wheel. Never thick, Lyle was thinner still. Older. "It's just going to be Sarah Pooley and the rest of her *banditas*. We don't have to be there. She'd like it to be a tribute —she even invited Carly. But there's no dinner and after the first two drinks the coven will close ranks. We'll be superfluous. I'm still an untouchable, better not seen anyhow."

"No dinner!" He mocked surprise. "I thought a bottle of schnapps and a six-pack of Keystone *was* dinner."

"Lunch."

He stretched his neck and affected a profound professional tone. "You think she's gettin' enough key-lated minerals?"

"Peppermint's a mineral, isn't it?"

"If taken with yeast." He drummed on the dashboard.

"There you go."

He hooted, I snorted. His shoulders relaxed. "Sometimes I don't know how serious to take her?"

"After all these years? Come on."

"Always scared the hell out of me." He sat back. "Even her smell is twisted. You ever smell her scalp?"

"It was all that shit she fed us about *tussers* and *mylings*—"

"*Vardøgers.*"

"Those too," I laughed. *Vardøgers.*

He stopped laughing.

"Oh come on, you've gotten over those spook stories of hers."

"Have you? I fuckin' hate graveyards." He put up his hand in defense of unseen phantoms. "I think there's somethin' to what she says, things we can't see. Too many strange, nasty things happenin'. Everywhere."

"You mean ghosts?"

"You're always talkin' to them. Least you used to. I think they follow us. That Harold thing was creepy." He caught himself and checked to see if he'd tripped my fears again.

"It's okay." I waved it away. A trace lingered.

He continued. "Somethin' was following him. Timmy K's wife. Same thing. That kid in Rochester, remember he took an ax to his whole family? Somethin's drivin' them, somethin' unseen."

"Unseen, maybe, but there's a sound reason for everything, usually scientific."

"Like Harold offin' himself."

I hesitated. "Yes, even that. Something logical, even if it was only logical in Harold's mind. I'm investigating his death." I wasn't going to mention it to anyone.

"Investigatin'? What's there to investigate? You're not still thinkin' you had somethin' to do with it?"

"I just want to be sure. I want to know why. Why'd he do it? Even in his mind, he rationalized it. That's what we do, all of us." Saying it started me simmering.

"Rational? You think life is fuckin' rational. You're swimmin'

in deep waters, Sis. I don't go there. I learned ya can't be sure —
of anythin'." He waved me off and peered out the window.

I'd pulled an axe handle from the shed and kept it by my
bedside, just in case Atara showed up at the farmhouse. And
now she and Victor . . . no telling what they'd done the night before. Harold and some woman. A guy named Johnny Ray.
Momma and her retinue of darkness, forever ranting.

"Holy shit!" Lyle signaled to my left.

"Shit!"

Carver's colossal taxidermy sign was gone, and the two massive support timbers that had borne it were whittled into
kindling. But there, way down and across the road, against an
apparently untouched grove of black spruce, sat the sign,
Carver's eyes staring at us. The tornado had come down that
corridor. The shop, sitting alone in the clearing, still sagging a
bit, was untouched.

Lyle's face froze, then he buried it in his hands and broke
down crying.

"Oh my god, Lyle. What's the matter?" I unbuckled my seat
belt and reached for him. He let me take him in my arms.
"Whoa, whoa. What's the matter? We can fix it."

"No," he said, voice choked and flat. "No." Carver's eyes bore
down on us. My brother subsided, regrouped. He wiped his nose
with his hand and the moisture from his eyes with his sleeve. I
handed him the sanitizer from the glove compartment.

He stared at the small bottle and laughed. "I'm a dead man."

The stillness cracked, a clap so loud we both jumped as if one
of Carver's timbers was splitting on top of us. The sound filled
the sky, flapping over the landscape in waves, an invisible flock
of white pelicans. A single resounding rifle shot. The car began
to buckle, a trophy deer going down. In the distance an engine
started and drove off. We looked at each other.

"What the fuck was that?" Lyle asked, sobering and getting
out of the car.

"Don't!" But he was out and I did the same.

"Your tire, somebody shot it out."

"Another warning," I said.

"Another?"

"Never mind. What do you mean you're a dead man?"

"Somebody's shooting at you?" He wore his disbelief like gravity, his face and shoulders weighed to the ground.

I must have looked the same. "What do you mean you're a dead man?"

He knelt by the flattened tire, then slumped with it. "Blood. In my urine. You ever see that? Chunks of red and black blood streamin' out of you? Out of *me*."

"It could be a lot of things."

"It could be, but it's fuckin' cancer, kidney cancer."

"Oh Lyle." I went around to him, crouched down and held him again, the two of us pinned against the fender, a cool draft tussling his thin hair, the smell of his old leather jacket against my cheek.

Who is warnin' you about what?" Lyle finally got to his feet and ran fingers through his hair.

"Somebody doesn't want me nosing around." Or wanted me to deliver a comb.

"About what?"

"Harold . . . or maybe I remind somebody of their past, I don't know. Anyway, about you, are you sure? Does Momma know?"

"Sure. Doctors agree. Momma don't know nothin'," he said with disgust.

"How much time?"

"A month, maybe three."

I gasped. "You should've told me."

"I'm tellin' you now, and you're the only one, and I expect you to keep it to yourself, understand?"

"Yes."

"Open the trunk. Let's fix this goddam tire and get outta here."

CHAPTER FIFTY

It was worse than most trailer parks. Just driving past the wagon wheel gate made me want to take a shower. I considered the glove box then started looking for numbers.

I'd decided to ask forgiveness rather than permission when I surprised Johnny Ray. *Come with me.* I saw Harold by his neck and something more: he reached out to me, hopeful. Then it went blank, that dark frame that followed me everywhere, something I couldn't or didn't want to remember. It was a slice more than I'd recovered before but I had to keep my focus.

My car crept through the afternoon shadows, no one in sight but a mangy tabby that frightened at the sight of me and limped behind a stack of plastic piping shrouded in tall grass. Project abandoned.

When I reached #72, it was a trailer home in better repair than most of the others, with a small fenced yard that was free of debris and a custom-made birdbath of small orange and blue tiles. As I passed it I admired the workmanship. *No reason to be nervous.*

The door opened before I made it to the front step. "Can I help you?" asked a sturdy voice, a hint of Creole from the darkness behind the screen door.

I stepped back. "I'm sorry to bother you but someone suggested you might have known Harold Cloonis."

"Someone?" asked the shadow. A puff of cigarette smoke ballooned through the screen.

"Look, did you know him? Because I'm his—"

"I know who you are."

That threw me off balance. "Well, can I come in?"

"You mean 'may' you come in."

"Yes."

"How about you stay out there and I open the door, just for a short time, because I've got things to do and you weren't expected."

"Sure, that would be fine. Thank you." I didn't know whether I should remove my shades. I didn't want to unsettle him. "How do you know me?"

"I know you, that's all."

My twisted history in town had been more on display than I'd realized. "Okay."

The door opened wider and a neatly cropped white-haired man in his late fifties, wearing a gray and white-striped cardigan, no shirt, and black jeans, managed to effortlessly wedge open the screen door with his wheelchair. He held the cigarette between his teeth and drew more smoke. "You're on the clock, lady."

"Okay, okay, then how did you know Harold?"

"Too long a story. Next."

"Maybe if we could—"

"Next," he repeated without rancor.

"I'm looking for people who knew him before his death."

"Hard to know him after."

I reorganized. "Yes, of course. What I meant was, you're aware that he killed himself?" Out loud, it hurt. Even then.

"So they say." Like I was a suspect.

"So, ah, did he seem despondent when you knew him and when was that exactly?"

"I knew him a year or two before his death. We both liked Dickens. I still do. At the time he wasn't at all despondent. He was very happy."

"*Very* happy?"

"That was my take."

"Does the phrase 'come with me' have any significance related to Harold?"

"No."

"Did he have any friends besides you?" I bit hard on it. "I mean, maybe a girlfriend?"

"There was a girlfriend."

I was a marionette, yanked up and down with every answer.

He pulled the cigarette out of his teeth with his thin lips and sucked in the bonus smoke. "Before my time." No smoke exhaled.

"Do you remember a name?"

"Connie or Constance. Figueroa, I think."

"Any idea where she worked or lived?"

"Worked at Itasca."

"The state park. How long ago?"

"Two years, maybe more. Like I said, before my time."

"Do you know what she looked like?" And then another question I really didn't want to ask, and an answer I wasn't sure I wanted to hear. "Was he . . . in love?"

Johnny Ray sniffed. "Don't know, but he wasn't in love."

"Did he tell you that?"

"Yes. And we've run out of time."

"Could we talk again?"

"I've got a guitar to re-string. But I'll ask *you* a question."

"Yes, of course."

"Why don't you let the dead rest?"

As I searched for a reply, he backed up his wheelchair and slammed the screen door shut.

☽☽☽

I resolved to give Victor a visit, to gauge his response to me, alone, and to squeeze out any information he might have concerning Johnny Ray. But when I arrived at the mayor's office, his secretary waved me off. "Not today," she said pointing to the crowd of people waiting for him, including his wife, the still extravagant Melissa. "He's even more backed up than usual." The only available chair was next to her, so I sat. Even after all those years and the encroaching crows feet, she was quite lovely and well toned. I gave her a pained smile.

"He's a busy man," I said.

"Yes." She wasn't pleased.

"Hi." I removed my shades, extended my hand; she'd never met me in person outside of The Beaver. "I'm Eunis, Eunis Cloonis."

She was clearly taken aback; then shook my hand. "You're Eunis." She was strong.

"Yes."

"I guess we all need appointments to see the great man." Her lips were tight, her perfect teeth hidden.

"Sorry."

"Yes, well, I guess it comes with the territory. But it would be nice to see him once in awhile. It's every night now."

I didn't know what to say.

"You're done with the Miss USA, right?"

"Yes."

"Ever find that guy you were looking for? I told Vic you called."

"I did, thank you."

She kept studying my face. Then checked the waiting throng; slapped her skirt and stood up. She flashed her perfect teeth. "It was nice meeting you." She walked out and I did the same a few minutes later.

〉〉〉

It had been almost four days since Atara confronted me in the parking lot and her subsequent silence was deafening. An hour didn't go by without me expecting her to show up at the farmhouse, violently. Yet now more than ever, with the threat of a tape, the comb was my best insurance against her attacks, even though her precious comb also brought the peril. A paradox.

I knew no exchange would guarantee my safety. The best I could hope for was a stalemate. Maybe spending time around Roddy had made me more tactical.

She wasn't the taciturn type. The suspense finally got to me and I found her number on my cell, from the call she'd made to me that final day in the pleasure ship. When I called I was surprised when Levi answered.

"Who's this?" His honeyed voice instantly recognizable.

"Eunis."

"How'd you get my number?" Train signal bells jangled behind him.

"You know she's here in Minnesota."

"I do."

"You too?"

"No, and I told her not to, but she's a women of great beauty and great will."

Beauty, absolutely; *will,* more likely malevolence.

"What do you want?"

"I don't have your comb."

"Don't tell me, tell her. It's not my business."

"Call her off. Tell her to come home."

I sensed his amusement across the space. "I'm not home, and she's got a mind of her own." More train noise. "The sun could be jealous of the stars. Would you like to meet me for a few days?"

"No." But part of me missed his body; part of me missed his admiration.

"Then good luck." He hung up.

I walked back into the house, watching the woods, the shadows, for any movement.

)))

"The hell you are," said Momma when I told her that Lyle and I were planning a drive. "My party," she growled.

"We'll be back for the party," I said. A lie. I expected her face to show the usual apathy, but she seemed genuinely hurt.

"I'll expect it. This could be my last. Please."

)))

The lodge ceilings were high, the dark logs rustic and grand. Rooms split off in different directions reminding me of the grandeur of Levi and Atara's palatial ship, although their apartment had become a kind of sinister museum, palatial but sinister. The lodge, however, reeked gravitas. Signs announced that it was built in 1905.

"You've never seen the headwaters of the Mississippi?" Lyle stuck his nose against the smell of the old wood.

"No."

And that's where the front desk sent us, a rotund formal man with especially small ears saying, "She'll be out along the trail somewhere. You can't miss Constance, can't miss her smile. She's an institution here."

So we began the walk, mud and puddles, passing interpretive signs and a few small families returning in the late Saturday afternoon light. Kinglets and vireos —I never could tell the difference— looping from tree to tree, chipmunks waiting for food to drop along the wooded trail.

"I used to dream of floatin' like Huck Finn down the Mississippi, get as far away as possible," said Lyle.

"Me too! But I'd start here, not in Missouri. All the way down."

"Coulda met Johnny Ray early on, maybe played New Orleans."

The trail opened up and I saw lake water beyond. A squat woman with a brown baseball cap talked to a young couple.

"Here we go." Lyle pointed at the lake. "All's we need is a raft."

"Thank you," said the young woman, letting her hand drop from the young man's, and as the squat woman removed her baseball cap to itch her head, I saw hair so thin her crown showed through, like the older woman at the Drink 'n' Dive.

"Did you know," I heard the squat woman say, "that Itasca means 'truth' of the 'head?' Yes. Walk around. It will be good for you. It will be good."

"Thank you, Constance," said the young man shaking her hand again because she'd offered it again, while he tugged his partner away with the other. "You've been very informative."

"No, thank *you*." Constance turned to bid them farewell and smiled broadly. "Thank you, thank you. Come again. En-joy!"

Lyle and I were no more than twenty feet from Constance, who turned to us as the young couple departed.

"Here you are at the headwaters of the Mississippi," she said to us, "where the mighty river begins its 2,552 mile journey to the Gulf of Mexico." Her yellowed teeth and shining blue eyes lit up most of her face, as her head bobbed left and right in pure pleasure at seeing us. "I'm Constance. Is this your first visit to Itasca State Park?"

"No/yes," Lyle and I responded in unison.

"Well, welcome. I'm Constance. I can tell you a lot."

She was mid-forties, I'd guess, but it was hard to tell because her face was out of proportion: flattened nose, wide curved eyes, like a child. She had a full or partial extra copy of chromosome 21: Down syndrome. A kind, happy face, despite its dysmorphic structure. Perhaps Johnny Ray had made a mistake.

Lyle made eye contact with me as if to question our purpose.

"I'm Eunis." I held out *my* hand, a rare initiation for me.

Constance took it with both of hers. "Hi, Eunis, I'm Constance. Welcome."

"This is my brother, Lyle."

"Hi, Lyle." Constance waved. He waved back.

"So this little stream becomes the mighty Mississippi?" I said. "I'll bet you've met a lot of people since you've been here at the park."

"A lot."

"Do you remember a friend of mine, Harold Cloonis?"

Constance's face went blank, then shined ever more brightly. "I remember. I remember Harold."

"You do?" Still, maybe Johnny Ray had been confused about their relationship.

"He was my boyfriend for a while," she said proudly. "You know him too? Is he your boyfriend now?"

I might as well have had sawdust in my head. I was dumbstruck. "No, not now." I thought about telling Constance.

"He is a nice man. I love him. I am glad I know him. He is a nice man."

I swallowed. I collected myself. "Yes, he is. What do you remember about him?"

"He was nice. He took care of me. He made me feel . . . " Her eyes were mischievous. ". . . well, like a woman. I like that!" She faced Lyle, tilted her head. He smiled at her.

I couldn't imagine. "Why did it end, you and Harold?"

"He had to go. Okay, it was okay. I knew he wouldn't be forever. Forever is long. He is a nice man."

I was on autopilot. "When did you stop seeing him?"

"I don't know time so well."

"Well, thank you."

"Do you want to hear about the headwaters of the Mississippi?" Constance's little engine was raring to tell.

"No, thank you, we have to go, but it was a pleasure meeting you, Constance." I turned, gathering Lyle in the process. The pattern was clear, and I fit perfectly in it.

"You too, Eunis and brother." She waved. "You too. Enjoy! Say 'hi' to Harold. Tell him Constance loves him."

If Lyle hadn't been with me I would have cried all the way to the car, and then I don't know what.

CHAPTER FIFTY-ONE

We didn't talk much on the way home, traveling through dense unsettled knob and kettle woodlands of virgin red pine and bloodroot. Now I understood why Harold was so resistant to bringing me to the park.

Without turning to Lyle I finally said, "I wanted us to be together. Spend some time."

His eyes went soft. "Thank you."

"You're the brother I never had."

"Right." He chortled and rubbed my shoulder.

We became quiet again, Lyle probably wrestling with his demons or perhaps contemplating his last visit to the Mississippi and never riding it to its end. Me gripped by my painful inconsequence, how easily Harold had exchanged us all. No more than a factory part.

Finally Lyle asked, "Who told you about Johnny Ray?"

I was struggling with my thoughts. "A text. Don't know who." *Or why.*

Again we reverted to silence.

We stopped at a bar restaurant in the middle of the woods because Lyle was particularly gaunt and there were few places *to* stop before Bemidji. The food —a plump lightly fried walleye with chips and a cheeseburger with slaw and chips— turned out to be pretty good, though the place was full and festive and rowdy with music. Neither of us fit in. We ate quickly, leaving an obscene amount on our plates.

On the way out I caught a glimpse of Victor in a booth, beyond the dance floor. He reached across the table, addiction in his eye, and met the hand of a woman. Fingers intertwined. I couldn't see her. He didn't see me.

I moved to the far end of the bar to get a better look. A cocktail waitress pushed past me through the crowd. He kissed the woman's hand then looked up and toward the bar, as if he was aware I was watching him. I turned away and ducked my head. I don't think he saw me. It was none of my business.

When we got to the car, my windshield was fissured in veins, a one-way assault from a crowbar or baseball bat.

"Oh shit," said Lyle.

Around the dark dirt parking lot nothing moved.

Lyle yelled, "Come out you fuckin' coward!" But there were only crickets and the music and laughter from the bar.

"I'm going back in," I said.

"Talk to the owner? I better come with you." But he leaned heavily against the car.

"Not necessary. Will you be okay?"

"I'm fine."

By the time I got back inside and fought my way to Victor's booth, it was empty. I scanned the dance floor. I corralled a waitress and yelled above the din. "Did you see the woman with the guy in that booth?"

She looked at me like I was insane, then yelled, "You kidding? You see this place?" She shrugged me off. "I got six tables, she's got nine. Fucking Juliette didn't show. No time for getting familiar with nobody tonight."

And with that she headed to the bar.

〉〉〉

The glare of the fractured windshield fought me all the way home. After we passed through Bemidji and non-existent Puposky, with the farmhouse minutes away, I broke the silence. "Your Martin," I said speaking of his once constant companion guitar. "You've stopped playing."

"What's the point?"

"I haven't heard you sing in years."

He managed little more than a sucking-air sound.

"It brings you pleasure. It's your thing, it's *your* beauty."

"Was."

"Your dad loved music, remember?"

"O'course. And he was your dad too." Even in the dark I could see Lyle turning to me to acknowledge it. "He gave me that toy ukulele. He got me started."

"And," I reminded him, "he hummed those songs, remember? What was the name of that guy?"

"Ralph Stanley. He loved Ralph Stanley."

Papa Karl would hum the songs just fine but he'd never *sing* any of them, like his mouth was sewn shut when it came to singing. Maybe that's why Lyle took it up, so he could sing *for* his father. "You brought your guitar to the hospital. You sang him a couple songs."

"I did."

"He couldn't speak. He could barely move a finger or bat an eye, but he could hear. You put a small curl on his mouth. I'd call it a smile."

"I don't remember."

"I do."

"Your point?"

"Play. Play for me. Play for Momma. Mostly, play for you. Leave us a piece of your beauty. Leave something of you I can hold on to."

Silence. We turned on to Smith Road. Pressure built around my shoulders, fatigue parched my eyes. I steeled myself. "I hope Momma's asleep." At the farmhouse, the kitchen light was on.

"You ungrateful little bitch!" screamed Momma when we entered. Bottles and shrapnel shelled peanuts surrounded her. "Your real sister Carly came all the way to see you, Lyle, and your freak sister ruined everything, as usual."

"Momma!" Lyle yelled without hesitation, a single searing accusation so damning I thought that, in that moment, my brother had shorn his fear and regained his health.

"She's a devil, Lyle. She'll drag you down like she has me." Momma spun around, clutched her chest and fell to the floor.

Lyle staggered, I ran to her. "Momma!" I squatted next to her and raised her to her elbows. "Momma, what happened?"

She reached out for him, quivering. "Lyle, my baby." She looked up at me. "You're trying to kill me."

"No, Momma."

Lyle brought her a glass of water. She sipped it. We sat her up. "Don't you touch me," she said flinging my hands away.

"Lyle." She reached for him, pleading, and with every once of strength he had left he was able to pull her to her feet.

Then *he* collapsed.

"Lyle!" I knelt by my brother, cradling his head in my hands.

He was dazed. "I'm okay," he said to me. "Just dizzy." He took slow, shallow breaths and stared blankly at the garbage can.

Momma faced me, hands on hips, teeth bared. "Ya see what ya done."

I was empty. There was no shelter from any of it.

☽☽☽

Over the next few days I did my best to avoid Momma, mostly working on the skin of the house. It also kept me out of town, where I had no interest in bumping into Victor. I was ever vigilant for Atara but there was no sign of her, which made me even more uncomfortable.

My plan was to stay, tending to Lyle until he passed and I'd solved Harold, and then who knew? I'd never planned on leaving Momma because I'd never planned on coming back in the first place. But now that I was there, a blunt pulse followed me around.

And when would be an appropriate time to leave, if ever? The allotted time, though, the appropriate *amount* of time, was already a concept I'd have to reckon with. It also suggested the possibility of a Sisyphean existence without parole. Every breath, in or out, was a breath of low-level depression. I couldn't shake it.

Momma wouldn't look me in the eye. We didn't speak. I heard Lyle strumming his guitar in his room, creating a warm, momentary micro-climate around my heart. Carly left the morning after the party without a word, just a note saying she'd be back within the week.

"You got a call from some guy in New York," Momma said when I came in for a bite of lunch. She held my phone.

"What are you doing?"

"Don't get sassy with me. Your damn phone just kept ringing, disturbing my peace and quiet."

"What guy?" More than ever I hoped it was Roddy, saving me from the isolation I'd created for myself.

"Anthony somebody, and he wants you to call him about the comb. He sounded scared. You bringin' your cursed demonkind down on him too?"

I grabbed the phone out of her hand. "Don't pick up my phone ever!"

"Why? You gonna hurt me like you did that *tusser* husband of yours?"

I closed my fist.

"You think I don't know?" She inched backward.

It was the second time I'd recognized the fathoms of my anger, and yes, my capacity to hurt someone. It should've scared me, but it didn't. "Then if you know, you'd better not fuck with me."

Momma lowered her eyes. "Ungrateful bitch."

I reckoned I'd go for a drive. It was time to try Harold's parents again.

"Anthony, this is Eunis," I said, leaving a message on his voicemail. "Please just sit tight. Nobody could have any idea you have it. Nobody." I believed that was true, I really did. "They're fishing." I didn't know what to say regarding Junior, so I said nothing.

I also believed that Carly had left town. Yet while pulling into downtown for groceries and Lyle's medications, I spotted Carly's fire engine yellow convertible, the luck or curse of a small city. As I slowed to be certain, Carly came out of a bright building, The Cosmetic Center:

Certified Laser and Injection Nurse
- Contour your body – freeze fat away
- Reduce unwanted hair – laser hair reduction
- Define your features – Botox, Xeomin, Juvederm and other injectables
- Rejuvenate your skin – remove spider veins and brown spots

And plastered across the window: "My skin lies about my age, so I don't have to."

On the go taxidermy for humans. But why say she was leaving town?

Carly ducked into the nearby pharmacy. My phone jolted me. I stared at the number almost long enough to lose the call before picking it up.

"Yes? Hello?"

"Eunis, it's Gordon. Can we get together one more time before I leave?"

"Gordon? Did you text me about Johnny Ray?"

"Who?"

"Johnny Ray Bardo. You texted me. Nearly a week ago. With his name. I'm pretty sure it was from your phone."

"Can we talk weather?" he said. "I'm really not familiar with this guy. I'd tell you if I was." That breezy earnestness I'd come to trust. "Would you be willing to come to our offices and meet my general manager? We'll have to fudge your experience a little bit, but he values my opinion. Your instincts and smarts, you'd really fill a void we have right now." He added, "You'd be behind the scenes, I'm afraid. Not on screen, I mean."

"Naturally."

"So you'll come?"

"When I'm done here; could be months. And on one condition: you'll check your phone for me. I got a text from your phone, I'm sure of it." I hesitated. "Victor King doesn't have access to your phone."

"Vic? Certainly not. Not my type." A quizzical silence followed. "You and I, we're always bargaining, aren't we? But sure, I'll check my phone's history. Just don't count on anything. But you'll come? I'll even pay for the trip, caramels and all."

At least I had one person in my corner. "Sure, unless my mother or the authorities get me first."

"Authorities?"

"It was a joke."

When I looked up, Carly's yellow Miata was gone. The least of my worries.

⟩⟩⟩

An hour later, I'd worked up enough confidence to slump down in my car as Rhoald Cloonis drove off in his truck. As I approached the Cloonis house, the orderly yard impressed me again, but for the first time I sensed the bone-drying weariness vaporizing the place. Perhaps it was always there and I'd simply repelled it; it was only my third visit. The other two —first with Harold, then the attempt to understand him— were like wading deep into desert.

Muriel answered the door, without surprise. She did not invite me in. "I don't think you should be here." She was impassive.

"I loved your son." *I think I loved your son.* "All I want is to put him properly to rest. If I could just have a moment."

She glanced over my shoulder, left and right. "Okay, but just for a moment."

But then Muriel, who was about to have one herself, offered me a cup of tea. Tea! Unlike my imagined encounter, it wouldn't include Daryl Hannah and Michael Jackson.

I accepted, and while she was in the kitchen, I scanned the living room in hopes of a clue. There were a few cheap antiques: a brass hurricane lamp, a woodcut terrier dog, a mantle clock, all of them subdued brown or aged yellow.

A small, stoppered urn, porcelain with thin ochre trim, stopped me cold. Harold's remains?

Only one photograph: Rhoald, quite a few years younger, in hunting gear with rifle and a dead trophy moose. The same rifle, it appeared, hung over the mantle, pressed against walls papered in a dull gray pattern. I stood to sniff the rifle to see if it had been recently fired, but Muriel returned.

"I hope this is okay. It's just Lipton's." Lankier and less attractive than I'd remembered, Murial had long ears and a concaved face.

"Thank you, you're very kind. This is great." *Be quick and strategic.* I didn't know when Rhoald might reappear.

As if she was inside my mind, she said, "Mr. Cloonis won't be returning for about three-quarters of an hour."

"Do you have any idea why Harold did what he did?"

"No, no I don't."

"We were happy, you know. Your husband is wrong about

me. Harold loved me."

"Then why?" Her dehydrated face withered downward.

"I want to know too. Did he say anything to you in those last few weeks?"

"He rarely spoke to either of us. He didn't like coming here. He must have told you. But no, nothing."

"Did he say anything about me?" The question scared me, even as I asked it.

"After that time you and he visited, he said he was going to marry you. I asked him if he loved you, and he said he did."

"That's all, nothing more?"

"He didn't like talking to us. He was always a private child. Wouldn't even let us take photographs of him, even as a little boy. Oh, but there was your mother."

"My mother?"

"Yes, he said she visited him. Unannounced. Wanted to know if his intentions were honest. My son! But I guess I can understand a mother wanting to know."

It took me a minute to process. Was Momma trying to sabotage my relationship or was she looking out for me? "What else did she ask him?"

"Don't know. He was just polite with her, I guess. My son's intentions were always good. He was that kind of boy."

"Did he have any other friends beside me?"

"You didn't know? Well, if you didn't, we certainly didn't. But even as a little boy he would say he wanted a perfect friend."

Muriel hadn't touched her tea. Staring at the hunting photo of her husband, she continued. "He'd say, 'a friend who will trust me, who will come with me whatever I do, the way I look, wherever I go.' And I told him 'you will, you'll have friends.' But that didn't raise his spirits. He didn't believe me. He was like that."

"Like that?"

Muriel wiped something from her eye. "He was a good boy. Rhoald is . . ." She tossed away the thought.

I studied her face, like studying the inside of a thin wooden bowl. "Does Rhoald —Mr. Cloonis— does he still hunt?"

"He's still a very good shot and he goes to the range occasionally but I don't think he hunts anymore. Arthritis."

"Before me, did Harold have any friends? *Anyone* that he mentioned?"

"Not many."

"But there were a few?" My chest lifted, hopeful.

"Not a few." I waited as Muriel burrowed into her concaved memory bank. "He had that friend, the one he met at the library. I guess they both liked the same books."

"Dickens?"

"No, that wasn't his name."

"I meant the author of the books."

"Oh, well, perhaps, but the guy had one of those southern names. Jimmy Bob Somethingorother."

"Johnny Ray Bardo." I was almost touching something concrete.

"Johnny Ray, that sounds familiar. He was at the cremation."

And I wasn't allowed. Another blow to my heart.

"Rhoald liked 'the shape of his jib.' Neatly trimmed. That's Rhoald's way." Muriel glanced at the clock on the mantel. "Maybe you should go."

☽☽☽

That Momma had weaseled her way into my investigation made me claustrophobic, like I was caught in a net. About to be hauled on deck to bake in the sun. Like my life was everyone's but mine. So I drove to Kingdom, just to get wet.

The deepest sections of the bogs still had occasional ice crystals and some small plates of ice, but the welcoming weather tempted the first greens out of hiding and the rivers were flowing. Kingdom Lake was there for the cold scrubbing, and I'd delayed my first swim way too long. It had a marked chill to be sure, but I made it to the east side where the sun had layered a blanket of gold and copper over roughly sixty yards of rocky shoreline. I remained there, face and chest to the sun, toes probing mud, for a while, cleansed and temporarily emancipated from my litany of questions, before swimming back across the placid lake to my pile of clothes.

When I got to my car I was surprised to find tire tracks alongside mine, possibly a truck's judging by their width, freshly marking the thin mud. I didn't recollect seeing them when I'd pulled in. Even while I'd been swimming, the trawl had closed in on me again. Paranoia? Absolutely.

☽☽☽

No sooner had I returned to the farmhouse with Lyle's inhibitor pills than Carly confronted me on the back steps. I tucked his medication in my pocket.

"What have you gotten us into?" Carly's usually playful eyes were dull with fear.

"Me?"

"A woman looking for you. She's going to hurt one of us, I'm sure of it."

"Slow down."

"You have something of hers."

"She threatened you?"

"No, she implied. She came close to burning my face. Like it was an accident, but it wasn't. Maybe we should go to the police." Carly's eyelids were puffy, her irises fractured like my windshield. I'd never seen her vulnerable, never seen her scared. And I was the cause of it, as usual.

"No, no, you can't prove anything, right? Where'd this happen?"

"The Cosmetic Center downtown. It doesn't matter *where*, just give her whatever it is."

"Did anyone see it happen?"

"No. She's creepy, really creepy. She's not fucking around."

"How'd she know who you were?"

"I don't know and I don't care. What do you have of hers?"

"I don't have anything."

"Well, she thinks you do, damn it. I always thought it was Momma's twisted mind, but you do bring bad juju. Just give it back to her."

"Black hair, green eyes, beautiful?"

"That's the one."

"She won't hurt you or Lyle or Momma, I promise."

"Then you'll give it back to her?"

"I will."

Carly threw her hands up in disgust. "You'd better. Geezus!" She stormed to her car and drove off.

A voice came from behind me. "I got nothin' to lose." Lyle clung to the back door. "I'll take care of it."

"No you won't, you stay out of this."

"I'll get her. She's the one messin' with you, runnin' you off the road, the gun shot, your fucked up windshield."

"We don't know that. And you're in no shape to be goin' after anyone. Now get back inside and get some rest."

He took my order, and I was ashamed to have spoken to him that way. I sounded like Momma. I stood in the late afternoon light, gazing at the caboose, trying to organize my thoughts. When the wind started nipping at me, I took the invitation, the gusts nudging me all the way back into the kitchen.

Momma, scornful and skulking around like she was plotting something, made sure it was just the two of us within earshot. I braced. She launched into me before I was halfway across the room. "What's the matter with you? You blind too? Your brother's sick. You've gotta do something. Lyle's dying!" She wanted me to contradict her, I'm sure, but I couldn't respond without recanting my promise. In my silence, age crept over her. "He's dying," she said again, her eyes pleading. "Don't just stand there like a dumb—"

"You're sure?"

"Oh god." Momma closed her eyes, trying to imagine the truth. "A mother knows."

I leaned forward, searching her face for a more reasonable explanation, but she gave none. "You mean like intuition? Like crickets and low-flying birds?"

"What?" The reference meant nothing to her. "Yes, intuition," she said smugly then sagged more sheepishly. "Maybe I overheard him on the phone with his doctor. Anyway," she snapped, quickly regaining her stock insolence, "what are you gonna do for him?"

Should I shake my mother by the shoulders or hold her? Both unreasonable. So I did neither. I nodded. "Okay. We should call

Carly."

"Carly! That girl wouldn't notice nothin' but her mirror. She don't know shit, might make a bigger mess of things than you."

"Momma! You want to help or do just want to fuck with me all the time?"

"Eunis Marie!"

"Don't Eunis Marie me. I'm past indignation, if you understand what that means, so don't bother laying yours on me."

"You always were too smart for your own good."

My eyes burned. "You went to see Harold."

Her eyes went left and right, she hung her head. "Maybe."

"Bullshit! You went to my fiancée and bullied him."

"I didn't bully nobody. I went for you. Look the guy in the eye."

"For me."

"Yes."

"You tried to talk him out of it."

"You don't know what you're talkin' about, like always."

"So tell me."

"Nothin' to tell. He said he loved you. Not sure I believed him, but there you have it."

"That's it? Anybody else there to corroborate?"

"Corrobo . . .?"

"Got any witnesses?"

"Damn you." Then she faced me straight on. "Yes, as a matter of fact. A man came while I was there. Long hair. Scruffy. Your weird boyfriend sent him away."

"Name?"

"Who do you think I am? It wasn't my place to—"

"Okay, about Lyle. You'll do what I say."

"What *you* say?"

I stood firm, peering down at Momma.

"Maybe, if you got a plan."

"I got a plan. I'm systematic."

She looked puzzled. "Okay, okay."

I wasn't sure what I'd do next. But at least I was still afloat.

CHAPTER FIFTY-TWO

"It was Aunt Mae, my great aunt," read Gordon's text. "She'd heard you were looking for connections to Harold. Used my phone when I went to the bathroom. Didn't know she even knew how to text. Sorry."

I texted him back, "Tell her I'll be by today or tomorrow. I need her help."

))))

I listened by my brother's door. A few sweet chords and his frail voice:

> *"The sun is slowly sinkin'*
> *The day's almost gone*
> *Still darkness falls around us*
> *And we must journey on . . ."*

"Lyle," I whispered, tapping on his bedroom door. His singing and strumming stopped.

"Come in." He brightened. "Sis."

"I'm sorry to bother you." He'd lost more weight, his hands stringy, his blue blood vessels the roadmap of someone twice his age. I was watching him drift away and I was helpless.

"Nah, you're the most welcome of all."

"I've got an idea."

"Better be soon."

The pain went deeper still. I took a breath. "Would you be willing to sing for a group of people?"

"I don't want no pity."

"Lyle, you can sing, I just heard you. If I set it up?"

"I don't want no one to know. Don't want them comin' cause they pity me."

"I understand."

He thought about it. "Only if you'd sing harmony with me."

"I don't sing."

"Who says?" He waited. As he breathed his whole frame deflated.

I couldn't lose him, not now. "Okay," I said. "If you teach me."

"I can do that." This seemed to revive him. His fingers did a little tap dance on the guitar, and seeing his fingers move with spirit loosened my strings.

❩❩❩

A little after noon I visited Mae at the Drink 'n' Dive, the place almost empty. We sat at the bar, none of the girls in the tank. Mae and I drank imported Vernors, her favorite.

"Never knew Lyle had more'n one sister." Her voice gravely as ever. She wiped excess soda off her lips with the back of her hand. "But I'm glad to meet you."

"Same."

"So you'll do that for Lyle?"

"Before we talk about Lyle, you're a friend of Gordon's." She set it out like a litmus test.

"I am." I felt good saying it. Gordon *was* a friend.

"Well, maybe you can tell me, does he have any girlfriends? I mean beside you, cause you're just a friend, right?"

"Well, we're definitely friends. But if you mean romantically—?"

"Yeah."

"No."

"That's what I figured. So does he?" She waited, steely eyed, for my response.

Lyle's gig perhaps contingent on my answer. "Well, I don't know about his life back east."

She leaned forward, conspiratorially, even though there was no one near us. "Do you think he's got a woman?"

I saw where she was heading. "You probably should ask him."

"I don't think I could do that. What do you think?"

"Well, I don't know. But he's a man of his word. And he's funny."

"I'll grant you that." She flicked the Vernor's can with her fingernail.

"So what more could you want?" A supportive smile.

"There are things I just don't understand."

"It's okay," I said placing my hand gently atop of hers. "Me too. Me too."

"I suppose you're right." She inhaled. "I just want him to be happy."

"I don't know him that well but I think he is. How many people can say that?"

"Mmm."

"So, Lyle? You'll do that for him?"

She took her time, evaluating me. "I will. He always had talent. Never could understand how he didn't get along. Pleasure to have him here."

"Well, thank you." I hesitated before lifting off the barstool. "There's one more thing."

"Shoot."

"Johnny Ray. How'd you connect him to Harold?"

"I seen 'em from time to time. Hard to miss JR with that hair a his, all funny and tied up. And Harold with those loud shirts a his."

"Right." The front door opened. Bright light and a couple of degenerates flushed into the bar. "And thanks for the Vernors."

I wasn't but a few steps outside the Drink 'n' Dive heading for my car, when I caught Victor leaning against the building in front of me, a bit startled and dismissing someone in a tan fishing jacket.

"Eunis, how nice to see you again." He took my hand, gripped it less tightly this time.

"Mr. Mayor. You going for a drink?" I had the sense he knew I'd be there.

"Oh no." He settled into easiness. "Not at this hour, and certainly not here." The big man afraid of mermaids.

"Did you show her around?" I searched for my car keys.

"Who?"

"Atara."

"Your friend from New York. No, we never did get a chance.

I've just gotten so busy. Politics, everyone thinks I have an answer for their problem." Still rehearsed. "And of course, I have my own business to run. Not easy being a small town mayor, I can tell you that. And Bemidji's not that small anymore."

"I can imagine."

"And you? You here for a while?" His iris locked around his pupils. He genuinely anticipated my answer.

"Not too much longer, I don't think."

His eyes let go. "Well, it was nice bumping into you."

"You too."

〉〉〉

I dialed the farmhouse. She answered. "Momma, " I said.

"Yeah, what do ya want?"

"This guy you saw with Harold. Was he in a wheelchair?"

"Yeah, so? Your Harold was weird. He had weird friends."

"Wheelchairs aren't weird, Momma."

"Yeah, well . . . what else you want?"

"Nothing, Momma. Thanks." I hung up.

I turned east, stopping at Little Bass Stump for a swim to clear my head. The smaller and shallower the lake, the warmer, especially so early in the season. But I found two fishermen and their loud portable radio so I moved on to Kingdom, which was the next most swimmable on the way home, more private and my favorite anyhow. The lake was still a cold 50-55 degrees but there was no wind. Just a quick dip.

After folding my clothes under the white cedar, I dove into the water and glided quickly through the velvet electricity, recalling the icy wind and Malcolm, my Charles Dickens. "Death is coming," he'd said. "Let's dance while we can."

And so I swam —my kind of dance— once to the center of the small lake and back, lost in thought as I considered the bravery of so many people I'd met in the past year: Malcolm, Elizabeth, Sydney, Roddy (!), Cherry, the blind young sailor, Lindsay, Constance, Harold's mother and, yes, my brother Lyle. Especially Lyle.

And there was something else, something that both Malcolm and Harold had said, about intuition, about not being blind to it, though it was hard to reconcile with verifiable data, tedious to even think of it.

A squawk box echoed. "Roger fifteen."

Then more voices. One hundred yards off the shore and almost 100 yards to the west of my neatly stacked clothes, two men sloshed around in the tall reeds, searching for something. As I got closer I saw holsters on their hips, and dread spiked in me.

Trembling from the cold, I pulled myself out through the reeds. Harold was near. I didn't resist. Between the cops and me, something protruded from the shadows, just north of the cedar, amongst the canes. Something Harold wanted me to see. Something beautiful. Five short crystalized shoots caught the light, evocative of a beckoning hand.

Still naked and shivering, I slipped out of the water, quickly dried and clothed myself. One of the cops saw me and yelled, "Stay there."

As he doubled back toward me along the ragged shoreline and his buddy kept combing the stalks, I waded over and through the clumps of tall grass to one of the still frozen clusters along the lake. Without my glasses I had to bend closer. It was a hand! And even through the thin layer of ice I couldn't mistake that face, those aquamarine eyes. Atara stared up at me.

Disbelief. Shock. And relief. I know it sounds cruel.

"Jim, over here." I heard the officer. "Did you do this?"

She was still beautiful.

"Lady, did you do this?"

"What? No. I just found her."

"Don't move."

I couldn't take my eyes off her. She didn't take hers off mine.

One of the officers pulled me to the shore and asked me a bunch of questions.

"No bumps, no bruises, no bullet holes," I heard one of them say. "Cause of death?"

"Coroner's call. Cold maybe, the waters pretty cold," said another.

"She's fucking gorgeous."

"And in great shape. Not much cloth wasted on that bikini."

"Lady? Lady!" He yelled at me.

"Yes," I said, still dazed.

"You can go, but don't go anywhere out of the county. You understand? Detective Sullivan will have further questions, I'm sure."

☽☽☽

The front of Johnny Ray's trailer showed more signs of wear and tear than I'd remembered, yellow water stains under the windows and the roof thick with leaves. Or perhaps it was that second look that revealed more.

How did that man traverse the front door steps in his wheelchair? Was there an accident? When could he drive a car? I moved quietly around to the rear where a wooden ramp angled to the ground a few feet from a dark blue car. A basketball net hung on a spindly, long-dead tamarack. I returned cautiously to the front yard.

The orange and blue birdbath, now somehow familiar, attracted me and, watching for Johnny Ray's imminent arrival at the front door, I drew closer to it, off the gravel path on which I was surely supposed to remain. A few cups of water sat at the bottom of the shell-shaped bowl gathering fragments of twig and leaf. The workmanship was quite good, each row of tiles carefully orchestrated, joined by an almost unerring spacing between them. *Not tiles, beads.*

"You're back." Johnny Ray sat behind the screen once more, his voice not quite as sturdy.

"I'm sorry to bother you again."

"No, you're not."

"Can I come in?"

"If this visit will be your last."

"I can't promise that." I ascended the two front steps. "My brother wanted me to pay you what he owes you. Four hundred and fifty-five dollars, for those lessons and the amp." I pulled the bills from my pocket, the dwindling remains of my back pay.

"Lyle," Johnny Ray coughed, "after all these years? Bullshit."

I waved the bills at him. "He wants things square, and I have to know about Harold. He was my husband. I have to know."

"Don't be so sure."

"May I?" I saw him wheel away from the door to allow entry.

I stacked the wrinkled bills on the closest counter top, away from an opened bottle of Red Bull. The trailer was cluttered but as orderly as the outside. I counted at least five guitars arranged in a semi-circle; others hung uniformly on the walls. The stench of cigarette almost suffocated me, small plates and ashtrays overflowing with remnant parts, incongruous with the otherwise pervading order.

"It was you who ran me off the road. You shot my tire out."

He swallowed a smile, like meeting a long-lost family member and not quite knowing how to react. "You don't know what you're talking about." He pulled a Lucky Strike from the pack and lit it.

"My mother smokes those. You have the same cough."

"Should I offer you one?" The first hint of sarcasm I'd heard from him. He answered for me. "I didn't think so." He didn't move his wheelchair back to make room for me to sit.

"I stopped at the Drink 'n' Dive, spoke to Mae. Lyle will be singing there in ten days; a Friday night."

"The thirtieth, day of the Cannonball crash. Not very lucky."

"Mae says you changed your famous braided hair."

"Change is good."

"Actually, you cut it sometime after he and I got serious. When my mother met you it was long. At the cremation, you'd cut it."

"And how were the Twins doing at the time? A two-game win streak? Maybe I was celebrating. Maybe it was in deference to my friend. Maybe I got lice. What's your point?"

I steadied myself against the small counter. "You changed your hair color on his death —your hair is naturally brown, not white like mine."

"I should have asked your permission." He stubbed out the cigarette before its time.

"You met at the library. You both loved Dickens."

"You're regurgitating." Johnny Ray sounded fatigued.

"You were friends."

"Friends." He spit out a rueful laugh. "He was a good man."

"Yes, he was."

"You don't know how good."

"You say that like I didn't deserve him."

"You didn't."

"So tell me."

"He was kindhearted. He didn't need bright lights. He didn't need a sex pot like you."

That tickled me. "Sex pot?! Me?"

"Throwing your tits and ass all over the place. He was perfectly happy before you came around."

"I didn't come around. He came to me."

He fell silent, grabbed the pack of Luckies again.

I steeled myself. "Did he love you?"

Johnny Ray set the pack of Luckies in his lap and searched for a place to wheel his chair, but he was blockaded. I was afraid he'd barrel over me.

"Did he?" I stood taller.

"He never said that, but he did. Do you even know what made him laugh?"

"Me."

"Shiiit."

"You were lovers. You sent him that Poe book with your hair, those beads; the same beads you used to create the birdbath out front."

"My college colors. Go wildcats." He was almost breezy.

"You wanted him back."

"We were a good fit. Happy."

"Was the hair a memento or a warning?"

He peered up at me, eyes glassy.

I relaxed, tried to speak tenderly. "It was, wasn't it . . . a warning? That's how much you wanted him back."

"I never meant . . ."

"For him to kill himself."

He wiped his eyes.

I struggled to be sympathetic. "You must have known his father would abandon him completely if he found out, if you'd made your relationship public. Rhoald's not a forgiving man, even if it was love."

Johnny Ray grew smaller. "Even if it was love?" He lit another cigarette. He blew smoke my way. "Maybe you killed him. Maybe he realized his mistake. You consider that?"

The cigarette trembled ever so slightly in his hand. I could see them together, arms around each other's shoulders. Not attractive men, but beautiful friends.

"Of course I did."

He rubbed his forehead, took another drag from the cigarette.

"We were all part of his collection." I couldn't see what they'd seen in each other's faces.

"Yes." I could barely hear him. "But he *married* you. Conventional. The others . . ." His eyes disconsolate. "The rest of us . . ."

His gaze drifted, reflecting the oceans of unknown that we shared. I didn't know what to say. Hadn't a clue. And nothing more was said.

CHAPTER FIFTY-THREE

The next day I was summoned to the police station, a peach brick building that was even less hospitable inside, walled in white cinder block. Harold's true cause of death was still unclear, as was Atara's, and Johnny Ray's jealousy aside, I couldn't believe he'd kill Atara and frame me for it. Or how he might even have accomplished either death given his condition. But Sullivan had his eye on me, and who could blame him. There was the very real chance that he would hold me in jail as a prime suspect. I shivered at the thought of incarceration.

As soon as we were in Sullivan's closet-like office and he'd closed the door, he said, "It's odd, isn't it, that we keep meeting this way. You knew her, correct?"

"Atara, yes. Atara Bukara."

"That wasn't her last name."

More particles in motion. *I was such a fool.* "That's the name she told me."

"And how did you meet?"

Oh shit, I didn't want to go *there.* "I was a patient in a hospital."

He leveled me with distrustful eyes. "What kind of hospital?"

I took a breath. "I had a mild concussion. I'd helped a man, but —"

"I don't need that level of detail. She was a nurse."

Thank goodness. "Yes."

"And . . .?"

"She and her husband were very generous to me."

"She wasn't married."

Naturally. "Oh, well they lived together."

He stretched to see the sheet of paper on his desktop. "Levi . . . Levi O'Brien."

"Levi, yes."

"Apparently you had something of Ms. Afaa's."

"That was her name?

He nodded.

I considered telling him the truth but I saw a small dirty jail cell with me in it. My breath became shallow, labored. "I didn't. I don't."

He held up his hand. "Two different people have testified that you do."

Water, I should have brought some water. "Two?"

"What do you say to that?"

"Levi, Mr. O'Brien, may have thought that. Atara certainly thought so, but I don't know who else—"

"A credible person."

"Who?"

"You know I can't tell you that. Did you introduce Vic — Mayor King— to Atara Afaa?"

"I did."

He opened a manila folder on his desk. "And apparently you had other questionable episodes, in New York."

That covered a multitude of possibilities. I was being pulled under. *Don't panic.* "I have no record. I've never been charged with anything."

"No, you haven't. Who might have a reason to intimidate or want Ms. Afaa dead?"

"I don't know. But she was no angel."

He raised an eyebrow. "How do you mean?"

"You can ask Mr. O'Brien, and maybe even . . ." I measured the wisdom of mentioning it, "the Mayor."

"Our mayor?"

"Could have been an accident. Some people underestimate the cold. Hyperthermia. She was wearing a bathing suit." I looked again at the mounted bass on his wall, then squarely at the detective, but he didn't meet my gaze. *There was something about that fish.*

"You like swimming in cold water."

"I do."

"Where were you the past two days, before we found her?"

I recounted that I'd been to the pharmacy for Lyle's pills, I'd talked to Gordon, I'd visited Muriel Cloonis.

"Your former mother-in-law."

"Yes." Then for a swim in Kingdom and then home with Carly, Lyle and Momma.

He wrote it all down. Poker-faced. "Anyone see you at the lake?"

"Not that I know of."

"Yesterday?"

"Home. The Drink 'n' Dive with Mae Scotts. I even bumped into The Mayor."

"Yes, he told me."

"Then Kingdom."

"Right." He scribbled something more. I started adding too.

"Anything else?"

"No, that's it for now."

A reprieve. My throat loosened, breathing came more easily. "You got a tip." I started to rise.

"What?"

"Strange that someone tipped you to look in the lake. In Kingdom."

"How would you know?"

"Detective, do your men usually beat around the bushes?"

He stared down at his notes. "That's it for now, Mrs. Cloonis. Thanks for coming in."

When I got to my car I found a stray receipt and on the back made one of my lists:

<u>Who killed Beauty?</u>

<u>Suspect</u>	<u>Impediment</u>
Accident	Would she swim in the cold?
Victor	Motive?
~~Lyle~~	~~Too weak~~
~~Carly~~	~~Too scared~~
Johnny Ray	Revenge on me? Capability?
Rhoald	Revenge on me?
Levi	Motive?
Other?	?

ⅅⅅⅅ

It was like the first time I'd jumped into a lake.

"Levi?"

"Yes."

"It's Eunis."

Silence.

"I'm sorry for your loss."

"You've got to be kidding."

"I had nothing to do with it."

"Quite a coincidence that of all people you found her."

I remained unusually serene. "Quite a coincidence that she was at my favorite swimming spot."

More silence.

"And that she drowned like her sister."

"She didn't have a sister."

Duped again. My turn to take a breather. "Well, I'm sorry."

"I don't suppose you have any ideas about who might have done it."

I had to restrain myself. "No. Perhaps it was an accident. Perhaps she miscalculated the cold water."

"That's what the police are saying . . . so far." He was remarkably calm. "Is that all?"

"The other day when I called you . . ."

"Yes?"

"You weren't in New York, were you?"

"No."

"Would you tell me where?"

"No. Is that all?"

"No. Both of you shared with me something of your arrangement." Actually, they'd hinted.

"You mean about our bodies?"

That was it! "Yes. You're in charge of her burial, not her family."

"So?"

"I thought I could be of service."

"What does that mean?"

I looked out over the farmhouse. Restored, it had come a long way, the yard not so much. I was halfway in two worlds. Having the discussion with Levi in New York made it even more dreamlike. "I want to make a deal."

"You don't have anything to deal. Are we done?"

"I think I do. Hear me out. In a few days, after the autopsy is complete, I'm going to send you some instructions."

"You can't be serious."

"You both signed papers, right? Legal but delicate."

He was silent.

"Levi?"

"This is madness."

Balmy weather had returned. The marshes would be filling with white and pink bog rosemary, and the woods showing red baneberry with its white spears and glossy rubicund fruit. "We all have our madness; she was yours. Don't force us to be adversaries. I can make this work for you. For both of us."

"You want to come back to the nest?"

I was silent. The luxury, the adulation. I wanted it but not if it cost me my purpose and self-respect. I'd come close to losing both.

Then he ended the silence. "No, I didn't think so." He hung up.

The farmhouse, as I stepped backward to get perspective on the fresh veneer, no longer matched the rest of the landscape. The bristles of unkempt weeds, the blighted shed, the rusted caboose, the crumbling equipment, the rotting trough, were all reminders of profound, unfinished business.

Inside the house, the peeling walls, the hobbled cabinets, the worn carpets, the neglected furniture, were all steeped in four decades of tobacco and delusion. Nothing had changed on the inside. It was past time for me to tackle the hard choices.

☽☽☽

Organizing my thoughts wasn't easy, not around Atara or Levi or Harold. I'd learned something about beauty that was part of the solution. But there were only two things I had to immediately attend to: organizing Lyle's performance and rehabilitating Carver's workshop, a place I could work, alone. I threw myself into both.

With but a few days till his show, Lyle could barely move without support. Perhaps I'd placed an unnecessary weight upon him by suggesting the performance. But he perked up during our brief rehearsals. When I proposed taking him out for dinner, he offered an appreciative rejection. "No point spendin' on a dinner that I'm gonna crap and puke out two hours later."

Momma visited him once every morning when he was barely awake, and when —I surmised— he was least likely to make any conversation, allowing Momma to generously offer, "I'll just let you sleep."

So in the mornings I was off to Carver's, first purging and cleaning, then hammering whatever was necessary for protection from the elements, if only temporary. The well and plumbing was still somewhat intact, and a call to Sparky took care of electrical support. Someone had returned the sign and leaned it against the front of the small building, creating more cover. I entered through the back. And while I worked, I mulled the sequence of my route the day the body was found, the autopsy, and Atara's final moments.

Despite all that, the week went by slowly, and on the Wednesday before his show, I came into Lyle's room with his medication, finding him clinging to his guitar and delirious. "Ya know," he said, heavy-lidded, "you should be out dancin' instead of here."

"What do you mean?" I sat on his bed, gently repositioning his ever-lengthening hair out of his eyes and off his face, and tucking it behind his ear.

"I'd dance if I could, you and me."

"Yes."

"Don't be mad." His eyes pleading.

"Why would I be mad at you?"

"Promise."

"Okay, I promise."

He smiled, hung his head over the Martin, and fell asleep. His emaciated face possessed the genes of a little boy I'd watched from first breath. Try as I might, I couldn't see them, another face I'd collected but failed to fully understand, even as his blood drained into mine, leaving me sadder still.

)))

When Detective Sullivan called me in for more questioning, familiar faces populated the reception area: Gordon, Victor King, Melissa, Rhoald and Muriel. No one looked happy.

"Ah, Mrs. Cloonis," the detective said. "Please, come with me." *Come with me!*

Gordon nodded. Victor's wife tracked me with a sullen glare. Victor didn't make eye contact. I thought Rhoald was going to leap up and hit me until Muriel laid a steadying hand on his arm.

The Detective ran me through many of the same questions he'd already asked. It was as if he'd marched me past the others in the reception area like a model on a runway, to elicit a response. So I tried to isolate each expression. Gordon looked confused, embarrassed and sympathetic. Melissa looked aloof and piqued to be in such a place. Victor was stoic. Rhoald, as I say, more determined than ever to close the door on me permanently, hostility forefront, but an anomalous hint of duplicity around his eyes, scarier than the anger. And Muriel, mawkish and almost shamefaced.

Somewhere in there, probably, was a clue. With me, the supposed expert on faces. *Ironies coming at me like locusts.* My track record not so good. But, as Lyle would say, it's all I had in my holster.

)))

I approached Harold's old office, the mid-day light flat and unwelcoming. I hadn't been there since returning a week after Harold's death at the detective's request, when Detective Sullivan manipulated me into moving Harold's oak desk. And now, as I ascended the staircase to the second floor office, I began to understand.

The detective's logic must have been if I could move the desk I could have snapped Harold's neck, I could have lifted or moved the body. *I could have. But why?*

My phone rang. It was Gordon.

"Hi." I got to the top step and stopped.

"I heard they're going to charge you."

"Charge me with what?"

"Two deaths. Something like, *you can come in on your own or we'll issue some type of document making sure you do.* What are you gonna do?"

"Fuck! Really?" I looked back down the staircase. The walls edged closer. "Alright," I said. Voices came from the corridor below. "First off, who told you this?"

"Vic."

"Right." I listened for Victor's voice. The voices came and went and came again. Short little bursts, but indefinable. I whispered, "Well, nothing's been served on me and you're my only recent call."

"But what are you gonna do? Is there something I can do? A lawyer?"

"Now they've got a record of you calling me."

"I don't care about that."

"But you may."

"You didn't do that did you?"

"No, I don't think so."

He chortled. "You don't think so?"

"I don't remember."

"That was Nixon's line. Are you serious?"

I looked down the corridor. "Gordon, I don't think I have time to talk to you. Will you have your cell with you?"

"Yes. But where will you be?"

"It's better that you don't know. Besides, it's uncertain. Like the weather." I hung up.

Two deaths. Another pattern? All those cases I'd read about, that had captivated me as a young girl. Sleepwalking killers, *usually* murdering family members. Schizophrenia, hearing voices, pleas of insanity and short-term memory loss from others. Killers of all sorts, none of whom remember what they did. Things they did, asleep or wake, that science could not resolve.

Harold irritated the hell out of me at times, and I often went to bed worried about him interfering with my work. Now the other lovers. The secrets. Maybe I already knew. Maybe I knew he was unfaithful. To me? To Johnny Ray? And my luxurious

Octagon apartment? Not without Harold's estate. *And . . .* The blank spaces. *Come with me.* Those damnable blank spaces.

I turned left into the narrow wainscot hallway that led, barely lit by a frosted transom, to his office. I moved quickly. At the door I found a handwritten note. I removed my shades. There, a phone number and a name to call if interested in renting the space.

Come with me. I tried the door. It opened. Someone else had inhabited the space since Harold. Walls painted sky blue. Same old oak desk, different chairs stacked in a corner, the freestanding lodge pole coat rack laid across them, one of its thin tines broken off. None of it well organized. Dusty. Atoms stirred; resonant water surrounding me as I submerged. Numinescence.

I closed the door behind me.

"Come with me," Harold said, holding out his hand, smiling beatifically, as peaceful as I'd ever seen him. "Together," he said. "Away from this world," he said. "Together always."

I took two steps back, confused. "Don't!"

He loves me.

"It'll be easy," he said. "Together. I'll show you. You're the only one. Nothing is so beautiful as us. Nothing can ruin this."

He climbed upon the desk. He threw the thick rope over the thick beam. "Forever." Once more he adjusted the cord. "In the drawer."

He pointed to the oak desk. "Together. Come with me." He placed the cable around his neck. "Forever."

He stepped off the desk.

"Harold!" I said aloud to the empty office, as much questioning my memory as him. But I knew I'd been there as he'd stepped off that desk. I'd been there and lost the memory in a squall of atoms, electrons and quarks. I had walked away. But his broken neck?

To get to the desk drawer I had to remove the damaged coat rack. I held it for a moment, distracted by the cracked tine. *Harold's neck; it had snapped because of his small bones, his brittle musculature.* I pulled apart the stacked chairs, shifted a cabinet, reached over and tugged on it. It was locked, just as I'd left it after his death, when I'd found nothing. That was the way Harold had always kept it, ever wary that someone might invade his space. And then what? So, out of respect, I'd re-locked it. But he'd given me permission to see anything of his and in fact had encouraged it, I'd thought until the recent revelations.

A voice in the hallway. I didn't move. After a minute, when I was sure the voice had disappeared, I locked the door.

Back to the desk. I felt for the key along the inner rim of the desktop, sliding my fingers this way and that till I came upon it, still taped there and surprised that the detective hadn't taken the time to unlock it. Or perhaps he had and had simply re-placed the key. I'd told him about it.

Reaching over, I considered the advisability of *knowing*. I en-visioned a nautical rope. *Stop imagining.*

One last breath before I inserted the small key and turned it, then pulled the middle drawer toward me. There was no rope. I swiped my hand back and forth. Nothing.

I relaxed. *It's all in my head*; Harold and sailors jumping to the call of something deep. I *had* been there! I had been part of this. But still there was blank space.

Then, remembering the smaller secret drawer to the left that simultaneously unlocked (and that especially pleased Harold), I leaned over the cabinet. Knowing that it frequently jammed in the warmer weather, I wrenched it open.

No rope visible. I shuttled my hand inside. There was some-thing! A folded piece of paper and, withdrawing it, I could tell it was a sheet of accounting ledger. It could have been anything: a faulty formula, a scrap notation. But not a rope. *Not a rope.*

I unfolded the perfectly quartered and scored paper. So Har-old. It read:

> *"If you find this, I know you loved me. You were will-ing to consider my offer. You can love. But I could not take you with me, as much as I wanted to. To-gether always, in this world and others. I love you –*
> *H"*

ꭰꭰꭰ

I ached. I cursed its untidiness, its lack of pure definition, leaving me without borders. But I knew at last what I'd found beautiful in Harold: his compassion. Not just for me, but for everyone, everyone but himself. He could see beauty where others could not. And it confirmed my earlier thoughts on the vulnerability of beauty.

No police cars in our driveway. I walked, disoriented, into the farmhouse. I was shaken into the present. Roddy sat at the kitchen table with Lyle and Momma.

"Come join us," Momma said merrily, raising a beer.

"You promised not to be mad," chipped in Lyle, as Roddy stood and wrapped his arms around me.

Momma, Roddy, Lyle! I could've died. But no one acted as if anything was wrong. So, for a luxurious opening in time —I can't tell you how long— I was diverted by Roddy's warm, singular smell: sweat, wood smoke and oranges. He wouldn't let go till I put my arms around him, which I did reluctantly, and then it was I who didn't want to let go. He was so . . . comforting.

"How nice," said Momma.

I opened my eyes. Roddy pulled away. I questioned Lyle with a glance. He showed no urgency.

"Lyle invited me," said Roddy.

"Everyone wants to hear my boy sing." Momma waved her Keystone triumphantly.

"*I* wanted him to hear me sing." Lyle was steadfast.

I knew better. I'd tell him it was preposterous, but I wanted no quarrel with Lyle, his eyes so ringed in red, doing his best to sit upright. "Really?" I said, still not looking at Roddy. "I never thought you were such buddies."

"Friendships arise." Roddy smiled at Lyle. Lyle nodded in accord.

"And," I continued to Roddy, "I never took you for a country music fan."

"I like all kinds of music, I'm open-minded."

Perhaps a jab at me but I quickly dismissed it. "Where are you staying?"

"On the couch." He pointed to the living room and his bag sitting by the sofa. "Lyle suggested it."

"The more the merrier," said Momma.

The old couch, lumpy and stained. I felt shame for Momma and the whole house, and that Roddy should see this as my environment. "It reminds me of my Aunt Maxine's sofa," he said. "As a kid, I always felt safe sleeping on it. I'll be fine."

Carly came through the back door. "Hi everybody!" Sport bag in hand, as if *she* was the party everyone was waiting for, she smiled. Then seeing Roddy she ran her hands through her hair, tossing it back, and running her tongue across her full lips. "And who is *this*?"

She came close enough to Roddy that her well-heralded breasts were quickly upon him, compelling him to steady himself on the kitchen table to avoid falling on it.

"Jerrod," I said instinctively, hoping to protect him.

"Roddy," Roddy said, trying to find room to raise his arms and shake Carly's hand.

"Lyle's friend." Carly held his gaze.

"And Eunis's," Lyle said.

Carly faced me, pursed her lips in a didn't-know-you-had-it-in-you expression, from which I didn't retreat. It occurred to me that even Carly could have disposed of Atara. She had the strength, though I doubted she had the guts.

"Hello, Carly." Momma's jaw twitched.

"Oh, hi Momma." Carly waved but didn't look at her. "Everyone should have *friends*." Carly sized up Roddy.

Prickly heat ran up my neck. Knocking Carly down was an option, but then I wondered why. Rather than explore the question, I asked, "Any calls for me?"

No one knew what I was talking about? Calling Gordon might make matters worse for him. I excused myself. "Well," I said, threading past the bodies in the kitchen. "I'll be downstairs if anybody needs me."

I passed Carly's duffel bag, all covered in bright stickers from Mexico, Costa Rica, even Paris, and I thought about asking her where *she* planned to sleep. Then I decided I'd rather not contemplate her choices.

CHAPTER FIFTY-FOUR

I stood by the woodpile, then walked away from the farmhouse to the rusted caboose and looked back. Even in the late afternoon haze the farmhouse showed its insincerity, ever more present seen at a distance, despite my good intentions. Its vanity and hollowness sadder even than before its rehabilitation.

That unfinished business again, thinking paint would hide the mind of the place. Because that's what it was: the mind, not the soul. It was too late to undo, and unless I aimed to work the *whole* property . . . I couldn't imagine that.

Yet unfinished was so undisciplined. And unfair. To what? To whom? To Papa Karlyle? It wasn't the work, I enjoyed the physical, the hands on. It wasn't the property, I could make it attractive, even in its scraggily environment. It was the mindset: Momma's. I was ashamed of Momma. And for a moment I was five years old and sitting in front of the vanity mirror, Momma applying cosmetics to my baby face.

It was all about choices. Momma's, Harold's, mine. Was Gordon truly my friend? Was his call premeditated to elicit a response? The police hadn't contacted me. I bounced down and did five quick pushups, stretched my neck a couple of times, then circled around to the shed. Even I knew better than to enter it, the slightest whisper liable to cave it in, first tearing, then burying, any trespasser. I was amazed it hadn't happened years before.

Nevertheless, wading through the spikey spring weeds, which left trails on my bare legs, I stepped over the downed barbed door and through cobwebs, ducking my head, careful not to touch the doorframe. Even so, I almost fell against it, losing my balance as I pulled viscid spider traps from my face and swatted at imagined creatures dropping into my hair.

Someone had added paint cans to the floor plan but otherwise it hadn't changed in thirty years, another graveyard of unfinished business. Choices. I stooped to the cans and, brushing aside their caked dust and mud, saw that they'd never been opened. I lifted one up to verify and sure enough, it was full, the weight of it surprising me so I almost lost my balance again before my arm anchored to a small patch of clear, dusty earth. I pondered what I was doing there.

Standing straight up was impossible lest I bring the roof down upon myself. I bent over and stepped tactically onto lattice that snapped under me, between a large perforated washtub and a shattered glass washboard, and over the boat paddle that had lain on the same dirt floor moldering for half a century. Stepping into the dingy in the corner where Nemo and I once cuddled, I settled in very carefully, the sides giving way with a crackle to my slightest pressure, a sizeable splinter wedging under my thumbnail as I let myself down. "Damn!" I shook out my hand and sucked on it.

Besides the front door, the only invading sunshine came from three small overcast shafts squeezing between slats on the far wall, never reaching me. For the first time I wondered how the dingy made its way into the shed through the door. It was as if the shed had been built *around* the dingy. Had the boat ever sailed? Who in my family had ever been a fisherman? No one.

Fishermen. The two at Little Bass the day they found Atara's body at Kingdom. One could have been Victor's friend whom I'd seen only a half hour earlier outside the Drink 'n' Dive.

My phone rang. "Yes?"

"Eunis?"

"Yes."

"It's Levi." He sounded tight.

It wasn't a train's signal but the clanging of a cable car. "You were in San Francisco when it happened, weren't you?"

"Yes."

No longer on my suspect list.

"I told them you were authorized to take the body for me," he said. "You'll have to go in to sign for it. They'll deliver."

"I'll take care of it." My confidence grew. But something still troubled me. "Levi?"

"Yes?"

"What about the tape? Atara mentioned something . . ."

"I don't know anything about a tape. She was probably bluffing."

"She didn't strike me as the bluffing type."

"I told you, I know nothing of a tape."

"Sis, you in there?" It was Lyle.

"I gotta go," I said to Levi. "I'll keep you apprised." I hung up.

"Lyle, don't come in here, it's dangerous."

"I can see that. What *you* doin' in there?"

An excellent question. "I needed a place to think." Both foolish and insufficient. "I'm too big for under the staircase." Even more ludicrous.

"Well come on out, we need to talk. An fer god's sake, be careful."

"Okay, okay, I'm coming out."

And when I did, he said, "What are you doin'? You've got more at stake 'an I do. Come on." He led me over to the old caboose where we sat against the sleeper timbers on the sunny south side, sitting side by side, looking away from the house, away from its cluster of black ash and box elder trees, and out the driveway, up the rutted road. We didn't speak for several minutes. The last remaining scent of creosote wafted in and out.

"You know why Momma never got rid of this caboose?" he finally asked.

"She was lazy?"

"Nope. I don't think that was it."

"She thought it was art?"

He turned to me with a surprised soft smile. "In a way, you're right."

I gave him a curious tilt of the head.

"If art comes from dreams," he said, his shrug signifying *seems right to me.* Then his eyes traveled up the road. "It was Papa Karl's hack, his caboose, ya know. He salvaged it from the Burlington. He loved it, with its cupola. It was considered a helluva caboose in its day with its coal stove. It was art. It was his dream, and it became hers too. Saw a picture of it once. It was red, I mean really red, alive, before nature and all the seasons got to it, before we ever saw it. Momma once told me that Papa Karl was gonna trick it out and they were gonna hitch it with his connections and ride it all the way to New Orleans when they'd saved enough money. They'd go on some high adventure."

He breathed deeply. "Course they never made it, what with Papa's accident and all. She blamed it on Papa Karl for not believing in the dark spirits, the *tussers*, the *mylings*. Or the Christian ones."

Lyle scuffled the dirt in front of him with his boot. "It was their boat down the Mississippi. They never made it. That's somethin' the three of us have in common —me an Papa Karl and Momma. Not like you and Carly."

It sounded too much like a farewell, and I didn't want him to go. "You've got time. Every day they're finding cures."

"Naw." He shook his head. "I've run out of time, it's okay. Had my chances. Danced up a storm, just never danced with any direction."

I put my hand on his arm. It was atrophied and, I suspected, brittle.

"I wanted to thank you, Sis."

I shook my head, resisted the clouds rising in my eyes.

"No really." He focused on the dirt, his eyes also beginning to brim with dampness. "Tomorrow night, that means a lot to me."

"We can talk about this later, after—"

"No, listen. That guy, that Roddy, he's a real man. You were in New York, what's the Jew word? Mesh?"

"Mensch." My dimple may have shown for an instant.

"He's that, and you should be nicer to him." Lyle scratched at the dirt. "I needed someone . . ." His voice caught. He stopped for a moment, wiped his nose with his sleeve, regained his composure ". . . but I thought I don't need no one. All that shit Momma told us, all that scary shit . . . those folktales, those myths. But you taught me better. Sis, you taught me better."

I rubbed his shoulders.

"So I got a lot to thank you for, and we ain't even sung our song yet. But you listen to your brother Lyle, okay? This ole caboose," he waved weakly at the lacerated hulk behind him, "it only has thirty-nine feet of track now, but it was a beauty and it could travel anywhere and people would notice —Papa had those plans— but now the only thing it has left is worn edges, which is all most of us will have at the end. You're strong, you got curves —I see the way men look at you— and you got brains and heart and somethin' else, somethin' not quite the same as everybody else. Somethin' special. Don't sit up on blocks yet, okay?" He started to cough.

"Okay," I murmured as his coughing escalated. "You okay?" His body quaked more and more violently with each cough.

"Lyle!"

They came faster, louder, deeper. He signaled: *Get me back to the house.*

☽ ☽ ☽

Once I had Lyle lying down in bed, his face regained color. But not much. I covered him in the stained white comforter and waited till he drifted asleep. I moved the hair off his face and tucked it behind his ears before quietly closing the door behind me.

There were voices in the kitchen. I turned away, routinely, the way I'd done at Little Bass Stump that day. Then, this time, I changed direction.

"It was, it was!" said Momma. Carly and Momma sat at the table, each with a beer: a Keystone for Momma, a Modelo for Carly, and no knives drawn.

"He was cute, wasn't he?" continued Momma. "Always that great voice."

"Yes, Momma, always that great voice." Carly saw me in the doorway. "Well, come on in, for chrissakes. Have a beer. Mom's are pisswater—"

"Carly Renay!"

"So I suggest you have one of mine."

"I'm good." I contemplated the empty chair.

Carly jumped up, snatched a bottle from the fridge and set it down with a clunk in front of me. "Sit." She placed both hands on my shoulders and pushed me down in the chair.

I threw her hands off. "Don't."

Carly raised both arms and backed away before settling into her own chair again. I sat eyeing both Momma and Carly. I wanted to talk about Lyle but I was afraid he'd hear and I didn't really know how to start the discussion or what the point was. We all sat there, suddenly quiet, each eyeing the other.

There wasn't even a spring wind to rattle the screens. "What you been up to?" said Carly sipping her beer, breaking the silence.

"Up to? Me? Like starting when?" *Like starting when you had no interest in me? Like forever?*

"Recently."

"Oh," interjected Momma, "you can see what Eunis did with the outside of the house." She smiled at both of us. *Unreal.*

"I was assisting genetics research in New York."

"Yes," said Carly. "That's what Roddy said."

Then why did you even bother to ask? But instead I said, "Where is Roddy?"

"Went to the lodge," said Momma. "A gentleman; said Carly should get the couch."

I turned it over in my head.

"You can stop worrying, Eunis," said Carly. "I'm not gonna hit on the guy. But I *do* like the lodge," she said with a leer.

My eyes definitely bugged out.

"Just kiddin', he's not my type at all."

"What *is* your type?" I lowered my head, ready for battle.

"All kinds, but they gotta be good looking."

"You bitch!" I accidently knocked over the beer then quickly righted it and blotted at the spill with a napkin.

"No, no, that wasn't meant as a swipe, really. If he's studly to you, that's all that's important."

I fixed her with contempt.

"*Really,*" offered Carly, rightly apologetic.

"He's handsome," I said, turning to Momma. "Don't you think?"

"Well," said Momma, "I think he's very nice. Seems very nice."

"But good looking, I mean."

She let out a rheumy cough. "I've seen handsomer, if you want the truth." Momma glanced at Carly and managed a swig from her Keystone.

I focused again on Carly. "You really don't think he's handsome?"

"Like I said, whatever blows your skirt. It's not like I think he's *bad* looking."

"What would make him better looking —in your opinion?"

"Geez, Eunis, what does it matter? Do you love the guy or not?"

"Love! Who said anything about love? The man is my lawyer."

"You have a lawyer?" said Momma, impressed.

All I could think of was how blind I'd been to his features.

CHAPTER FIFTY-FIVE

The next morning after checking the fishing regulations on the Minnesota Natural Resources website, I entered the kitchen, surprised to find Lyle already up and sipping his coffee at the table. "Well, the early bird," I said pouring myself a cup. "You beat everyone."

"Yeah." He wrapped his boney hands around his Johnny Cash mug, the one giving the finger. "This is gonna be a good day."

I smiled and secretly prayed that I wouldn't screw up his song, although I've never held much belief in prayer except when I prayed with Papa Karl because he believed in it. "Can I do anything for you before I meet Roddy at The Drink to set up?"

"I'm good. Don't worry 'bout me. I got one more practice after breakfast then I'm gonna take a hike."

"A hike?"

"Nothin' special. Thought I'd drive out to Carver's then walk to Kingdom Lake." He saw my reaction. "Sorry, that has bad memories for you."

He didn't know the half of it. But I'd camouflaged my work at Carver's pretty good, and he never was one to poke around scary places. "Driving, walking? You strong enough?"

"It's a short walk, I'll be fine. Beautiful there, peaceful. That week I worked for old man Carver I'd take my breaks at the lake, just to get away from all the dead parts." Again he winced. "Sorry."

We did have some things in common. "You want to wait till I get back?" Out the window to the northwest, dark clouds gathered over Thief River. Another quick temperature drop could bring rain or another tornado. "I could go with you."

He lingered on his reflection in the coffee. "I'll be fine." He wanted to be alone, and if anything happened to him it'd be better out there in the open, amongst the comfort of the trees and next to the water, than in the house. But I wanted him to know that I'd gladly walk with him. "You're sure?"

"Sis, I'll be fine."

And even as he smiled and zigzagged laboriously to his room, I knew I was going to miss him, that another hole was going to be left in my heart.

$$\mathcal{D}\mathcal{D}\mathcal{D}$$

Before leaving the farmhouse I paused in the vestibule, feeling for the incoming weather. Nothing struck me as imminent though I smelled the potential for rain. I hoped against it. I wanted no excuses; I wanted that small room packed for Lyle's performance.

On the drive down to Bemidji I cast an occasional eye toward the Thief River clouds, which thankfully seemed painted in one place and lacking intention. I hoped that would be true of the police as well. If they jailed me before Lyle's event I would be letting him down, like I'd done to so many others.

When I arrived at Bemidji Funeral Home & Cremation Service, there wasn't a car in the lot. But the door opened and I went to the front desk. "Hello," I called out. No response. A little bell sat on the counter, the kind you'd find in a dry cleaning establishment or the post office. So I tapped it.

"Be right there," came the voice from out back. And in a moment I stood face-to-face, and alone, with Victor King.

"This is your place? *You're* the uncle?"

"Excuse me?"

"Are you the owner?"

"What do you need, Eunis?" He was all business.

"I came to sign for the body. For Atara's body."

"You! Mr. O'Brien spoke to us, but I had no idea." I saw the wheels turning. He sniffed. "This is highly irregular."

"Melissa doing well, I hope? She seems like a lovely woman. Not just beautiful, but a nice person."

"She's great, yeah. What did you say to her?"

"I said nothing." Beauty was most vulnerable to other beauty, especially beauty perceived to be equal or greater.

"And the police?" He lifted an errant pen off the counter and dropped it into an open drawer.

"Not much *to* say. I just found her."

"I'm surprised you haven't been arraigned." He slammed the drawer shut.

I didn't flinch. "Yes, I'd heard rumors, don't know where they started, but I don't run, I swim." A slightly befuddled expression crossed his face. "Do you like to fish?"

"No, I don't have the time." His mouth tightened, fed up. "What does that have to do with anything?"

"Well, Detective Sullivan does; likes to fish. You ever see the largemouth bass mounted on his wall?"

"What?"

"It does seem like someone wanted me to look guilty. Maybe someone knew how regular I am in my patterns. I am rather systematic. But the thing is, I checked. Little Bass Stump is closed to fishing till May 23. Has been since April 1st. Seems they spawn now, the bass, I mean. What were those fishermen fishing for if they couldn't legally catch fish?"

"Fish. Not everyone abides by the rules."

"With their radio blasting? I think someone sent them there. Maybe just told them to take a day off at Little Bass. Gave them permission."

He shook his head. "You make this stuff up as you go along."

"I think someone knew that I'd move on to Kingdom Lake if I couldn't swim naked at Little Bass."

Victor remained stony-faced.

"Anyway, I was never attractive enough for you."

"What does that mean?!"

"Anyone with an eye for beauty, like you, *like your wife*, would know that you wouldn't waste time with me. Certainly not a whole evening, till late. And then night after night."

His face lost some of its color.

I pressed on. "What I thought was providential was how much you and Atara had in common."

Impassively, "I don't know what you mean."

"Mermaid tattoos. I guess it's a universal fascination."

He instinctively reached for his groin. "How do you—?"

I smiled. And then it must have resonated, because his mouth hung open, his eyes fled mine.

"I don't have time for this." But he didn't move. At the very least he knew he really was vulnerable. As was his wife, Melissa.

"Jealousy can get so ugly."

He swallowed. "I'm going back to my work."

"I'm sure you and Melissa will be very happy for many more years. Children need the mother's touch, don't you think?" The irony didn't escape me. "Anything you can do as Mayor to explicate me from Detective Sullivan's consideration, well . . . it's a shame Atara went into *that* water. Colder than she was used to, no doubt."

He'd turned pale grey, like the charred powder that came out of his furnaces.

"Please have it delivered on Monday, without fanfare. Here," I said handing him the directions. I walked out, my legs strong, my body upright, my gait nimbler.

ᴐᴐᴐ

Roddy was already at the Drink 'n' Dive when I arrived, setting up, his back to me. The gloomy windowless room and the bleached barroom smell overpowered my ability to focus, but I was finally drawn to a tabletop screaming with yellow and gold tulips, a large basket with a note rooting Lyle on: "Be the boss, hugs from Ruthie, Brytney, Vinnette, Anthony, Simone and Anthony Jr." A natural oasis and reassuring fragrance. I could see their faces.

With Roddy's back still to me, I tried to reconstruct *his* face and calibrate the disconnect between what I saw and what Carly and Momma saw. The empirical criteria had seemed to fit. Yet the divide was too great. I thought I was immune to such things. Perhaps I'd ask Mae when she came in, but by then the invited would already be streaming in leaving me no time to attend to research. And Mae was in her eighties. How would that twist the results? *Focus.*

I stood watching Roddy. He pulled inverted chairs from tables and arranged them. Why had I thought he was handsome? I suppose I shared that view with Elizabeth. Already I sensed myself recalculating his attractiveness. Another study gone awry.

And what about imperfections? Could they be what set off a face as beautiful? That little mole on an otherwise unblemished cheek? Or the straying eye on an otherwise perfect canvas? The scar? The tilted nose? The errant eyebrow? The cleft chin? The crooked smile? Perhaps that was the factor that turned a face beautiful, made it more appealing. He had none of those.

I didn't make a sound —barely breathed really— yet he must've sensed me because he turned and, seeing me, smiled. "Hey," he said.

I refused to be fooled again, a researcher examining and evaluating her subject, nothing more. "Hi." I smiled. "You didn't need to get here so early."

His eyes: cerulean, reasonably symmetrical, although his right eye was perhaps a fraction lower than the left, with a hint of puffiness that suggested poor sleep. His skin quality: a bit wrinkled, yes, with some sun/age spots, but the *color* of his skin was a perfect blend of brown and white.

What would others say? The ratios, from eyes to nose to mouth, weren't squished together, like Harold, or too distant from the forehead, like Gordon. His nose was a bit large, but not outside the "average" for the population, its skew only marginally to the right.

"I'm happy to help." He reconfigured the space between two chairs. "You okay? You've been under a lot of strain."

Smell, a definite factor in attractiveness according to the research, often correlated back to the facial proportions. The more balanced the face, the more enjoyable the body odor. At this, I inhaled the scent memory of him and decided I'd found my researcher bias. I could no longer be objective, his odor clearly an aphrodisiac —if I was honest with myself— that couldn't be resolved in my study.

"I'm fine." I walked as slowly as I could toward him to extend my calibrations a few more seconds. His face was masculine, though the research was splintered on the effect. Women may marry neutral-faced men but want to have sex with the masculine-faced male for his genes, aware that such men are more aggressive and less faithful. Then there's the suggestion that, when the woman is in a weakened position, say pregnant or nursing, that she prefers the smell of a man that replicates those of her closest relatives. Lyle, Carly, *Momma!*

"This place smells awful, doesn't it?" he said, his nose lifted. "Maybe we can do something about it before tonight. It's like sitting in a urinal."

"Yes, it is," I said, charmed that he somehow read my mind. "I feel like I'm being pickled." Mr. Carver would have said *preserved*.

Roddy coughed out a small laugh, set down another chair, and came to hug me. I was disinclined, but not because I was unenthusiastic about pressing my body next to his. I tried not to breathe him in, and he noticed.

"Breathe," he said, misunderstanding my motivation. "This will all go fine, you'll see."

We finished organizing the tables and, finding some large floor fans in the storage room, set them on opposite sides of the stage and turned them on full to blow away the malaise, though the smell of *him* was still with me. The shrill tin sound of the fans drove us into the main barroom, mostly empty at this hour, where we scooted into the booth in the corner, the same one in which Sparky and I had conversed.

"How is he?" he asked.

"Oh, he seems particularly upbeat this morning. He was up early, says he's going for a drive and a short walk." I removed my hands from the tacky tabletop and searched for the hand sterilizer in my coat pocket. "Was this a mistake?"

"The performance? You just said he's upbeat."

"But this place . . . I'm not sure what's up or down anymore." I tipped a couple of drops of hand disinfectant onto my palm and massaged my hands together.

"If he's happy, you're doing all the right things. What can I do?"

"Nothing, he really likes you." I offered him the small bottle of sanitizer. He mouthed *no thanks*.

"And you?" he asked.

Meaning do I really like you? The question flustered me.

"What do you mean?"

"Is there something I can do to help you?"

I sat back.

"I mean, with Lyle or the house or your research?"

"Oh, everything's taken care of." I was relieved and hoping the one waitress on duty would see us in the corner and bring us some water. My mouth was a desert; lips bonded together as if grout had been layered in. Probably the coffee.

"So you've come to conclusions about beauty? Because I've got questions galore."

"Just a lot of research and nothing final." I didn't want to cross-reference him against additional criteria, at least not in that moment.

"Well maybe you can explain; like if someone has a beautiful face and a mangled body, are they still beautiful?"

"Scientists have been working on those solutions for years. I don't take that on. I'm interested in offering facial beauty from the get-go. Getting it genetically right at inception."

"But?"

"But defining what that is, is more difficult than I thought." I signaled the waitress, who waved back.

"I'm not surprised," he said perhaps smug. "Different cultures, like you say, see beauty differently. I'll bet even climate plays a part."

"You're right. Think how differently a Tahitian and an Eskimo might consider what's beautiful."

"Based on what they can even see." His eyebrow went up, roguish.

"Yes," I said thinking *damn he's cute* and warming to his interest, "and there are specific criteria analyzing the face, like symmetry using numeric calculations, and perceived visual cues, say about our immune system, and," I hesitated, "smell. The research indicates that even smell impacts our perception of beauty."

"So many ways to skin a cat." He mugged, put both hands behind his neck and stretched.

"Yes," I flashed on Levi.

He leaned forward, his hands back on the table. "So the day is coming when my pitch to you for a date is 'I was down there at the end of the bar with my buddies and I couldn't help notice that your immune system looks very cool. I think your symmetry and my smell would be great together.'"

I laughed. "Something like that."

"And then the more you see and smell me, the more attractive you'll find me." His eyes and cheeks closed in on each other: his pocket smiles.

"Could be." My crescent moons out of my control.

"Hmmm. But besides my getting a date with you —which I admit is critically important— what is the *purpose*?"

"To make life easier, to make people happier. At least looking like this wouldn't be a deterrent."

Something like a hiccup erupted before he covered his mouth, coughing out something between a belch and a small laugh. I couldn't be sure.

"What?!"

"I'm sorry." He took my hand across the table. "Has your research shown that to be true?"

I removed my hand from his. "I can't solve every problem but it seems obvious."

"Obvious, like the nose on your face?"

That *was* an affront. "Yes."

He leaned over the table and kissed my nose. "I don't think it works that way."

"Can I get you two a drink?" The waitress, a once-attractive thin woman approximately my age had reversed the beauty process by introducing botoxed lips. I flashed on Carly leaving The Cosmetic Center.

"Water," we said in unison.

"That's it?" The waitress searched for roving mascara in her eye.

"For now," Roddy said.

And she left, tossing two menus to the table.

What to do with his kiss? My respiration was up, his eyes searching for a place to land. "Let's get back to work."

CHAPTER FIFTY-SIX

The afternoon sun filtered through the copse of still-barren black ash, a fall-like backdrop of gold filigree framing the farmhouse. Inside, I hung up my jacket. I could already hear Momma and Carly at the kitchen table in a celebratory mood. They quieted down when I came in.

"All set up?" asked Carly, and I could see for the first time how her good looks had come from Momma; the full lips, the small balanced mid-face, the smile so seldom seen on Momma.

"I think we're good. There are some flowers and we put up some posters —Roddy's idea, he gathered them online— places Lyle had played before: Butte, Cheyenne, Laramie, a couple others. It gives the room some color. Is Lyle back?"

"Not yet." Momma took a drag from her cigarette. "But I think we're outta the woods." She smiled, nodding at Carly.

"What do you mean?" I asked.

"Lyle," answered Carly. "He's much better today."

"I think the medicine is working," Momma interjected. "He went for a drive *and* a walk."

"Momma." I was trying to be sympathetic but I shook my head.

"What? This is what we're all hopin' for." She picked a fleck of tobacco from her tongue.

"Momma," I said, "his blood vessels, the tumors . . ."

"Can't you ever be positive?" She twisted to Carly and back. "Damn it, Eunis, do you have to be so fuckin' negative? Be more like your sister." She snuffed out the cigarette.

"Momma," said Carly trying to downplay comparison.

"He's really sick," I said.

"Yes, but he's gettin' better, anyone can see that. Look for the beauty, for godsakes." Momma gaining steam. "Look for the goddamned beauty!"

"Momma, I want this as much as—"

"Shit." Momma rose from the table and stormed out. "You can spook wine into water."

I exhaled slowly, fully. "Do *you* understand?" I asked Carly.

"Hey, don't ask me," said Carly, also getting up. "This house is as fucked up as ever."

))))

Lyle hugged his guitar, the last raging scarlet light from the horizon rippling over him.

"You look tired." I took my eyes off the road for a moment. "You okay for this? We can head back if you—"

"A course he's fine," said Momma from the back seat, requisitioning endorsement from Carly, who looked away. "This is his big night, the beginnin' of big things, isn't it, Lyle?"

"I'm good," he reassured me. "I probably carried a *myling* walkin' to Kingdom, but I'll be fine. We're good." He tapped the Martin. In the rearview mirror, I checked Momma's reaction. She averted her eyes.

))))

The Drink 'n' Dive was filling up; mostly men, hands clenching their half empty glasses, ogling the mermaids in the tank, waiting for the night's lucky break, a few women trolling for the same. From the stage, Mae waved to Lyle and me as we entered, and Roddy appeared from the side toting a mike stand.

Lyle took shaky steps to the stage and Roddy reached out to help him up the last two. I caught Roddy's eye and thanked him.

"I'm looking forward to this," said Mae, kissing Lyle on the cheek. "It's been too long." He gave her a weak hug and patted her on the shoulder; Mae gazed past him to me with dismay. I'd given no explanations to anyone, just as I'd promised, but Mae was no fool.

"Oh," she said, "looky here." She reached down and provided a bottle of Jim Beam. "A present from Gordon. He wishes he could be here. Says 'break a leg.'"

"That's awful white —nice of him." Lyle lowered himself onto the stool behind the mike. "You thank him for me."

After the three of us fussed over Lyle for a few minutes, bringing him water, moving the basket of tulips closer, adjusting the mike, he checked his sound levels, and Roddy and I proceeded to our front row table, next to Momma and Carly and Sparky. Seeing Carly next to the multi-pierced Sparky was surreal. The whole thing was.

Two of the off-duty mermaids —big-busted redheaded Sherry and a hawkish younger woman named, appropriately, Birdy— sat close-by and introduced themselves, shaking my hands and inclining me to pull out the hand sterilizer. I refrained.

The house lights went down, the clinking glasses and drifting talk softened, and the spotlight came up on Mae. "I want to introduce someone I've known for years, a wonderful local musician who has the voice of one of those —what dya call them, sirens— that can pull you into worlds you probably couldn't reach otherwise. He's been gone for a while now —just returned from some engagements in New York City— and we're so glad he's come back home. Please welcome Lyle Kind." Middling applause.

"Thank you, Mae." Lyle lifted his hand in front of his face, diffusing the spotlight. It was turned down. "And I want to thank my family, friends, all of you for being here tonight."

He peered into the dim lip of light cast upon the first row of tables, and found Roddy and me. He gave us a small nod, a wan smile. "By the way," he said, exploring beyond us into the darkness, "Kind is my stage name, but my real family name is Kindsvatter."

He started his final tuning and I swung around. The community had rallied. Thanks to Mae and Gordon, Carly, Sparky and Sherry, the room was half full with some familiar faces and two surprises: Sandy, the lamb-faced Miss USA judge, and Johnny Ray Bardo.

In the darkness I could imagine the other faces, the ones I'd been studying for years —DeCaprio, Pitt, Anniston— I wasn't sure I found them beautiful anymore. Not that they were ugly; they just left me numb —and not the refreshing numb of the water, just numb. And there it was: I'd reached the end of my research because the faces and the answers kept changing; there were too many of them for any one of them to be definitive. I could look all I wanted, but I couldn't see.

Except . . . except in those odd moments particular to me, though I still didn't understand the lineage of what brought me to those moments any better than when I made the promise to Nemo. I could *see* him. Maybe his smile and his lick meant *you're so foolish, little girl; I love you because of it; you're beautiful because of it*. Because that's how I felt about him too. To see his little face, that smile, the hope. Even now I see him and I suffer. I tell myself to move on. And I do, but I also —always— suffer.

It's what happened with Lyle. Sensory not intellectual.

Staring up at him, so handsome in the spotlight . . . I'd never seen him that way before. Handsome. Beauty forever shifting — at least for me. Weird. Like a spell got me, like it gets everybody. Unique stories chemically infused in each of us from birth. Triggers of all sorts, everywhere: the neighborhood, the room, the smell, the time of day, the language, the familiar expression (of hope or desperation), the person *next* to the person, the music, the background TV, the smile, the soft voice, the eyes. Message after shadowy message transmitted from within. Treasures and curses from the DNA swamp.

So after all, my weakness was everyone's weakness; objective versus subjective was beside the point. It was both. I couldn't outrun my cells, my primitive lineage. I had no choice, I was going to have to be attentive to them, maybe even accept some of them. And I guess, those of others.

Still, I had to be careful. It was, after all, a mire of switches. I'd seen beauty as a virtue. I'd also seen it as subversive. I wasn't always quick to decipher between the two. I'd needed to work on that, especially as so much of it was out of my control. All of us at the effect of our shadows.

"This'll be a short set," said Lyle. "I'm feelin' a little under the weather but I hope you like 'em, they're some of my favorites. This first one is a Lowell George tune." And cradling his D-35, he splayed his palm on its amber body, and his hand trembled for a moment before he closed his eyes and launched into a slow version of Little Feat's "Willin'":

"I've been warped by the rain

> *Driven by the snow*
> *I'm drunk and dirty, don't ya know*
> *But I'm still . . . willin'. . . "*

I settled in, shut my eyes, the room full of people falling away and leaving me alone, every grainy word verifying his journey. He was steady to the end:

> *". . . And if you give me weed, whites and wine*
> *And show me a sign*
> *I'll be willin' to be movin'"*

The small crowd waited to be certain he was done and then extended an almost reverent applause; as if the audience wasn't sure that they'd really heard such intimacy and if so, what they should do with it, while I marveled and applauded loudly.

He didn't wait for the audience to be sure. He pressed on with two Johnny Cash tunes: the itinerant "Guess Things Happen That Way" and "God's Gonna Cut You Down," which sounded to me like heavy raindrops on a cortege. He paused, and his eyes traveled out and beyond the audience, not saying a word, even after the applause subsided. He reached down and took a sip of water and began again, this time Hank Williams' "May You Never Be Alone." And as the last chord lingered, the room filled with louder but still reverential applause, the audience stunned by his ache, and their own.

"Just two more," he said, and there were groans and someone yelled out, "No!"

"I'm afraid so." Then, "This one was written by Kris Kristofferson and Danny Timms and is especially for my sister, Eunis." I eyed him in surprise. He shared his crooked smile with me, me alone. He closed his eyes once more and embarked on "Moment of Forever:"

> *"Was it wonderful for you*
> *Was it holy as it was for me*
> *Did you feel the hand of destiny*

That was guiding us together

You were young enough to dream
And I was old enough to learn something new
I'm so glad I got to dance with you
For a moment of forever"

A wellspring broke open in my belly, frightening me. *That recurring susceptibility.* I wanted to reject it but it rose like a rocket through my chest to the surface, and tears emerged. I didn't wipe them away. Lyle was . . . inexpressible; *he* was beautiful.

Attempting to quantify that beauty would have been an attack on the sacred. I couldn't have that; I wouldn't want to take that away from anyone. *May beauty live on wherever it's felt.*

"Come whatever happens now
Ain't it nice to know that dreams still come true
I'm so glad that I was close to you
For a moment of forever"

He was done, and the crowd leapt to its feet, applauding and calling out. I sat stunned and cleansed.

The applause receded. He said, "For my final song . . ." —and again "No" rang out from multiple locations in the audience— " . . . I'd like my sister Eunis to join me on stage."

What had I been thinking?! Not only was I going to sing, I was going to step onto a stage in front of 100 people. The hot terror of facing the Octagon Homeowners fell in folds over my spine and shoulders. I was burning up *and* frozen.

"Ralph Stanley was one of my father's favorites; he'd hum Ralph Stanley all day long . . . "

I wasn't worthy. I wasn't prepared. But I'd promised.

" . . . So we're gonna sing one of Papa's favorites."

I found myself rising from the table and walking toward the stage.

"A Man of Constant Sorrow," yelled a man in the audience.

"No," responded Lyle, "I've sung that one enough."

I made my way up the steps and across the stage as Lyle stood stiffly. I discovered myself next to him, eyes downcast. He embraced me and whispered in my ear, "Together."

Up and out, past Roddy into the darkness, fear vibrated my entire body, my legs ready to buckle.

"They say Ralph found the title in proverbs or folklore. Anyways, they sounded right to my Papa, and they still sound right to me. Ralph used to sing this with his brothers. It's a song that takes harmony, and I can't imagine a better partner than my sister."

At that, he began picking in ¾ time and singing, his voice clear and coarse and angelic:

> *"The sun is slowly sinkin'*
> *The day's almost gone*
> *Still darkness falls around us*
> *And we must journey on . . ."*

He turned to me and closing my own eyes, I found the space above his voice, the one he had taught me, and I discovered myself singing harmony:

> *"The darkest hour is just before dawn*
> *The narrow way leads home*
> *Lay down your soul at Jesus' feet*
> *The darkest hour is just before dawn"*

Lyle played the instrumental bridge, my body swaying willingly. I was in water.

He began singing again:

> *"Like a shepherd out on the mountain*
> *A-watchin' the sheep down below*
> *He's coming back to claim us*
> *Will you be ready to go . . ."*

And I joined him, opening my eyes this time, our voices intertwined in an ecstatic home, so exquisite and so comforting I hoped it would go on forever:

> *"The darkest hour is just before dawn*
> *The narrow way leads home*
> *Lay down your soul*
> *Let Jesus in*
> *The darkest hour is just before dawn*
> *The darkest hour is just before dawn"*

Then it was over. We had stopped singing. He had stopped playing. My molecules tingled; I was purified. Slowly, the sound around us came thundering alive, bathing us in adoration. He was crying, making no attempt to wipe away the tears. He hugged me once more, and we clung to each other.

CHAPTER FIFTY-SEVEN

At home I helped Lyle into bed, his body wind-shivering like a twig of sandbar willow. I pulled covers over him and, holding his hand by the bedside, we both fell asleep.

I woke to the sound of raindrops plunking one-by-one on the roof and —our hands still interlaced— the coolness of his touch. Despite the rain the morning sun streamed into the room, across his bed. Lyle's chest wasn't moving. I stretched over him and tucked the hank of his hair behind his ear.

☽☽☽

The day after the funeral was another cool clear spring day; smells emerging from the earth as I walked behind the farmhouse in the thicket of black ash, balsam and mostly dead-standing tamarack. Roddy tried to keep up with me. He finally halted and called out, "Goodbye," and extended his hand to me.

I stopped.

"I've got to go," he said standing his ground. "Come here, please."

As much as I had deconstructed him into a variety of weathered or incompatible parts, he felt like family. I couldn't deny that.

I pried away the branches and took four long, strong strides, pulling up to him quickly. Our heavy breathing syncopated and our breaths coalesced, almost visible in the moist air. He rested his hands on my shoulders and I smiled up at him.

"You're a friend," I said wrapping my arms around his waist. "Family too. Thank you for Lyle."

His eyebrows lifted in mild surprise and he drew me to him, rather sadly. "Yes," he said.

"Yes," I repeated, still talking into his chest. "Where do you go next, back to New York?"

"New Jersey. Eliz is in New York. I live in New Jersey."

"Aah, I see." I gave him a little smirk.

"Yes, I'm a lawyer, in case you need one."

"A lawyer. I've heard all sorts of stories about lawyers." I separated from him, looking up, examining him. "You don't look like a lawyer."

"I get by on my good looks. And you?"

"Me too." If I could have blushed, I would have.

He smiled and reached for my face. "No, I meant what's next for you?"

"Oh, I thought . . ."

"Yes, I know what you thought and you know how I feel about that, don't you?" He brushed the top of my cheek.

I closed my eyes. Was there ever a place for him? With so much still to learn. Reality rushed over me. I opened them. "You're a wonderful man, and you'll always be welcome in my home, wherever it is. But I don't know where I'm going. The money's run out and this isn't my home, not really. And I'm not sure the lab's the place for me. Anyway," I sniffed, "we'll see."

"I want to see you again."

I lowered my eyes. "Maybe."

"No, that won't do."

"I can't predict . . ."

"I thought you had a gift?"

"Maybe."

"You equivocate on every answer. Not very scientific."

I looked back up, admiring him. "Hanging around lawyers will do that. You know, consider every possibility, admit to none."

"You want me to admit." He was unflinching.

It was too much for me. I quickly put my hand to his lips. "Ssh. Please don't say anything."

"Then . . ." He rolled his hand over several times, meaning give me an answer.

"Okay. Okay, we'll see each other again."

"Good."

I flexed both hands. "But I can't promise when."

He kissed me on the mouth. Hungry *and* tender. And then he was gone, out the driveway and past the caboose in that silly little blue rental car, leaving me questioning my sanity. Again.

⟩⟩⟩

"Can I ask you something?" Carly leaned out of her yellow Miata.

Momma, on the back steps, turned and went into the house.

"Sure." I hovered over her, supporting myself by leaning against the car's top.

"Did you kill her?"

"Do you really think I could?"

"Well, you do have a temper, but no."

"Any other questions?"

"Yes. How the hell do you do it?"

"Do what?"

"Keep going."

"What are my options?"

She sat with that for a moment. "You know she's gonna blame you." She signaled toward the farmhouse.

"Probably."

"You sure you don't want to come with me, at least to Minneapolis?"

I skimmed over the property. "I've got a few more things to take care of."

"If you say so."

"But could we, maybe, talk every once in a while? Check in?"

"I've never been very good at that."

"Could we try? I think we have things we could teach each other. We carry some of the same DNA."

"Always the scientist."

"Not always."

She digested the idea. "Sure. You're probably right. A check-in might be nice."

"Good." I hoped she would be the one to call but I guessed otherwise.

"Momma'll be back on her feet in no time." It was Carly's way of giving me permission.

"Thanks," I said reaching my hand to hers and gently squeezing it. "You be safe." I stepped away from the car.

She cranked the ignition. "You too."

)))

May 8th

"Harold,

Roddy stuck around a few days to help with the funeral while Momma barricaded herself in her room. Carly left and came back several times saying, 'I can see you two have it handled.' Some things don't change.

But some do. I was mistaken. I'd originally assumed that Lyle had fabricated the return to Bemidji as another of his selfish ploys, with me as his protector and concierge. Now I'm not so sure.

Somewhere in that skinny self-indulgent man-boy there was a yearning, perhaps not even obvious to him that he wanted to connect with one person before he died. Why he chose me, I don't know. Maybe he wanted Momma but knew she couldn't handle the task, or wasn't particularly interested. Maybe I was just convenient. Maybe he had tried in his own perverse way all along and I was his last resort.

But somewhere along the way it changed, and I'm thankful, because he did his part too. There was a poet in him. I think his last performance was his gift to me, a type of map. Anyway, I wouldn't be here without him, not the way I am now, which is the way you suggested: a little less systematic. Certainly I'm more out and about because of him —and you.

So thank you. I wish you'd been able to see your own beauty. I wish you hadn't been afraid of it. I'll think of you from time to time, even consider your advice and your beautiful heart. But it's time now to say goodbye.

Love, Eunis."

)))

Carver's eyes followed me into the darkness. My work was almost done, and when it was I could call Anthony and he'd be able to convert the comb for Junior's medical bills, maybe even with something left over. The hardest part, of course, was the skinning, which is why I started at the feet, where it would be least noticeable. And I counted on Carver as much as I did myself, because he inhabited the space for more than thirty years. His energy and skill were still contained in the workshop, and we both had an eye for beauty. We worked together.

"Your hair," I said to her, "is as magnificent as ever." And I affixed it the way she'd have wanted it, down and flowing to her impeccable shoulders. I tugged carefully at the cheeks, those ageless, transcendent cheeks, so there wasn't a wrinkle, not even around her mouth, not even around those still provocative lips.

Her eyes, the singular most mesmerizing aspect of her beauty, of course had become clouded —potassium in the red blood cells breaking down— and were the one element that couldn't be salvaged, but I'd had some made that came close. I owed that to Levi. Though I'd sealed the workshop from the elements, I felt air pass behind my neck and I knew that Carver was cautioning me not to make the same mistake I'd made with the skunk.

"No," I said, "not one hundred percent symmetrical, or she'll look mean."

☽☽☽

As with Sam's funeral pyre, I held the flame to the corner of the workshop. And like Sam's box it caught quickly, given its weary dryness. The flames spread and engulfed the building. It had served me well over the years but it was time to move on, time to investigate new mysteries.

Along the path to Kingdom Lake there were signs of spring, but winter's chill still eddied through the trees, moving them left and right, not wishing to leave. The trail, too, still showed winter's mark. Where the track dipped there were puddles, and on the sides the tall tangled grass bulged in large wet clumps, mounds of them stretching out over the forest floor. I stepped on them and water oozed, almost a swamp.

I carried nothing more than a towel. It was likely still too cold for crickets, but I could hear them in a month or so, especially if the warm temperatures returned and sustained over the next few weeks.

Around the bend and up ahead, my favorite white cedar stood alone, naked against the uncertain sky and isolated from the jack pine, black spruce, and balsam that were ringed at their base by thick moss.

The tall reeds weren't so tall this time of year, bent by the winter snows and not yet certain of the spring. There was little camouflage. I lowered the towel to the ground beneath the cedar. I disrobed, folding my clothes into a manageable pile and placed my shades on top of it.

At the water's edge I shivered at its overture. Goosebumps. "Okay, be kind." *In the original Hans Christian Anderson version of* The Little Mermaid, *the despairing mermaid hurls herself into the sea and her body dissolves into foam.* I waded quickly in, my breath sucked away by the snowmelt water. Once beyond the stems and stubble, I dove in and swam vigorously toward the center of the lake, at first gasping, my wake of white hair following behind me. I was in the middle faster than I'd imagined, treading water and breathing hard, turning 360-degrees and taking in the magnificence around me. It gave me strength.

Out there I'd always felt invincible, but now with Lyle's death, *saudade*, a longing had opened, perhaps permanently, of unending vulnerability. I would need to find a way of including it, a new way of considering *everything*. Even the pain. That included Momma and her pressing demands. Roddy would say, *"Human behavior: an acquired taste."*

I swam back to shore watching the workshop's orphaned wisps of smoke dissolve above the treetops and, in passing, surveying Beauty's final place as it disappeared behind tattered stalks.

I toweled off rapidly and imagined all the suspects besides me the police had had to consider, given Kingdom's frigid temperature, which could easily have broadened the time of death by a day or two.

"Well," Detective Sullivan had offered, "Mr. O'Brien said you could be trusted. He couldn't imagine you were involved in all this. And Mayor King also thought you were an unlikely suspect. Naturally, I'll be the judge of that. We have concluded that when you found her she'd been in the water maybe twenty-four hours or so."

A single soft trill pulsed, hidden in the grass; the first of the spring field crickets. I threw the towel over my shoulder and turned up the path, my feet at home on the ground, the last vestiges of winter gusting lightly in my face, then at my neck, teasing my hair. Victor's hearse had picked The Beauty up and she was on her way back to New York. At least for the moment it was all very orderly.

"Moths, and all sorts of ugly creatures,
hover about a lighted candle.
Can the candle help it?"
Charles Dickens,
Great Expectations

PG LENGSFELDER began his writing career at 7 years old, co-editing a neighborhood newspaper with Annemarie, his next-door neighbor. His lifelong passion for writing and telling stories include awards for storytelling on national television, NPR and in print, including 17 years as a television writer/director and 16 years consulting on themes and storylines for litigators telling *their* stories in courtrooms across the country. *Beautiful to the Bone* is his first novel.

PG Lengsfelder is available for select readings and lectures. To inquire about a possible appearance or to be kept updated on his newest books, please visit www.pglengsfelder.com/contact.

My mind, as author Anne Lamott has cautioned, "is a neighborhood I try not to go into alone." So it is with great appreciation that I thank the following people for their willingness to wade into my neighborhood with bon homie and guidance as I navigated this, my first novel.

To fellow writers, Larry Watson, Marina Endicott, John DeDakis, Katherine Reay, Leslie Budewitz and William O. Joseph, your insight and encouragement has kept me moving. Let me add Jim McCarthy at Dystel & Goderich Literary to this list.

Then too, there are my editors, Peter Gelfan and Brenda Windberg, who saw through the clutter of my thoughts and gently suggested weeding here and there and there and there. Oh, you were so right!

The enthusiasm and affirmation of my beta readers —Apple Williams, Eliza Lape, John Finger, Terry Byrnes, Lorin Oberweger and Teresa Pugh— remind me what a circuitous and eye-opening journey it's been.

My dear friends and some new acquaintances, experts in their respective fields, kept this work of fiction grounded in the historical facts and the remarkable science of today. Thank you Dennis Stark, Rena Falk, Halyna Breslawec, Jeff Welch, Leo Soukup, Barry Babcock, and the other wonderfully supportive people at the Bemidji Historical Society.

Credits

Lyrics from the following compositions are used by permission:

"Guess Things Happen That Way" words and music by Jack Clement, © 1986 Universal – Songs of Polygram International,

Other quoted text:
Essentials of Cell Biology, Unit 2.3, © 2014
www.nature.com/scitable

Dickens, Charles:
The Old Curiosity Shop, 1841.
American Notes for General Circulation, 1842.
The Haunted House, 1859
From a letter to Marguerite Power, 1847

www.ingramcontent.com/pod-product-compliance
Lightning Source LLC
Chambersburg PA
CBHW051208120726

47905CB00004B/1032